T0278627

INHERITANCE OF SCARS

INHERITANCE
OF SCARS

CRYSTAL SEITZ

Margaret K. McElderry Books

New York   London   Toronto   Sydney   New Delhi

MARGARET K. McELDERRY BOOKS

An imprint of Simon & Schuster Children's Publishing Division

1230 Avenue of the Americas, New York, New York 10020

Text © 2024 by Crystal Seitz

Jacket illustration © 2024 by Marcela Bolívar

Jacket design by Greg Stadnyk

MARGARET K. McELDERRY BOOKS is a trademark of Simon & Schuster, LLC.

Simon & Schuster: Celebrating 100 Years of Publishing in 2024

For information about special discounts for bulk purchases, please contact Simon & Schuster Special Sales at 1-866-506-1949 or business@simonandschuster.com.

The Simon & Schuster Speakers Bureau can bring authors to your live event. For more information or to book an event, contact the Simon & Schuster Speakers Bureau at 1-866-248-3049 or visit our website at www.simonspeakers.com.

Interior design by Irene Metaxatos

The text for this book was set in Adobe Caslon Pro.

Manufactured in the United States of America

First Edition

2 4 6 8 10 9 7 5 3 1

CIP data for this book is available from the Library of Congress.

ISBN 9781665959926

ISBN 9781665959940 (ebook)

To Grammy Seitz,
for all your stories.

And to my dad, Peter
Seitz, for encouraging
me to write my own.

I love you both.

AUTHOR'S NOTE

Astrid's experience with Crohn's disease, while different from my own, is inspired by mine. Your circumstances may differ even if you share the same disease, or know someone who does, but my hope is that you can still relate to Astrid's experience, as I do.

While this story is inspired by Norse mythology and Scandinavian folklore, I've given it my own twist. One of my favorite things about myths and folklore is how varied they are, always changing and evolving and told differently by different people. This is my own variation.

Similarly, the religion in this story is fictional and is not representative of any modern religious beliefs or practices. This work is also not meant to be historically accurate. Although the Icelandic staves are relatively modern, in my story they are much older and thus use Old Norse names. Thank you to Jackson Crawford for consulting on the Old Norse. Any mistakes are my own.

Please note that this book portrays a number of difficult subjects, including death, animal death (non-pet), grief, ritualistic self-harm, graphic violence, and allusions to cancer and suicide.

A pronunciation guide is available on crystalseitz.com/inheritance.

PROLOGUE

TEN YEARS AGO

"Get to bed before I use a sleep thorn on you."

Amma *always* threatens this. But the only magical staves my grandma uses are for boring things like keeping her barrels from leaking, or to catch me sneaking some of her fresh butter.

I cross my arms. "I'm too old to have a bedtime."

I'm almost eight. My best friend, Johan, doesn't have one, so neither should I.

Amma gives me that stern look she gets a lot. "Astrid, I mean it."

I pout. "Johan's mom lets him stay up as long as he wants."

Amma scoops me up in her arms. "Well, I'm sorry to say, you are stuck with me." She plops me into bed and tucks the soft crochet blanket around me, protecting me from winter's chill. "Which means you will go to bed when I see fit."

I give a great big sigh. "But I'm not sleepy."

"You will be once you close your eyes."

So much for that.

"What about Daddy? I need my kiss good night."

Amma's face crinkles like paper. "He's not here right now."

"Oh." Why am I surprised? He never is. Dad might as well be one of the Hidden Folk from Amma's stories.

"So," Amma says, leaning forward, "I suppose I'll just have to give you one myself."

She presses her moist lips to my forehead. She smells like pine needle tea. Not like Dad and his gasoline stink from working on cars all day. Amma always says he prefers them to people because cars can be fixed.

Amma heads for the door, walking past the Fell King, who lurks in the corner of my room, too tall to be human. His face hides in the shadows, except for his glowing blue eyes, which are always watching me. And Amma is about to leave me alone with him.

"Wait!" I blurt out. "My bedtime story. You forgot."

Amma stills. "What would you like to hear? Perhaps that time Freyja turned into a falcon and outwitted the Hidden Folk?"

I roll my eyes. "Not the goddess again."

Amma hesitates in the doorway, frowning. "Oh, so you've outgrown the goddess as well as your bedtime, have you?" She shakes her head. "Very well, Asta. Since you are such a big girl now, why don't I tell you a scary story instead?"

Gulping, I reach for my stuffed bear, Björn, stealing a glance at the Fell King. I don't need scary stories to give me nightmares. But Amma pulls my least favorite picture book from the shelf: *The Hidden Folk*. The mattress sinks when she sits beside me, drawing us closer together. With every turned page comes a creature more terrifying than the last.

"What about the huldra, hmm?" Amma asks, reaching a picture of a beautiful woman standing in a forest. "Once there was a man who lost his way in Tiveden. He wandered the woods so long, his stomach began growling like the monsters roaming the forest. Eventually, he spotted another human. Not only was she the most beautiful woman he'd ever seen, but she promised to help him return home, so long as he wed her after. He gladly agreed." On the next page, the woman's back opens like a giant Venus flytrap. "But once they set off, he spotted her tail. Knowing she could no longer pretend to be human, the huldra decided to devour him—"

"Actually, I want to hear about Freyja after all."

"No, no, you've had enough of the goddess." Amma flips through the book, monstrous creatures leaping out from its pages. "What other story shall I tell you instead?"

"Perhaps you would rather hear about the Fell King," she says, lowering her voice. "He who wears a crown of twisted roots, marking him as Tiveden's ruler. His army is as numerous and vast as the forest. On his hip hangs a bone horn, and all who hear its thunderous call awaken— even the dead. So powerful is the Fell King, only a mountain can serve as his throne. Seated high upon it, he can see everything in the entire land." She leans forward and taps my nose. "Even *you*, little Asta."

I gulp. Amma is wrong. The Fell King isn't on his mountain.

He is right here.

Amma walks right past him and flips off the light. "As the days get shorter, the Fell King's power only grows greater," she says, her face floating in the darkness. "He is most powerful during Midwinter, when we're lucky to feel the sun warm our skin at all and Freyja, the Bright Lady, is at her weakest."

Despite the cold, I'm suddenly sweaty. The Fell King visits me most this time of year. "Isn't tomorrow Midwinter?"

"That's right," Amma says. "Which is why you must be a good girl and go to sleep now, or else he will come for you."

Staring at the glowing eyes in the darkness, I ask quietly, "What if he already has?"

Amma turns my night-light on and the Fell King disappears.

"Oh, Asta." She takes my hand in hers. Her palm is comforting, familiar and soft like my blanket. "You don't have to worry. You're safe so long as you're with me. I promise."

"Are *you* safe?"

Amma sighs. "This is why I don't tell you these—"

"I'm not scared," I insist.

"Oh?" Amma offers a knowing smile. "Then I can turn your night-light off?"

I pull Björn closer. "No."

Amma shakes her head. "Tomorrow, I'm telling you a happy story about the time Freyja was finally reunited with her lost husband," she says before she leaves. "Good night. Love you."

The hairs on my arm rise as I stare at the empty corner of my room. The Fell King may be gone, but I can still *feel* his gaze.

"Goodbye," I tell Amma. Maybe by mistake. Maybe just in case I disappear too.

"Oh, Asta. I told you." Amma's smile is small and sad. "We need no goodbyes."

PART ONE

The Sleep Thorn
Svefnþorn

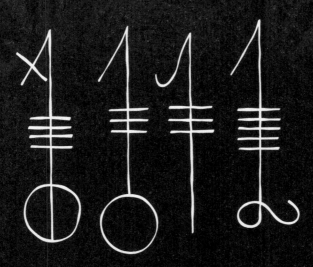

ONE

People don't just disappear. Not anymore.

But that's the reason we're heading home for the first time in nine years. Dad drives down the winding road, and the seat belt cuts across my throat as I lean closer to the window. Tiveden forest presses in around us, ragged pines reaching for our car like thousands of outstretched hands.

I peer out at the snow-drenched woods, half looking for the creatures my grandmother used to warn me about. Anytime something went wrong in Unden, Amma blamed the Hidden Folk. Food spoiling too quickly, covered with crawling flies. Power outages leaving us in cold darkness. Birds dropping out of the sky like stones.

When I first got sick.

No matter how long I stare out the window, I don't see any monsters. I'm sure Amma would say what she always said about the Hidden Folk: *Just because you can't see them doesn't mean they aren't there.*

Except now she isn't here either.

We got the call no one wants to get a month ago while Dad and I were out for yet another doctor's appointment. Because *of course* Dad still uses a landline. The voicemail was waiting when we got back, a blinking red light.

This is Officer Lind from Unden. No one's seen Ingrid in a few days. We checked her house, but she wasn't around. Thought maybe she'd gone to visit you in Stockholm? Well, just give us a call—

"We should be there soon," Dad says, startling me back to the present.

"Took long enough," I mutter, fiddling with the radio.

Dad ignores my barb and flips the radio off, leaving us in sudden silence. Now our soundtrack is bitter December wind blasting the car and tires grinding over gravel. Something about the motion makes me sick to my stomach. Or maybe it's because I'm finally going home.

To Unden.

Maybe this is another before-and-after moment and I just don't know it yet.

Before the voicemail, I hadn't heard Amma's name spoken aloud since we moved. After, dread doused me like ice water. Dad rubbed his mouth like he always does when he doesn't know what to say, which is most of the time. He didn't need to explain. I already knew. Neither of us had seen Amma in nine years. She was too old, too stubborn to ever leave Unden. So if she was missing now, it could only mean one thing.

Something had happened to her.

I'm sure she'll turn up, Dad offered eventually.

She didn't, and so here we are. Sighing, I slip my cell phone out of my pocket. I pull up my messages, scrolling through the most recent texts from Zuri:

> soooo when are we getting Mr. Cake again??
> Astridddddd
> since when do u not want cinnamon rolls lol
> hey, everything ok?
> ok girl you're actually worrying me now. are you ok??
> it's not another flare, is it?

I tap my thumb on the reply bar, but I don't know what to tell her. No service either. Great.

The rest of my messages are texts from people I never answered. Hey, how are you? and Want anything? and Wanna hang out? Maybe I'm just pushing Zuri away like I do everyone else. At least now I can use no reception as an excuse.

But it also means no distraction. The drive to Unden feels endless, like the hours I spent waiting for any update from Officer Lind. I remained right by the phone, because the alternative was staring blankly at homework or, more likely, Netflix. Each time it rang, I bolted over, but it was always Dad's work or my gastroenterologist.

Days passed. Weeks.

Then finally Officer Lind called.

We're going to find her became *I'm so sorry.*

I press my forehead against the cool glass of the window, hoping it will calm me, but I've felt sick to my stomach since that last call. This better not be another flare-up. Not long ago, I could barely get out of bed to make it to the bathroom, never mind travel hundreds of kilometers. Dad didn't want me to come. *You never even let me say goodbye,* I reminded him. Dad sighed. *Fine, Astrid. This is your opportunity, but then you have to move on with your life.*

He's barely spoken to me since.

We've been driving for hours and in the car, there's no escaping Dad. I can't retreat to my bedroom or slam the door in his face. As the forest blurs outside the window, I catch a flash of something between the trees—

No, not something. Some*one*.

A wrinkled, pale face floating in the darkness of the forest. A white braid hanging over her shoulder like a rope. If I'd blinked, I might've missed it. Missed *her*. My breath catches in my throat. Amma is here.

"Stop!" I shout.

Dad slams the brakes, and the tires scream in protest. Momentum throws us forward in our seats. We skid off the icy road toward a tree, but Dad swerves away at the last moment. A low-reaching branch digs into the side of the car like nails scraping over a chalkboard. We screech to a halt, my heart pounding wildly.

Dad grips the steering wheel, white-knuckled. He turns to me, breathing hard. "Shit, Astrid. Are you okay? What is it?"

"Amma," I choke out. "I just saw Amma in the forest."

My eyes dart between the tall trees. Broken branches jut out like rib cages. Pine needles shiver as a breeze blows through the forest. My skin tingles, dread washing over me. Amma was *right* there.

Now no one is.

I stare at the empty space between the trees, trying to make sense of it. I jab the cold glass. "She was right there!"

Dad rubs his mouth, his large hand scratching over his beard. He barely glances in the direction of my finger before pulling back onto the road. My focus remains glued to the side mirror as the trees recede into the distance.

"You know," Dad says, hesitating a moment, "when I lost your mother, I saw her everywhere."

I blink. We don't talk about Mom. Ever.

Even though I never knew her, I've felt her absence my entire life. Mom died shortly after giving birth to me. Sepsis caused by postpartum infection. Though he's never said it, I know Dad blames me instead of her shitty immune system. I'm a living reminder of everything he lost. That's why he's always angry. Why we always fight. He wants to forget, when all I want is to know her. If it weren't for Amma, I wouldn't even know that Mom loved to bake semla year-round and sing along off-key to ABBA.

But then the shock wears off, and the rest of his words hit me.

"Don't act like Amma is dead," I say tightly.

His jaw flexes, but he doesn't respond.

"We don't know anything, not without a body." I twist toward him, and my seat belt is the only thing restraining me. "Maybe if you hadn't delayed for a month, we would've found her by now." Maybe I would've noticed something everyone else missed. Maybe *I* could've found her.

Maybe I still can.

"We're not here to find her." Dad glances between me and the road, his shoulders tense. "We're here to lay her to rest and evaluate the estate. Take care of loose ends. Once that's finished, we're getting the hell out of here and never coming back. We agreed, Astrid."

"Lay her to rest?" I give a sharp, disbelieving laugh, and drag a hand over my braid. "How, exactly? She hasn't even been found."

Dad takes his eyes off the road long enough to give me an irritated look. "Unden is holding a vigil for her." His brow furrows, deepening the creases in his forehead. "That's the only reason you're here. So you can say goodbye this time, like you said."

I look away. Stare out the window. "We never should've left. We should have been here to take care of her. If we were, this never would've happened."

"I took you away for your own good," he says tightly.

I have to blink back tears. "Bullshit."

"Stop blaming me." Dad smacks his palm against the steering wheel. "Stop blaming *yourself*. Do you want to make yourself sick again?"

He's seriously doing this. Acting like I can't handle any stress just because I'm sick. If I hadn't been there when he played the voicemail, I'm not sure he would've even told me. Or if Amma's disappearance would've just become another thing on the long list of topics we never talk about. All kinds of messy feelings well up in me, threatening to overflow.

"I love her, Dad." My throat aches with the words. "Is that so wrong? I need to know what happened to her. I can't just move on and forget like you do."

Silence forms a wall between us.

"She was old," he says finally. "Her mind wasn't all there anymore. She wandered into the woods and got lost. It happens more often than you'd think."

I shove my hands into my coat pockets. "Amma isn't senile—"

"She *was*." His voice is harsh. "You were too young to realize it, but she was. You don't know her like I do."

My palm grazes the paper tucked inside my coat. The last letter I received from Amma. We've been communicating for years, but Dad has no idea, and I'm not about to mention it. After we left, he forbade any contact with her. He'd be furious and ground me if he found out.

"Whose fault is that?" I ask instead. Even the question leaves a bitter taste in my mouth.

Dad sighs heavily. "I won't talk about this, Astrid."

I curl my left hand into a fist, until my nails bite into the scar that runs across my palm. He always does this. Every damn time. The air in the car turns suffocating. Almost as suffocating as Dad. As I lower the window to a blast of cold air, part of me wishes *he* was the one who disappeared.

No.

No, I don't. Even the thought of it feels like a swift punch to the stomach. I can't imagine my life without him. Dad has been my only constant. He's the one who takes me to my doctor appointments and colonoscopies, who spends the visiting hours at my bedside when I'm in the hospital, who makes sure I never forget my medicine.

I'd miss him even more than I resent him.

So I stare out the window, even though no blue sign declaring VÄLKOMMEN TILL UNDEN is going to greet me. Unden doesn't appear on any map. Amma always said you can only find it if you know where to look. Our remote village has been forgotten by time. Unden is like a drying river, slowly diminishing. No one ever comes here.

No one ever leaves, either, not unless they die.

Except me and Dad.

As we drive down the only road into Unden, it feels familiar and foreign at once. Some kids chase our car down the street, and I have to fight a smile. When I was their age, I used to race like that too, laughing and screaming with friends, back when it was still easy to fit in. Back before I was too angry, too sick, too *much*.

Old houses stand out bright as blood against the snow. Unlike the colorful pastels of Stockholm, the homes here are all the same shade of Falu red. Instead of tall buildings crowded together, the village spreads over a generous swath of land, and in the distance, the tiered roof of the stave church darkens the bleak gray sky.

We pass a pole that looks like a lamppost, but instead of a light, a giant animal skull rests on top of it. The animal's empty eye sockets stare at me while we drive by Old Ulf's house. Unease scrapes across my skin. *That* is certainly something I'd never see in Stockholm.

A níðstǫng pole for cursing enemies. Or neighbors, in Ulf's case. He's famous around here for his unpleasant attitude. When I was a kid, we all called him Old Ulf and whispered about how he was over two hundred years old. I'm surprised he's still around—and Amma isn't.

A group appears ahead, erecting a large wooden structure using ropes. A rune for protection. Other giant rune effigies are being raised all over the village ahead of Midwinter on December twenty-first. Eight days from now they'll be set ablaze to protect us from the Fell King while the Bright Lady is at her weakest.

Midwinter was the one night of the year Amma would leave me. As Unden's foremother, it was her duty to lead the community and preside over the town-wide celebration. Not that I ever saw the ritual. Dad never let me attend. We stayed home instead. All I could do was watch from my window while everyone else gathered in the streets and lit the effigies.

Amid the group, I catch a glimpse of a long white braid—

My heart sticks in my throat.

As her face comes into view, my mistake becomes clear. Those stern features could only belong to Helga, the village healer and Amma's best friend. Of course it's not Amma. I swallow my disappointment. Part of me wishes we could stay until Midwinter, but Dad made it clear we had to be back in Stockholm by then. This is just a quick weekend trip, and I can't miss any more classes.

A few houses down, Ebba Karlsson watches us from her window. She's the typical middle-aged nosy neighbor who needs to know everything that's going on. Our eyes meet momentarily. She disappears, lace curtains fluttering in her wake.

Tires crunch the snow like glass as we roll to a stop. Not in front of our house, but the police station. If you can even call it that. It's more of a converted barn, which leans sharply to one side, looking ready to collapse at any moment.

"What are we doing here?"

"I told you. Taking care of loose ends." Dad rubs his forehead. "There's some paperwork Officer Lind needs me to sign, and I want to get it over with as soon as possible. Be right back."

He slams the car door, putting a punctuation mark on this conversation.

I climb out after him. "What paperwork?"

Dad heads toward the police station without even looking back. "To declare my mother legally dead."

Dead.

The word is sharp and sudden, cutting through my thoughts. At least *missing* holds the possibility of being found. Tears build behind my eyes until I feel like a dam about to burst. We don't even have a body—or any answers.

I chase him inside the station. "You can't."

Lights blink and hum overhead. Paint peels off the clapboard walls like scabs.

Officer Lind sits at a large wooden desk, chatting on the phone. Behind him, a series of photos line the wall. Portraits of Unden's past foremothers. Since cameras existed, anyway. The six frames are eclectic, but the photos are eerily similar. A smiling woman standing in front of the stave church with a crown of braided hair.

My stomach flips when I reach the last picture. *Amma.* I used to believe mine would hang in the empty space beside hers one day. Since I was young, I've dreamed of leading Unden, like Amma always said I would. It's why I chose to focus on business administration in high school. A big part of me still wants that title, but not yet.

Not if it means Amma is gone.

Dad clears his throat loudly.

"Sorry, they just got here, Ulf." Officer Lind looks relieved to see us. Old Ulf was probably complaining again. "Talk later." He drops the phone into the receiver and pushes up from the desk, holding out a hand to my dad. "Rick, good to finally see you again. You too, Astrid. Will you be joining us for the vigil tomorrow?"

Dad stands as still as a statue. "I'm here for the paperwork, Adrian. Save the pleasantries for someone else."

I glance between them, shifting uncomfortably. The tension is palpable. And I'm caught in the middle. Amma once mentioned they used to be best friends but had a falling-out over my mom. Eventually they became drinking buddies after her death. Right now, it sure seems like they can't stand each other.

Officer Lind drops his hand. And his smile. "Fine, Rick. Have it your way." All pretense of politeness vanishes as he shuffles through the piles of papers on his desk. "I just need you to sign these here."

Whatever is going on between them isn't important. Finding Amma is.

"Shouldn't you still be searching?" I ask.

Officer Lind doesn't glance up. "We searched for days. Everyone helped, but there was no trace of her anywhere in Unden."

"People don't disappear here," I say, recalling the flash of Amma I saw in the forest.

"I suspect she went into the woods," he says as if reading from a report. His voice is flat. Factual. "Used to be somewhat of a tradition. When resources were scarce, the elderly would sacrifice themselves for the communal good. And while I was doing interviews . . . well, it turns out Ingrid was sick. Helga said she didn't have long, anyway."

His words hit me like a hard slap, nearly knocking me over. *"What?"*

It takes a moment for me to realize what he's saying.

What Dad didn't tell me earlier.

"You think she went . . . to die?" The words drop from my mouth, heavy. Silence is his only answer.

Amma never mentioned she was sick. I shake my head so hard my braid sways. They're wrong. Amma wouldn't just . . . abandon me. The letter I have in my pocket is proof of that.

I bite the inside of my cheek. "Then why haven't you found her?"

"Because she didn't want to be found." Officer Lind's mouth twists. "She went beyond the stave church. I'm not risking any more lives, simple as that. Tiveden is too dangerous."

"Too dangerous? What about *Amma*?"

Wait. He's not talking about the dense forest, or treacherous terrain, or even the freezing temperatures, is he? He's talking about that stupid superstition: *never go beyond the stave church.* Supposedly, if you do, you'll be devoured. Drained of blood. Bones broken like branches. Superstitions I was only scared of as a kid.

"The Hidden Folk aren't even real," I say.

I look to Dad for backup. He's always hated his mother's stories. The word he used for them was *nonsense*, or if he was feeling less generous, *bullshit*.

Now he has nothing to say.

He must not care *why* as long as he gets to clean his hands of this. Case closed. Time to move on.

"What if there's proof she's alive?" I ask before I think better of it.

Officer Lind's chair creaks as he leans forward. "Do you know something?"

I hesitate, fingers brushing over Amma's letter. Mail takes forever to arrive from Unden, so I didn't get it until a week ago. The smooth paper is creased from how many times I've reread it since, enough times to know the words by heart:

> As your birthday approaches, I cannot help but recall the day you were born. You were absolutely perfect. Your hair was blond as wheat cream, your eyes the color of fresh hazelnuts, your little laugh like birdsong. I cannot remember ever loving something so much. For so long, I begged Freyja to give me a daughter. Finally, she blessed me with you.
>
> And now soon you will turn eighteen yourself. How time passes! You must return to Unden before Midwinter so we can celebrate your birthday together. I've prepared a special gift for you, one that can only be given in person. We have much to celebrate this year! You will become an adult, and not even your father can keep us apart.
>
> We need no goodbyes.
> Amma

I grip the paper as Officer Lind watches me, waiting.

Dad stares at me so intensely, it feels like I'm being raked over hot coals.

This letter is proof they're both wrong. She was in her right mind. She didn't just wander off or abandon me. She was waiting for me to come home. But it's also damning proof that I've been secretly communicating with her right under Dad's nose. Years of swiping the mail will be undone in a second. Knowing Dad, this letter would be enough reason to turn around and go back to Stockholm, vigil or no vigil.

"No." Sighing, I slip my hand from my pocket. "Not yet."

Officer Lind glances between us uncertainly. "Well then." He slides the papers across the desk like he's handing out a death sentence. "Here's that paperwork. Sign right here, Rick."

As soon as Dad signs, no one will ever look for Amma again.

I grab his arm. "You can't, Dad. Don't."

Dad scrawls his legal name, *Erik Skarsgård*, across the line. "It's already done."

My eyes sting as I stare at the dark, permanent ink. I want to scream at him, beg him to do *more*, but my teeth are clenched together tight enough to crack. He will never relent. Once his mind is made up, there's no changing it. Just like mine.

I storm out of the station.

If no one else will, then I'll have to find her myself.

Once I'm outside, Amma looks out at me from a missing poster plastered to a telephone pole. Her face is wrinkled and warm as she smiles, a long white braid draped over her shoulder like a rope. The same face I caught a flash of in the woods, but this photo is faded like a memory.

The bold capital letters above read: *MISSING*. Swallowing hard, I scan the rest of the poster's information. *Ingrid Skarsgård. Age: 68. Height: 165 cm. Weight: 58 kg. Last seen November 11 at her home.* I don't know what Amma would have been wearing when she disappeared or even who the last person to see her was. She might have been *dying*, and I had no fucking idea.

It's pathetic how little I actually know. How little Dad has actually told me. As I peel the poster from the telephone pole, it rips down the middle. I stare at Amma's torn, smiling face through my tears.

No matter what Dad says, I won't give up.

TWO

This is the house I was born in. The house my mother died in.

But now no smoke rises from the chimney.

The windows remain dark.

Our home waits ahead, black as a stain against the snow. The steeply pitched roof and rotting sides look older than I remember. Older than a lot of homes in Unden, almost as ancient as the stave church. Unlike the red-painted houses in town, its wooden planks are bare, exposed to the elements. Amma prefers it that way. More natural, she always said, like the trees in Tiveden. Which is fitting since our home sits on the edge of town, not far from the forest. Only a short walk and the stave church separate us.

My breath steams in the cold December air as I climb out of the car.

"Don't forget your medicine," Dad says, slamming his door.

"I know, I know."

I sling my Fjällräven backpack over my shoulder and grab the mini-cooler from the trunk. Ice sloshes around inside along with my weekly injection. Thanks to this heavy-duty biologic shot, I'm in remission. For now. But it also means I can get life-threatening infections. To control my Crohn's disease, the biologic drug stops my body from attacking itself—but also makes it harder to fight off infections. If I get one, I have to stop my medicine until I can recover.

I think of Mom. *If* I can recover.

"Need some help?" Dad asks, hefting his duffel bag over his shoulder.

Shaking my head, I carry the cooler toward the house. "I got it."

Dad holds the door open for me.

As I walk inside, I'm confronted by an empty house. The empty sofa. The same sofa we used to sit on while Amma braided my blond hair, saying how it reminded her of sunlight, soft and beautiful. The whole house used to smell of pine and chaga mushrooms while Amma boiled tea for our daily fika; now, only the stale scent of dust greets me as I step inside. The chair she once sat in, bouncing me on her leg and singing "Rida Ranka," is empty.

The memories press down on me.

In the living room, bundles of dried herbs dangle from the ceiling like outstretched arms. Their musty smell wafts over me as I walk by, transporting me back to my childhood. Amma considered herself a spákona—a wand woman, as she called it. She would draw magical staves in the bottom of my sneakers so I would never get lost. We would pluck bright red mushrooms together and plant henbane seeds in the garden. For a long time, I believed Amma was a witch; now I know it's foraging and herbalism.

As soon as I reach the kitchen, the stench of something rotten fills the air. For a split second, I imagine Amma lying on the other side of the counter, sprawled on the floor, no one to help her. *The house was searched,* I assure myself. That was one of the few details Dad actually shared with me. Then I spot the blackened fruit sitting on the countertop, fuzzy with mold.

The floorboards groan as Dad joins me. "I'll deal with it."

"Thanks." I pull open the fridge, greeted by milk and eggs and jars full of lingonberry jam and bilberry preserves. Every summer, Amma and I would pick berries together. We'd pluck so many, the juice would stain our hands. Grinning, I would hold up my palms. *Look, blood!* And every time, Amma would shake her head and laugh.

I unload my shots quickly and snap the fridge shut. Her absence is everywhere. It permeates every centimeter of this place. Her last letter to me, all this food, the fruit waiting on the counter . . . Officer Lind is wrong. If Amma left, she intended to come back.

So why didn't she?

"I'll figure out something for dinner." Dad dumps the rotting fruit in the trash bin. "The vigil isn't until tomorrow afternoon. Try and get some rest before then."

Wait—the vigil. This could be my opportunity to speak with Officer Lind alone. Everyone in Unden will be there to offer their condolences, so Dad won't be suspicious if we exchange a few words. If he notices at all.

"Sounds good," I say before retreating to my old bedroom.

The door creaks as it opens, but my room is the same as I left it. The same forest-green walls that I used to imagine were Tiveden. The same crocheted blanket Amma knitted for me is tucked in neatly on the bed.

The only thing missing is my teddy bear, Björn. He's been with me all my life, through everything, ever since Dad gave him to me for my third birthday. Björn was one of the few things I took with me to Stockholm since we left in such a hurry.

I still don't know what the rush was for.

Looking around my old room, I grip the straps of my backpack. It feels heavier now, pulling down my shoulders. Every night in Stockholm, all I wanted was to be back here. Now I finally am.

But Amma isn't.

My bag drops to the floor along with my heart.

A sob escapes me. I clap a hand over my mouth before Dad can hear. Tears slide between the valleys of my fingers, and it feels like my chest is cracking in two. I haven't let myself cry since we got the call. Now I can't stop. Grief squeezes the air out of my lungs, leaving me gasping.

I don't know how long I cry, or if Dad can hear me.

If he does, he never interrupts.

‡

After dinner, I return to my room, ready to start my search. Hopefully, the gift Amma mentioned is here. Somewhere.

Old toys lie scattered around the floor. All wooden, of course. I'll never forget how amazed I was when I visited Zuri and saw she had a plastic Barbie. I nearly stumble on a figure of Freyja. Her feet are still charred from when I held her over the fire years ago. Amma yelled at me, saying I could hurt myself, but I just wanted to see if the toy would survive being burned like the goddess.

Suddenly I spot it: a book waiting for me on the nightstand. I wipe a thin layer of dust off the cover, exposing the title: *The Hidden Folk. This* is why no one will search beyond the stave church. Because of superstitions. Stories.

There's less dust on it than I would expect. I was reading this book with Amma before I moved. That had to be the last time this book was opened. When I crack the cover, some of the pages stick together. On the blank spread, Amma's familiar handwriting is scrawled there.

> Remember, Asta.
> Just because you can't see them doesn't mean they aren't there.
> Love, Amma

A smile tugs at my lips. When I was really little, I could never say my name quite right. Instead of Astrid, the best I could manage was Asta. Amma said it made a wonderful nickname.

I flip the page and an ancient draugr stares out with glowing blue irises, his snarl exposing wicked fangs, his fingers tipped with claws as sharp as knives. *Draugr, plural draugar,* the caption reads. *An undead creature from Norse mythology, sometimes referred to as an aptrganga, literally again-walker, or one who walks after death. A draugr refuses to die, drawing animate will back into the corpse. Only ash wood through the heart, beheading by cold steel, or fire can deliver a final death.*

A shiver runs through me.

Amma used to warn me about the draugar, but especially the Fell King. He was the most dangerous—the most bloodthirsty and terrible—draugr who ruled over Tiveden. He used to terrify me. I would see him, standing in the shadows of my bedroom, watching me with his otherworldly gaze. Now that I'm older I know it was just my imagination. When we moved, he no longer haunted my nights.

In Stockholm, Amma's stories felt further and further away, until I eventually outgrew them altogether. Curiosity keeps me flipping through the book. None of these made-up monsters scare me anymore. Not when I've faced worse things, like being diagnosed with severe Crohn's disease at ten years old. I live in constant fear of another flare-up, not the Fell King.

As I turn the page, a slip of paper falls onto the floor.

I pick it up and pore over the letter.

> Asta,
>
> How I longed to finally welcome you home, but I must leave Unden. The time has come for me to join our ancestors at the Shore of Sacrifices. Follow the path Skaga first walked through Tiveden, and you will find me. Remember all I've taught you.
>
> I know you are capable of making this journey, as I did, and my mother did before me. Before embarking, go down to our cellar. There you will find your birthday present, as well as the legacy you will soon inherit. I promise I will explain everything once we are reunited.
>
> We will be together again in Tiveden.
>
> All my love, Amma
>
> P.S. Accept your gift from Freyja. You will need her protection.

My hands shake as I stare down at her words, struggling to make sense of them. Shore of Sacrifices? Skaga? What is Amma talking about? And since when do we have a cellar? No one around here does. This isn't Stockholm. Not to mention, how can I accept a gift from a goddess who doesn't exist?

Dad's warning comes back to me.

Her mind wasn't all there.

Maybe he's right. I put the note on my nightstand.

A huldra stares up at me from the book. When I was young, Amma and I would go on long walks together, my little hand clutching her warm, wrinkled one. If a pine twitched, she'd point at it. *Did you see, Asta? A huldra's tail disappeared behind that tree!*

Amma always had an explanation for everything. Usually involving magic.

But magic isn't *real*.

After spending so much time in and out of hospitals, I stopped believing in Freyja. The longer I lived in Stockholm, the more I questioned my memories, until I realized what Amma did weren't spells at all but superstition. Maybe that's why her note makes no sense to me now.

Once my phone is charging, I flip through some more pages. A horse-like monster illustrated mid-gallop grabs my attention. Rather than a field, it runs along streams and lives on the bottom of lakes. The nykur appears beautiful at first, but the longer I stare at it, the more unsettling it looks. Instead of four legs, it has eight like a spider.

My eyes grow heavy as I thumb through the book.

Eventually, sleep takes me.

"What do you think, Skaga?"

Father wipes sweat from his brow as he takes in the newly finished house.

Frowning, I peer at the steep slanted roof and bare wood exterior. The house is rather plain, absent any intricate carvings like the ones that decorated our longhouse in Birka. But I know how hard Father has worked on this new home, toiling for months to build it with his bare hands. The work was back-breaking, but he did it without complaint. Liv and I helped when we could, but for the most part, our days were spent spearfishing in the lake or foraging in the forest so our bellies would be full enough to continue working the next day.

Finally, it is finished.

"It's perfect," Liv and I say in unison.

Liv is like a mother to me, unlike the woman who birthed me. My father first met Vanadís in a faraway land, and he lay with her, unable to resist her alluring beauty. But as soon as I was born, Vanadís left, abandoning us both. Something I know Liv would never do.

Father swells with pride. "I will call it Ramunder's Abode."

I wrinkle my nose. "A rather boring name, isn't it?"

"Skaga," Liv scolds.

As always, my tongue moves quicker than my mind. Liv has been with us long enough that she should be accustomed to it by now.

Father gives a booming laugh. "Next time, I will leave the naming to you, little one."

I'm about to argue I am not so little anymore, that I have seen thirteen winters already, but Liv grabs my shoulder. She pulls me to her side as she wraps her other arm around Father's waist.

"A fine name for a fine home," Liv says. "One where we can all be together, like you always wanted, Skaga. Your father will no longer need to go raiding for the king anymore."

I remember standing on the shore, waiting for my father's ship to return. Every time before he left, I begged to go with him. He was gone more than he was ever home. But when he returned, he would bring me all sorts of gifts: golden necklaces, silk clothes, little trinkets from faraway worlds. Gifts that are now left behind in Birka, along with our home.

For all her scolding, Liv is right. I have my family, and that is more precious than any treasure.

"Let me show you inside," Father says. Suddenly, he picks up Liv, much to her surprise and mine, and carries her over the threshold.

I follow them, stepping over the raised doorway, careful not to trip.

Father sets Liv down on the creaking wooden floorboard.

"What was that for?" she asks.

"I would carry my wife into our new home for the first time." Father grins. "Shall I show you our bedroom next? Perhaps here, you will give me a son."

"Not in front of your daughter, Ramunder," Liv says, though she fights a smile of her own.

I roll my eyes. When Father first wed her, I feared Liv giving him a child, and that Father would forget me for his new family. But since fleeing to

Tiveden, I find myself longing for a sibling now. It would be nice to have a companion closer to my age. Not to mention another pair of hands to help with the work.

Father gives Liv a meaningful look. "I suppose that tour can wait till tonight then."

Sighing, I sit on one of the benches along the walls, kicking my feet back and forth. The wood is still stiff and sharp, unlike the benches worn smooth from use in our former home. I do not have my piles of fur to sleep on either. All I have now are the apron dress I wear and the dagger hanging at my hip.

And Lady, of course. My forest cat rubs against my legs leisurely, purring. When we were forced to leave, I carried Lady, hugging her close. I complained that I couldn't take more, but Liv said we were lucky to keep our lives.

"What is it, little one?" The bench creaks as Father lowers himself beside me. "Are you not pleased?"

I grab fistfuls of my apron dress, unsure what I should tell him.

I settle on the truth.

"For a longhouse, it is not very long at all," I admit quietly.

"Skaga," Liv scolds. "You should thank the gods you will have a roof over your head again."

My cheeks burn hot with shame. She's right—better a hard bench than the ground we've slept on for months with only a tent over us. Father even prepared a fire pit in the middle of the room that will keep us warm during the cold months. Still, I cannot help but miss what we left behind. Now that I see our new home, I realize it is not the same. It never will be.

Father laughs. "She's right, Liv. It is small. That is why I built us a cellar, so we can store the many barrels of mead we will make."

Liv shakes her head. "You and your mead."

When we were exiled, the villagers allowed us to carry one possession each, but Father took two: his axe and some mead for the long journey.

"Speaking of which, we will feast tonight to celebrate our new home, and I will finally enjoy my mead again." He slaps his knees and rises from the bench. "Let's feed the fire, Liv. Skaga, fetch the fish from outside."

"Yes, Father."

Eager to get away, I race outside to where the fish we caught hang from a makeshift spit, their stomachs sliced open. After months of perch and pike, I'm starting to get sick of eating the same fish, but our options are few. Liv and Father are doing their best. So must I.

I remove a few fish, their unseeing eyes staring at me as I drop them into a woven basket.

A branch snaps nearby.

I turn quickly. "Father?"

But it isn't him. A young man approaches me instead. He barely has a beard, and half his short brown hair is pulled into a bun. He's wrapped in a shaggy animal-skin cloak and carries a spear like a walking stick. Has he been sent to hunt us? I shake my head slowly. I have never seen him in Birka, and Father said no one would follow us into Tiveden. We are supposed to be safe here.

I reach for my dagger. "What do you want?"

"Don't be alarmed." He holds his hands up, trying to placate me, as if he's encountered a feral animal and not a girl. "My name is Torsten. I only seek shelter for the winter months. I can help around the house however you need."

I narrow my eyes. "Why should I trust you?"

"Because I—"

"What's going on here?" Father emerges from the house, clutching his axe. He smiles when he recognizes the young man. "Torsten!"

"Ramunder!" Torsten exclaims.

Father embraces him like an old friend. "Look how much you've grown, boy."

"I was gone raiding, but once I heard what happened, I set out to find you. I don't care if they call you Ramunder the Evil now. You have always looked out for me like a father would."

"Come inside, boy," Father says, slapping him on the back. "Tell me everything."

"What did happen?" I ask. Father never told me why he was exiled.

Torsten looks between us, his expression uncertain.

"It matters not," Father says. "What matters is that we are here now."

We sit around the table while Father and Torsten talk. Apparently, they used to go raiding together, and Torsten was like the son Father never had. It is almost insulting how overjoyed Father is to see him, when I am right here. I always have been. He even pours Torsten some of the mead he's saved since we left home. Mead he has never offered me.

As Torsten speaks, I study his sharply chiseled features. He's younger than Father, but still years ahead of me. I must admit he is handsome. Noticing my attention, Torsten offers me his drinking horn, but I shake my head swiftly. Maybe it's the fire, but I feel my cheeks growing warm as Torsten laughs. He is the first person close to my age I've seen in many months, and the sound of his laughter warms me in ways no mead can.

"What will you do now?" Torsten asks.

Father takes a long swig of his drink. "I will start my own settlement here, far better than Birka."

Torsten raises his horn of mead. "Then I wish to stay, if you will have me."

"Of course." Father knocks his drinking horn against Torsten's. "All will be welcome here. Outlaws, freed thralls, migrants from faraway lands. I care not so long as they work hard and live honestly."

"What will this fine settlement of yours be called?" Torsten asks, sounding more than a little drunk.

Father turns to me. "Well, Skaga?"

I'm unable to hide my surprise. "Won't you name it yourself?"

"It will be your home longer than mine," Father says, and his words send a stab of sadness through me as he continues, "so I would give it a name that you approve of. And anyway, I promised I would let you choose the next name."

I must come up with something good, something that will endure. Birka was named after the island, but here there are none. Only the lake called Unden. The lake I have drunk from, spearfished in, and bathed myself and my clothes in. It seems fitting to name our new home after the lake that has already helped us so much. "Unden."

"Unden," Father repeats before nodding his head. "Very well. Unden it is, then."

‡

A knock on my bedroom door startles me awake.

"Time for the vigil," Dad calls.

"Already?" As I sit up, something crashes to the floor beside me. *The Hidden Folk* lays there, spread open to an illustration of a smiling little girl with needle-like teeth and milky eyes. A mara. The giver of nightmares.

My dream was so vivid, lucid enough to be a fever dream. I'd better not be sick. When I feel my forehead, it's dry and cool. Just a bizarre dream, then. Stretching my arms, I look around my bedroom, trying to get my bearings. Probably because I'm back in Unden. The house I dreamed of even looked like ours, but the inside was completely different. All this stress is finally getting to me.

Another sharp knock on the door.

"Astrid," Dad says, growing impatient. "We're going to be late. Isn't this the whole reason you insisted on coming?"

"Okay, okay," I say, climbing out of bed. "I'll be right out."

Before long, the stave church looms over me: tiered rooflines, black shingles covering the wooden walls like scales. My neck prickles as if the church watches us approach. The structure sits at the edge of the woods like a warning. This is as far as anyone in Unden goes into Tiveden. Any farther and you risk never returning. Supposedly.

A sense of misgiving scrapes over my skin as I stand here.

Why did Amma go beyond it?

Carved dragon heads stare down from the gables, looking more like they belong on a Viking longship than a church. This place reaches back through Unden's history, before even my great-great-great-grandparents' time. Skaga had it built centuries ago after her father, Unden's founder, died. Instead of nails, magic staves were used in its construction, or so the story goes. Not long after, Skaga became our first foremother.

Now this church continues her legacy.

So does my family.

According to Amma, Skaga is a distant ancestor of ours. Until that dream, I've never really given her much thought. She was just another story of Amma's—though less interesting because she was real. I'd never particularly cared about her or our family history.

I was always more interested in magic.

Before heading in, I tug my face mask over my mouth like a shield.

We pass through the doors, greeted by the sharp smell of cedar and a swarm of people. The whole damn town is packed into the old church. The chatter cuts off and every head swivels toward us in unison. No one moves. The wooden walls close in on me as we stand there. My breath is hot beneath my mask, trapped with nowhere to go.

I hate being close to anyone, since getting close means I can get sick. Very, very sick. *Immunocompromised* is the official term, but I hate that word. It sounds like I'm not enough, like part of me is missing, even though I don't feel that way. Or maybe I just forgot what it's like to be healthy.

Crowds are one of the things I never liked about living in Stockholm. With my mask on, people avoid me like I can get *them* sick, not the other way around. My illness may be invisible, but my mask isn't.

Everyone here is staring at my mask. I should be used to it, but I'm not.

I scan the sea of faces, hoping to find Officer Lind.

Ebba Karlsson, the nosy neighbor, bumps into me instead. Her gaze lands briefly on my mask before she meets my eyes. "Oh, I'm so sorry."

And there it is.

That's what people always say once they learn I'm sick. They look at me with pity, even though it's the last thing I want from anyone. *I'm so sorry*, they offer, but what they're really thinking is *Thank God I'm not you. Thank God I'm healthy*. I swear I can see the relief in their eyes. And I hate how it makes me feel.

Suddenly, Unden doesn't seem so different from Stockholm.

"It's just terrible what happened," Ebba continues. "We all loved Ingrid so much."

She throws her arms around me. Maybe I'd misread her apology? But I guess we're hugging now, which is even worse than pity. I try not to recoil as she squeezes me. Too tight. *Too close*. Now I'm grateful for my mask, even if it doesn't seem to faze her at all.

Ebba releases me with a warm smile. "So good to see you again, Astrid."

"You too, Ebba," I say, and I mean it.

Until she turns to my dad and looks him up and down. "And it's *really* good to see you again, Erik. Or can I call you Rick?"

I cringe. Please tell me she is *not* flirting with my dad.

I'm grateful when two of my old classmates approach us.

"Astrid!" Linnea pulls me into a hug. "We miss you!"

It takes me a moment to recognize her without her long red hair. It's cropped short now, but her face is still full of freckles and her green eyes sparkle. She looks happier than I've ever seen her.

"Hey," I say, patting her back awkwardly. "I missed you all too."

I'm surprised to realize how *much* I missed them. In Unden, making friends was effortless. Unlike Stockholm, everyone wanted to sit next to me and be my friend. Well, everyone except Nils. He sat behind me so he could yank my braid every chance he got until one day I turned around and punched him. The braid pulling stopped after that.

Now, even *he* looks happy to see me.

I guess a lot really has changed.

"Are you two together?" I ask, looking between them.

"Gods, no," they both say at the same time.

Linnea laughs. "My girlfriend, Emma—you remember her, right?—is over there with her family."

"Speaking of which," Dad says, resting his hand on my shoulder, "we should take our seats too. The service is about to start. This way, Astrid."

He steers me to the front of the church.

Looks like I'll have to find Officer Lind after the service.

Sighing, I slide into the front row beside Dad.

A towering wooden sculpture of Freyja looms over the altar. The religion here is ancient and wild, like the thick roots that run through the soil. The goddess watches her worshippers, but even the careful carving can't capture her beauty. She's called the Bright Lady not only because of her flowing hair, which shines like the sun, but also because she brings daylight with her as she walks the world, weeping tears of gold. Everyone gathered here believes they'll be reunited with Freyja in Sessrúmnir one day.

Once, I believed it too.

When we moved, Dad forbade me from talking about Freyja. He said we no longer needed that religion. No one else believed it anymore. Only Unden hadn't moved on from the past. He was right about that part, at least. Anytime I said þǫkk sé Freyju to a classmate, everyone laughed at me. When I drew a stave for good luck on a pop quiz, I got detention for using my blood. And then grounded. Suddenly, the stave didn't seem so lucky anymore.

Those old beliefs didn't last long in Stockholm.

Ulf walks to the pulpit. "Thank you for gathering today," the old man says, his raspy voice filling the church. "Normally, Ingrid would be the one standing before you. Unfortunately for us all, she is no longer here, so you'll have to tolerate me."

Wood creaks as someone sits beside me. "Long time no see, Astrid."

Johan. Unlike Linnea and Nils, he doesn't seem thrilled that I'm back, even though we were inseparable when we were younger. His black hair is just as curly as I remember, but he's a lot taller and wears glasses now. He looks more tired too, with deep circles underneath his eyes, dark against his brown skin. Not even his glasses can hide his exhaustion.

I nudge him with my shoulder. "Hey, Janne."

He winces a little at the old nickname.

"No one calls me that anymore," Johan whispers. He's so quiet I can barely hear him. Clearly, he doesn't like talking during the service. He's never been one to break rules.

"Right." The bench creaks beneath me as I shift my weight, suddenly uncomfortable. "Sorry."

It's been years since we last spoke, and even longer since I've seen him. After I left, I pushed Johan away like everyone else. I was hoping to see him today, but now that he's next to me, I don't know what to say.

Johan twists his hands in his lap. "I'm sorry for your loss."

I stiffen, my body as rigid as the pew under me. I want to tell him I haven't lost anything, that Amma is waiting for me in Tiveden, but I bite my tongue.

"How are you doing, Astrid?" Johan asks.

He sounds genuinely concerned. It's the first time anyone here has even bothered to ask me. My hands ball into fists as I tell him the same thing I always tell Zuri. "I'm fine."

Mostly.

Not really.

Johan frowns like he wants to say something more but doesn't.

Dad clears his throat, shooting us a warning glare.

"I think we can all agree Ingrid was a gift to Unden," Old Ulf continues. "During her time as foremother, our community flourished under her care. Skaga and Freyja must be proud of the work she's done. We will never forget all the sacrifices she has made on our behalf. Ingrid may have left us, but she is never truly gone."

"þọkk sé Freyju," Johan murmurs next to me.

Praise be to Freyja.

Everyone repeats it except for me and Dad. Even Officer Lind says it with such conviction. Freyja and the Hidden Folk are just stories to me, but not to everyone else gathered in this church. They all *believe* it.

That's why Officer Lind won't even look for Amma.

As I study him, something seems off. His eyes are dry, his face devoid of any emotion. The people sitting on either side of him are the same. They barely even blink. I look down the row of so-called mourners, but everyone wears the same emotionless mask. Even Helga, who knew Amma longer than anyone.

No wet eyes, no quiet sobs, *nothing.*

This isn't right. Amma is their foremother. Everyone loved her— almost as much as I did. When we walked around Unden, everyone would go out of their way to greet her. If she ever forgot to bring her purse to the butcher, Áki would wave his hand and tell her not to worry. Wherever we went, everyone beamed as soon as they saw her. It creeped me out a little. When I asked why, she smiled. *Freyja has blessed our family. Without us, Unden would not exist.*

So if everyone believes Amma is gone, why is no one mourning her?

This is all *wrong*. A month isn't even enough time to declare a missing person dead. I've watched plenty of true crime. Typically, it takes several years. Longer. Maybe Dad was right not to trust Officer Lind.

Suddenly, I'm not sure I can trust anyone here.

My skin prickles with the sensation of being watched. I turn slowly, looking over my shoulder at the rows of staring faces. Maybe it's because we're up front, but it sure seems like no one is actually paying attention to Old Ulf.

They're all staring at me.

THREE

By the time the service ends, the sun has nearly set.

As Midwinter nears, we're lucky if we have five or six hours of daylight. As I look over the sprawling grave field, sunset bathes the centuries-old stones with an eerie red glow. The gravestones, each as tall as the person it commemorates, send shadows reaching over the hill like long fingers. For an instant, it appears as though hundreds of dead people stand stone-still on the hillside.

Shaking off that unsettling image, I join Johan.

Everyone from church slowly makes their way up the hill toward Amma's newly added gravestone, careful not to trip over any of the smaller, sunken rocks. Johan and I walk side by side, just the two of us. The last time we were together like this, we were little kids, scrambling up boulders and shouting, *I'm king of the mountain!*

Maybe he'll be willing to come with me still.

"Why don't we search Tiveden?" I ask. "We can hang out like old times."

Johan frowns. "We can't go beyond the stave church," he says harshly. "You know that."

I roll my eyes. "Don't tell me you still believe in the Hidden Folk."

"If you don't," he asks, suddenly defensive, "then why are you wearing that trollkors around your neck?"

I glance down at my necklace and reach for the twisted piece of cold steel dangling from it. "Amma gave it to me. That's why."

I can still feel her hands placing the cord around my neck and tugging my braid free from its clasp. *You must always wear this,* she told me, her face grave.

Johan shakes his head. "Just because you can't see them—"

"Doesn't mean they're not there," I finish. "I know. Don't you think that's a little convenient, though? How can you believe that and still want to study science?"

"It doesn't have to be one or the other," Johan says, his expression hardening.

"That's how I feel about Amma," I insist. Maybe I just have to put this in a way Johan will understand. "To me, she's like Schrödinger's cat right now. Alive *and* dead. Until I find her, I won't know which she actually is."

"That's not how it works." Johan shoves a hand through his curls. He's been obsessed with science since we were little. "That thought experiment is about quantum superposition, and—you know what, never mind, I'll go along with it. Whether or not the cat is observed doesn't change if it's alive or dead. It can't exist as both simultaneously. Actually, that's why Schrödinger designed the whole thought experiment. He wanted to disprove the—"

I give an exasperated sigh. "You don't understand. I just . . . I need to know."

Mom's loss is an old wound: a scar, swollen but still tender. Amma's disappearance is more like a slit throat, sharp and sudden. There's no explanation. No closure. Nothing. It turns out the only thing worse than knowing is *not* knowing. No one can really understand until it happens to them.

I fold my arms across my chest. "I'm telling you, there must be a reason why she went into Tiveden. And don't you *dare* say it was the Hidden Folk."

Johan glances away. "It doesn't change the fact that she's been missing for weeks, and, well . . ."

His silence says more than any words could. My gaze lingers on the stones dotting the hillside. I may not believe in the Hidden Folk, but I know how freezing it gets here. I know all about the risks of dehydration and starvation and . . .

No.

I can't even consider it. So I focus on all the questions I'm left with instead. Why would Amma go beyond the stave church? Why is Officer Lind in such a rush to declare her dead? And if everyone really believes she died, then why is no one mourning her?

He sighs, pinching the bridge of his nose. "I know what you're thinking of doing, but you can't go beyond the stave church. It's too dangerous."

"I won't," I lie. "Don't worry—"

My foot catches on a rock, and I almost stumble.

"Watch out," Johan says, grabbing my arm. "Don't step on Ramunder's longship."

"Longship? Oh. Right."

The boulders by my feet aren't scattered randomly. Each one was deliberately placed to form the shape of the slender ships the Vikings once went voyaging in. Ramunder's body was never recovered, so I guess this is the closest Skaga could get to a ship burial.

To me, the stones look like waiting jaws, ready to devour me.

Shuddering, I step over them carefully. "Do you come here often?"

"Of course." He glances at a nearby gravestone. "My mom is here."

Guilt pinches me. Growing up, I always envied that Johan had a mom. His family was everything I longed for: supportive, happy, *whole*. It hurt me to see it sometimes. But I never wanted him to lose his mother. I wouldn't wish that pain on anyone.

"I'm so sorry."

Johan stills in front of the grave covered with fresh flowers. He must visit a lot, even though she died shortly after I left.

"You didn't even attend her funeral," he says.

"I wanted to."

I should've been here for him while he went through that, like he used to be there for me whenever I missed my mom. He always invited me to his house and tried to make me feel like I was part of his family. Once I left Unden, it wasn't the same anymore. Nothing was.

"But I couldn't," I add weakly. "Not when my dad—"

"That was years ago, Astrid. You're telling me you couldn't have visited, not even once?"

"I *tried* to."

When I was thirteen, I took the train here, but it only went as far as Laxå station. Since I couldn't afford a taxi, I tried walking the rest of the way but ended up getting lost instead. After Dad had to leave work and drive three hours to get me, I was grounded for months. Next time, I cut class so I could take the bus, but the school called the cops on me. They threatened to remove me from Dad if I kept skipping school or running away, so I had to stop. I didn't want another new home. I just wanted my old one back.

"It isn't that simple," I finish.

Johan sighs. "You could have called, or at least *responded* to me."

"You're right," I admit. "I should have."

While I was in and out of the hospital, I forgot to respond to his messages. Eventually, he stopped reaching out.

Now we're standing right next to each other, but the distance between us widens the more we talk. Soon, I'm not sure either of us will be able to cross it. I never felt like I belonged in Stockholm, but maybe I don't belong here, either.

Not anymore.

"I'm sorry about your mom," I say. "I really am."

"She's held by Freyja now, in a field that goes on forever, surrounded by golden wheat swaying in a warm breeze, someplace the sun never sets." The words are a refrain, spoken each time someone in Unden dies.

Now that I hear them again, it strikes me that no one said them for Amma.

When we reach Amma's gravestone, bright yellow cowslip are heaped before it. I stare at the delicate flowers until my eyes start to ache. In Unden, they're known as Freyja's tears, and are grown indoors year round. The villagers believe the flowers first sprang from the goddess's tears as she wandered the world, weeping for her lost husband.

I swipe my tears away. I don't care what Johan or anyone else says. I'm going to find Amma, no matter what.

"Hi, Mr. Skarsgård," Johan says.

Dad joins us. "Johan. You've grown up, haven't you? The last time I saw you . . ." His voice trails off.

I know exactly what he's thinking, and I'm sure Johan remembers too. The memory is lodged in my mind like a splinter.

Johan and I were outside playing when Dad dropped my suitcase into the trunk with a heavy thud. I had no idea what was happening as he shoved my teddy bear into my arms and dragged me over to the car. *I'm doing this for you, Astrid,* he said, buckling me into the backseat. *One day, you'll thank me for it.*

I still haven't.

Dad never even gave me the chance to say goodbye to Amma. I've reminded him many times since, every opportunity I get. I still haven't forgiven him, and he knows it. It's the only reason he broke down and let me come at all. That, and how I refused to apply to any university before I could say goodbye. He thinks that once I do, we can both move on.

Johan clears his throat. "Well, uh, I'll leave you two alone to talk."

"No, don't." When I realize how sharp my tone is, I quickly add, "We were in the middle of catching up, Dad."

Johan glances between us nervously.

"You'll have plenty of time to talk at the reception," Dad says after a beat.

"Sure," Johan says, not unkindly. "See you there."

He offers me an apologetic smile before heading back down the hill.

"What reception?" I ask, raising an eyebrow.

Dad turns to me. "Ebba was just telling me they're holding an event at the rec center to honor Ingrid."

"And you're actually going?"

"Everyone is." He rubs his forehead roughly. "I need to iron out some details with the lawyer so we can leave first thing tomorrow. Oh, and talk to Helga. Apparently, she's interested in buying—"

"Dad," I say, lowering my voice. "I think some people here might be involved somehow."

He frowns. "Involved with what?"

I chew my lip, recalling the scrap of paper I found in my book. Amma said she *had* to leave Unden . . . almost like she was being forced to. "Amma supposedly disappearing."

Dad stares at me. "You haven't been watching those true crime documentaries on Netflix again, have you?"

I roll my eyes. "I'm being serious."

"So am I." He shakes his head. "Anyway, like I was saying," he continues, brushing aside my concerns like they're nothing, "as soon as I sell the house, we can get out of here tomorrow."

My heart misses a beat. He's selling Amma's house? *My* home?

"We just got here, though." If he's really planning on leaving tomorrow, then tonight is my only chance to search Tiveden. "Actually . . . I'd better not eat. Especially not if we're driving back tomorrow. I'm not really feeling well," I lie. Sort of.

"Are you okay?" His brow furrows. "It's not another flare-up, is it?"

For a moment, I almost feel bad.

I shake my head quickly. "I'm sure I'll be fine. I just need some rest."

"All right," he says, looking unconvinced. "I'm going to stop by your mother's grave. You should say goodbye to Ingrid before you go. This is your last chance to get some closure."

Dad walks away, leaving me alone.

I inhale deeply, breathing in the soft scent of the cowslip flowers. Her memorial looms over me, runes snaking around the stone. I trace the carved symbols, the stone cold under my fingertip. It takes a long time to translate: *Erik and Astrid had this stone erected in memory of Ingrid, their beloved mother and grandmother.*

Despite the fragrant flowers, my stomach turns. Beloved? I stare at the stone until my eyes are so wet, the runes begin to blur. Dad never loved Amma. *He* is the one who abandoned his own mother. *He* is the one who took me away from her. *He* is the reason this happened.

What he feels is *guilt*. Not love.

My throat closes as I stare at the runes. I can't say goodbye. I won't, not until I know for sure what happened. So I leave the grave field behind and set off in the opposite direction from everyone else—back home to prepare for my search.

I don't need a goodbye. I need answers.

‡

Amma's house is dark and silent.

I have to hurry. Before searching for the cellar, I should grab some things I *know* I'll definitely need. I head straight for my bedroom, not bothering with the lights or even removing my coat. I can't risk alerting anyone.

Rifling through my backpack, I assess what I've brought: water bottle, bags of pretzels, another pair of dark jeans, plenty of socks and underwear, and a few T-shirts. If I'm going into Tiveden tonight, I'm going to need some warmer options. Temperatures drop below freezing fast. I try my drawers, but these clothes would only fit me if I was still eight years old.

I'm sure Amma won't mind if I borrow some sweaters. I walk down the hall, floorboards creaking with every footstep. My hand rests on the cold doorknob of Amma's bedroom. Swallowing the lump in my throat, I push open the door.

Her room is just as I remember: small bed, large wooden dresser, an old lamp, canvases lining the walls. Whenever I couldn't sleep with the Fell King watching me, I would crawl into bed with her and cling to her linen nightgown.

Pulling open the dresser's top drawer, I find one of the sweaters Amma always wore. The one with gray wool and snowflakes spread from shoulder to shoulder. I bring it up to my face, inhaling deeply, the lingering scent of pine filling my nose. If I close my eyes, I can almost pretend Amma is still here.

When I finally pull myself away from the sweater, wetness blooms on the wool.

Wiping it off, I tuck it carefully inside my bag.

I try to think of anything else I might—

Backup cell phone battery.

I'm sure I won't get reception in the woods either, but my phone is also a compass, GPS, flashlight. Definitely all things I'll need. And I don't want it dying on me while I'm in the woods. Luckily, Dad never leaves home without a spare battery pack.

His room is barren. Only an empty metal bed frame sits here, its iron bars reminding me of a prison. Not even a mattress remains. He must have slept on the sofa last night. His duffel bag is the only thing on the bed. I unzip the bag and look through it. Dad will probably be back soon. I'm running out of time.

I grab the charger quickly.

When I look up, I notice a framed photograph hanging above the bed. Two people stand together, but the glass is cracked. Carefully, I work the photo free. Dad is grinning, his arm wrapped around Mom while she laughs, blond hair blowing in her face. Staring at her smile, I trail my thumb over her cheek. She looks so . . . *happy*.

They both do.

My chest grows painfully tight. I set the photo down and head for the kitchen.

As I pull open the fridge, I'm bathed in its bright, unnatural light. My next injection is tomorrow morning, so I grab a shot just in case I'm not back by then. My shots can be stored at room temperature for up to two weeks if necessary. I'll be back long before—

The floor in the living room creaks behind me.

My heart shoots into my throat. Dad is back already? I swivel my head toward the living room. A familiar silhouette stands there, right beside the sofa. That thin frame. *Amma.*

I race over to the light switch and flip it—

Just a narrow cabinet. That's all.

What the hell's wrong with me? My hands shake as I stuff my shot into my backpack and hastily zip it up. I can't risk leaving my bag behind, so I pull it on quickly. Time is running out.

Looking around the floor, I search for any sign of a cellar.

But there isn't any. Only the rug Amma crocheted. I stare down at the pattern of bright yellow flowers. Freyja's tears. Again. Amma used to say intuition is how the goddess guides us.

Right now, I'm desperate enough to listen.

Crouching down, I peel back the rug like a page of a book.

Sure enough, there's a trapdoor.

The cellar.

I try the door—

Locked.

There's no hole for a key, or any sign of a locking mechanism. Only a strange symbol carved carefully in the wood. Damn it, I don't have *time* for this. How the hell do I open a locked door that has no key?

Rubbing my hand over my mouth, I look around the house. Maybe I can pry the door up. The crack around it is just a sliver, too narrow for a hammer. I need something else. The silverware drawer squeals as I pull it open, utensils rattling around like all the questions in my head. I grab a knife and wedge it into the crack for leverage.

I push down, my arms shaking.

The door groans . . . but stays put.

Frustrated, I pound my hand against it. A jagged edge stabs my skin, making me wince. I stop abruptly, studying the strange symbol carved into the surface more closely:

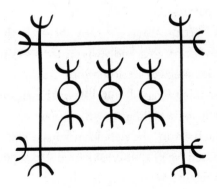

A magic stave.

Amma always said they could do the impossible. Make an enemy dream of unfulfilled desires, produce an endless supply of coin, turn yourself—and whomever else you touch—invisible, open locks without a key . . .

It comes to me like I learned it yesterday. Lásabrjótr. The stave on the door means *lockbreaker.*

I try the door again, pulling on the handle with all my strength. It still doesn't open. I shake my head. Why would it? Magic isn't real. Before we found out I had Crohn's, I would get horrible, unexplained abdominal pain. Amma tried painting staves on my stomach with her blood. But it was only the doctors in Stockholm, with their antibiotics and anti-inflammatories, who actually helped.

I trace the carving, only to nick my finger on the sharp wood. The twinge of pain makes me wince. Blood splatters the stave like drops of paint. I blink a few times. Amma always said the staves need fuel. More specifically, *blood.* I can't believe I'm about to do this, but . . . slowly, I drag my finger along the stave, smearing red into the grooves.

Nothing happens.

I sigh. Of course it wouldn't *actually* work.

But then—something clicks, so quiet I almost don't catch it.

I suck in a sharp breath as the wood groans.

Impossible. Just like Amma said.

I'm still not sure I really *believe* it, but the cellar is unlocked.

That's all that matters.

Hinges rasp as I lift the door. The room below is thick with darkness. I pull my phone from my coat and turn on the flashlight. Light illuminates rotting wooden steps descending into the darkness below.

Swallowing my misgivings, I start down the rickety stairs. The first step groans. I reach for a railing, but there isn't one. There's nothing I can hold on to. The hairs on the nape of my neck rise. Cautiously, I take another step. Another. Each stair creaks louder than the last.

As I descend, the air grows damp and heavy.

By the time I reach the bottom, a ripe, musty odor stings my nose. It's so freezing down here that I'm glad I kept my coat on. Slowly, I pan my flashlight around the cellar, cutting through the darkness like a knife. Dust motes swirl through the beam. The walls are packed earth, roots poking out like exposed nerves.

A sense of dread comes over me as I step forward, batting aside thick cobwebs. In the middle of the cellar stands an imposing wooden pillar, carefully crafted to resemble Freyja. Amma always said the goddess was known for her beauty, with blond hair flowing down to her bare feet and a soft, heart-shaped face.

Unlike the statue in the church, this Freyja is terrifying, all severe lines and sharp edges. The goddess's eyes are empty, her two palms extended out to form a wooden ledge where something rests. A sheathed knife, I think.

Accept your gift from Freyja.

As I pick it up, an image flashes—*large, calloused hands hold the dagger out to me, and I take it from them like a treasured gift.* I blink and reality returns, the statue of Freyja still staring at me. What *was* that? Am I hallucinating now too? And those glimpses of Amma I've seen since returning . . .

Maybe I am starting to lose it.

Shaking off that unsettling thought, I examine the knife more closely. It's heavier than I expected, but the handle fits my palm perfectly, whorls covering the wood like tangled vines. I slide off the sheath, revealing a gleaming dagger with a single edge. It looks deadly, nothing like the knives in our kitchen.

Right. Freyja isn't just a beautiful goddess of love and light.

She's also a brutal goddess of battle—and death.

Runes are engraved down the blade, spelling out *Skaga*. The same name as the girl in my dream last night. Our ancestor, according to Amma. Another shiver spreads through me. Why would Amma have something like this? She said I needed Freyja's protection in Tiveden. Is this what she meant? Full of foreboding, I slowly sheathe the dagger and slip it into my coat pocket. Just in case.

Amma also mentioned something about a legacy.

I keep searching, but there's only some iron rods and big wooden barrels. Storage, probably. Cobwebs curtain off the opposite side of the cellar. Holding my breath, I push them aside. My flashlight pans over a wet rock wall covered by a mural with three distinct scenes.

On the left, trees are painted over the rock, their roots as twisted as writhing snakes. A solitary figure stands in the forest. His face has been scratched away, leaving no distinguishing features, only a long cloak pooling around his feet. Above him, a name is written in runes: *Soren*.

On the other side, a girl wearing a long dress walks toward the woods, leaving her home behind. The roof is all sharp angles, the house reminding me of ours. Even the girl looks familiar.

I step closer, examining her features. All I can see are my own—we have the same sharp chin and pert nose. Even her simply drawn eyes fit her face like mine. My breath catches. She clutches a dagger in her hand, exactly like the one in my pocket.

This must be Skaga.

Of course it wouldn't—couldn't—be me.

In the middle of the mural, the two figures lock hands, the forest behind Soren, the house behind Skaga. A long string of runes are painted above them. It takes me a minute to translate.

The blood oath must not be broken.

I trace a fingertip over the wet stone, and goose bumps spread up my arms. What blood oath? I read the runes again and again, trying to fit the pieces together, to make sense of what I'm seeing, but I can't. In all her stories, all her lessons, Amma never mentioned a blood oath.

I look around the cellar, searching for some kind of explanation—

My gaze trips over something lying on the ground.

No, not something.

Someone.

⇒→FOUR←⇐

My throat closes up. "Amma?"

Seeing the body is like the sudden shock of plunging beneath an ice lake. I rush toward her, heart lodged in my throat. "Amma!"

No. *No.*

Only it isn't her.

A boy not much older than me lies there, deathly still. The flashlight illuminates silver hair. Waxy skin. No matter how long I stare, his chest doesn't move a millimeter. My mind finally catches up with what I'm seeing: a dead body in our cellar.

My phone crashes to the dirt. Oh my God. My breath comes in short bursts as I stand here, unable to move. The air down here tastes damp and moldy on my tongue. Suddenly, it registers that this is *real.*

I scoop up my phone and punch in 112, but nothing happens.

Right, no reception. *Damn it.*

Did Amma *kill* someone? Swallowing, I shine the flashlight over the corpse again. Fur pelts spread beneath him, framing his tunic, loose trousers, and leather boots. He could've stepped out of a page from my *History of Sweden* textbook. Except for his silver hair. It must be dyed, but it's unlike any dye job I've seen.

No signs of decomposition, though. He must have died recently.

But how? I don't see any blood.

Something sits on his chest. A stone with a stave painted on it . . . almost like four bent fishing hooks with lines cutting across them. I try to recall the symbol from Amma's lessons, but I can't. I need to get a better look. Squinting, I carefully pluck it off his chest—

A spark shoots through my fingertips, and I drop the stone like a hot iron.

The corpse inhales sharply.

His eyes shoot open, bright blue irises staring at me.

Holy shit. Suddenly, I forget how to breathe. My hands shake so much I drop my phone again, its watery light barely illuminating the cellar. I watch in horror as the dead body starts to *move*. Stumbling back, I get as far away from him as I can, but my legs give out, sending me smacking onto the ground. Hard.

No fucking way. He wasn't *breathing*.

Now he's getting up.

As he rises to his full height, silver hair falls around his sharp jaw, his long bangs framing ice-chip eyes. His features appear cold. Cruel. He focuses on me with an intensity that sends a slow shiver tracing down my spine.

My mouth goes bone-dry. "You . . . you were dead."

This must be a nightmare. In a moment, I'll wake up. I pinch my arm as hard as I can, but nothing happens. The dead boy—well, the *not*-dead boy—takes a step closer. His bright blue eyes remain fixed on me.

"So you have returned to me at last," he says, fury and something rougher rolling off his words.

My response to his voice is visceral, like he's stolen the breath from my lungs.

"What?" I gasp.

As soon as the word escapes, it dawns on me he's speaking Old Norse, not Swedish. Until the vigil earlier today, I hadn't heard that language in years. Amma taught it to me when I was little. *Our secret language*, she always said with a wistful smile.

"Hvat?" I try again.

He stalks toward me, his boots grinding the packed earth with each step. His presence fills the entire cellar. A thick fur-trimmed cloak hangs from his broad shoulders, framing his powerful physique. Not even the simple tunic he wears can conceal his muscles.

I reach into my coat pocket and slowly unsheathe the dagger. A small pouch hangs from his belt. No weapons. At least none that I can see.

"*Skaga,*" he practically growls.

I climb to my feet, holding the dagger between us. "You have the wrong . . ." I struggle to come up with the word for it in Old Norse. "Person," I settle on. I'm getting rusty. "My name is Astrid . . . wait." My voice rises in disbelief as I look at the mural. "Skaga—like the stave church? *That* Skaga?"

No way he actually knew her. That church was built *centuries* ago, but he barely looks older than me. Nothing he's saying makes any sense. Maybe he hit his head and has a concussion. Maybe he's drugged.

Or maybe he's out of his mind.

My head buzzes as I back away from him, only to bump against the wall.

Shit.

Before I can blink, the not-dead boy closes the distance between us and grabs my wrists, pinning me against the dirt wall. His cold grip sends shock waves shooting through me. Who the hell does he think he is? Hasn't he ever heard of personal space?

Gritting my teeth, I struggle against him. "Let *go.*"

Our gazes lock. I try to pull free, but he tightens his hold until my dagger clatters onto the floor. *Damn it.*

He leans over me, lowering his face—beautiful in its deadliness—closer to mine. "Do not dare deceive me again."

The words are barely a whisper, but it's enough to make the little hairs on my arms stand on end. Centimeters separate our faces. His nose practically skims mine. My heart pounds, ready to burst through my ribs.

I cannot get sick. Not now.

"I don't know what the hell you're talking about," I say, the ancient language coming more easily with every word. Amma would be proud.

"Do not feign ignorance." He narrows his eyes. "I know it was you who used the sleep thorn on me, Skaga. You cannot lie your way out of this again."

Sleep thorn? He must mean the stave I found on him. The one that, as soon as I removed it, woke him up. Whenever I wanted to stay up past my bedtime, Amma used to threaten me with one if I didn't cooperate. But I saw him—he wasn't asleep, he was *dead*.

"Who the hell are you?" My voice shakes.

"Do not take me for a fool," he snarls, baring his teeth.

No, *fangs*. Those are definitely fangs.

My breathing quickens. The illustrations of the draugar flash in my mind, but those creatures are stories. They're not *real*. I finally tear my gaze away from his mouth and look up into his bright blue eyes instead. They glint like ice, even in the dark.

"*What* are you?" I amend.

Those unforgiving eyes narrow. "You already know."

I look down his long blue tunic to his baggy linen pants tucked into tall boots. He's dressed like some historical reenactor. A really, really good one. But then there are also his ice-blue eyes. Skin leached of color. Hair like cold steel. Long, wicked fangs.

My mouth goes dry. The truth is unavoidable, staring me right in the face.

He is a draugr.

A *monster*.

Staves. Draugar. I can't deny it any longer. They're both terrifyingly *real*.

The ground shifts under me, making me unsteady on my feet.

All those stories Amma told me . . .

A memory comes back unbidden. *Dad said I shouldn't listen to you,* I told Amma tearfully as she pulled me onto her lap. *Why is that, little Asta?* I rubbed my cheeks roughly. *Because. He told me it's dangerous to believe you.* Amma spread the *Hidden Folk* book on her lap. *Don't you see, little one? They are the dangerous ones. That's what frightens your father—*

Amma was right.

They *are* real. And the one in front of me is clearly dangerous.

"What are you even doing here?" I try to pull away from the draugr. If he wanted to, he could crush my wrist. But instead he loosens his hold slightly, like he's restraining himself. Or trying to.

"You know very well why I am here." His claws brush over me like the tips of knives—claws capable of shredding flesh into ribbons, but he doesn't leave a scratch.

Even if he doesn't harm me, he could still infect me.

I twist my head away.

He grabs my chin, forcing me to look at him. "Because of *your* betrayal."

I stare at his cold face, too aware of my pounding pulse. Blood is the only thing capable of sating a draugr's immense appetite. And he must be starving after being asleep for so long. Looking at his fangs, it isn't hard to imagine him sinking them into my throat.

He leans forward, his face drawing dangerously close to my neck.

Then he whispers harshly against the shell of my ear. "Say my name."

I shiver at his words.

My attention shifts to the mural behind him, to the figure wearing the cloak. Both have sharp faces. Broad shoulders. The runes—his name, I think. It can't be a coincidence the draugr was imprisoned down here with that mural. Or that he's mistaken me for Skaga.

"Um . . . Are you Soren?"

His brow creases in confusion. "Have you forgotten?"

He looks as though I've wounded him. His grip loosens, and I slip free, my skin still buzzing. I double-check my hands quickly, making sure there are no scratches or cuts that could get infected, then brush the spot where he held me, my fingers lingering a moment too long.

So it *is* him. The figure in the mural.

Except it's not just a mural. *It's a warning,* I realize too late.

If Skaga really was the one who imprisoned him . . . she died a long, long time ago. Which means this draugr in front of me must be ancient.

And powerful, if Skaga had to use a stave like that on him. Hopefully I didn't break the blood oath by waking him.

I lived in this house for half my life and had no idea he was right below me. How many times have I walked above this very spot? In all of Amma's stories, she never mentioned a draugr existing outside of Tiveden. Especially not one asleep in our damn cellar. How could she not *tell* me?

What other secrets is she keeping from me?

Soren takes a slow, menacing step closer.

I have to protect myself. But how?

Cold steel—the *dagger*. I grab it off the floor and grip it so hard my knuckles turn white.

"You would betray me again?" he asks, his face full of fury. "After everything I have done for you? Everything I have sacrificed for you?" His eyes soften. "I am not your enemy, Skaga."

Something stirs within me.

Skaga believed he was, or she wouldn't have imprisoned him. The dagger trembles in my hand. There must be some reason no one was supposed to wake Soren. But I did. And now I might've done something that can't be undone.

"It is not too late," Soren says, stopping before me. "We can still break the blood oath. Together."

"I don't even know what the blood oath *is*."

Soren looks startled. "Do you truly not remember?"

When I say nothing, staring at him blankly, he adds, "The oath we made to each other before the gods."

I blink. "Yeah, still nothing."

He glares at me. "The oath we made for the Folk to remain in Tiveden so that Unden's settlers could live safely—"

I walk past him and pick up my phone, brushing it off. "You're in Unden right now," I point out before thinking better of it.

Soren gives an exasperated sigh. "Our blood was used to make the oath, so it does not limit me, just as it does not limit you."

I pocket my phone. "Then why do you care if it's broken?"

"Because it never should have been made," Soren says, lowering his voice. "Whether you recall or not, you must help me break it."

I reread the runes across the mural. *The blood oath must not be broken.* Yeah, the instructions seem pretty damn clear: that is *not* what I'm supposed to do.

I shake my head. "I can't do that."

He gives me a dark look. "Then I will make you."

>>→FIVE→←←

"I told you," I say, breathing hard. "I'm not Skaga."

Soren looks me up and down, taking in my boots and jeans and coat. "You are dressed rather strangely."

"*I'm* the one dressed strangely?" I scoff, staring at his ancient attire. "Someone needs to look in the—"

Soren grabs my free hand. He uncurls my fingers, inspecting my palm and the scar running across it. I've had it for as long as I can remember. I don't even recall how I got it anymore. Probably climbing a rock or a tree when I was little.

Soren lingers on the scar, tracing the pearly mark gently with one of his claws.

He nods like he's come to a decision. "You *are* Skaga. Here is the proof."

"What?" Air hisses between my teeth. "No, I've always had this."

"You can lie, but your scars cannot."

He tightens his grip and, without warning, twists my hand behind me.

"What are you *doing*?" I struggle against his hold, my shoulder pulling, but he won't release me. "Let go of me."

"Then do not resist me," he says, voice low.

Like hell I won't. Fighting back is all I know how to do.

With my free arm, I throw my elbow back as hard as I can—

He blocks the blow, forcing that arm behind me too.

The pain leaves me panting. "Let me go."

"I will not." His fingers dig into my wrists like he's desperate to hold on. "I *cannot*."

He mutters something, quick and low beneath his breath.

A strange sensation spreads through me like crackling frost.

"What are you doing?" I gasp.

My arms grow stiff, suddenly full of pins and needles. I try to flex my fingers, but my hands won't cooperate. My breathing turns quick and shallow. I can't even tighten my grip on my dagger. I can't move my hands at all. My wrists must be tied, but when I pull against the bindings, no rope chafes my skin.

Nothing does.

My blood runs cold as I face him. "What did you do to me?"

"You wouldn't listen," he says harshly. "I had to use a galdr on you."

"Galdr?" I ask in disbelief.

"Have you forgotten everything?" Soren looks lost, but then his cold, distant mask returns. "A galdr is similar to a stave, except spoken instead of painted. This spell binds an enemy without rope."

"Yeah, I know that," I spit. I just didn't think they were *real*.

I don't feel any awe, just frustration as I struggle against the spell. I can't move my arms no matter how hard I try. My body is betraying me. Just like a flare-up, I'm at the mercy of something I can't control. Panic sets in. Helplessness.

Anger.

"Walk," Soren says harshly. "You can still use your legs."

I turn away from him. "I'm not going *anywhere* with you."

When I don't budge, Soren pushes me up the stairs. The old wood groans under our weight, threatening to snap. I force myself to climb quickly, not wanting to fall and break a bone. The stairs creak loudly, one after the other, until I stumble into the living room.

Please, let Dad be back.

I scan the house desperately.

He isn't here.

Of course he's not here when I need him.

The old telephone in the kitchen. I have to call him. Call Officer Lind. *Someone.*

There's just one problem: my hands won't move.

Soren stares at the ceiling light, wincing at its brightness. "What magic is this?"

"Electricity," I say in Swedish. Not like there's a word for it in Old Norse.

He gives me a puzzled look.

Maybe this is how I can convince him he's mistaken. "A long time has passed since you went to sleep. Like a really, really long time. By now, Skaga is—she's . . ." I bite back the rest of the words.

Soren scowls at me.

I swallow hard. If I reveal she's dead, I have no idea what he'll do. Probably blame me.

"Skaga isn't here," I say weakly. "Does this look like her house to you?"

His cloak sways as he walks around the living room, surveying the red sofa, the bundles of dried herbs, the wood-burning stove.

"Your home is . . . not as I remember," he says, his voice strained.

His words remind me of my dream about Skaga, how different her house looked inside.

"What *do* you remember?"

Soren frowns. "There was one main room with benches running along both walls, and a bedroom in the rear of the house. A fire pit sat in the middle. Unlike most longhouses, its floor was not beaten earth but wooden planks—"

"Okay, okay. I get it."

What he's describing sounds exactly like my dream.

This couldn't be the same place. Not only is it impossible for me to have seen Skaga's actual house in my dreams, I know Amma inherited it from her mother. If Soren is right, that would mean our house has been here since the beginning of Unden over nine hundred years ago. That Skaga is the one who handed it down through countless generations.

Along with the secret hidden in the cellar: *Soren.*

He searches the house like he's desperate for a trace of her to hold on to. His reaction seems genuine. I must have looked the same way to Dad when we arrived yesterday.

"I told you," I say, my voice softening. "Skaga no longer lives here."

He gives me a long, dubious look.

So much for that. "I'm *not* Skaga."

"Do not continue lying to me." Whatever hesitation he had dissipates like fog. "Go," he says, pushing me through the house. "Now."

"Wait." My voice rises in desperation. "Where are we going?"

I look around, scrambling to come up with something.

Anything.

Then it hits me. "Check my coat pocket—my identification card is in there. You'll see, my name is Astrid. Unbind me, and I'll show you."

A sharp, sudden laugh escapes him, exposing his long fangs. "I think not."

Damn it. "Then *you* get it. The card is right in front. Near my hip."

He reaches around my waist, feeling for the pocket. His hands are so cold, his touch burns through my coat, and I can feel his finger on my hip, sending sparks shooting through me.

Soren slides my student ID card out with a claw and examines it. "What is this?"

"See? My name isn't Skaga. It's Astrid, like I've been trying to tell you."

"This means nothing to me," Soren says, discarding my ID like trash.

Anger flares in my chest, bright and hot, but I bite my lip. He can't read Swedish. Of course he can't. How the hell do I convince him now? He doesn't give me the chance.

Before I know it, we're out the door.

"Where are you taking me?" I demand.

A sudden blast of frigid air hits me. Now I'm really glad I kept my coat on. Moonlight turns the snow-drenched world outside a weak blue. Soren lays a hand on my backpack and pushes me forward—toward the stave church.

"To break the blood oath," he says simply.

Like I'm supposed to know what that means.

"How?" I ask.

"Together" is all he offers.

"You have the wrong person," I say, breath rushing out of me. "I have no idea what you're talking about. Skaga, the blood oath, any of it. Until I found you in the cellar, I had no idea you even existed. I had no idea draugar were even real."

Snow crunching underfoot is his only response.

I glance back over my shoulder at Amma's dark cabin as it recedes in the distance. I try to memorize the snow blanketing its steep roof, the wooden door that squeals every time it opens, and the short, welcoming steps. This might be the last time I ever see my home.

I lick my cracked lips and turn until I'm facing him. "I'm not Skaga. I swear it." I know how desperate I sound. I don't care. "Soren, please. Let me go."

He stills at the sound of his name. Something flashes across his face, there and then gone. "Your beseeching words will not fool me again." He sounds sad, but quickly steels himself. "Now walk."

I dig my heels in. "I'm not going anywhere until you tell me what's going on."

Without Amma here, Soren might be the only one who can answer all the questions I have.

He levels an icy look at me. "The blood oath is destroying Tiveden," he says reluctantly. "As I've already tried to tell you, we cannot allow it to continue."

I'm guessing Skaga didn't agree. That must be why he was imprisoned in the cellar, along with the mural and its warning. "Why do you need me?"

"Our oath can only be ended by both of us, as it was once made."

From the scowl on his face, it seems like he's loath to admit it.

I sigh. Every answer I get creates more questions—questions he's unlikely to answer. I chew the inside of my cheek. There must be a reason why Skaga, and maybe even Amma, didn't want the blood oath broken. I doubt Soren would be able to answer that. Even if he knew, it's not like he'd tell me.

"Now go, or I will make you."

Damn it. While trudging through the snow, I start going over my options. I still have my dagger in my hand, but it does me no good when I can't actually *move* and there's no rope to slice through. I could run, but if I can't use my arms, how fast will I be? Fast enough to outrun Soren?

Unlikely.

The stave church is meters away.

I'd better figure out something fast.

With each step I take, I'm getting farther from Unden. Farther from Dad. What will he think when he returns, only to find Amma's house empty again? What if I don't come back either? What will Dad do then? He lost his wife, his parents. I'm all he has left in the world. No matter how mad I am, I can't do that to him. I won't.

I refuse to disappear too.

SIX

Never go beyond the stave church.

Dad and Amma never agreed on anything except that.

Yet here I am, standing before the church at night. A full moon hangs above us, ringed with murky light, bright against the dark church. I steal a quick glance at Soren. Moonlight carves out his cheekbones, and his silver hair gleams like a blade.

"We are going to end this once and for all," he says roughly.

I struggle against the stave. He wants revenge against Skaga, and as long as he thinks I'm Skaga, that means *me*. Because of this freaking galdr, I'm completely defenseless. I won't stand a chance against him.

I have to free myself.

But I know next to nothing about staves or spoken spells.

Until today, I didn't even *believe* any of this.

Soren shoves me toward the church.

Think, Astrid. Think. I blow out a long breath. If staves are real, then all those times Amma drew those symbols in the soles of my shoes or carved them into the bottom of her barrels, she was doing magic. Actual magic. And Skaga—she was able to craft a stave powerful enough to put Soren into a supernatural sleep for centuries.

Maybe I have some of that magic too.

If I can break free, I'm willing to try anything.

Remember all I've taught you, Amma wrote. I close my eyes and concentrate, blocking out the sound of Soren's heavy footfalls in the snow.

Amma used to tell me how our family was blessed by Freyja. Supposedly, the goddess even rescued Skaga from Tiveden and taught her the magic of the gods.

I focus on the ache in my shoulders. The muscles straining in my arms. The weight of my hands behind my back. I imagine magic wrapped around my wrists like an invisible rope. A thin thread. I can almost sense it, like the crackling energy in the air before a storm strikes.

I think of Amma. How badly I want to see her again—

Suddenly, I can feel my blood rushing through me like a river. From my heart to my limbs to the tips of my toes and fingers. It carries something with it. Something ancient and unfamiliar. Something powerful. I think of the power Skaga had, the power Amma has, the power I might have.

One finger twitches.

Then another.

All at once, my fingertips dig into the dagger handle as the pins and needles disappear. My eyes pop open, and I blink in disbelief. Holy shit. I can *move* again. I bring my shaking hands in front of me and stare down at them. My body . . . it's mine again. I flex my fingers slowly. Deliberately.

A laugh escapes me. *I did it.*

Soren inhales sharply behind me. "Impossible."

I turn to face him, holding the dagger out between us. "Stop." No way am I letting him use another spell on me. "If you try, I'll just break the galdr again," I say with more confidence than I feel.

"Since when can you break spells?" he asks.

"Since now, apparently."

Soren stares at me. I'm guessing Skaga couldn't do that.

He looks alarmed. Scared, almost.

Good.

Then he grabs my lower back, pulling me against him with a sudden start. Before I can resist, Soren presses his cold lips to mine.

I gasp at the icy shock of his mouth.

His lips are . . . softer than I expect. I stand frozen, my body pressed against his. My fingers curl around my dagger as he kisses me. I don't know what to do. No one has ever kissed me before. Certainly not like *this*. There's a desperation as his mouth moves over mine. He kisses me like he's trying to prove something. To me, or himself.

I want to push him away, but I grab his cloak and pull him closer instead.

My mouth betrays me, returning his kiss with equal intensity.

Soren stifles a groan. He applies more pressure, more force, until my lips ache underneath his. My heart races. I don't stop him, even as something sharp slices my lip and the coppery tang of blood spills into my mouth. His tongue traces the tender cut, making me shiver—

He withdraws immediately.

"Your taste," Soren says slowly, disbelief lacing every word. "Who are you?"

His breathing is uneven. So is mine.

I can't believe this any more than he can. Still reeling, I swipe a finger over my lips. The cut there stings, making me wince. He—he *kissed* me. A draugr just kissed me. I run my tongue over the cut, again and again, until the metallic taste of blood fills my mouth. My first kiss was supposed to be something awkward and sweet. Not *this*.

So why do I want to kiss Soren all over again?

"What the hell?" I rasp. "What—"

"You are not Skaga."

I rub the back of my hand over my mouth. He wasn't kissing me. He was kissing Skaga—or trying to. My cheeks burn hot with humiliation. Oh God, and I actually kissed him back. Even worse, some part of me enjoyed it.

"Yeah," I snap at him. "I *know*."

He grabs my wrist, a sudden jolt of cold. "Who are you?" he asks, searching my face.

"Astrid. I told you."

Soren stares at me. "You are her descendant, then."

I force myself to nod.

His expression turns pained. "I understand."

We stand there in tense silence, neither one of us moving. What can I possibly say? Her loss must feel as sudden as a slit throat, like Amma's disappearance felt to me.

"What is your father's name?" Soren asks reluctantly.

"Erik, but he prefers Rick. Why?"

"I see, Astrid Eriksdóttir."

I bite back a laugh. "That's not my name. That's a little . . . old-fashioned. My family's surname is Skarsgård."

"Your surname matters not." Soren presses his lips together, clearly at odds with himself. "Is Skaga satisfied with him?"

"What? No, no, no." I hold my hands up, waving them both wildly. "She isn't—my mom was named Alicia. Skaga is my distant relative. *Very* distant."

Soren considers that for a moment. "But you dwell in her home. Where does Skaga reside if not with you?"

Sighing, I look up at the stave church and the bright moon behind it.

He still doesn't get it, but I can't blame him.

Change is one of the hardest things to accept. I would know.

I walk over to the nearby memorial stone, its engraved runes worn by time. "Here. Read this."

His brow furrows as he takes it in: *Dagny raised this stone in memory of Skaga Ramundersdóttir, her beloved mother, and Unden's first foremother. May Freyja hold her in a field that goes on forever, surrounded by golden wheat swaying in a warm breeze, someplace the sun never sets.*

I grip my dagger, unsure how he'll react to my next words. There's no easy way to break this to him, so I just say it. "Skaga died like nine hundred years ago."

Soren falters. "What?"

He looks at me like I slapped him. I know that look: *denial.* Ever since Amma disappeared, I've seen that same expression staring back at me in the mirror. Seeing it on someone else is unsettling. Unexpected.

"She's dead," I say softly.

Then I remember Dad saying the exact same words to me.

"*No.*" Soren drops to his knees before the stone and splays his hand against it, hanging his head. Silver hair curtains his face, making it impossible to read his expression. His shoulders slump as if her death has defeated him. "Skaga . . . she couldn't."

As I watch him kneeling there, his grief reminds me too much of my own. Apparently, nothing helps lessen grief, not even an answer to what happened to someone you cared about. And that terrifies me even more than Soren does.

A moment passes.

His hand closes into a fist, so tight it trembles. "What happened to her?"

How many times have I asked myself that since Amma disappeared? Over and over and over. Curled up in bed, legs drawn to my chest, staring into the quiet darkness of my room. Waiting by the window, forehead pressed against the cold glass. Walking down the cobble sidewalks, hands stuffed in my coat pockets.

But I don't have any answers for him, either.

"I . . . I don't know," I stammer. "I'm sorry."

When he speaks, the words are sharp and sudden. "Leave me."

Finally.

I turn around, ready to head home even if it means facing Dad's fury. But my feet won't move.

I can't just leave Soren. Who knows what he's capable of? Skaga must have had good reason if she imprisoned him. He could go on a rampage through Unden. If anything happens, I'll be responsible too. I'm the one who woke him, even if it was accidental.

I turn back to him, my breath misting in the chilly air. "What will you do?"

Soren nods like he's come to a decision. "I will find her."

From the determined set of his jaw, the glint in his eyes, I know he means it. Soren will do anything to find Skaga. Like I will do anything to find Amma. It seems we might be broken in the same ways.

For some reason, that comforts me.

"Even if Skaga is dead, she will be in Tiveden." He rises to his feet, his cloak stirring frost around him. "This changes nothing. If it truly has been as long as you claim, then it's even more important I find her—"

"Why would she be in Tiveden?"

He inhales deeply. "Because of the blood oath."

Could that be why Amma went too? She did mention joining our ancestors at some Shore of Sacrifices. Maybe that includes Skaga. After all, Amma said something about following Skaga's path. As I look out at the forest, it seems even closer to the stave church than I remember. The sharp scent of pine washes over me, cold and crisp and familiar. Tiveden—no, *Amma*—beckons.

"Then I'm going with you," I say, cold air cutting my throat.

No one else in Unden will step foot in the forest—except Soren. Based on the mural in the cellar, he belongs to Tiveden. He has no reason to fear it. He and his kind are the reason why no one in Unden will go beyond the stave church.

But maybe his presence is why I can.

"Are you so desperate to die?" Soren looks me over. "Tiveden is not meant for the living. The Hidden Folk reside there, and there are many other dangers besides."

I glance back at the stave church. Now that I've broken his spell, I could go back to Unden. I probably should. Tiveden is even more dangerous than I could've imagined. No wonder Officer Lind refused to send anyone to search the forest. If draugar are real, who knows what other monsters lurk in these woods?

Soren is right. I *could* die.

But if I go back now, Dad will drag me to Stockholm tomorrow. I'll never find Amma. I'll never *know*. I'll spend every damn day of my life desperate for answers I can no longer get. Like why Amma went into Tiveden by herself. Why she wanted me to follow her. Why I didn't when I still had the chance.

"I need to find my grandmother," I say, voice firm. "Just as much as you need to find Skaga."

He scoffs. "I doubt that very much."

"I mean it."

Soren gives me a once-over. "You will only slow me down."

"Or I could lead you straight to Skaga." I try to sound more confident than I feel. "My grandmother mentioned going to join our ancestors at some Shore of Sacrifices. Amma even told me to follow the same path Skaga once walked, and she'd be waiting at its end. Skaga likely is too. You need me."

Soren falls quiet.

He searches my face, his cold gaze piercing.

Goose bumps spring up on my skin as I meet his stare.

I hold my breath until my lungs burn.

"I suppose you might have your uses." A slight pause. "Fine. Then accompany me, *Skarsgård*," Soren says, his cloak billowing as he walks by me. "But be warned, once you enter Tiveden, it is likely you will never leave."

He glances over his shoulder with an amused expression, as if he expects to find me hesitating and afraid. But he doesn't. Squaring my shoulders, I stride after him. His countenance suddenly shifts.

I've surprised him a second time.

Soren's eyes gleam. "How far are you willing to go?"

I exhale. Tiveden is the only place I can get any answers. There's so much I still don't know. About Soren. About Skaga. About Amma. About *myself*. But I can feel those secrets waiting for me in the woods, drawing me toward them.

"As far as I have to," I say, and take my first step beyond the stave church.

PART TWO

The Helm of Concealment
Hulinhjálmr

SEVEN

Going beyond the stave church feels like breaking a law.

Stillness settles over Tiveden, as if the forest is holding its breath. Waiting. As I walk beside Soren, unease seeps into my bones along with the biting cold. It's so quiet I can hear the scratch of my winter coat and the crunch of snow with each apprehensive step.

Towering trees surround us, dead branches limned by moonlight. Even the snow has an eerie glow. I draw in a steadying breath, but the air is cold as a razor down my throat. This is why I wanted to head into the forest while it was still light, but it's now or never.

I cannot relax. Not for a second.

A bitter wind blows at our backs, pushing us deeper into the fog-shrouded forest. Branches knock together overhead, and the sound is like rattling bones. Or the old, creaking stairs descending into the cellar. I force myself to keep going.

The farther we get from the stave church, the tenser I grow. No one from Unden will follow me. Not Johan. Not Dad. If anything happens, I'm on my own. I can't expect Soren to help me, not after what my family has done to him. I curl my left hand into a fist, nails biting into my palm.

Something darts between the trees in the darkness. I catch a flash of a tail and pause. When I look again, there's only the still forest. My stomach drops. An animal. I'm sure it's just an animal. Not a huldra ready to devour me.

I stand frozen, dagger ready.

I'm barely able to hear over my pulse pounding in my ears. "Soren?"

"Ignore them," he says harshly.

Them.

I look out at the darkness. How many are already there, watching us? I can't see anything but trees. *Just because you can't see them doesn't mean they aren't there*, Amma always told me. As I got older, I started thinking of it as a convenient, albeit ridiculous, explanation. Now I see it for what it is.

A warning.

Cold terror pushes through my veins like ice. As we head deeper into Tiveden, the trees grow thicker and the moonlight weaker until darkness smothers us. I can barely see Soren beside me anymore. Amma said I'd be safe, I remind myself. That Freyja would protect me, so long as I follow the path Skaga left through Tiveden. But how am I supposed to know *where* that is, especially in the pitch black?

I slip my cell phone out of my coat pocket and flick the flashlight on.

Skeletal branches reach toward me. Swallowing hard, I pan the light around slowly, trying to get a bearing on my surroundings. My flashlight sweeps over fallen trees and brush poking through the blanket of snow. Little flakes spiral around us, spots of bright light.

My cold breath fogs in front of me. There's no path—

Soren steps before the beam and winces. His illuminated face is just as harsh as the light, shadows tracing the cut of his cheekbones. "What are you doing?" His large hand swallows my phone, leaving us in sudden darkness. "Do you want to draw every creature toward us?"

"How else am I supposed to see?" I ask. "Days are super short already, and they're only getting shorter. I need to be able to keep going at night, or I'll never reach Amma."

"Then I will be your eyes."

I hesitate. "Why would you help me?"

"We both want the same thing," Soren says slowly. "To find your family."

"But we haven't found the path yet."

"For now, our best bet is to follow the river. Otherwise, it is far too easy to get lost and wander the forest forever."

"What river?"

In the darkness, I can't tell there even *is* one, and I'm not about to take his word for it. I shine the flashlight around quickly. Sure enough, a river—if you can even call it that— carves out a space between the rocks. It's hardly more than a trickle. "No wonder I didn't hear it."

"It once was a powerful stream that flowed from the stave church into the heart of Tiveden. It is vital to the forest, like an artery."

His heightened senses will definitely be helpful to navigate, not to mention his knowledge of the forest terrain. I need to find Amma as soon as possible. I don't know how long she'll last—or how long I will. Which means I have no choice but to follow him for now. And I hate it. Soren is the last person I should be relying on.

"Fine." I stuff my phone back into my pocket. "Lead the way."

Soren continues without another word.

After walking for a while, I see something moving out of the corner of my eye. My breathing turns ragged as I look left. Something pale vanishes into the darkness. My skin crawls as I peer between the trees, but it's too dark to see. Tiveden is too dense. Not even moonlight can pierce it—

Bright blue eyes stare back at me, two glowing fixed points.

Draugr?

As soon as I blink, they're gone.

Just darkness.

I try to focus on something else. Anything else. "What were you doing in Amma's house, anyway?"

"*Skaga's* house."

I blow out a long breath. "Right. Sure."

"I would visit her there," Soren says, but he sounds sad. Like it's still painful for him to talk about—though I guess to him, her betrayal must seem recent. An old wound that feels fresh. "I went to plead with her to break the blood oath, but she would not listen."

"Why not?"

He gives me a scathing look. "Because she cared more about power than anything else."

I must remind him of Skaga still. Then again, as I recall his fury when he thought I was her, I'm not sure that's a good thing. His feelings for her seem balanced on a knife's edge between love and hate. She betrayed him, and yet he wanted to kiss her in spite of it.

"What happened between you and Skaga?" I ask carefully.

Soren gives a warning glare. "Why do you ask so many questions?"

My teeth grind together. I've always asked questions. I hate not knowing. I hate not being able to make sense of things, like why I got Crohn's disease or what happened to Amma.

"Because. I need answers."

Soren sighs. "You are as stubborn as her."

The hint of longing in his voice is unmistakable, but he offers nothing else.

We continue in uncomfortable silence.

"So huldra really exist?" I ask eventually.

Soren walks ahead. "They do."

I push through the snow after him, but I can barely feel my legs. "What about nykur?"

He nods.

"Obviously draugar are real." I try to recall the other creatures from Amma's stories. But the book of Hidden Folk is so thick, I can't possibly remember them all. Now I wish I'd brought it in my bag. All those stories she told weren't to frighten me, like Dad always said. They were meant to *prepare* me.

I keep talking, trying to distract myself from the cold. "What about the Fell King?"

"You already know the answer to that," he says, his lip lifting in a cruel grin.

Before I can reply, the forest comes alive.

I spin around, searching frantically, but I can't *see*.

Branches snap to my right, loud as a gunshot.

I grab hold of Soren's wrist without thinking.

A look of surprise flashes across his face. He's almost as surprised as *I* am. He looks back at me, making eye contact briefly before looking away.

I let go of him. Now that we are in Tiveden, Soren could betray me at any moment, like Skaga supposedly betrayed him. *Maybe he already has.*

"This had better not be a trap," I mutter.

"This is not my doing," he growls at me.

Soren is a draugr. One my family kept imprisoned for centuries. Can I really trust anything he says? Would he actually tell me if I *was* in danger?

Something shoots through the trees.

Soren pulls me behind him, as though acting on instinct, when a draugr comes to a sudden stop before us.

The draugr looks familiar, though I don't recognize his face. Long silver hair slides over his shoulder as he nods to Soren. His exposed chest is covered by tattoos, but everything about him seems off.

"Greetings," the draugr says, sharp fangs glinting.

My heart beats harder than a jackhammer. Why is Soren shielding me from him?

Do they know each other?

"So you're finally awake." The draugr smirks. "Took long enough."

Clearly, he's familiar with Soren.

Soren remains silent.

The draugr observes his claws idly. "Why return? You are no longer welcome in Tiveden."

I glance between them. Is *that* why Soren brought me? So he can hand me over in exchange for passage? I'm not going to wait around to find out. But before I can so much as shrink back—

"What do we have here?" The draugr raises a brow.

He pauses. "Skaga?"

Not again. I turn and run, but I'm no more than a few steps away when a massive shape lands before me, blocking my escape. His tongue flicks out and runs over long, wicked teeth.

"It's me," the draugr says. "Torsten."

Where have I heard that name before?

My dream. But this can't be the same person. He's a lot older. Crueler. His skin is drained of life, his brown hair turned to silver. He is not human at all, but a *monster*.

I back away slowly. "You have the wrong person."

Torsten lunges for me.

Without thinking, I swing my dagger, slicing through—

Fingers.

Black liquid oozes as Torsten holds his hand up, examining the stumps. Only his thumb and index finger remain. He peers at me through the gap where the rest of his fingers were. "Is that any way to greet your husband?"

"What?" Soren and I say in unison.

Stunned, I shake my head.

I don't even have a boyfriend, let alone a *husband*.

Soren glances between me and Torsten, toward the golden ring glinting on his severed finger.

Could Torsten actually be Skaga's husband? I never paid much attention to history, but I haven't been able to forget the pained look on Soren's face when he realized that I was her descendant. Even if it wasn't Torsten, Skaga married *someone*. Someone who wasn't Soren.

"Enough," Torsten snarls. "Come to my side, wife."

Soren makes no move to help me. Even though he knows I'm not Skaga, he's looking at me like I am. He's as likely to let Torsten take me as he is to protect me.

Looks like I'm on my own after all.

"Fine," I say, playing along with Torsten.

At least if her husband thinks I am Skaga, he's less likely to harm me. Hopefully.

And now I know my dagger is capable of hurting *him*.

I take one last glance at Soren. Something inside me tells me not to leave him, but right now, Torsten seems safer. He was her husband, not her enemy.

I approach Torsten cautiously.

"Wise choice." He smiles, but it's all teeth. "We belong together, Skaga, even if I must turn you."

My body goes numb. *Turn.* There's only one thing he could mean.

Torsten wants to make me into a draugr too.

But first, he'd have to kill me.

A mistake. This was *definitely* a mistake.

Lunging forward, I drive the dagger into his side with both hands. I feel it in the pit of my gut as it lodges into his flesh with a sick squelch, sending rivulets of black liquid down my hands. *Blood.* It reeks of rot. Of death. I retch but drive the blade in deeper—

Torsten backhands me.

Pain explodes as I fly through the air and slam into a tree. My cheek is on fire. He must've busted my damn face open. *Damn it.* Touching my cheek, I wince at the angry gouges I can feel there. My fingertips come back wet.

Torsten is unable to look away from my blood. Even Soren stares at it, appearing more conflicted than before. The sight seems to bother him, though I can't tell if it's because he hungers for a taste or wants to kill Torsten for harming me. Or both.

I reach for my dagger, but it's not there.

"My wife would never harm me," Torsten says, drawing the words out menacingly. "She would do anything to be with me."

I'm about to bolt—

His uninjured hand closes around my throat. His fingers are like icicles, and as soon as he touches me, images flash before my eyes—*a golden ring dipped in blood being slid onto my finger, Torsten smiling at me as he takes my hand in his and calls me wife.*

The sudden onslaught of memories makes me gasp as Torsten chokes me. Those images—the lack of oxygen has me seeing things. He slams me back into the tree with such force it knocks the breath from my lungs.

He leans in closer. "Who are you? And why do you wear my wife's face?"

Soren watches with an unreadable expression. His body is tight with tension, but he remains rooted where he is, like he's at war with himself.

You can't count on his help. He's one of them.

My teeth grind. I didn't survive flare-ups and infections and everything else just to die now. I buck against Torsten, raking my nails down his hand. He doesn't release me, so I dig deeper, leaving trails of dark blood in my wake.

His tongue flicks over my bloody cheek, wet and slimy as a snake.

The wounds close quickly.

Blood heals them, Amma's words come back to me. *And strengthens them.* I struggle against Torsten, but it's no use. His grip has grown even stronger. His fingers dig into my windpipe until my lungs burn.

"Answer before I rip your throat out," Torsten growls.

I wheeze, barely able to keep my eyes open as I look to Soren. "S-Sor . . ."

Something in his countenance shifts.

"Enough," Soren says through gritted teeth. "Release her this moment."

Torsten grips my throat harder. "I don't obey you."

Stars pop in my vision. *Can't breathe—can't—*

Soren grabs hold of his wrist with such force that Torsten drops me.

I fall to the snow, gasping for air.

Torsten starts swinging wildly, but Soren dodges left and right, his cloak whipping with each step. Torsten finally manages to land a blow, sending Soren slamming into a tree.

"Soren!" I scream.

If anything happens to him, I'm as good as dead.

Before I can blink, Torsten is in front of me, gleaming claws coming at my face. I barely duck in time as he slices through the tree behind me.

Sharp splinters fly through the air. *Shit.* Each of his claws is sharper than my dagger, and I have no weapon. Nothing.

"Do not dare harm her," Soren says, his voice turning lethal.

He sounds almost . . . protective of me now, even though he knows I'm not Skaga.

Soren lunges for Torsten.

Then they're nothing but a blur, moving too fast for me to track. But I can hear the impact of each blow as they strike each other with hurricane-like force. While they're distracted, I scan the snow until I spot my dagger and quickly scoop it up.

Suddenly, Soren stops Torsten, catching his fist.

He wrenches his hand down with a swift, sure movement.

There's an awful tearing sound as Torsten's arm rips right off.

Soren drops the severed arm beside me with a heavy thud.

Torsten screams, clutching his shoulder as oily blood gushes from it. "The Fell King will have your head for this."

The Fell King.

My chest rises and falls rapidly, but Soren only scoffs.

Torsten retreats into the woods, disappearing as quickly as he appeared. As if he were never here at all.

Except for his severed arm staining the snow.

"H-how . . . ?" I manage to get out.

"The more ancient a draugr is, the more powerful they are," Soren says simply, a cold glint in his eyes. "And I am very old. If not for the lingering effects of the sleep thorn, there would have been no contest at all."

Soren stands there, his presence as towering as the trees surrounding us. A gust of wind opens his cloak, exposing his athletic, muscular body. His ice-chip eyes remain fixed on me. Out of all the draugar, *Soren* was the one Skaga felt dangerous enough to imprison. Just how ancient is he? How powerful? Since entering Tiveden, I've been afraid of what lurks in the shadows or waits behind the trees.

But Soren might be the most dangerous thing in these woods.

I scramble backward, desperate to get away from him.

"If I wanted you dead," Soren says casually, "I would've killed you already. Or let Torsten do it."

"Is that supposed to make me feel better?"

He smirks. "I suppose it wouldn't."

Except it kind of does. As soon as I woke Soren, I never stood a chance against him. He could've killed me numerous times, but hasn't. In fact, when he grabbed my wrists in the cellar, I could tell he was holding back. Not only that, but he *protected* me.

My hands are slippery with sweat and blood. I can barely hold my dagger. "Why haven't you?"

Soren looks me over, his attention lingering on the slices across my cheek. My heart speeds up. I'm keenly aware of the blood welling there, and from his intent expression, so is he.

His throat bobs. "Because of Skaga."

I know she's why he kissed me. The memory of it makes me bite my lip. The cut his sharp teeth gave me still stings. He lowers his gaze to my mouth, like he's thinking about it too.

I force myself to swallow. "Is she why you helped me?"

"Helped you?" he says coldly. "I owed you a debt for waking me from the sleep thorn. That is all. Consider it repaid." After a moment, he adds, "Besides, you may prove useful to me. I might require you to gain Skaga's cooperation."

Soren holds his hand out to me like an offering.

My body aches as I reach for him, ready to accept his help—until I notice the scar across his right palm. The soft, swollen skin looks identical to the scar on my left. A mirror image.

I freeze at the sight of it. "How did you get that?"

He grabs my hand, our palms pressing together.

Our scars line up, exact matches for each other.

"The blood oath," Soren says, helping me onto my feet.

I slip my hand from his and stare at my palm, my mind reeling. How do *I* have the same scar, then? Skaga made the blood oath with him, not *me*. And that was centuries ago. But I doubt Soren knows the answer to that either. If he did, then the scar wouldn't have been enough to convince him I was Skaga.

If anyone knows, Amma would.

The sooner I find her, the sooner all of this will make sense.

EIGHT

Dread coils in my stomach while we walk through the cold, dark forest. After the run-in with Torsten, part of me wants to turn back. Even though Soren drove him off, Tiveden is teeming with monsters. I can't see any other draugar, but I can *feel* their presence.

Watching.

Waiting.

Is the Fell King watching too? Maybe he always has been. A shiver shoots up my spine as I recall how his specter haunted me when I was a child. All those sleepless nights I spent terrified as I saw him standing in the shadows of my room, a nightmare come to life.

I grip the dagger so hard my knuckles turn white. "You don't think the Fell King will find us, do you?"

"You should be more concerned about Tiveden." The way Soren says it isn't threatening so much as a statement of fact. "The deeper you go, the more dangerous it will get. The more difficult it will become to ever leave."

Maybe he's right. My teeth chatter, aching from the cold. Maybe I don't have to worry about the Fell King. At this rate, I'm going to freeze to death first. I don't even know how long we've been walking or how much farther we have left to go. My legs are already numb, and—

I tumble forward, and my hands and knees disappear into deep snow. My skin burns, painfully cold without my gloves. *Damn it.* Frustrated tears fill my eyes.

"We can stop," Soren says.

"No," I say, panting. I don't want his pity. "I can keep going."

I *have* to.

My lungs burn more with each frigid breath. If Amma was able to make this journey, so can I. Even if deep down, I know Soren is right. I should stop. If I push myself too hard, I could get sick or trigger another flare-up. Then finding her would be impossible.

Soren stands over me, staring down as I kneel in the snow. "How inconvenient."

I glare up at him. "Excuse me?"

"Being human," he says coldly.

Our eyes lock in wordless battle.

It's not just that I'm human. I'm chronically ill. It *is* inconvenient, but I won't let it stop me. Something sparks inside me, my chest growing tight and hot. Even though his stare is intense and powerful, I refuse to look away.

"You've now seen what you are up against," Soren continues. "It is not too late. You can still turn back."

"I can't." I clench cold snow in my shaking fist. "Not without Amma."

"You would risk your life to find her?"

Everyone else has given up on her.

Except me.

I climb to my feet. "She's like a mother to me. If our roles were reversed, I know she would do anything to find me. She wanted nothing more than for us to be together again. I *will* find her. No matter what."

"I see," Soren says, but he sounds distant.

I look away and brush the snow off me.

Soren clears his throat. "We will stop here until morning."

"Why?" I blink a few times. If I didn't know better, it almost seems like he's trying to be considerate. Unless this is some kind of trick?

Soren frowns. "You make so much noise, you are drawing every draugr toward us. I would like to avoid another fight until I have fully regained my strength."

So much for being considerate.

Fear ripples through me at the rest of his words. I don't know which is more terrifying: being surrounded by unseen draugar, or that Soren wasn't at his full strength when he tore Torsten's arm off.

Shuddering, I drop my backpack onto the snow and sit down. "Okay, fine."

"I forgot you humans need warmth," Soren says.

That's not why I shuddered, but he's not wrong either. I slide my dagger back into its sheathe and return it to my coat pocket. "Well, it is freezing. Aren't you cold too?"

Soren gives me a quizzical look. "Of course not."

"What, you're telling me you can't feel the cold?"

"I cannot feel anything."

Our kiss returns to my mind unbidden. Could he feel *that*? It sure seemed like he could. I lower my gaze to his lips, remembering how they felt pressed against mine. Cold and invigorating and—

I clear my throat. "Must be nice."

To my surprise, Soren doesn't make a snide remark.

Wordlessly, he unfastens his cloak.

He tosses it to me. "Here."

I catch it, staring down at the blue fabric and soft fur collar. "Are you sure?"

Without his cloak, I realize just how broad his shoulders are.

"I don't need it." He averts his gaze. "As I said, the cold doesn't bother me."

Now he sounds like Elsa from that Disney movie Zuri and I watched in the hospital together. She couldn't believe I had never seen *Frozen* before, but it's not like we had a lot of recent releases in Unden. Though I can say with 100 percent certainty that Soren would not get the reference.

I'm not going to refuse his offer when I need the warmth. So I wrap myself in his cloak, enveloped in the smell of wood musk and moss. Soren's scent. The soft fur collar brushes my skin as I pull it around me, nestling inside it.

All those monsters I used to fear are *real*. Not just bloodthirsty draugar, but huldra with hollow, hungry backs; spiderlike nykur larger than any horse; and the mara with her razor-like teeth. As I pull Soren's cloak tighter around me, I feel like a little girl again, wrapping myself in Amma's crocheted blanket to hide from monsters.

Now Soren is the only thing keeping me safe.

"You'd better not leave," I tell him.

"I won't."

For some reason, I believe him. Maybe because he wants to find Skaga as much as I want to find Amma. Or maybe because he offered me the comfort of his cloak even though he didn't have to. Its fur collar is soft and fluffy as a pillow as I wrap the wool around myself like a warm, familiar blanket and curl up in the snow. I always thought the night terrors were something I grew out of, but now I'm not so sure. Maybe they only stopped because I left Unden.

Bundled in Soren's cloak, it doesn't take long until sleep swallows me.

"Careful, Skaga," Torsten says, reaching for my spear.

After three years, I've grown tired of his coddling. I pull the spear away before he can grab it, water splashing around me, and give him a wicked grin. "I am better with a spear than you. Perhaps you ought to be taking lessons from me."

Torsten sighs, standing ankle-deep in the shallows of the lake. "I'll admit you are the better spear-fisher, but spears are still weapons, and you must respect them as such, or you might harm yourself. You are no warrior."

A fish darts past our feet.

I stab my spear into the lake, taking my frustration out on it. "I don't need you to remind me of that."

Red clouds the clear water. My strike was true.

I toss the fish into the basket on the rocky shore. As it flops down, a putrid smell stings my nose. The fish we have caught are all rotting, as if they have been left out for months instead of moments. I wade through the shallows to get a closer look. Their scales turn slimy, their flesh melting off their bones until only carcasses remain.

A full day's worth of fish gone.

"Torsten." My throat constricts as I speak. "Something is wrong."

His spear drops from his fingers with a splash.

"I know" is all he says.

I turn slowly, afraid of what I will find.

The entire lake is red. Suddenly, the water around my ankles turns sticky and hot. Horror dawns on me as the lake of blood stretches before me. There is enough blood here to belong to Ragnarok, the great battle when even the gods themselves will die. A fish floats to the surface, lifeless. Another rises, and another, until hundreds of dead fish drift through the blood.

"No, this cannot be." I stumble backward, my legs unsteady.

I slip on one of the stones, but Torsten grabs hold of me before I can fall and hurt myself.

"How . . . how is this possible?" I ask, searching his face desperately.

He shakes his head. "I do not know."

As Torsten helps me onto the shore, I stare down at the bloody hem of my dress in disbelief.

This must be another nightmare. I have them often since coming to Tiveden.

Sometimes, I wake in a cold sweat, only to find myself staring into a little girl's face. A mara, the giver of nightmares, sits crouched on my chest. Her gown is bright in the darkness, almost as bright as her empty white eyes. She smiles at me, but her mouth is too wide, her lips stretching around rows of sharp teeth. Her small body crushes my chest, impossibly heavy, until my ribs scream in protest, threatening to snap. But I can't move. I cannot even cry out. All I can do is stare as the mara slowly brings a finger to her lips—

Surely if I can only wake myself, this will be over.

Shouts rise from Unden.

Torsten and I exchange a look.

Leaving the spoiled fish and lake of blood behind, we race toward the village, now full of houses and people from all over. Word spread of our settlement, where all are welcome, even those on the fringes of society. Outlaws like my father with nowhere to call home. Freed thralls looking for a fresh start. Even migrants from faraway lands. Unden has become home to all of us.

Now everyone is in an uproar.

The fences we've built to protect our livestock have been smashed through, scattered across the village.

"What happened here?" I ask, panic rising.

"The animals went wild," Valens, one of the traders from Constantinople, says. "They trampled their pens and took off into the forest, frothing at the mouth."

"It was madness," his wife adds, "unlike anything we have seen before."

Hundreds of hoofprints leave a frantic trail into the forest.

"Our lake is filled with blood," I say, forcing the words out.

"And its fish are all tainted," Torsten adds gravely.

I look around at the panicked faces as people gather in the streets, drawn from their homes by the commotion. If this is a nightmare, why does it feel so horribly real? Why do we all share the same terror?

"Everyone, stay calm," Father calls, arriving at last. "Torsten, Valens, come with me. We will bring back the livestock. Skaga, let Liv know what has happened. Everyone else, repair the fences."

I grab Torsten's arm. "You can't go." I turn to Father. "Neither of you can. It's too dangerous."

"We have no choice," Father says. "Winter is approaching. Without our animals, we will starve." He lays his hand on top of my head. "Do not worry. I will be back before you know it, and I will keep Unden safe as I always have."

"Let me go with you," I insist.

"Tiveden is too dangerous and you are too gentle." Father ruffles my hair like he used to when I was a child. "You are no warrior, little one. Go tell Liv."

I am tired of being left behind. I am tired of being told I'm too gentle or kind. Father never allows me to venture very far into Tiveden anymore. Biting the inside of my cheek, I force myself to nod. "Yes, Father."

Under my breath, I murmur a prayer to Freyja. As I watch Torsten leave, I tell myself he will be safe. So will Father and Valens. They have to be. If anything were to happen to them, Unden would not survive.

I would not survive.

Grabbing my bloodied skirts, I race toward our home.

My breath comes in quick bursts as my bare feet pound down the dirt path. "Liv!" I shout. "Liv!"

"Skaga?" She appears in the doorway and immediately notices the blood on my clothes. "What happened? Are you all right? Where is—"

"Something is wrong," I say, breathing heavily. "The lake—our animals—Father—"

Liv grabs hold of my face. "Slow down. You're not making any sense."

After she leads me to the fire pit, I tell her of our mounting misfortunes. By the time I finish, I've only grown more frantic.

Liv runs a hand over her copper-colored braids. "I told your father this would happen one day. Tiveden belongs to the Hidden Folk, and we are uninvited guests."

I sigh. For years, she has shared her misgivings about the Hidden Folk. It's what Liv calls the supernatural beings created when the gods first fashioned the world from a giant's skull. She insists we cannot speak their true name or else we will bring their misfortune upon ourselves, though it seems we already have.

She stokes the fire, sending hot sparks shooting into the air. "As Unden grows, so must their anger. They are trying to expel us now."

"But Unden is our home." More than that, it is my father's dream. We cannot abandon it, not after the years of blood and sweat and tears that went into making it reality. "Father will never leave, and neither will I. There is nowhere else we could go, even if we wanted to."

"I know," Liv says quietly. "I know."

"Can we not make Unden work?" I ask, huddling before the flames.

Liv shakes her head. "That I cannot tell you."

Before I can respond, the door bursts open.

Father rushes inside, a wild look on his face. "The animals did not get far. They dashed themselves against the rocks in their madness. Their bones snapped like branches, their meat already rotted and thick with flies."

His words chill me even more than the blast of cold air he brings with him. "What will we do?"

Without the lake's fresh water or its fish, we cannot survive. Not without our livestock. Lately, our hunters return from Tiveden with less food. The wood grouse and other animals that once flourished in the forest grow scarcer. Soon, I suspect our hunters will return empty-handed.

"We only need make it through the winter," Father says, but his voice is rough with worry. "We will eat bark from the trees if we must. In the spring, our fortunes will improve."

My stomach growls like an animal. As hunger claws my insides, I long for the familiar taste of perch and pike again.

"What if winter never ends?" I tremble with sudden cold.

"It will." Liv pats my hand. "It always does."

She's right, of course.

But I fear none of us will be alive to see it.

NINE

Something nudges my side. "Wake up."

When I open my eyes, long lances of light slip between the trees, making the mist around us shimmer. Amma used to say this phenomenon was the Hidden Folk dancing in the mist. But the draugr standing over me isn't so pleasant.

Soren is staring down at me, impatient. "Come on, Ska—Skarsgård."

His near slipup makes me twitch with annoyance.

At least he didn't leave me. I'm grateful, especially after my nightmare. I swear I can still smell the stink of rotting fish, still taste the revulsion on my tongue. I can still see the blood spreading through the lake around me. Still imagine bones crunching as animals dash themselves against rocks.

I sit up slowly and rub my face. Maybe it was a mara. Or maybe the terror of this place is getting to me. I not only dreamed of Skaga again, but Torsten was there too. He seemed so different from the monster we encountered in Tiveden. A coincidence, maybe.

"We need to go," Soren says, his voice insistent.

His eyes are shadowed. It doesn't look like he rested at all.

"You didn't sleep?" My voice comes out unsteady. Actually, I'm not sure if draugr even *do*. I know so little about them.

Soren hesitates. "I've slept long enough."

"But . . . oh."

The sleep thorn.

And now I'm sitting here, bundled up in his cloak. Its soft fur collar brushes my throat like a feather as I run my tongue along my dry, cracked lips. Soren might not need this, but he didn't have to offer me it either.

Standing, I remove the cloak and hold it out to him. "Thank you."

"Keep it," he says.

I shake my head. "It's heavier than it looks. And anyway, it's so long, I'd probably trip over it."

His lips twitch briefly, almost as if he's fighting a smile.

Soren takes it, and our hands brush briefly before I pull away.

Clearing his throat, Soren sweeps the cloak around his broad shoulders, but his fingers tremble as he fastens the pin in place. Or maybe I'm still seeing things.

"We should go," he says, voice rough.

I pull on my backpack. "Fine by me."

Now that I'm looking at Soren more closely, I can't tear my gaze away. His skin looks like freshly fallen snow and feels just as cold. In bright daylight, his complexion has a blue tinge. As he swallows, I notice a scar across his throat. It doesn't look like the kind of wound anyone recovers from, yet it's healed over, pearly and swollen.

"What is it?" Soren asks.

Shit. My cheeks grow hot. I'm definitely staring.

"Nothing," I say too quickly.

Stretching my arms out, I take a look around. The snow is white and powdery as chalk, the dark trees standing out in stark contrast. In the daylight, the forest looks peaceful and still.

Tiveden appears . . . beautiful.

Like when I was little and would walk along the edge of the forest with Amma, my hand clutching her warm, wrinkled one. For the first time since entering Tiveden, my muscles ease a little.

I don't see any trace of her, though.

The longer I look for Amma, the more the mist seems like thick smoke, turning everything a bleak gray. The sun becomes blinding, a hole punched into the sky. *It's pointless,* a raspy voice whispers behind me, far too close. My neck prickles. *You will never find her—*

I turn quickly. No one is there.

"What?" Soren asks.

"I was just surprised," I say by way of explanation. "That's all. I thought draugar are supposed to be nocturnal."

"We are," Soren says simply. "Daylight burns our eyes."

The snow all around us reflects the glare. Soren has to be in pain right now. But he's still willing to go out in the daylight. For Skaga.

"We normally prefer to remain someplace dark while the sun is up," Soren adds.

"Like what, coffins?" I tease, trying to lighten the mood.

Soren misses the joke entirely. "No, beneath the earth. Many are below us this very moment."

Now it feels like he might be trying to pull one over on me. But he sure doesn't look like he's joking. I stare at my boots pressed into the snow. "What, seriously?"

Soren nods solemnly. "We can pass through the ground at will. Though many draugar are never buried, they prefer the earth because it feels like a burial mound."

My mouth goes dry. So some soil is all that's separating me from countless draugar? I might as well be walking through a grave field. Suddenly, my joke no longer seems so funny.

"Is that why you were in the cellar?" I ask.

Soren winces. I can't tell if it's because of what I said or the dappled sunlight moving over his face.

"The sunlight doesn't harm you, though, does it?" I ask quietly.

His eyes widen, as if he's surprised by my concern.

But then his face returns to his usual scowl. "Worry about yourself."

"As long as it's light out, I'll be safe."

"Are you certain about that?" Soren asks meaningfully. "It may be light, but the Folk are never far. You may not see them, but they are everywhere, all around us. They live not only below ground, but beneath boulders, in the hollows of trees, inside caves. In Tiveden, there is no such thing as 'safe.'"

I scan the forest. Tiveden's beauty only makes it more dangerous.

I can't let my guard down.

As we walk, I search for some sign that Amma might've come this way, some sign that I'm on the right path: footprints, broken branches, scraps of clothing. *Any* sign. I don't know how I'm supposed to find the path when I don't even know what I'm looking for. I blow out a long breath. Amma should've been a little more specific.

Suddenly, I have the distinct sensation that we're being followed. I check over my shoulder. No one's there. If someone was, I tell myself Soren would know. Even if he can't see as well during the day, his other senses are heightened. Tiveden must be making me paranoid, that's all.

Out of the corner of my eye, I see a hand wrapped around a thin tree.

Heart racing, I turn slowly toward it.

The hand shrinks back, but no one stands behind it.

No way. There's no way.

I blink, and it's just another tree, no different from the ones around it.

I'm exhausted. Either that or I have a fever and I'm hallucinating. Just to be sure, I hold the back of my hand up to my forehead—I'm so cold, I can't tell. But fevers can cause chills, too. A cold tingle travels down my spine. This had better not be another flare-up or infection. Just exhaustion. I hope.

Wait. Something is carved into the tree trunk.

It's a symbol. Squinting, I step closer.

No, a rune. Not just any rune either. It's the rune used for the wooden effigies raised throughout Unden for Midwinter. Goose bumps spread over my arms at the sight of it. The rune represents protection. Spiritual connection. The higher self.

"Look," I breathe.

Hope blooms inside my chest, like the first buds of green breaking through frozen ground. Maybe, just maybe, Amma is the one who carved this. This is what she meant by following the path.

"That's nothing," Soren says. "Just the mark of an outlaw trying not to get lost in the woods."

I glance over at him, recalling my dream of Skaga and her family arriving here. "Why would outlaws come to Tiveden?" It's hard for me to wrap my head around when no one will set foot in the forest anymore. Except for Amma.

And now me.

"They are driven to desperation," Soren says gravely. "Being outlawed is the harshest punishment society has. To be alone is worse than death. You not only lose everything, you are no longer even considered *human*. Anyone wandering by themselves is presumed an outlaw, and none will aid them. Outlaws are unwelcome everywhere and can be killed without punishment, so they are often hunted down like animals. Many fled here to hide in the woods, since Tiveden was the only place no one would follow."

I'm about to ask why when I realize. "Because of the Hidden Folk."

Anyone who risked their life entering Tiveden must have had no other choice. Like I'm doing now. Amma must have felt similarly for her to come here. Still, it's strange to think that our home started out as a place for outlaws. Was Soren an outlaw? That scar running across his throat seems like a clue.

"Did you live in Unden too?" I ask. "Is that how you met Skaga?"

"I resided in Tiveden long before Unden ever existed," he says, sounding almost defensive.

But if that's true, then . . . My legs weaken at the vast amount of time that separates us. How ancient he is. How much time he lost to Skaga's sleep thorn. I look him over carefully, considering. What is his story, anyway? How did he become a draugr in the first place?

"You were human once, right?" I ask carefully.

Something like anger flashes over his face, and his body tenses. "Once."

"You say that like it's a bad thing."

"Because it is," Soren says tightly. "Humans are weak."

My nails sink into my palms. "I am *not* weak."

I've fought off fevers, life-threatening infections, flare-ups, fatigue, you name it. Being weak isn't an option when you're sick. Just getting through each day takes so much strength.

"All humans are," Soren says. "You are fragile things. Your life is no more than a spark. Mine is a wildfire."

"Yeah, I'm well aware."

When I was diagnosed with Crohn's in the hospital, I asked if it meant I was going to die. I was ten years old. My doctor gave a small, sad smile. *The disease shouldn't reduce your life span,* he told me. *As long as we keep it well controlled.* It still seemed like a sentencing anyway. A lifetime of injections and infections, surgeries and side effects.

"But that doesn't make us weak," I add, steeling my voice. "And you're wrong about this rune, too. Amma left it for me to follow."

Soren gives me a skeptical look. "Are you certain?"

I trace a fingertip over the rune's edges. My breath catches as another vision takes hold of me—*standing here, dragging my dagger through the bark, wood peeling around the blade. The movement is practiced and sure, my hand never so much as shaking with the fear I should be feeling*—

"Skaga," I gasp.

What the hell *was* that? I saw flashes like that before, but that was when Torsten was choking me. I assumed it was the dire situation I was in or the lack of oxygen, if not both. But that doesn't work as an excuse now.

Sure enough, this rune is smooth beneath my fingertips. Worn by time, not sharp and fresh. I swallow my disappointment. Maybe it wasn't Amma who left this for me. Maybe it *was* Skaga.

Soren tilts his head. "What?"

"I think Skaga carved this," I say, barely able to breathe.

Follow the path Skaga first walked through Tiveden, Amma said. Maybe she didn't mean just physically. I stare at the rune before me. Spiritual connection. Could the dreams I've been having actually be glimpses into Skaga's past? Not just dreams, but things that have actually happened?

It seems impossible, but so did magic yesterday.

"This way," I say, feeling encouraged for the first time since entering the forest. I spot another rune marking a tree ahead of us. And another. With each one I see, my confidence grows. Amma is waiting for me ahead. We'll be together again soon.

Suddenly, I catch a glimpse of something between the trees. I turn, staring out of the corner of my eye. Cold crawls down my spine. Nothing's there.

Soren stills. "What is it?"

"Nothing," I say, trying to convince us both.

A branch cracks underfoot. Only it doesn't sound like a branch snapping. It sounds like the hollow crunch of bone. Slowly, I force myself to look down.

Just a tree limb.

But as soon as I look up, I gasp.

A man. There's a man strung upside down from one of the trees. Bile burns my throat at the sight of him dangling in front of me, his ankles tied together with rope and his arms hanging limply. For an instant, I think he's reaching toward me, and I stumble back.

My legs give out. "Oh—oh my God."

Soren catches me before I hit the ground. "So it's already infecting you."

"What?" I glance up at him. "What are you talking about?"

When I look back to the tree, the man no longer hangs there.

"Tiveden is not meant for the living anymore," Soren says. "It is full of ógipta now."

It takes me a moment to translate.

Ógipta. Misfortune. Ill luck.

Amma used to say that the Folk could wield misfortune like a weapon. Anything that went wrong in Unden, she blamed on them. But that was just when her butter spoiled, or she lost her purse. Not like in my nightmare. The lake of blood. Animals dashing themselves against rocks. Food rotting while everyone starved. I thought it was all impossible, but was that the work of ógipta too? Did those things actually happen?

I pull free of Soren. "How? *Why?*"

"One consequence of the blood oath was that all the Hidden Folk began spreading ógipta, which infects living things," Soren continues. "In humans, it alters your mind until it eventually drives you mad. It will only get worse the deeper into Tiveden we go."

The pale hand wrapped around the tree. The hanged man. The sensation of someone—or something—following me everywhere I go. The unease scraping across my skin ever since setting foot in this forest. All because of ógipta.

Being in Tiveden is messing with my mind. Somehow, the forest knows everything about me. Things I would never tell anyone else. It knows what I want more than anything—and what I dread most too.

I swallow hard. "Right."

Instinctively, I reach for the trollkors around my throat, rubbing my fingers over the twisted metal. Amma gave it to me when I was little. She said it would protect me from the Hidden Folk and their misfortune. So far, it doesn't seem to be working very well.

Soren lowers his gaze to my throat, making my heart pound. The way he's looking at me . . . I don't think anyone ever has looked at me like this before. Almost as if he's in a trance. He reaches out for me, about to caress my neck. I swallow in anticipation—

His hand lands on my necklace instead.

My face must betray me, because his mouth lifts at the corner. "Did I make you blush?"

"Wh-what?" If I wasn't blushing before, I definitely am now. "No," I say, forcing the word out. "Of course not."

Soren looks me over with an amused grin. "Sure, Skarsgård."

I glance away. Am I that easy to read? I'm not. I know I'm not. No one else can read me, yet we only just met and somehow Soren is already getting under my skin. It's *unnerving*.

One of his claws grazes my collarbone as he lifts the necklace. He inspects it, careful not to touch its steel, but his fingers brush the sensitive skin at the hollow of my throat. My pulse leaps. His touch feels somehow familiar, as though I've felt it many times before—

Soren withdraws his hand suddenly, pulling away from me.

"That will not protect you."

Blinking, I close my fingers around the trollkors defensively. "Why not?"

He clears his throat. "You somehow have the ability to nullify magic, as you've already shown. Because of that, your necklace is good for its steel and little else."

‡

While we continue walking, whenever I glance at Soren, he's focused on my face. As soon as he notices my attention, he quickly looks away. I bring my hand up, testing my cheek, and wince. The skin is swollen and tender. Probably bruised. But my fingertips come back clean. At least I'm no longer bleeding.

Soren is staring again.

"What is it?" I demand. "Why do you keep looking at me like that?"

He must want to deny it but can't. "You are the one looking at me."

"Not at *you*," I say quickly. "At the forest. You know, for the markings."

Soren gives me a long, knowing look.

"Speaking of which." I focus back on Tiveden, but the trees are different, and the terrain has turned treacherous. "Amma told me how ancient this forest is. Primeval, she called it. She said it was so vast, it was like multiple kinds of forests. But actually *seeing* it is . . . something else."

"Did your grandmother tell you about the blood oath?"

"She never mentioned it." I shake my head. "My dad took me away from Unden when I was almost nine. He cut me off from her. Or he tried his best to, anyway." The thought makes me feel sick. "She still wrote me sometimes, but . . ." My throat closes up. "Apparently there are a lot of things she didn't tell me."

His mouth twists. "Did you know she kept me imprisoned?"

"I—I didn't." After a moment, I add, "I'm sure she had her reasons not to tell me."

Soren's eyes are cold fury. "Skaga may have betrayed me first, but her entire line continued it. Every last one of your family is the same. Nobody freed me."

"I did."

Silence settles over us, heavier than before.

I swallow the lump in my throat. "I just want to see Amma again. So badly."

"I am familiar with the feeling."

"What will you do when you see Skaga?" I ask him.

"I . . . do not know," Soren says, the words strained.

All I can think about is when he kissed me, believing I was her. The idea of him kissing *her* like that bothers me now, even though I don't know why. I stand in front of him, blocking his path. "Well, pretend I'm her. What would you say to me?"

Soren stares at me blankly.

"Here, I'll help." I clear my throat. "Oh Soren, how long it has been," I say, doing my best imitation of how she sounds in my dreams.

"Ska—" Soren searches my face. He's so close now that all my little hairs stand on end, like my body is beside a magnet. The moment draws out.

"Skarsgård, don't be ridiculous."

He brushes by me, his cloak swaying in his wake.

My legs ache, but I chase after him.

I have to make the most of the daylight. As Midwinter nears, the days are getting shorter. I have to keep going, no matter how tired I feel. So I distract myself with thoughts about Soren and Skaga. How did they fall in love? Did Skaga even return his feelings? And if she did, why would she betray Soren and imprison him?

Eventually, I spot another rune carved in a nearby tree.

Testing it with a fingertip, I make sure it's real. The edges are as worn as the others.

"Do you think we're getting close?" I ask Soren.

"I do not know. Tiveden is vast, and it's taken on a life of its own since I've been gone."

I swallow my disappointment like a bitter pill.

The rest of what he said strikes me like a match. "What?"

"The forest is sentient and has a will of its own," Soren says. "It's moving toward Unden, testing the limits of the blood oath's magic."

The trees come alive at his words. Their limbs strain toward me like stretched fingers, roots snaking through the snow. I can feel them crawling up my ankles, wrapping around my body, until Tiveden holds me in its embrace—

Soren lays a hand on one of the branches. "It wants to free itself of the blood oath's poison."

At his touch, the roots retract, withdrawing from me slowly.

The forest is still once more.

Tiveden *had* seemed much closer to the stave church than I remembered. I assumed because I hadn't been back in so long, I was misremembering. Or that Unden seemed smaller since I'm no longer a child. But maybe it was more than a misperception.

A blaring noise cuts through the silence like a knife.

We both jump.

Heart pounding, I look around, startled. That annoying chiming.

"What is that terrible sound?" Soren's head swivels, scanning for threats.

My phone. Wincing, I scramble to silence the alarm. "Sorry. Just my alarm."

"Alarm?" Soren asks.

"Yeah, for my next injection," I say absent-mindedly, pulling up my text messages automatically. "I have to set an alarm on my phone or else I'd never do it."

My stomach sinks when I see the last message from Dad. Want anything?

We'd stopped at a gas station on the drive to Unden. I hadn't even bothered replying, but he'd gotten me a protein bar anyway. I stare at his message another moment. I wish I could tell him that I'm okay and not to worry. Of course, there's no reception. I planned on leaving him a note before I left, but then I stumbled across Soren. I should've at least texted him while I still had the chance. Not as just an afterthought.

Soren stares at my phone. "What is that?"

"It's, um . . ." I try to think of how to explain it in a way he would understand. Not like there's any word for it in Old Norse. "It lets you send messages to people."

Soren looks around us. "I see no messenger nearby."

I can't help laughing.

He scowls. "What?"

He's surprisingly sensitive. I wave my hand. "Nothing, don't worry. No one is here." Back at the house, he assumed electricity was magic. Maybe that's the easiest way for him to understand.

I hold the phone up. "This is modern magic."

"May I?" Soren asks.

When I nod, he takes it from me and examines my phone with a furrowed brow, turning it over so he can inspect every angle. "Where is the stave? I cannot find it."

"Uh . . . there isn't one."

"Impressive." He looks at the phone in awe. "It must use galdrar instead."

Actually, he's not too far off. Voice commands aren't *that* different. Siri will really blow Soren away. Unable to resist, I switch to Swedish. "Siri, set an alarm at this time next week."

When Siri responds, Soren's eyes widen. "A woman is trapped inside?"

Right. Siri is short for Sigrid. Of course he'd recognize the name.

"She likes being in there," I assure him.

Soren considers that. "I do not think anything, living or dead, likes to be imprisoned."

Like my family kept Soren locked in our cellar for centuries. Like the Hidden Folk are now trapped in Tiveden.

For once, I don't know what to say.

"So this magic can send messages," Soren says. "Can you contact Skaga?"

I shake my head. "There's no reception—"

Soren gives a puzzled expression.

"Its magic is too weak in Tiveden," I try instead.

Soren looks disappointed as he hands the phone back to me. "I see."

"Astrid!" someone shouts somewhere in the distance. "Astrid, are you there?"

Dad. That's Dad.

I spin around, looking desperately, but I can't see him.

"Dad!" I scream.

Soren grabs my mouth, pressing his cold hand over my lips. "Keep quiet unless you want to summon every draugr to us."

"But my dad—"

"It's the forest, you fool." Soren gives me a dark look. "So long as you are in Tiveden, you cannot trust *any* of your senses."

My chest deflates. "Right."

Of course it's not Dad. He wouldn't go into Tiveden, not even when his own mother disappeared. Maybe he's relieved I'm gone now too. He won't have to see Mom every time he looks at me anymore or be constantly reminded that I'm the reason she's not here.

"No more shouting," Soren says, removing his hand from my mouth.

I bite the side of my cheek and nod instead.

We continue in uneasy silence. The only sounds are branches creaking in the breeze and snow crunching like glass with each step.

Eventually Soren asks, "Would your father really follow you?"

I shake my head. "He wouldn't go beyond the stave church. No one would."

"You did."

"That's different." I hug my arms, rubbing my hands up and down my coat. "My dad and I aren't really close, not like Amma and I. She's the one who actually raised me."

"Why is that?" Soren asks.

"My dad wasn't around much," I say. "Until the day he decided to bring me to Stockholm. Supposedly to start over, but . . . by then it was too little, too late. It only made me hate him more."

"Skaga and her father had a troubled relationship as well."

"Really?" They seem close in my dreams. Then again, all I know about her father is that he founded Unden, and before that was called Ramunder the Evil. I liked the nickname as a child. So did Amma, because we started to refer to Dad as Erik the Evil instead. She said it had a nice ring to it. "I don't know all the history, I guess."

"Who do you think allowed Skaga to be left as a sacrifice?"

"What?" I ask, unable to hide my shock.

"Unden was little more than a fledgling settlement then. It wasn't an easy life for them, and admittedly, we Folk made it harder, trying to drive them from Tiveden. In exchange for us easing their suffering, they began to leave some of their own in the woods as offerings for us. Those they thought too weak to survive—their ill, their old, their injured."

Their ill. People like *me*.

Like we are worth less just because we aren't healthy.

But we're not worthless.

We're *not*.

I can't find the right words in Old Norse, so I say in Swedish, 'That's fucked up."

Soren gives me a puzzled look.

"That's . . . horrible," I clarify.

"It is the way things are."

"Were," I say quickly. "We don't do that anymore."

Although, even today in some countries, the ill and old and disabled are still abandoned. Maybe society hasn't changed as much as we like to think.

"Wait . . . their suffering?" Realization dawns on me. "Like the lake turning to blood?"

"I thought you said you didn't know what happened."

"It was just a guess. Maybe Amma mentioned it in passing, and I only remembered now."

Soren gives me a skeptical look. "Skaga was to be left as an offering. . . ."

He continues talking, but I'm not listening anymore. So the Hidden Folk actually turned the lake to blood? Maybe those dreams really aren't just dreams. My skin prickles. The runes carved into the trees. *Spiritual connection.* The strange onslaught of images I've been getting recently. When Amma said I had to walk the same path as Skaga . . . was it not just literal, but figurative, too? Did Amma see the images as well?

Since discovering Soren, *anything* seems possible.

"Why didn't her father save her?" I ask, as if I've been listening to his story all along. I'm surprised how bitter I sound.

Tiveden must be getting to me again.

"I do not know," Soren says. "He was willing to sacrifice her for the settlement, I suppose. But she could not forgive him for it afterward."

Like I couldn't forgive Dad for taking me away.

Suddenly, Stockholm doesn't seem so bad. There were plenty of things I liked about living there, too. Eating frozen pizza with Dad and watching reruns of *Bonusfamiljen* together. Exploring the ABBA museum to feel closer to Mom and then blasting Billie Eilish back in my bedroom. Going ice-skating at Kungsan with Zuri and enjoying fresh cinnamon rolls at Mr. Cake after, laughing about how many times we both fell.

Just admitting that feels like a betrayal of Unden and Amma.

I sigh. "Can we stop for a minute?"

As soon as Soren nods, I slide my backpack off my shoulder and start digging through it. "I need to do my injection while it's still light out."

Soren tilts his head to the side. "An . . . injection?"

I peel open the package and hold up the shot. "Medicine that I need to inject beneath my skin."

As I unzip my coat and lift my sweater up, the cold bites my stomach. I rip open the alcohol wipe that comes with the shot and swipe it over my skin, its sharp smell pricking my nose. Even Soren grimaces.

"You are ill?" Soren asks.

I nod and brace myself for the usual comments I get, like *I'm so sorry,* or even worse, *you don't* look *sick.* But Soren doesn't say he's sorry. He doesn't say anything at all, and I'm grateful for it. I hate talking about my illness with people.

"So was Skaga," he says eventually. "She told me how she turned feverish and had severe pain in her abdomen before we met. She began wasting away. Her exhaustion left her unable to move sometimes, though her healer could not explain why."

"Really?" I grab my shot. "That sounds like a Crohn's flare-up."

I would know after all. As much as I hate injections, I love being in remission. So I pinch some skin between my fingers, and with a swift stab, I press the button on the injection pen. The needle punches into my stomach. I barely flinch anymore. The shot stings, but at least it's done for the week.

When I look up, Soren is staring at the small bead of blood forming on my skin. He stands completely still, his body rigid. *Right.* As soon as he notices my attention, he quickly averts his gaze.

Clearing my throat, I zip up my coat and turn away.

As I do, I notice someone standing in the forest ahead.

My heart pounds in my chest.

Amma. It's Amma.

TEN

Relief bubbles up inside me. "Amma!"

She stares at me through a shroud of mist, her hand resting on a short, split tree branch. No matter how much I squint, her features are murky . . . but I'm sure it's her. It must be.

That's her long white braid standing out against the dark trees. Her favorite gray knit sweater with a pattern of snowflakes spreading from shoulder to shoulder. She still looks the same as I remember her. Unchanged after all these years.

And she's alive.

Cold air stings my throat as I call out to her again.

Stepping closer, I can make out her face. Her mouth moves like she's speaking, but she's still too far away for me to hear what she's saying. I try reading her lips. It isn't hard, since they keep moving in the same shape. She's repeating the same word over and over.

Help. Help. Help.

"Astrid!" Soren shouts somewhere behind me.

I'm already running toward Amma.

But then she turns away, retreating toward the forest depths. It feels like a slap to the face. She may not have changed, but I have. I'm no longer a little eight-year-old girl. Amma is right there, yet somehow, she's never felt more out of reach.

"Amma, it's me!" I shout between cupped hands, but she won't listen.

She beckons for me to follow and disappears between the trees.

"Astrid, no!" Soren calls, panic in his voice.

Soren.

Amma must be afraid because of him. Because I'm not alone.

I chase her, my arms pumping. "Amma!"

My boots punch through the snow. Trees fly by. My lungs pull, each breath bursting from me. I catch a flash of her white braid before it disappears again.

"Amma, wait!"

I crash through the branches behind her. Tree limbs scrape my face and hands, and I grit my teeth at the dull pain. But I don't stop, don't slow.

She's so close.

Momentum carries me down the hill, and it feels like flying. My coat catches on a tree limb, tearing with a loud *rrrrrip. Damn it!* Stumbling forward, I keep going. Keep moving.

I burst through the trees and skid to a stop.

No sign of her.

Impossible. It's impossible. My eyes leap between the trees. Sprouts poke out of their trunks like thousands of unnaturally long fingers, each one pointing in a different direction. My heart rate turns frantic. Branches jut out all around me, sharp and jagged. The forest goes on forever—

Which way? I scan the snow for tracks, but the footsteps stop where I am. Panting heavily, I spin around, but there are no footprints *anywhere.* Just the two holes underneath my boots. Unbroken snow stretches in every direction. My pulse pounds in my ears as I look around.

I lost her.

A choked sob escapes me. "No."

I was close. So close. She was *right* there, and I let her get away. Cold air slices my throat as I try to fill my lungs, but my chest is too painful. Tears freeze on my lashes.

"Damn it." I smack my palm against the nearest tree, again and again, until it stings like a hive of bees beneath my skin. *"Damn it!"*

A branch snaps behind me, the sound traveling through me like a gunshot.

Soren must have caught up.

I spin around, but a young woman stands there instead. Loose blond hair falls around her neck and her pale lips pull into a faint smile. Her eyes are the color of hazelnuts and hold a glimmer of amusement. A white dress spills down her thin frame like a waterfall as she strides toward me.

She looks vaguely familiar, but I can't place her—

Wait. Blond hair. Hazel eyes.

"Mom?" I choke on the word.

The world stills. We stand there, staring at each other. Everything goes quiet, and all I can hear is my heart knocking against my ribs. A damp breeze blows through the forest, making the trees shiver.

It can't be.

Mom holds her arms out like an invitation.

Her face blurs as my vision fills with tears. I rub them away roughly, not wanting her to disappear. Every birthday since I can remember, *this* is what I wished for. To get to see my mom, even for a moment. Dad didn't even bring any pictures of her to Stockholm. When I found the old photo of them in his room, I couldn't stop staring at her face.

I still can't. *"Mom."*

My feet start moving on their own.

I'm drawn helplessly toward her as she stands there with open arms.

Mom smiles, her lips pulling back, but instead of teeth, her mouth is full of wet, rotting moss. It pushes out of her mouth and pours down her dress, staining it green.

Panic grips me. "Mom, what's happening—?"

She turns slowly. Her dress falls open like a hospital gown, revealing the pale skin of her back. Only there's a large gaping hole down its middle. She reaches around, grabbing the sides of her back until it splits apart with an awful cracking sound. I watch in horror as each side of her rib cage spreads like gruesome wings.

I can no longer breathe. "Mom?"

My feet move on their own, as if I'm being drawn toward her.

As the distance closes between us, I can see her cavernous insides. Where her organs should be, there is only soft moss, and peeling bark where muscle and tissue belong. It's as if I'm a child again, peering inside a hollowed tree to find the perfect hiding spot.

A sudden, inexplicable urge to climb inside strikes me.

No one will find me here. I grip her sides of bark, looking into her body. Balmy air blasts my face as I stick my head inside. There's some kind of spatial distortion, a sense of wrongness and impossibility. Wood lice scuttle down her damp insides. A soggy bed of moss awaits within her, someplace I can finally rest without worry or fear.

"Help," Mom says, her voice like scraping stones.

When she speaks, vibrations travel through her body, making the bark tremble underneath my hands. The reverberations spread through me until my bones resonate with her voice. She's trying to help me. I understand that now. I could easily slip inside her skin and dwell there forever. Safe.

I start to climb in—

"Skaga, no!"

Something knocks into me, slamming me into the snow.

I look up, blinking through the tears until my vision settles. Soren is lying on top of me, looking as shocked as I feel. His breathing is shallow, and his hands are shaking at his sides.

"What were you thinking?" Soren asks.

There's a desperation in his voice I haven't heard before.

"Get the hell off me," I say, pounding my fists against him, but his chest is unyielding. "My mom—"

"Whoever you think that is, it isn't them."

I tear my eyes away from Soren and look at Mom.

That isn't a belt wrapped around her waist.

It's a tail—*her* tail.

A sickening realization spreads through me. That isn't my mother. It's a *huldra*. Her back retracts, folding in on itself until she looks human again. Almost. Her eyelashes are pine needles and her papery skin peels off her body like birch bark. Of course. Huldra can wear the faces of anyone to lure their prey closer. First Amma. Then Mom.

My body won't stop trembling.

I should've known something was off as soon as I saw Amma. She was wearing her favorite gray knit sweater, the one with snowflakes covering the collar—the same sweater that's in my backpack. She couldn't have been wearing it when she went into Tiveden. And even if she somehow had an identical one, it's been nine years. It would be impossible for Amma to look the same. I knew—at least some part of me did.

But I saw what I wanted to see.

Soren snarls at the huldra, the sound deep. Protective. Claiming.

She turns and takes off through the woods barefoot, her tail swishing behind her. Within moments, she's gone, swallowed by the forest.

I stare up at Soren.

Worry softens his sharp features. His lips are parted and his icy gaze roves over my face, making sure I'm unharmed. Right now he looks . . . almost human. Has he always looked like this? Have I never looked closely enough to see it?

"You could have been killed," Soren says, the words practically a growl.

He *was* worried about me. He still is.

"Since when do you care?" I try to keep my voice even. Soren hates Skaga and the rest of my family. He didn't have to rescue me, but he did. I search his face for answers, but there are none.

His bottomless eyes look deeply into mine.

"I always have," Soren says quietly. "I will never stop."

It's not me he cares about.

It's Skaga.

His longing is so obvious, I can't help but feel a twinge of jealousy. My tongue brushes over my lips; the cut from when he kissed me is still sensitive, even though it's already scabbed over. Some part of me wants to feel his lips on mine again. The sharp graze of his teeth. Only a breath separates us now—when did I lean closer? Or did he? I could easily close the distance between us. He lowers his gaze to my lips.

He looks conflicted, as if he might want to kiss me, too.

The last of my adrenaline drains away. Suddenly, I'm too aware of Soren's body pressed against mine, his arms wrapped around my waist. My cheeks flame hotter than any fire. It's hard to breathe under his weight.

"You're *crushing* me."

Soren clears his throat. "The huldra was about to consume you." He climbs off, peering down at me as I lie there, sprawled on my back in the snow. "I had to act quickly."

"I am *not* Skaga," I remind him.

"You are right," Soren says. "You are far more annoying."

I glare at him.

"I . . . don't think the huldra wanted to hurt me." As I sit up, my mouth fills with saliva, and I feel sick. "It's hard to explain. Like she thought she was helping me or something. I don't know."

"Every one of their victims thinks that until the moment the huldra devours them." His face is grave. "You would have died had I not intervened."

My hands spread over the ground, snow stinging my palms. All I can see is her back splitting apart, opening like a hungry maw. Soren is right. I could've died. I almost did. I heave again and again, throwing up bright yellow bile.

What terrifies me the most is that I wasn't scared like I thought I'd be. I didn't even *realize* I was in danger. Not like a year ago, when I got a really bad infection. My fever shot so high I had to be hospitalized and hooked up to IVs. My greatest fear was finally coming true. I was going to die the same way Mom had.

After a few days, I started to improve. Until I started coughing up blood, thick and red as lingonberry jam. Pulmonary embolism. I had no idea at the time, but apparently, Crohn's makes you two to three times more likely to develop blood clots.

I start sobbing. My skin is too tight. Too hot. *Damn it.* I always cry whenever I throw up: I don't know why, but it's been like that since I was little. And I hate it. I hate it even more that Soren is seeing me like this.

"I wasn't thinking," I choke out. "But Amma—my mom—I had to follow them."

Even if I almost died, some part of me is grateful I got to see my mom. Even if she wasn't actually real. Until then, I'd only seen a few photographs. Whenever I look in the mirror, I'm always trying to find her in my reflection.

"If you saw Skaga, wouldn't you do the same?" I ask. He called her name out before tackling me to the ground. "Isn't she why you chased *me*? I thought you of all people would understand."

The words drain the anger from his face. "I do."

Soren reaches out for me, his longing plain. He brushes the loose strands of hair from my face. Skaga's face. One of his claws gently grazes my skin like the tip of a feather. "Do not cry." His voice is as tender as his touch. "We will find them. *Both* of them."

Nodding, I rub the back of my hand over my eyes.

I take in our surroundings, trying to reorient myself. There's only one problem. I don't see any runes. Spinning around, I scan the forest surrounding us, growing more and more desperate. There are no runes anywhere. The forest closes in on me as panic pulls my thoughts apart.

Lost—we're lost.

ELEVEN

Tiveden might as well go on forever.

My socks are soggy inside my boots from trekking through the snow all day. A coppery taste fills my mouth from my chapped, bleeding lips. My hands are painfully cracked, just asking for an infection. *It will only get worse the deeper into Tiveden we go.* Soren was right about that.

Right now, it feels like I'll never find my way out.

I drag my hand over my braid, giving an exasperated sigh. My frustration finally gets the better of me. "Isn't there some kind of magic you can use to help us get back to the path? A galdr? *Something?*"

"It's too late." Soren narrows his eyes. I can't tell if the daylight is bothering him or I am. "Once you're lost in Tiveden, magic is no use. I would not only need to know our destination, but also have traveled there already myself."

I rub my hand over my face. "Great."

"A long time has passed since I was last here."

"Right." Guilt stabs me in the gut. "Sorry. We just have to keep going, then."

My stomach grumbles. Okay, so maybe it wasn't just guilt. When was the last time I ate? I pull my protein bar out of my coat pocket. Now I'm really glad Dad grabbed me one at the gas station on our way to Unden.

I'm about to take a bite when I realize Soren is staring at my lips. My cheeks warm. Suddenly, I'm aware of every little movement my mouth makes. I haven't eaten in more than a day. He hasn't eaten for *centuries*. I don't know if he even needs food, but I should at least offer.

I hold the protein bar out to him. "Want some?"

Soren seems shocked, but quickly recovers.

He shakes his head. "Keep it. I wouldn't be able to taste it, anyway."

"Really?"

"Blood is the only thing I can taste."

"Oh." I don't care how much he helps me. I'm not offering him that.

I take a bite instead. As soon as I do, it tastes like someone dumped an ashtray into my mouth. Gagging, I spit the half-chewed bar out on the snow. *What the hell?*

"It's progressing quickly," Soren says solemnly.

The Tiveden sickness, he means.

"It alters my sense of taste, too?" I ask, still rubbing my mouth.

"So you will starve."

It reminds me of the awful enteral nutrition I used to have to do. Since I got sick so young, they tried the liquid-only diet before resorting to a stronger, riskier medicine. They stuck a tube up my nose and down my throat so I wouldn't have to eat anything.

As I stare down at the protein bar, tube feeding doesn't seem so bad. But I have to eat *something*. So I force myself to take another bite. My tongue is coated with ash, gritty and disgusting. All I want to do is gag. My eyes water as I swallow, forcing the thick, painful lump down my throat.

Soren watches with a sympathetic expression. "I know that taste well. It is unpleasant."

"Is this how everything tastes to you?" I ask, horrified.

"Everything save for blood."

I think of all my favorite foods. Warm, savory köttbullar covered in brown sauce. Raggmunk fried to crispy perfection with thick slices of bacon and sweet lingonberry jam on the side. Semla full of almond paste and whipped cream, just like Mom loved—

Soren can't enjoy *any* of that. All he can taste is blood.

But he's a draugr.

I hold my hands in front of me, staring down at them. Somehow, my arms look like they belong to someone else. My skin . . . it's paler than usual. Maybe it's the grim daylight. Maybe Tiveden is just messing with my senses.

Or maybe it's slowly turning me into a draugr too.

I swallow hard. "If the ógipta is infecting me . . . will I turn into a draugr?"

Soren shakes his head. "You would have to die first to become one."

"Is that what happened to you?" I ask carefully.

"I was never infected."

"But you became a draugr."

Amma always said the draugar were humans who refused to die. They possessed a strong enough will to draw their life force back into their bodies after dying. Revenants, basically. But even then, certain conditions had to be met. At least according to Amma, they either had to be infected by another draugr, or otherwise corrupt and evil.

"Did you do something terrible, then?"

The words slip out without thought. As soon as I say them, Soren stiffens.

"You are mistaken," he says, walking ahead of me. "We should go."

The only sound is our footsteps breaking through the snow. I definitely messed up. As we walk, the growing silence soon becomes unbearable.

"So all of this is because of the blood oath?" I ask.

"Our ógipta infects Tiveden as well as humans," Soren says, weighing his words. "Corrupting the forest, spreading through it like a disease. Skaga and Unden benefited from the oath, while the Folk were imprisoned here with its unintended consequences. The longer the oath continues, the worse it will get, until Tiveden will overtake Unden. I do not know what will happen then." He hesitates. "It is already worse than I feared."

Tiveden is eerily quiet. Instead of birdsong, there is only silence, constant and unnerving—the absence of any *life*. My stomach turns queasy. In the safe parts of the forest, there are plenty of wood grouse. But here, animal life isn't just scarce, it's nonexistent. Not just animals, either. *Everything.* Even the trees seem like they're dying.

"What happens to Unden if the oath is broken?" I ask. Skaga must have had a reason for refusing to do it, especially if Amma still believes the same thing all these years later.

Soren remains quiet.

Nothing good, then.

Clearly there's still something he doesn't want to tell me.

Sighing, I glance around, not knowing which way to go anymore. Wandering through the forest, directionless, I try to make sense of everything Soren has told me. Can I really believe him? But now that I'm seeing Tiveden for myself, I'm starting to understand where he's coming from.

I don't know what—or who—to believe anymore.

‡

Now that the sun has set, my teeth won't stop chattering. "I have to make a fire."

It's still only midafternoon, but the temperature has already started to drop. I scan the trees around us, unsure where to begin. I haven't gathered firewood in a long time. Not like I ever needed to in Stockholm.

"Would you like me to assist you?" Soren asks.

"I can do it. I've made plenty of fires in our wood-burning stove."

Soren leans against a tree. "Very well."

There. That one seems sturdy.

As I approach it, Soren stiffens. "Not that tree. It's ash."

"I know." Amma always said ash wood produces a steady flame and good heat. She kept plenty of it around the house, enough to feed our wood-burning stove all winter. But ash wood is also one of the few things capable of killing a draugr. That must be why Soren is frowning at me now.

I reach for one of the branches—

Something scurries over the tree limb toward me. I yank my arm back as sharp teeth snap down, biting the spot where my hand was a second before. Rubbing my wrist, I stare at the small, bony creature. Its pitch-black eyes are too large for its face, and twigs are tangled in its long brown hair. When the creature smiles, its mouth is full of needlelike teeth. If I had pulled back any slower, those teeth would have taken my hand, or at least a few fingers.

"I did warn you," Soren calls.

"Yeah, thanks for being so specific. Really helpful."

Soren smirks at me.

"What the hell is that thing, anyway?" I ask.

"She is one of the vættir. She's bound to the ash tree, as a wife is to her husband, protecting it from harm. If anyone so much as tries to hurt it, she will harm them instead."

I stare at the small creature in wonder. "An askafroa."

The wife of the ash tree. "I thought ash harmed the Hidden Folk, though."

Soren considers my words. "Do you know that when the gods created Ask and Embla, the progenitors of humanity, they fashioned their bodies from ash trees?"

I nod. It was one of many myths Amma told me.

"Ash trees are sacred," he continues. "Even the world tree, Yggdrasil, is one. It can only harm draugar, as it represents life and everything we are not." His voice grows more bitter with every word.

Soren almost sounds resentful of what he is. I get it. Sometimes I feel just as bitter about being sick. That this is my life now, like it or not. But I don't know how to say that. I don't even know if I can say something like that to Soren.

"It would be wise to choose a different tree," he finishes.

I shoot him a wry look. "Clearly."

The other trees surrounding us appear skeletal.

I scrape bark off one, and it sloughs off as easily as skin. "What's wrong with these trees?"

"They are poisoned." His voice is grave. "The ash isn't only because of the askafroa's protection."

The tree underneath the bark is dead, so I break off a branch.

It doesn't sound like a branch snapping. It sounds like bone. The same blood-chilling sound as when I broke my arm as a kid. My teeth chatter, and not just from the cold. Sap pours down the tree trunk like spilled blood.

Revulsion overwhelms me, but I have no choice.

I need fire.

I snap another branch, shuddering at the awful sound. "Poisoned by what?" I throw the stick onto the ground to start a pile. "The ógipta?"

Soren nods. "The blood oath is thorough."

There's accusation in his voice. He means that all this is Skaga's fault—and my family's. Tense silence settles over us while I finish gathering wood for the fire. I grab a brittle stick and press it into another piece of wood like a spindle. Without a lighter or match, friction is my best bet. Rubbing furiously, I work my way down the stick over and over, taking out all my frustration on it.

No smoke. Nothing.

Soren folds his arms across his chest. "You're not very skilled at this, are you?"

I wince at his words, even though I know he's right. All I've managed to do is give *myself* a friction burn. If this doesn't catch soon, I'm going to rub my palms raw and bloody. Worse, I could get an infection.

"Come on," I mutter, pressing harder on the stick. *"Come on."*

Not even a spark.

I lean back, blowing out a long breath. Soren is right. I suck at this.

"Do you still not want my help?" Soren asks.

I flex my sore fingers and stare down at my bright red palms. At this rate, I'll freeze to death before I can get a fire going. I know what Amma would say. *Your stubbornness won't keep you warm.*

"I do," I admit begrudgingly.

Soren crouches next to me.

As he takes the spindle from me, our hands brush. The quick contact sends a spark shooting through me. His skin feels soft. Surprisingly so. Almost as soft as his lips. I shake my head, trying to get rid of the thought. What is *wrong* with me? He's a draugr.

He drags the stick through the frozen dirt, drawing a symbol.

No, a *stave*.

"You can use staves too?" I ask. "Amma always said seiðr magic practitioners could use staves *or* galdrar. Never both."

Soren snaps the stick he's holding in two. "Those are limitations humans set on themselves," he sneers. "They believe staves are womanly magic, while only galdrar are suitable for men. Men practicing staves is considered taboo, but both have their uses. Staves generally last longer than galdrar but are more difficult to create."

"Are you sure you can't use both because you're a draugr?"

"No." Something dark passes over his face. "I learned the staves long before I was killed for it."

I glance at the scar across his throat without meaning to.

He must notice, because he grows quiet. "Not just me. My parents as well."

I meet his eyes. "I guess I can understand why you would hate humans."

Soren seems surprised, like my words caught him off guard.

"We can be pretty awful," I admit. "Unfortunately, that's one thing that's never changed. Even today, some people are full of hatred. Because of that hate, they hurt others."

"That is not unique to humans," Soren says, but he sounds sad. "Hate can infect us as well. As draugar, if we are not careful, such emotions can easily consume us."

"Has that ever happened to you?" I ask carefully, thinking of Skaga.

Soren stills. He stands, clearing his throat. "The stave is complete."

I'm grateful, even if Soren is trying to divert my line of questioning. I'm so cold that I can think of little else besides a fire anyway. But nothing is happening yet. The stave still needs blood.

I reach for my dagger defensively. "You are *not* getting any of mine."

"Who said I needed it? A stave requires the blood of its creator."

I blink. But the lockbreaker one worked for me. Maybe it only did since I share the blood of whatever family member drew the stave? I can't make sense of it otherwise.

His lip quirks, exposing one of his pointed teeth. "Besides, my blood works better."

Soren brings his thumb to his mouth and bites into the flesh. Black blood beads on his pale skin like an onyx jewel.

"Why is that?" My voice comes out breathy.

Soren grins. "We are more powerful than the living."

"So the blood itself influences the stave's strength?"

Soren nods, pressing his thumb down. He drags it slowly over the stave, the same way I imagine he might swipe his thumb across Skaga's lips. Or mine. Ever since he kissed me, I can't stop thinking about it. No matter how hard I try.

"Even the Allfather of the gods sought the dead for our wisdom and magic," Soren finishes.

A small flame flickers to life. It snakes along the path of his blood as if it were oil, growing stronger as it goes. Soon, a fire blazes where there once was only frozen dirt and snow.

Magic.

Maybe that's why I keep thinking about the kiss. Because of Tiveden's ógipta. Falling for a monster who craves your blood does seem pretty unfortunate. Only a fool would do that.

I hold my freezing hands over the hot flames, trying to focus on the warmth instead. The fire pops and snaps, soothing my skin. I sigh happily. I could've spent hours and never gotten a fire going. Certainly not one as large as this.

Sparks rise from the fire as I study Soren over the wavering flames. Silhouetted against the fire, he looks almost human. But his body is rife with tension. He must be keeping his distance from the fire. He might appear human, but he's still a draugr. Fire is one of the few things that can destroy him.

And he still made one. For me.

"Thank you," I say, surprised to realize how much I mean it.

Soren sits across from me, and the firelight carves out his features. His silver hair spills around his face, his bangs skimming the bridge of his nose, almost like he's trying to hide behind them. The urge to brush them aside strikes me, but I clamp it down.

"You should rest while you can," Soren says.

Pushing thoughts of him away, I stretch out on the snow. It's not even that late and my body aches with exhaustion. If I want to find Amma, I need rest. I lay my head on my backpack like it's a pillow and stare up at the sky. Dead branches reach into the darkness like long fingers, firelit shadows shifting all around us.

I roll over, peering at the forest. As my vision adjusts, I can barely make out the silhouettes of creatures in the darkness. They surround us, standing as still as trees, but their legs and arms stretch too long to be human. Some must be at least three meters tall. They remain far away, unmoving. I hope.

As I lie there, Soren drapes his cloak over me without a word.

"Thanks," I murmur, pulling it around me.

I'm not sure how to feel about his kindness. Or about *Soren*. Ever since he stopped Torsten, the initial iciness between us has started to thaw. But he is a draugr and dangerous. I can't let myself forget that or else I'm as good as dead. Even if some part of me is drawn to him.

Especially if I'm drawn to him.

In Tiveden, the things I'm drawn to will kill me.

TWELVE

"We will never forget your sacrifice, Skaga," Gorm says, leading me by a rope.

Each time he yanks me forward, I curse the day the disgraced priest found Unden. His rope chafes my wrists, rubbing my skin raw, nearly as infuriating as the mischievous tone of his voice. But when Gorm speaks, people listen. *You suffer because you have angered the Hidden Folk,* he proclaimed when he arrived. If you are to survive, you must appease them with offerings.

Gorm's solution was simple if brutal: we had too many mouths to feed, so we must reduce our numbers. It started with the old. The injured. The ill. One by one, they were taken into Tiveden to die. With each offering, Gorm amassed more followers, until he led nearly all of Unden. People followed him because they were afraid if they didn't, they might be next.

Now, I am.

Everyone in Unden gathers outside their homes to watch me go. Once I became ill, I knew it was only a matter of time until I took this walk. Humiliation burns my cheeks as I'm led like a captured thrall through the village my father founded. I search the faces of people I once thought I knew well. Liv. Torsten. Even Father watches with wet eyes, but he will not interfere.

No one will.

Not even Freyja can save me now.

As we walk toward the forest, I recall when I first learned of Tiveden.

Our exile was not enough punishment to some in Birka. They hunted us down like animals. I nearly had my throat slit by one of the men who hated my father—until Father's axe split his head like a tree stump. After that, Father gave me a dagger of my own so I would always have something to protect myself with. It was heavier than I expected, the handle carved with twisting roots, smooth in my palm. Excited, I unsheathed it. Even the blade was beautiful, finely carved with runes along its edge—

"It says my name!" I said, filled with delight.

"All things deserve to be named," Father said. "And since this will be your first blade, I named it after you."

"I love it, Father."

"As I love you, little one." Father's large hand swallowed mine as he closed my fingers around the handle. "You must carry it with you at all times, do you understand?" He lowered his voice, sounding grave. "Where we are going now, you will need it."

"Where is that?" I asked.

His long beard looked rougher than usual, and deep lines marked his forehead. Only then did I notice how weary he looked. "A treacherous forest known as Tiveden." Father helped me sheathe the dagger and tucked it carefully into the belt around my apron dress. "Somewhere no one will dare follow us."

Fear curled in my stomach. "Why?"

His expression darkened, but he offered no response.

"So we can all remain together," Liv offered, not answering my question. She exchanged a look with Father, her hand resting on the longsword tucked into her belt. Suddenly, my little dagger no longer seemed enough.

Now I do not even have that.

As I walk through Tiveden, weaponless, reality grabs hold of me, like a giant crushing me in its fist. I will never return to Unden. Branches and stones scrape my bare feet, and each step brings me closer to my death. When Gorm and his followers came to get me, I didn't have a chance to slip on my leather shoes. The time has come for you to go to the gods, Gorm told me, Will you go willingly, or must I force you? His followers held Liv and Father as Gorm tied my wrists and led me outside like an animal to the slaughter.

Now I will never stand in my home again.

Gorm moves cautiously through the forest, his hood swiveling as he glances every which way. Everyone accompanying me is fearful, even *though I am the one who will be left behind. Their unease makes mine grow. I'm the one who will have to face the Hidden Folk once darkness falls over the forest.*

If I am to die either way, part of me hopes that the Folk find us before we reach Trollkyrka. After Gorm has led so many to perish out here, it seems fitting for the Folk to claim his life too. But I am not so lucky.

I am surprised how short the walk seems.

Soon, the mountain looms over me like a slumbering giant turned to stone by Freyja's light. As all things deserve names, Gorm has taken it upon himself to call this place the Troll's Church. Supposedly, it is sacred ground, the only place suitable to leave our offerings for the Hidden Folk.

As we climb the mountain, I realize trolls are all around us. They peer out from crevices in the rock. They scuttle across the cliffs, sending crumbling stones down on our heads. Briefly, I catch a glimpse of a beautiful troll woman—she looks like she could belong in Unden, save for her snakelike golden eyes, sharply pointed ears, and eerily long fingers.

A stone altar waits for me when we reach the top of Trollkyrka.

Gorm's followers surround me, cutting off any escape, even though it's obvious I cannot run. My body still has not recovered from my sickness. I barely made it up this treacherous mountain. When they force me against the altar, I'm too exhausted to fight back. In fact, lying down is almost a relief.

Maybe dying will be too.

Gorm peers down at me from his hood, with his kohl-smudged eyes and dark lines trailing his cheeks like tears. His followers pull the rope tighter as they fasten me to the notches in the stone. Gorm extends his arms with a great flourish, his robes spreading wide. "We leave this girl's life to those who have always dwelled in this forest—"

"My father will never forgive you," I say, interrupting his foolish speech. I have grown tired of Gorm's words. I do not wish to hear more, especially if they will be the last words I ever hear. "Be it days or months, he will kill you for this, priest. I only regret I will not be there to bathe in your blood afterward."

Gorm cocks his head to the side, considering.

Then he grins, exposing the horizontal lines cut into his teeth. "Is that so?"

He seems amused by my threat, which only stokes my rage further. "How fortunate you will be there to greet me in the afterlife instead." He glances over to one of his men. "Gag her so we can finish."

They bring a rope to my mouth. I bite down hard, hoping to take a finger, but only get coarse rope. They force it deep into my mouth as I push my tongue against it. I glare up at Gorm, willing every ounce of hatred within me into my gaze as if it could sear him alive. I recall the last time someone tried to kill me—how my father's axe swiftly cleaved his head in two, hot blood splattering my face—and how I long to see the same happen to Gorm.

Gorm's eyes roll back, turning white as wool.

"Is this a vision or a threat? You wish to see my head split by an axe, do you?" Gorm asks as though he is seeing—experiencing—exactly what I want him to. As though I have projected the memory into his mind.

But that is impossible.

So why does Gorm appear so unsettled?

After blinking a few times, his eyes return to their normal shade of brown.

Gorm lets out a barking laugh and the sound echoes over the stone. "How remarkable."

Of course death would not frighten Gorm but delight him. I bite down harder on the rope, tight enough to crack my teeth. We should have killed him the moment he first set foot in Unden.

Something wets my cheeks.

"Look," one of his men says, in fear or awe, I cannot tell. "She weeps tears of gold just as Freyja does."

Panic seizes hold of me. I am no spákona. I possess no power. There is nothing remarkable about me.

It should not be possible, and yet my cheeks are wet with magic.

Gorm looks down on me. "So the blood of the gods flows through your veins," he says with a laugh. "It is almost a shame to leave you here knowing that, but we have already come all this way, and an offering must be left."

Gorm's and his follower's faces float above me. Of course he will not offer himself or one of them in my stead. He is only playing games with me. Though I do not know my birth mother, it is ridiculous to think she could be a goddess.

Surely, my father would have known. He would have boasted of it to all who would listen.

"Hear me, mighty and ancient Folk," Gorm calls out, still grinning, "I offer you Skaga Ramundersdóttir so that you will do us no harm."

He lets the weight of his words settle over me.

Gorm leans closer and whispers, "Farewell, Skaga. I hope you do not suffer too long."

With that, their faces vanish.

Their footsteps are heavy over the rocks, and I have to twist my neck to watch them leave. My scream is trapped by rope as I pull against the too-tight bindings with what little strength I have. They don't so much as glance back in my direction. They will return home.

I will not.

I don't know what to expect; I only know that those who are brought to Trollkyrka never return. Which of the Hidden Folk will find me? Will it be one of the trolls, or a draugr, or perhaps one of the vættir? Will I die of thirst before they kill me? Or perhaps the cold will finish me first.

Only one thing is certain: I will die.

The silence turns suffocating as I wait, and wait, and wait, the bindings burning my skin. My stomach growls, reminding me of the long winter when we all starved. My clothes became so loose they hung off me, and my bones protruded from my skin. Hunger drove us all to desperation, eating bark or anything we could find to fill our bellies. Unden seemed on the verge of ruin.

That was when Gorm arrived.

After the offerings, things began to improve, which only strengthened his hold over Unden. Everyone returned to normal. Except for me. Even when there was plenty of food again, I did not gain my weight back. My parents and Torsten lavished me with every fish and wood grouse they could find, but it didn't matter how much I ate. I continued to waste away—

A branch snaps, startling me.

I twist my neck from side to side, trying to see who—or what—is approaching.

No one is there.

I am alone.

The cold slab of stone presses into my back, its chill seeping into my bones. I'm so cold, I long for the feverish nights of my sickness, curled beside the fire pit, sweat soaking my clothes. My entire body begins to hurt as it did back then, when exhaustion would swallow me like a great chasm.

As I stare at the bright sun, I think of Freyja. This high up the mountain, the Bright Lady's light is radiant, and I concentrate on the warmth of her heat upon my skin. Lying alone before her like this, I might as well be naked. Tears burn rivers down my cheeks.

I do not want to join the gods, not yet.

I only want my family. I can still feel Liv's soft lips on my forehead, still feel Father's strong arms encircling me. I can still see their faces as they watched me leave for the final time. Silently, I beseech Freyja: let me live. Return me to them.

Something splatters my arm. Then my foot.

Rain.

Although there are no clouds, fat raindrops fall from the sky, and sunlight turns them to gold.

Freyja weeps for me.

Her tears shower me, warming my skin and soothing my aching bones. In the gentle patter of the rain, I hear her voice, soft as a whisper. "Live, my daughter. I did not birth you so you could die here. A fantastic future still lies ahead of you. If you wish to see it, you must survive." Her voice is so rapturous, so beautiful, it can only belong to Freyja, the goddess whom I have worshipped all my life—

Daughter, *she called me.* Freyja . . .

My birth mother.

It feels as though I am breathing for the first time.

I cry freely, my tears mingling with my mother's. For so long, I have wondered who my birth mother was, and why it was easier to abandon me than to love me. But now I understand. Every question, every doubt, every struggle—they are replaced by calm certainty.

That must be why I always loved her most of all the gods. I know well that

Freyja goes by many names as she walks the world. Gefjun. Mardöll. Sýr. And of course, the name my father said was my mother's: Vanadís. Even the name itself means lady of the Vanir.

The tribe of gods that Freyja leads.

I hated my birth mother for leaving, but if she was the goddess, she had no choice. Not because she did not love me, but because the gods cannot remain with humans for too long.

All this time, Freyja has been within me, her magic in my veins. That is how I was able to use a power on Gorm that I did not know I possessed. My mother is the first practitioner of seiðr, and the most powerful. She has shared her gift with me.

As sunlight washes over me, I am no longer afraid.

A wound I have carried my entire life has been healed at long last.

But just like when I was born, my mother cannot remain with me for long. Eventually, the sun sets, taking her love with it.

I am alone once more.

Darkness settles over me like a blanket, and I long to feel my mother's warmth again. My eyelids grow heavy. If I allow my eyes to close, they may never open again. I stare up into the vast night sky and imagine it is the primordial void, where fire first met frost and all existence began, that I peer into.

I have to hold on. I will see the future my mother promised me—

Footsteps echo against the stone like thunder.

My heart drums against my chest. Has one of the Folk found me?

I twist my head to the right.

Nothing.

Slowly, I force myself to look to the other side.

A creature lurks in the shadows.

His eyes glow in the darkness, bright as blue moons. A spike of dread shoots through me as the draugr nears. His silver hair gleams like a blade, and his lips press into a line as he stands over me.

A broken, keening noise rises from deep within me. The sound is something like the lamb makes when it sees the blade slip free for the first—and final—time. I pull against the bindings, struggling with what little strength I have.

The draugr peers down at me, like he's savoring the terror he surely sees on my face. Then he lifts his hand, each claw sharper than the dagger my father gave me.

I thrash wildly against the rock. Rope muffles my screams as I beg and cry.

I am not ready to die. I cannot.

He brings down his claws—

I can't move. I can't even scream.

My muscles lock up, painfully stiff. My arms and legs won't work. I can barely twitch my fingers. No ropes hold me, but it feels as if I'm lying there on the altar, hard stone against my back, helpless. I force my eyes open, only to be met with the same piercing blue stare.

Soren.

Cold spreads through me. It was *him*. He stares at me with the same intensity as when he stood over Skaga, ready to take her life. I whimper.

"Are you all right?" Soren asks.

No, I try to say, but my mouth won't move.

I can't even shake my head.

My eyes water as I stare up at him. My chest is so tight with terror, I can barely breathe.

His forehead creases with concern.

"It's okay," Soren says, his voice softening. "I'm right here. You're safe."

With a great gasp, I finally manage to sit up.

"Just a night terror," I say, but my voice is unsteady.

Soren says nothing. He's waiting for me to continue if I want to.

So I do.

"I used to have them as a child," I say once my breathing steadies. "I would see the Fell King in the shadows of my room. Sometimes, I would wake in the middle of the night, unable to move or scream, as he stood by and watched. Amma never believed me. She couldn't see him. No one else could. But it felt so vivid. So *real*."

"Is that so?" Soren sounds intrigued.

I swallow hard before continuing. "It would terrify me. But I haven't experienced one in a long time. Not since moving to Stockholm. I always assumed I grew out of them. Now . . . I'm not so sure."

Soren hesitates. "Did you see him again?"

"No, this was . . . different. I was left to die in Tiveden," I say quietly. "Well, it wasn't even me. It was Skaga. But I could feel her terror as if it were my own."

Soren goes still. "Are you certain?"

I nod. "I've been dreaming of her since I returned to Unden."

He looks lost in thought. "Not dreams. Projections."

"What?" I ask, leaning closer.

"Skaga has the ability to project her memories and thoughts onto people, which means we must be getting closer to her if she's communicating with you."

"She can do that?" I ask, wondering if Amma saw these projections too.

Soren nods. "Just as you can break magic."

Was Skaga calling Amma here too? I recall the power she used on Gorm, his eyes rolling back in his head while he saw what Skaga wanted him to see. If these haven't just been nightmares but Skaga projecting her memories onto me . . .

But why would she? Is she trying to tell me something?

Or warn me?

"It was you, wasn't it?" My hands start shaking, so I stuff them into my pockets. "You found her on Trollkyrka. What happened next?" In Amma's stories, this is when Freyja arrives to save Skaga, but I'm curious to hear what Soren has to say.

He gives me an uncertain look.

"Well, I know Skaga survived," I prompt.

Soren leans against one of the trees, arms folded while he watches me. "When I first saw Skaga in the woods, the world went silent and still. I had never seen anything so beautiful."

My cheeks flame. The reverence in his words . . . he's talking about Skaga, but I can't help feeling he means me, too. His gaze is fixed on me. Something in my chest squeezes. Soren looks at me like no one else ever has or ever will.

He continues. "Normally, by the time I came to claim their offerings, they were already dead. Frozen, or another one of the Folk had found them first. But not Skaga. She was still fighting to hold on, like she wanted to live so badly that she refused to die. The terror on her face reminded me of how I had once felt, long ago. So I carried her back to Unden and returned her home—"

"You mean Freyja did," I say automatically.

Soren stiffens. "What?"

Amma told me the story often, so I repeat it to him. "After Skaga was abandoned in the woods, the goddess walked through Tiveden and found her daughter near death. Freyja lifted Skaga up in her arms and carried her home. On the way back to Unden, the goddess taught her the staves, and shared the sacred knowledge of the Vanir with her. Our family has been blessed by Freyja ever since."

Now Soren looks shocked.

His shock quickly dissipates, replaced by anger. "You give your goddess too much credit." Soren's response seems to slip out, almost without him realizing. Once he does, his mouth snaps shut. "I am the one who taught Skaga the staves."

I narrow my eyes. "You expect me to believe that?"

"I cannot lie."

"Yeah, right," I say with a laugh.

"I am incapable of it." Soren holds my gaze. "I am bound by the ancient laws of the Hidden Folk, so I cannot tell a lie or break my word once given."

Amma never mentioned *that*. But Soren looks genuinely hurt. As if he's actually telling the truth. I've never seen Freyja, but Soren is sitting in front of me. He's ancient and knows the staves. If he's being honest, it suddenly makes more sense *why* he keeps insisting that Skaga betrayed him. She didn't just imprison him; she used a stave he taught her to do it.

I try to think of a lie he's told me. Any lie.

"Do you still love her?" I ask slowly. "Skaga, I mean?"

Soren remains silent. Is it because he really cannot lie like he claims, or he can't bring himself to admit the truth? Either way, his silence tells me everything I need to know.

Even if Soren can't lie, it doesn't mean I can *trust* him.

THIRTEEN

Soren and I continue as soon as it's light out. My neck aches from constantly searching, and I still haven't spotted a single rune. We walk until my legs turn raw and stiff from the cold. This is all my fault. How could I be so *stupid?* Blowing out a foggy breath, I drag my hands down my face. The huldra didn't devour me, but she still might cost me my life—

Wait.

My coat. Amma always said that if you were lost because of a huldra, there was one thing you could do to find your way back. At this point, I'm willing to try anything. I take off my coat, reach into the sleeve, and pull it inside out. Now I'm really glad Dad insisted I get a reversible one.

Soren raises an eyebrow. "What are you doing . . . ?"

Once my coat is turned inside out, I transfer my dagger into the outside pocket and pull it back on. "It's supposed to help us find our way back."

"I see," he says, fighting a smile.

I must look as ridiculous as I feel. But if it works, I don't care.

Before I can tell him off, his whole body goes rigid. "Something is coming."

What could be horrible enough to set *Soren* on edge?

Gripping the dagger, I look around the forest. Torsten again?

Or has the Fell King found us?

Trees tremble around us. Fear climbs my ribs like the rungs of a ladder. I can't tell if it's a breeze or something approaching us. Whatever it is would have to be massive. I catch a glimpse of a creature moving through the forest. Large. Leopard-like.

Soren grabs my wrist. "Run!"

The creature gives a menacing growl.

We take off at a sprint, crashing through branches.

I check over my shoulder, but the forest is too thick. I can't see what's chasing us.

Trees snap behind us.

Soren pulls me along as we run, and I stumble after him. My breathing is loud. Too loud. Branches block our path.

But we have to keep moving.

I check behind us again.

A nearby pine shivers, sending snow spilling to the ground with a loud plop, startling me. We dash ahead, not even knowing which way we're heading anymore, if we're going deeper into the forest or getting closer to the path.

Trees blur past as we run, feet flying over the snow—

Soren stops suddenly.

He draws me behind a tree, tipping his chin toward it. "Get in. We'll be safe inside."

The tree has an opening, almost like a doorway, and the inside is hollow. Suddenly, it's like I'm peering into the huldra's cavernous back again. Dread prickles my skin. He wants me to climb in there?

I shake my head, panting. "No way."

"Hurry."

I hesitate until a massive leopard-like creature prowls toward us. Its flesh has been flayed, leaving wet, glistening muscle exposed. Those muscles bunch and pull as it moves through the forest with predatory grace.

Swearing, I duck inside the tree hollow. Soren climbs in after me, hunching his shoulders, but the space is too small for us both even when we straighten out inside. His body is pressed against mine, far too close.

The creature growls, so close the sound rumbles in my ears.

My breathing turns shallow. "What the hell is that?"

"A kattakyn."

I gulp. It looks like a monster out of my nightmares, as if I'm experiencing sleep paralysis again. But I'm not. I know I'm not.

The kattakyn pads closer.

Closer.

It's so close all I can see are its massive paws. Sharp, wicked claws. Each longer than my hand. Ropes of saliva drip from its sharp teeth. I don't dare *breathe*. Suddenly, a large, yellow eye with a slitted pupil fills the doorway.

I clench my jaw to keep from screaming.

The creature withdraws, and I let out a small sigh—before Soren pushes me back as the kattakyn scratches at us. We flatten ourselves against the tree trunk. There's nowhere else to *go*.

Claws swipe through the doorway—

My heart races as the kattakyn strains to reach us. It gives a frustrated howl, raking at the tree desperately. Wood curls and peels under its claws, leaving ribbons around us.

Soren shields me with his body until the awful scraping stops.

The claws have vanished.

Finally, with one last, frustrated screech, the kattakyn lopes away.

The forest seems quiet. For once, the unnatural silence is a welcome relief.

I sag against Soren. "Will it return?"

"We should wait a while longer to be sure it doesn't," he says roughly.

Even though the kattakyn is gone, my heart is still pounding. Soren's body remains flush with mine, pinning me in place against the tree. The hard plane of his chest presses against mine as I draw in a shaky breath.

Somehow, this feels just as dangerous.

‡

When we finally climb out of the tree, we're in a different part of the forest entirely. I suddenly feel nauseous as if I have a bad case of motion sickness. "What happened? Where are we?"

"Huldra live within the trees." He sounds annoyed as he adds, "They use those doorways to travel between trees in the forest quickly."

I stare at him. "A huldra lives there? Why didn't you *warn* me—"

"We needed someplace safe from the kattakyn." He sounds annoyed as he adds, "If a huldra had been inside, the tree would have been sealed."

Horror dawns on me as I take in the forest around us. All the tree trunks of various sizes. How many have huldra hidden inside? No wonder that huldra seemed to appear out of nowhere, taking Soren by surprise, and vanished into the forest so quickly after.

"So the trees are like portals throughout the forest?"

"Something like that," Soren says. "But only the huldra know where they lead."

"Too bad we don't."

As I look around, I spot something moving between the trees. *The kattakyn?* No. Whatever it is, it's fluttering in the distance like a white flag. My breath mists in the air as I push through the snow toward it.

My coat. It's a scrap of my coat, snagged on a branch from when I'd chased the huldra.

"See, told you it would work," I say, gesturing to my coat.

Soren raises an eyebrow. "Or the huldra's tree would have led us here regardless."

I roll my eyes. "Either way, the path is over here."

"Are you certain?" Soren asks.

I snatch the fluttering piece of fabric from the tree, smoothing it out in my fingers. "Look." I hold it up to him and then motion to the rip in the sleeve of my coat. "We definitely came this way. Let's go."

At least now I know we're headed in the right direction.

We keep going for hours until a putrid stench makes me gag.

A corpse is lying in the snow.

No, not any corpse—*Torsten*.

His head has been hacked off and rests gruesomely beside his body. His face is frozen stiff, mouth stretched into a scream. His pale, unseeing eyes stare at me.

I shake my head, trying to clear the horrific sight. I should be grateful he's dead, since he tried to kill me, but I can't help feeling remorse. He genuinely seemed to love Skaga. If my dreams really are projections of her life, then Torsten was teasing, protective, caring.

No one deserves this, not even a draugr.

"What happened?" I manage to get out.

I didn't know anything in Tiveden could *do* this to a draugr.

Amma always said they were the most powerful creatures in the forest.

As Soren examines the corpse, his face seems paler than usual. "I can't tell."

I've never seen him so shaken.

"Could the huldra have done this?" I ask.

"There would be no body left behind."

Right. I swallow hard. "What about the kattakyn?"

"Perhaps, but this is a clean cut," he says, examining the neck more closely.

"Another draugr, then?"

"We do not kill our own kind," Soren says.

I blink, recalling how he savagely tore off Torsten's arm. It sure seemed like Soren *wanted* to kill him. And from what Torsten swore, it sounds like he and the Fell King both want Soren dead.

"Even the Fell King?" I ask. "Could that be something else that's changed while you slept?"

Soren looks rattled. "It's possible. Perhaps he wields a human weapon, but their handles are often made of ash wood, so we cannot."

As I stare down at Torsten's severed head, I can still see him drinking mead by the fireside, still hear his easy, familiar laughter filling the longhouse. His hands rest at his sides, but I can still see him holding them up in surrender as Skaga pointed her dagger at him when they first met.

His legs are stiff, but I recall his pants rolled up his calves while he stood shin-deep in the lake, splashing through the water and spearfishing as Skaga teased him.

"Whatever did this, we can't just leave him here," I say. "We should bury him. Burn his body. *Something.*"

"There's no time. He hasn't been here long. Whatever did this likely isn't far away."

I recall how thick the *Hidden Folk* book was. How many monsters were depicted in its pages. The forest is still and unmoving, as if holding its breath—

"Wait," I tell Soren. "Let me at least say something. I know it's not like I actually *knew* him," I say quietly. "But . . . it kind of feels like I did."

He sighs. "Be quick."

Soren can't say no to my face. *Skaga's* face.

But what should I say?

All that comes to mind are the words Johan recited at his mother's grave. The words everyone in Unden recites whenever we lose one of our own. It seems fitting, actually. Torsten was part of Unden. He was there when it first began, when it was just an idea Ramunder had, when Skaga first named it.

"May Freyja hold him," I start, my voice shaking a little. "In a field that goes on forever. Surrounded by golden wheat swaying in a warm breeze. Someplace the sun never sets."

As I finish, a hot tear slides down my cheek. I can't recall the last time I said those words.

Soren looks me over. "We should keep going."

Swiping my cheek, I give a quick nod. Soren is right. Better not hang around. I really don't want to find out what killed Torsten. Kattakyn or not, who knows what it would be capable of doing to *us*?

We pick up our pace. Finding Torsten like that has given both of us an added sense of urgency. Each time I hear a noise, my eyes dart around nervously. I can't shake the feeling we're being hunted.

We continue until the sun sets.

Even after Soren makes a fire and I have some food, I'm still on edge. I feel queasy despite finishing off another protein bar. As I pull his cloak tighter around me, I search the dark forest. What if there's something even worse than the kattakyn waiting in Tiveden? Something more deadly than any draugr.

Something capable of killing Soren.

FOURTEEN

"You may leave this offering to Freyja," Father says, holding out a pitcher of our finest mead, "but do not stray too far into Tiveden, Skaga."

"I'll be back soon," I say, accepting the pitcher from him and acting the obedient daughter. "Don't worry."

Just as you did not when I was left to die, I almost say.

That would not be fair of me, and I know it. Father was just as overjoyed as Liv when I returned. Neither of them could believe I had truly come back until they held me.

Then they asked how I escaped the forest.

I knew the truth might get me killed, so I lied.

You know how I have always loved Freyja, I told them, the story already forming on my lips. The goddess saw me and took pity on me. She picked me up in her arms and carried me back here. To Unden. To you.

Father asked how, still disbelieving. So I told him the truth I discovered atop Trollkyrka as Freyja's tears fell on me. That my birth mother Vanadís and the goddess have always been one and the same.

Father began to sob. It was the only time I ever saw him cry.

Now, as I head through the village, everyone nods as I pass by. Word spread like wildfire that Freyja herself had saved me, her mortal daughter. Now I am untouchable. Not even Gorm dares defy the gods. He claims he did not realize who my mother was, not until I used her magic on him at Trollkyrka.

I do not mention he still left me to die.

But I will not forget that fact. As I pass the villagers, I cannot forget how they all stood and watched as I was taken into the forest. Torsten. Liv. Father. They were all willing to sacrifice me so Unden could survive.

All except the monster.

I was certain I would die as he brought down his claws. Instead of my throat, he sliced the ropes binding me to the stone altar. He picked me up in his arms and carried me down the mountain when I was too weak to walk on my own. The monster who was supposed to kill me returned me unharmed instead.

But who would believe that tale? I hardly believe it myself. I don't even know who my savior is, or why he chose to spare me when he could've killed me just as easily.

Why was only a monster willing to show me mercy?

As I look at my neighbors, my village, my family, resentment fills me like bitter poison. I will never forgive a single one of them. Even now, I am only safe so long as I lie. I loathe dishonesty, but if I must lie to continue living, I will do so gladly.

Gorm stands ahead, and I make eye contact with him. If anyone knows why one of the Folk would spare me, perhaps he would. He knows the most about the Hidden Folk of any of us, always saying how their whims can change as quickly as the weather. Perhaps that is why I was spared. Or perhaps my mother's hand guided the draugr.

Gorm glares at me.

As I walk past, I cannot help but whisper, "Do not worry, Gorm. I did not suffer at all."

His hands clench into fists.

I am beyond even his reach now, and he knows it.

I head into Tiveden of my own free will this time. Even though I wear leather shoes now, the soles of my feet are still raw and painful from that brief but treacherous walk. I am not afraid any longer. I have nothing left to fear.

The pitcher grows heavier in my arms the farther into Tiveden I go. My body is still in a weakened state, but I continue until I find a satisfactory spot to make my offering. I reach a small clearing that seems as good a place as any.

Slowly, I begin to pour the mead into the soil. "I give thanks to you, Mother—"

A branch snaps, startling me before I can finish.

The draugr stands there.

I clutch the pitcher against me. "It's you."

In the light of day, I can see his features more clearly. His skin is pale as snow, his blue eyes cold like ice. A long cloak hangs from his shoulders. He is dressed like a warrior king of old. I have never seen anything quite like him before. Even knowing what he is, I find him rather appealing.

I step toward him. "May I know your name?"

"Why?" he demands.

His voice is deep and low, drawing me toward him.

Something spreads through me, thrilling and dangerous. It feels like being at Trollkyrka again, standing on the edge of its cliff, looking down at the sheer drop.

My breath quickens. "So I can thank you properly."

His gaze roves over me.

"Is that why you have returned?" is all he says.

I glance down at the pitcher in my hands and nod. "I hoped to thank you for sparing me. But I also selfishly wanted to know why you would."

The draugr presses his lips together. "Do I need a reason?"

"I do," I say firmly.

He considers a moment before answering, "Because I know what it is like to want to hold on to life desperately."

My fingers tighten around the pitcher. "Is that why you became a draugr?"

He seems startled.

"Of course I know," I add quickly. I could tell the moment I saw him, from the unnatural pallor of his skin and his dagger-sharp claws, that he was one of the undead. Now, I confess, it only makes me more intrigued by him.

"Aren't you frightened?" he asks, the words bitten off.

"Why would I be? You saved me." I take a step closer. "Will you tell me your name?"

He stiffens, watching me approach, but doesn't move.

"Soren," he says. "Soren Thrainsson."

"Then this is for you, Soren." I hold the pitcher of mead out to him. "Please accept my offering."

He hardly glances at the pitcher. "Keep it. I would not be able to taste it, anyway."

"What can you taste?" I ask slowly, though I suspect I already know.

This is a dangerous game to play. But I want to play it all the same.

"Blood," he says.

The question escapes before I can think better of it. "Shall I offer you that instead?"

Soren's entire body tenses.

A strange thrill shoots through me. I'm certain he wasn't expecting me to say that. Neither was I. I feel so reckless and foolish, I might as well be drunk on mead.

As Soren looks at me, his eyes darken with desire. But his mouth remains pressed into a tight line, as if he is fighting his own nature.

I decide to help him lose.

"I must thank you properly." I tilt my head slightly, exposing my throat. "Please accept my offering, Soren."

Soren steps closer, like he is no longer able to resist. "You would offer yourself to me?"

My pulse runs wild. "I would."

Soren draws me against him, his hands cool on my skin. I shiver with pleasure at his touch. He leans closer to me, his breath a whisper on my neck. I cannot breathe from anticipation. I close my eyes, waiting to feel his teeth. Will it hurt? Will it be sharp and sudden . . . or slow and savoring?

At long last, he gently bites into my neck.

I gasp with pleasure.

The pitcher slips from my fingers, all but forgotten.

The next morning, I rub my throat in the same spot Soren bit Skaga. As my fingers brush over my skin, it's almost like I'm disappointed I woke up. Like part of me wants to share her experience. . . .

I shake my head. What the hell am I *thinking*?

Soren watches me intently.

I drop my hand, suddenly embarrassed. He doesn't know what I dream of, I tell myself. If he did, he wouldn't have been surprised when I told him about the dream I had of Skaga.

But if it wasn't just a dream, if it really was Skaga's projection, then Soren told me the truth. *He* is the one who spared Skaga, not Freyja, like Amma always told me. If she saw the same thing, then she too would know the truth. But she's never mentioned him in any of her stories.

My focus should be on finding Amma, not . . . him.

Unzipping my backpack, I grab my water bottle and chug some before tearing into one of the bags of pretzels. They taste like gritty ash, but I force myself to eat as many as I can stomach. If we're going to be walking for hours again, I'll need the energy.

When I'm finished eating, I stand and pull my backpack on quickly. "We should get going. Hopefully we can get back on track today."

"Indeed."

As we continue our trek, branches grab my hair and scratch my skin like hungry hands. I bat them away, searching the forest for some sign of the rune carvings or even the river we followed the first night in Tiveden, but my mind keeps returning to that dream. To *Soren*. It has to be some kind of aftereffect from Skaga's projections. Like her feelings are lingering within me. I can't explain it otherwise.

I rarely get crushes. When I was little, I had a crush on Johan. We announced we were getting married shortly after we held hands. I'm pretty sure we even had a pretend wedding once. In Stockholm, the only boyfriends I had were in books. I missed so much school that I wasn't around enough to get crushes on classmates. And anyway, it's hard to date when you never know when you'll need to run to the restroom.

Crushes aren't really my thing. Not that this is one or anything.

We've been walking for hours when I see something in the corner of my eye—

Hundreds of arms retreat behind the trees.

"Wait." I still.

Now that I'm looking around, the area looks familiar. "Haven't we already been here?"

Soren squints. "I don't believe so."

Right. It's so bright out, he probably can't see very well. If we already walked through here, I should have been paying closer attention. We've been wandering in the forest for so long, it's hard to tell anymore. Everything is starting to look the same.

Something lies in the snow a few meters away—

Torsten's decapitated body.

A sight I never wanted to see again. "We have. Look."

Panic rises in my chest.

Shit, shit, shit.

Soren's mouth presses into a line. "Impossible."

"We've been going around in circles this whole fucking time." I blow out a long breath, dragging my hands down my face. "We walked for a whole day only to end up back where we started? How is that possible? We went in a completely different direction!"

We are so fucking lost. So screwed.

So much for turning my coat inside out working. It's hard to breathe. How the hell will we ever get out of here? The huldra didn't kill me, but I'm starting to think that maybe this is worse. Wandering directionless through the woods, dehydrated and slowly starving. The wash of acid in my stomach and the parched dryness of my throat keep getting worse with every passing hour.

I can't die in Tiveden. I can't. If anything happens to me, Amma will never be found. And Dad? I'm all he has left. I don't know what he'll do if something happens to me, too. He'd never forgive me. Never forgive *himself*. I can't do that to him. I need to get out of here.

But as I look around, these trees are all the fucking same.

No runes mark—

That's it. I pull my dagger out of my coat pocket and lodge the blade into the trunk of the nearest tree.

"What are you doing?" Soren asks.

"Taking Skaga's idea." Wood peels back around the blade as I drag it down. "If I mark our path, we'll be able to tell if we've been here before or not," I say, carving an arrow into the bark. "This way we'll know what direction we went in and won't confuse it with Skaga's markings."

Soren nods.

As we walk through the woods, I stop regularly to leave a mark. Hopefully now we'll actually be able to find our way out of this. As soon as we spot another mark, we'll know we've already been through there and can redirect ourselves.

This is going to work. It has to.

Stopping before a nearby tree, I wedge the tip of my dagger into the bark, the movement already familiar. My mind keeps returning to Torsten. To the terrible end he met. "How did Torsten become a draugr?"

"I do not know."

I stare at the tree in front of me. "Did he do something terrible?"

"Some become draugar because of misdeeds or malice," Soren says, his voice guarded, "but many others simply cannot let go of life. Others, like me, are not given a choice."

"What do you mean?"

"There is another way to become a draugr." He hesitates before adding, "A stave so powerful it is forbidden. Few know of it, and fewer still would ever use it. But my parents did. With the last of their life's blood, they painted that stave onto my chest as I lay dying."

The weight of his words settles over me. His parents died so he could live.

Just like Mom did for me.

Blinking back tears, I struggle to find words. "I had no idea that was possible."

When I look up, Soren is assessing me.

"My mom died giving birth to me," I add softly. "She was sick, so her pregnancy was considered high risk. But she still had me even though it ended up costing her life. I wouldn't be alive without her, but she's also why I have Crohn's disease."

I doubt he knows what that means. Even though they likely had the illness back then, or something similar, it wouldn't have been called that.

If she really did have Crohn's, Skaga wouldn't have known what it was, or how to treat it. I remember the terrible uncertainty before I got a diagnosis. For her, it never ended.

"A chronic illness," I clarify.

Sometimes I forget everyone doesn't know, since it's just part of me. Unlike becoming a draugr, my illness is mostly invisible. It's like what Amma always said about the Hidden Folk. Just because my illness can't be seen doesn't mean I'm not sick. For a long time, no one believed me. Some still don't.

"I wasn't given a choice either," I say slowly, "with my disease and everything that comes with it. No one even knows why I got it. I just happened to inherit it from my mom. And it changed my life forever."

Soren watches me. "Is there no cure?"

I shake my head. "I'll always have it."

He looks . . . almost sad. "It is the same for draugar."

His tone makes me think maybe some part of him longs to be human like I long to be healthy again. Maybe he just can't admit it to himself. After I was diagnosed, it took me a long time to accept I was no longer healthy. No longer *normal*, whatever that's supposed to mean.

"Don't get me wrong," I say quickly. "I'm glad to be alive."

Being a draugr is better than ending up like Torsten. Anything is better than being dead. Anything. Soren may no longer be human, but he's still alive, even if his experience is different from mine. I glance at the scar across his throat.

"Your parents wanted you to live, no matter what." My blade scrapes through the bark, too loud. "The circumstances might be different, but that's the same thing Mom wanted for me—"

My dagger catches on a knot in the wood.

The blade slips, slicing my finger open.

I wince at the sudden sharp pain. "Ow, shit."

Soren's entire body stills.

I clutch my finger, but blood is already dripping down, dotting the snow red. "It's nothing," I tell him.

I'm not sure Soren is even listening.

The whites of his eyes disappear, eaten away by midnight black, his irises glowing like blue moons in a dark sky. My heart is about to burst out of my chest. Soren steps closer, a predator closing in on his prey. His eyes don't leave my finger or the blood I can feel welling there.

My breathing hitches. Soren looks just like he did in my dream, when Skaga offered herself to him.

Something stirs deep within me.

"Here." I hold my finger out to him before I can second-guess myself.

He reaches for my hand in an almost trancelike state, as if his curiosity is gone, replaced by something more dangerous. Something primal. His eyes darken with desire. I'm not sure I *want* to stop him.

"Are you certain?" Soren asks, his voice husky.

No one has ever looked at me the way Soren is looking at me right now—as if he's starving and I'm the only thing that will sate him.

I nod.

His cold touch startles me as he brings my wounded finger to his mouth. The nape of my neck tingles as I stare into his glacial eyes, half-lidded with desire. His tongue slides over my fingertip, making me shiver with pleasure. Then he takes my finger in his mouth and starts to suck it gently.

My belly turns liquid. My body is responding to his touch on its own. A memory comes to me, unbidden. *Soren's cool lips moving over mine, his tongue exploring my mouth, his teeth grazing my already tender lips*—I gasp. No, not my memory. Skaga's. My skin feels feverish with her desire for him. The wanting becomes so bad it aches, until it's no longer a want but a need. I *need* Soren—

Shit—I jerk away, remembering myself. Shaking my head, trying to clear my thoughts, I back away from him. I don't know what got into me. Since when am I so *stupid*?

A bitter taste floods my mouth. Skaga must be influencing me. Her thoughts are still clouding my head, making me think I want this. Want *him*.

Soren rubs his mouth. "I apologize if I got carried away."

I scrub my skin, trying to erase the lingering feeling of his tongue on my fingertip. My heart kicks against my chest, and I try to steady my breathing. Some part of me doesn't want his apology.

Some part of me wants him to do it again.

Unlike when he kissed me, he knows I'm not Skaga now. And yet he still . . . wanted me. Or my blood, at least. I swallow thickly as I remember how he stared at me. How he slowly took my fingertip into his mouth. How the brush of his tongue was cold yet thrilling, like sinking my bare hand into snow—

Okay, I'm pretty sure I'm the one getting carried away now.

God, what am I even thinking?

He's a *draugr*.

I turn away, shoving my hands into my pockets. "You could get me really sick."

"But I cannot get ill, nor am I capable of carrying any disease."

"You can't get sick—like ever?"

He nods.

I quickly look away. What must that be like? I try to imagine not having to scrub my hands constantly. Not having to stay home or wear my mask in crowds so much. Not having to fear getting close to anyone.

"Maybe being a draugr wouldn't be so bad," I say slowly.

It's not so different from the choice I had to make. Take medications that might kill me, because it's the only way to treat my disease. Or don't treat it and give up any quality of life, then eventually get complications or cancer. Either way, I could die. But the medicine gives me a better chance of controlling my symptoms and actually living my life.

"Skaga wouldn't agree," Soren says slowly. "At first, I think she was drawn to me because I was different from anyone in her village. But once she truly saw for herself what I am, it repulsed her."

Soren is looking at me like he's seeing *me* for the first time.

His gaze is so intense I have to look away. Using the scrap of my coat I grabbed earlier, I tie it around my finger as best I can to stop the bleeding, then clear my throat. "We'd better keep going."

Soren follows without another word.

Pine needles scratch my skin as I bat aside a branch, taking my frustration out on it. Pushing ahead, I try to ignore the stinging pain and all the mixed-up emotions inside my chest. I can't trust any of these feelings either. Not when I can no longer tell if they belong to me or Skaga.

I pick up my pace as if I can outrun them.

⇒►FIFTEEN◄⇐

Another day gone, and we're no closer to Amma or Skaga.

Dusk leaves the forest a cold, forbidding blue. My breath clouds in front of me as I keep walking. The only sound is our footsteps punching holes in the snow. I suppose I should be grateful we haven't come across the kattakyn again. Yet.

Swearing, I stab my dagger into another tree. We'll be forced to stop soon, and the only markings I've seen are the arrows I made myself. We're never going to find them at this rate.

A haunting, otherworldly sound fills the forest. It's almost like . . . the distant echoes of whales calling to each other. Somehow, it sounds near and far, high and low, all at once. I can't decide if the noise is soothing or sinister.

I turn to Soren. "Do you hear that?"

"I do."

"It's not the kattakyn, is it?"

Soren shakes his head, leading me through the trees. "Look."

A massive frozen lake stretches before us. Thin white cracks run through the ice like veins. My breath catches at the sight of it lit by the bright moon, cold and impossibly beautiful. A mountain rises above the trees in the distance.

As we get closer, the eerie sounds grow louder.

I stop in front of the frozen lake, letting its otherworldly song reverberate through me. "Oh. That's why it sounded familiar. There's a lake near our house that used to freeze over like this."

When I was little, it seemed magical. Now I know it's something that happens every winter when it starts getting colder. There's so much built-up pressure, the ice cracks, creating these sounds. I haven't heard the sound in years—it's not something you hear in Stockholm over the buses and noise.

Soren turns away, heading back toward the forest. "This way."

"Wait." I look out over the wide-open lake, inhaling the crisp, cold air. It's a welcome sight after the claustrophobic feeling of the trees closing in on me, a moment of respite from being lost in an endless forest.

A split echoes across the ice. I have to raise my voice so he can hear. "Why don't we cross the lake? It'll be faster to cut straight across instead of going all the way around. And that mountain is the first landmark we've seen. We can use it to orient ourselves."

Soren glances over his shoulder. "We will have no cover if the katta-kyn attacks."

"True, but we'll also see it coming from far away. If it can even cross the ice. And it'll be a lot faster than taking the long way around, won't it? We might be able to find them sooner."

"That mountain marks the heart of Tiveden," Soren says slowly, but he doesn't sound pleased. "It is likely that is where the river leads."

"Great, let's go."

But for some reason, Soren seems reluctant still.

"Come on," I call, carefully walking out onto the ice.

Soren stops at the shore, his arms folded. "I will remain here."

Is he afraid he'll fall through? "Don't worry, the ice is strong."

I jump up and down to make my point.

Soren gives me a dubious look.

"I guess I'll understand if you're too scared," I add teasingly.

"I am *not* afraid." He takes a cautious step onto the ice. And another.

I slide along on my boots, pretending I'm skating at Kungsan with Zuri. "See? Not so bad."

Soren scowls as I skate beside him until the forest is far away.

"You know," I say as the sounds' vibrations travel through me, "the first time I heard this, I thought whales were trapped beneath the ice."

"Whales?" Soren lets out a low laugh. The sound is nice to hear.

"I was five, okay?" I say, laughing. "After that, Amma told me some Vikings mistook whales for sea monsters. Hafgufa, or something."

"People often make monsters of what they cannot understand," Soren says, shaking his head. "But I can assure you, they were not whales. I once sailed alongside a hafgufa—"

That catches me off guard.

I don't know what surprises me more: that sea monsters are real, or that Soren ever sailed. "You used to sail?"

"Long ago." Soren smiles and it makes him seem different, softening him somehow. "My mother was a powerful spákona, revered throughout the lands, so we were always traveling. I've never smelled anything fresher than the ocean's salty air. I'd climb to the front of the dragon ship, watching waves lap against the prow. The horizon was always ahead of us, full of possibility."

His face is lit up talking about it, like he's invigorated.

"Why did you stop?"

"I no longer can," he says reluctantly. "Draugar are too heavy. We do not swim, we sink. Though I once loved the water, I do not want to be trapped below it."

I stare at the bright white cracks running through the ice under my feet.

No wonder he was so cautious stepping onto the lake. "Oh. I didn't know."

Guilt stabs me as I remember how scared I was the first time Amma took me on the lake near our home. I was certain the ice would break, but Amma told me to lie down on my back if I was worried. So I did, spreading my arms and legs out as if making a snow angel, and let out a triumphant laugh when the ice held.

"Here, I think we've gone far enough for now. Why don't we lie down for a bit and rest? It helps distribute the weight so you won't have to worry about falling in."

Cold seeps through my coat as I get on my back. Only it doesn't burn but soothes. It reminds me of Soren's touch, and I can't help but wonder if this is how it would feel to lie in his arms.

Soren eases himself down beside me. "How do you know this?"

"During winter, Amma and I would lie out on the frozen lake, just like this," I say, looking up at the cold and clear sky, full of bright stars. "We used to listen to the ice cracking together. At first, it terrified me. But then Amma told me it was the ice singing. She made it sound like magic, and it wasn't so scary anymore."

"Magic can be terrifying too."

His words startle me. I wasn't expecting an admission like that, not from him. Not when he's the one who used the binding galdr on me. My body tenses as I recall it: my arms unable to move, no matter how hard I struggled, powerless.

Soren is right. That *was* terrifying.

"Like the sleep thorn?" I ask carefully, recalling what he said by the fire.

Only the eerie splitting sounds answer.

After a moment, Soren says, "You asked me before if I've slept while you were resting. I haven't, not since you broke the sleep thorn's spell. I am afraid that if I do, I will not awaken. Or that I will, only to discover the world has changed on me again."

I try to imagine the magnitude of that. Closing my eyes only to open them to an unfamiliar and upside-down world, one where everyone I love is gone. Not just lonely, but completely alone.

My throat aches. The closest I can think of is Stockholm. When I saw it for the first time, with its streets bustling with cars and people and bikes, it felt like I had entered another world. Even then, I still had Dad. I was lonely, but at least I wasn't alone. I didn't appreciate that until now. What Soren is going through is so much worse.

I turn my head against the ice and study Soren like I'm seeing him for the first time. Lying here like this, with his silver bangs spilling around his face, his normally sharp features appear softer somehow. The deep blue of the ice brings out the different facets of his eyes. They look beautiful.

How did I ever fear those eyes?

My stomach sinks as I notice the haunted shadows beneath them. Soren was under the stave's spell for so long, unable to move or see anything. Was he aware of anything, or was it complete oblivion? Which would be worse?

Even though I released him, it suddenly doesn't seem like enough.

"Did you dream, at least?" I ask, thinking of Skaga's projections. "While you were under the sleep thorn's spell, I mean."

"No," he says quietly, "but I was still aware, trapped within my mind. Within my regrets. Skaga would sometimes visit, talking to me as though I could not hear, but I could. I heard many things about her life, but it only pained me, because I could no longer be part of it. Or perhaps I imagined it all. I do not know."

Like my sleep paralysis, but that only lasts minutes. Not years. *Centuries.*

If I hadn't found him, his sleep might never have ended.

Soren hesitates. "As soon as I woke, some part of me knew you weren't Skaga. But I wanted so badly to believe you were her, that maybe all those lonely years had only been my imaginings, that she had not betrayed me. But she did, and there is no changing that."

I don't know what to say other than "I'm sorry."

The words don't feel like enough.

Now Soren is the one staring at *me.* "Do not apologize," he says, his voice surprisingly soft. "It was not you who betrayed me, Astrid."

Lying here on the ice, I'm suddenly too aware of how close our hands are. How I could reach out and wind my fingers through his. *You don't have to be alone,* I could tell him. *We can be lonely together.*

But he doesn't want me.

He wants Skaga.

That's why he's so desperate to find her, even though she's the one who used the sleep thorn on him. He must be trying to find some familiarity in this unfamiliar world. I have been too, ever since Stockholm. That's what Unden became to me. Someplace familiar. Someplace I could always come back to.

Home.

Skaga must be like home to him.

I can't help but feel a hot stab of jealousy.

Something cracks between us, even as the ice holds.

When I close my eyes, their time together flashes behind my eyelids—*lying in Tiveden in his arms, him feeding me berries until I lean forward and bring my lips to his.* Her feelings for Soren ache inside my chest. Or maybe I'm mistaken. It's hard to tell if they're Skaga's feelings . . . or mine.

I think of his smile. Despite his initial coldness, he's starting to thaw, and I'm seeing a different side of him. A side maybe only Skaga has ever seen.

But I'm selfish. I want *more.*

"I cannot remember the last time I saw the stars," Soren says, sounding lost in thought. "They are the only thing that hasn't changed."

I open my eyes. His words remind me of something Amma used to say: *when we look at the stars, we can glimpse the past.* Some of the stars are already dead, but we see them as they used to be. I didn't get it before, but lying out here, seeing Soren like this . . . I think I do now.

I reach for the sky, pointing out Amma's favorite constellation. "That's Freyja's distaff."

Soren follows the path of my finger. "How so?"

"Not literally," I say with a laugh, and grab his wrist. His eyes widen, but he allows me to slowly guide his hand over the sky. "See? The stars right there are shaped like her staff."

"Beautiful," Soren says quietly.

He's no longer looking at the sky. He's looking at me.

Our faces are already so close.

I start leaning in, and he moves closer—

The lake's vibrations grow violent under us. My skin buzzes, an eerie feeling overcoming me. This isn't right. Something smacks against the ice. I push up on my elbows, looking around. "What the—"

As the reverberations travel through me, I realize they're not coming from on top of the lake. They're coming from *below*. Like something is trying to break free from the depths. Quickly wiping the drifts of snow off the surface, I peer under the frozen lake.

Something stares back at me.

Instead of my reflection, an emaciated horse looks up through the ice. Its skeletal face stares at me, and its gray flesh is rotting, falling from its bones. Its eight legs are bent at odd angles. The creature whinnies and the otherworldly song grows louder. As it strikes the frozen lake with its hooves, the ice separating us no longer seems thick enough.

My breath won't come. "A nykur."

Its hooves crack the ice. The lake starts splitting beneath us.

"We have to go," Soren says, jumping up in a swift movement. "Right now."

We break into a run.

Underneath our feet, the horse gallops against the ice. Cracks spread under us like spiderwebs. I try to keep up with Soren but slip.

Soren catches me. "Hurry."

With an earsplitting shriek, the nykur slams against the ice once more.

The frozen lake shatters like glass, dropping out from under us.

A cold shock hits me along with sheer panic. I gasp involuntarily, and frigid water pushes up my nose and down my throat, slicing my insides like sharp glass. My lungs are screaming for oxygen.

With a great gasp, I burst to the surface.

I choke on the water as I cough it up. A rank, pungent odor fills the air like surströmming. I could never stomach the fermented fish because of its smell. This stench is so putrid, I can taste it on my tongue. It must belong to the rotting nykur.

I can't see Soren anywhere.

"Soren!" I scream, scanning the dark water.

Chunks of ice drift around me, but Soren doesn't resurface.

I plunge back down and force my eyes open. Cold stings, blurring my vision—but I spot his glowing eyes. Soren is sinking, disappearing into the depths. *We do not swim, we sink.* He only went onto this lake because of me. I kick toward him, straining to reach his hand.

The nykur darts toward us.

Hooves slam into my stomach, knocking the wind from me. Sharp pain explodes as I tumble through the water, head over heels. All I can see is darkness. Moonlight. Darkness.

The horse opens its mouth. I throw myself to the left at the last moment, narrowly avoiding the snap of its jaws. I swim toward the surface—

Something grabs me, stopping me with a sudden jerk.

I bite back a scream as there's a sharp pull at the nape of my neck.

My braid.

The nykur is using my braid like a rope to pull me down. My scalp feels like it's on fire. I grab at my hair, trying to free it. But the creature's jaws are locked. Panicking, I thrash desperately, but it's no use.

The nykur drags me down into the depths of the lake.

Down.

Down.

Down.

My lungs burn. If I don't escape soon, I'll drown. And this time, Soren can't rescue me. I have to save myself. There must be some way I can beat the nykur. All of the Hidden Folk have a weakness. *Think, Astrid, think!* I struggle to recall Amma's stories as my head throbs.

Water squeezes me tight as a fist, until I'm about to burst.

Sinking lower, I strain my hand toward the surface, but the moon is a bright pinpoint, shrinking away from my fingertips. It's as far away as my childhood, cocooned in the house with Amma. I close my eyes, fighting the intense urge to breathe.

And I see her.

Amma sits on the couch, a book spread on her lap as she reads. *Nykur hate the sound of their own name,* she says. *Like Dad?* I ask. He hates being called Erik, preferring Rick instead. Amma laughed. *Yes, Asta. Except a nykur will actually obey you once you call its name. If only your father was so obedient.*

Bubbles explode as I gasp, my eyes popping back open.

"Ny—" As soon as I open my mouth, water floods down my throat like it's coming from a broken dam.

Dark water closes in as I sink lower.

The trollkors floats in front of me. *That's it.*

Grasping the necklace, I twist around and slam the steel against the nykur's face.

With an otherworldly screech, it releases me.

My arms slice through the water, my body buoyant.

I explode to the surface.

My skin stings as I gulp mouthfuls of air. Scrambling forward, I hook my fingers around the lip of ice, clawing my way up. My arms shake as I struggle to pull the rest of my numb body out of the freezing water.

"Nykur!" I scream, cold air cutting my throat.

Something shoots toward me through the dark water.

It's not working. My fingers slip on the ice as I struggle to hold on. Unless . . . the Hidden Folk have many names. Draugar are also called aptrganga. I need to use the right name.

The nykur gets closer. Closer.

"Näcken," I try.

Its jaws open wide—

"Bäckahästen!"

The horse's teeth snap shut, just shy of my ankle.

It swims by my legs, its mane floating like rotting seaweed. Now that it heard its name, it must be retreating to the depths. Before it disappears, I grab hold of it, hooking my legs around its body. Its rotting flesh isn't slimy like I expect, but *sticky.* My legs might as well be superglued to it. Bony ridges bite into my thighs, but I can't adjust my position. According to Amma's stories, I won't be able to get off until I utter its name again.

But first, I have to find Soren.

"Take me to the draugr," I command the creature.

I take one last deep breath before we plunge back under the lake. The horse shoots down, down, down, until its hooves touch the bottom, stirring sediment around us. When the debris finally settles, Soren is standing there. His eyes are wide as he takes me in.

I hold my hand out to him.

Soren doesn't hesitate. He pulls himself up behind me, penning me in with his legs. His thighs press against my hips, sending another wave of adrenaline shooting through me. He's so *close*. I struggle to swallow, grasping the horse's mane tighter.

The nykur sounds displeased, bucking like it's trying to get us off its back. But we're both stuck to it now. No matter how hard it kicks, it can't shake us off.

I slam my heels into the horse's sides before I run out of air. It shoots toward the surface, sending me lurching backward into Soren. He wraps his arms around my waist, securing me to his body. His touch is oddly comforting, even though it *shouldn't* be. My heart starts to race, and it's not because of how fast the nykur is swimming.

The horse doesn't slow even after we resurface. It continues racing across the lake, gathering speed to try to throw us off. Biting wind whips my braid as we fly over the water at a full gallop. I'm hyperaware of Soren's strong arms around me. Hooves pound against the frozen lake rhythmically, smashing through thick ice like a sheet of glass. I am weightless. Invincible.

Alive.

We reach the shore too soon.

"Bäckahästen," I say. As soon as the word escapes, I can *move* again.

The nykur releases its hold on us and kneels at the edge of the lake. This is as far as it can go. I brush a palm over the bumpy ridges of its ribs. Soren jumps off quickly. He's even paler than usual, his brows drawn tightly together.

I bring my leg over the horse's back and slide down to my feet. I'm unsteady, my knees wobbling. By the time I turn around, the nykur is already disappearing beneath the dark water.

There's no going back now.

SIXTEEN

The frozen lake is completely shattered.

From where I stand, the surface looks like broken glass. Dark waves lap against the rocky shore, dragging stones back into the water. My clothes are drenched, plastered to my skin. A cold wind cuts through me. I stand there a second longer, my entire body numb.

"You came back for me," Soren says in a low voice, so quiet I almost don't hear him.

But I do.

Slowly, I turn until I'm facing him. Moonlight shines on his wet skin, his silver hair dripping as water sluices off him. Like this, he looks . . . beautiful. I want to go to him, but something stops me. My feet are frozen in place.

Silence grows between us like a living thing.

Soren tips his head back. It draws my attention to his lips as he says, "You could have left me at the bottom of that lake."

At the sound of his voice, my body responds.

I step closer. Since entering Tiveden, I've been afraid Soren would abandon me.

Maybe I'm not the only one with abandonment issues.

"No, I couldn't. I wouldn't do that to you."

Only a few paces separate us.

It's *Soren* who reaches for *me*. His touch startles me as he grasps my waist and draws me close. I don't know who he's reaching for right now—me or Skaga.

"Thank you," he whispers, his voice cracking like frost. "You are different from Skaga. I'm sorry I didn't see that sooner."

Words fail me.

I hesitate before wrapping my arms around him. "Mhmm."

As his arms encircle me, his embrace feels familiar, as though he's held me many times before. I start trembling.

Soren pulls away, looking me over. "You must be freezing."

My teeth chatter as I nod.

"I'll start a fire for you," he says.

"Hold on." My hand shakes as I grab his arm. I'm not ready to let him go. "Can you . . . teach me the stave? Moving will help me warm up. And I could use the distraction."

Soren looks me over, considering. We both know how it ended when he taught Skaga.

But then he says, "Very well. Begin with a straight line."

My breath hitches. *He trusts me.*

Crouching beside him, I stab my blade into the ground and drag it down, not wanting to disappoint him. Unfortunately for us both, I don't possess an ounce of Amma's artistic talent. Even drawing a straight line is a challenge for me normally, and now my hand keeps shaking. From adrenaline or the freezing temperature, I can't tell. Probably both.

"Make another one beside it." He shakes his head. "Not that close."

I reposition the blade. "Here?"

"Yes."

My body tingles with awareness as Soren moves closer. I can feel him watching me intently while I work. Clearing my throat, I try to focus. "What is this stave called?"

"Bálspretta." His voice sounds even closer than I expected.

Firestarter.

"Make two more lines farther apart, on opposite sides." Soren blows out a breath, shaking his head. "Like this."

Before I realize what he's doing, he reaches around and covers my hand with his large one. The contact of his skin sends a shiver of excitement through me. His hands don't feel as cold as they did before.

My first instinct is to protest, but I bite my lip, locking the words up. I have to learn how to do this right.

He guides my hand, strong and sure. "Here."

It's hard to concentrate when I can feel the press of his body against mine. His breath on my neck. The little hairs there rise in anticipation, but of what? I don't even know what it is I want. My pulse beats wildly in my throat. This is dangerous. Soren is a *draugr*.

We both fall quiet, until the only sound between us is the dagger slicing through the snow.

"How did you learn the staves?" I ask eventually.

His grip on my hand tightens. "I grew up learning them. My father seduced a traveling witch and lay with her so she would share her magic with him. Even though society viewed it as women's magic, my father didn't care. He respected her and revered her power, and so my mother fell in love with him before long."

His hand stills.

"After I was born, she taught us both the staves," he says, applying more pressure to my hand. "But knowledge always comes with a cost. My father was scorned and reviled for practicing womanly magic. We traveled from village to village, until one day a chieftain grew distrustful of my family. He assumed my father was plotting to overthrow him."

My skin tingles under his grip as he continues.

"So one night the villagers snuck into the longhouse we were staying in. Since I was closest, they slit my throat first so I could not warn my parents. Clutching my bloody throat, all I could do was listen as the villagers stabbed my parents savagely, again and again and again. After the villagers left, my parents dragged themselves over to me, their blood streaking across the dirt, and painted their final stave on me together."

The staves had cost Soren so much. Not only his family, but his whole life as he knew it. And yet he still uses one to keep me warm every night. He makes me fires, even though fire is one of the few things capable of killing him. And now, despite his complicated feelings about the staves—and Skaga—he's willing to share them with me, too.

Even more than the staves, I want to know *him*.

Before I can find the words to tell him that, Soren's other hand lands on my hip, just for a moment, as he stands and brings me with him. "This is finished. Look."

I've caught glimpses of the symbol before when Soren started the other campfires, but this time is different. This time the two of us created it. I take in the entirety of the stave that we carved.

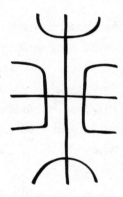

But the stave still isn't finished. Not yet.

It needs blood.

"I want to do it myself," I tell him.

I slice my finger and drag it slowly over the stave. . . .

Nothing happens.

I sigh. "Well, that was anticlimactic."

"I will use mine," Soren says. "Your blood must be incompatible with staves because of your magic-breaking."

"But I've used a stave before. Lockbreaker. It was how I got the cellar door open. Otherwise I wouldn't have found you."

"Or your blood broke its magic without you realizing."

I chew the side of my lip. I guess that makes sense.

As soon as Soren finishes adding his blood, something flickers.

Our blood starts to burn, but it isn't an ordinary fire. The flames are a gleaming gold, warm and bright as sunlight. My breath catches in my throat as I stare into the shimmering flames, entranced. *That* has never happened before.

"It's beautiful," I breathe.

Soren swallows hard, his throat bobbing. "This is Freyja's fire."

"What do you mean?"

"Skaga could create divine fire as well." Soren seems lost in thought as he stares into the flames. "When the goddess's blood flowing through her veins ignited, it would become Freyja's fire. She said it was part of the Bright Lady's gift to her."

"So your blood ignited the firestarter stave," I say, piecing it together, "but once mine burned, it turned the flames into Freyja's fire, like some kind of unique reaction?"

Soren nods.

I hold my shaking hand over the fire, but it doesn't burn my skin. The flames aren't harsh with heat; instead they have the bright warmth of sunlight. I move my hand closer. Closer. The fire doesn't harm me, only soothes.

"Why doesn't it hurt?" I ask, unable to hide my awe.

"Freyja's divine fire only burns the dead. It purifies everything else."

Another shiver spreads through me. "I see."

I'm still too cold. I want to feel this fire's warmth all over me. These wet clothes certainly aren't helping any. Peeling off my soaked coat, I drop it beside the fire.

Soren's eyes widen. "What—"

"I can't get warm as long as I have these on," I say, shucking off my sweater. Out of the corner of my eye, I can tell Soren is staring as I remove my wet jeans.

When I reach for my shirt, I lift it a little more slowly. I can feel his gaze on my skin, thrilling, as I strip off my clothes. I take my time undressing before him until just my bra and underwear are left.

Fire burns in his eyes along with desire.

As I curl before the flames, Soren looks me over like he's savoring the sight. My cheeks feel hot and not because of the fire. Especially after my illness, I've struggled with my body image, to say the least. Since I got sick when I was still growing, I was always made fun of for being small and underweight.

Now, I don't feel vulnerable at all.

I feel perfect just the way I am.

SEVENTEEN

"Skaga," Soren says, *and I savor the sound of my name on his lips.*

We walk through Tiveden as we often do while I gather firewood. Unlike other times, we don't speak of our homes, our lives, our dreams. We have run out of topics to distract us from the most obvious one: the feelings growing between us like the first buds of spring. Now we continue in silence, close enough that our shoulders nearly brush. My fingers twitch. I'm too aware of how close his hand is to mine—and how much I long to take it.

"Why do you continue coming here?" Soren asks quietly.

Every day, I offer to fetch more firewood from Tiveden. We have never had so much. Father and Liv thank me, amazed at my determination to help. When Torsten offers to accompany me, I refuse, saying I am eager to prove my own usefulness now that I have returned from Trollkyrka.

But that is not really the reason.

"You know why," I say, slowly turning to Soren. "The same reason you always wait for me."

Soren searches my face. "Skaga—"

Before he can say more, I grab his neck and crush my lips against his. I've longed to do this from the moment I first saw him here. He is the last person I should desire, but it only makes me want him that much more. Soren returns my kiss with equal intensity.

When I finally manage to pull away, he gasps.

The sound encourages me, making me grin like Lady after she steals a lick of milk. This is something forbidden. Something as profane as it is sacred. Unden would never approve of us. No one would. I know this, and yet I cannot resist Soren. It feels like a small revenge.

For the first time in my life, I am choosing myself.

I fumble for the fastener on his cloak, my fingers clumsy and uncoordinated at first. As it slips from Soren's shoulders, exposing the broad expanse of his chest, my hunger only grows. I am starved by my need, as hungry for him now as I was for food last winter. I rip open the collar of his tunic and kiss his throat in the same spot he once bit mine.

Soren lets out a low growl and grabs me, pushing me against a tree. Rough bark digs into my back as he kisses me harder, more urgently. The way I meet his lips with mine feels almost savage, wild with raw need. It's like being in battle, the way we explore each other's bodies. The trees surrounding us are dead, but I feel more alive than I ever have been.

Why do I continue to come back? The answer is simple.

With Soren is the only place I feel safe.

‡

Summer arrives with its sticky heat.

Soren's touch is as refreshing as my beloved lake, cool and brisk against my hot skin. His eyes are as blue as the lake's water, beautiful enough to drown in. Tiveden has exploded to life around us, insects singing everywhere, and the lingonberries have grown ripe.

Soren and I lie together on a soft bed of moss, my basket full of berries resting beside us.

"Why Tiveden?" I ask, staring at the green canopy above us. Sunlight shines through, illuminating little leaf maidens perched on the tree branches, their dresses of woven leaves dangling around their sticklike legs. They watch Soren and me, tittering and chattering among themselves, their voices like birdsong.

"What do you mean?" Soren looks at me, his silver hair spilling around his jaw.

"Why did you and the rest of the Folk choose this forest?" Soren frowns at my words, so I quickly add, "Besides its beauty, of course. This forest is also rather treacherous, is it not? Surely you could have found a better one to call home."

"It is not so simple," Soren says. "Do you know where Tiveden gets its name?"

"It means forest of the gods, right?"

Soren nods. "The Allfather was once exiled from his homeland. So he came to this realm, as the gods sometimes did, but he could not return home for three years. He created Tiveden and its treacherous terrain so that he would not be bothered by any humans.

"But years of solitude is a long time, even for a god, and he grew lonely. Allfather fashioned the Folk from the forest and breathed life into them, as he did when he made the first humans. So grateful were the Folk, they gave him a crown of twisted branches, a great bone horn, and a new name: the Fell King."

"A bone horn, hmm?" My hands wander down his chest, veering closer to his belt and the bone horn that hangs from it. "Like the one you carry?"

"Do you wish to hear the story or not?" Soren scolds me.

"I am sorry." I let out a small laugh. "You are more skilled in storytelling than any skáld, so please, continue. What happened once Allfather's exile ended?"

"He returned their gifts to the Folk," Soren continues, "and told them to keep what they had given him until someone worthy of wearing his crown appeared. He had grown fond of the Folk and did not want to see them harmed by humans, so he instructed them to remain hidden until he could return."

"So that is why your kind are called the Hidden Folk." I brush my hand over his cheek, leaving smudges of berry juice. Against his pale skin, its red color reminds me of blood upon snow. "Well, I am glad you did not hide yourself from me."

He captures my hand with his clawed one. "So am I."

Silence settles over us as Soren traces my palm idly, studying my berry-stained fingertips.

He brings my hand to his lips and presses a kiss to my palm. "I am in love with you."

My stomach fills with fluttering wings. "Are you really?"

"You know I cannot lie," Soren says softly.

Smiling, I lean over his face, my blond hair dangling between us. "Then tell me more how you love me."

He looks up at me, returning my smile. "I have loved you since the moment I saw you."

"I did not think you shallow enough to fall for appearances," I tease.

His smile disappears. "I am not."

"Do not get defensive," I say, still grinning like a cat. "What else could you have possibly loved about me at first sight?"

"Your defiant spirit." Soren kisses me gently. "I first fell in love with your will to live. And now, I love how alive I feel with you. You do not fear me. You treat me as though I am still human."

My throat is suddenly thick, my eyes wet.

Before, I never truly understood how love could drive Freyja to wander the world forever, searching endlessly for her lost husband, and I resented her for leaving us. But lying here beside Soren, I finally understand. Some love is so strong it renders even the gods powerless.

A tear slides down my cheek. "I love you, too, Soren."

Soren wipes my tear with his thumb, his touch tender. "Then why do you look so sad?"

"I fear that soon I won't be able to see you," I admit. "My father has been questioning why I go into the woods alone so often."

"But you return with these," he says, reaching for a berry from my basket. Every day he feeds me so many my lips are stained with crimson juice by the time I return home. Soren pops another one into my mouth. The too-ripe berry bursts open on my tongue, filling my mouth with sweetness as Soren kisses me deeply.

"I can't continue using berries as an excuse," I whisper against his lips. "Soon we will have plucked all the berries in this forest. And winter will come before we know it."

We lie in silence as the weight of my words settles over us.

Soren reaches for something at his hip. Not his horn, but a small pouch I've often wondered about. He takes my hands in his, placing a piece of soft coal in my palm. "Then use this."

I look down at the piece of lignite, small and fragile. "What for?"

"It bears a stave," Soren says. "So long as you hold it, you will remain

hidden until it crumbles. We can continue seeing each other in secret this way. I will make more, as many as it takes to be with you every day." He hesitates before adding, "I need you, Skaga."

Suddenly, the stave seems as precious as a jewel. "And I need you."

Freyja created staves to channel her seiðr magic. Staring down at the delicate symbol, I understand why this power was more treasured than her golden tears. The staves made her mightier than Odin, Allfather of the gods. Her magical knowledge won the war of gods, and it was the reason Odin wed her, uniting the gods beneath them.

"Will you teach me the stave instead?" I ask, hungry for my mother's power.

Soren studies me. "I will do anything you ask of me, Skaga."

With her staves, Freyja became powerful. No one dared to hurt her again. She could have anything she wanted. Become anything she wanted.

Maybe so can I.

≫EIGHTEEN≪

A cold hand covers my mouth.

Soren leans over me, panic in his glowing eyes. It's still so dark, I can barely see the rest of his features.

"What?" I mumble against his freezing palm. "What time is—"

"It's still the middle of the night, but we have to go," he says, his voice low with warning. "A swarm of undead is approaching."

My rough breathing is too loud in my ears. A breeze sweeps through the branches, knocking them together, but otherwise the forest is quiet as a grave.

Branches snap nearby. I look to my left—

A skeleton stands in the distance, its bones bright in the dark woods.

A small, choked sound escapes my throat. "What *is* that?"

"Aptrganga," Soren says.

Again-walker.

Everywhere I look, I see more skeletons wandering through the forest.

"Get dressed," Soren tells me. "Quickly. They haven't noticed us. Yet."

My hands shake as I shimmy back into my jeans and boots. At least my clothes are dry now.

"I thought that was another word for draugr," I whisper, pulling on my sweater.

"They were draugar. Once." Soren's voice is grave. "Our ógipta comes with costs, even for us."

Slowly, I zip my coat as quietly as I can. "How did they find us?"

"Draugar must be close by. They often act as bloodhounds."

My blood. We used it for the fire. They must be drawn to my blood, the same as Soren. I suck in a sharp breath. Something sniffs nearby like a dog. *Shit, shit, shit.*

"Can you walk?" Soren whispers.

His breath is a cool breeze on my neck, his lips nearly brushing over my pulse, reminding me of the pleasant dream I woke from. Now reality feels like a nightmare as the skeletons close in. I nod, not trusting myself to speak.

"Take my hand," he says, his voice low. Urgent.

I hesitate. Soren is asking me to trust him. And yet I don't, not fully. But I do trust him to keep me safe. I take his hand. His strong grip is reassuring, despite his claws. Before we can get far, a pair of glowing blue eyes appears ahead of us.

My palm goes damp, my heart palpitating.

I'm about to run when Soren stops me. "Wait."

Have you lost your mind? I want to shout.

A draugr is staring right at us. I shudder, frozen with fear, but his eyes appear vacant. The draugr doesn't react, as if he can't see us. He turns, continuing past us into the woods.

I catch my lip between my teeth. "What just—"

"A helm of concealment."

Soren guides my hand toward something in his other palm. It feels like a lump of charcoal. One that's started to break apart. Exactly like in the dream I was having of Skaga. I noticed the small pouch at his hip before, but I didn't know what it held.

"A stave?" I ask quietly, feeling the thin lines grooved into the surface.

"Yes, but it only works for as long as the lignite lasts."

Lignite. Amma kept plenty of the soft coal around our house, but I never understood why. The stave Soren holds has already started to crumble. Blood must be needed to activate it, but also causes the lignite to disintegrate.

"Can't they hear us?" I keep my voice low.

"The helm of concealment cloaks everything—sight, sound, smell." Soren squeezes my hand. "As long as you hold on to me, its power will keep us both hidden."

"What now?" I whisper.

Even with the stave protecting us, I can't bring myself to raise my voice when monsters stand less than a meter away. The stench of decay fills the air, like a moldy grave. It must be the aptrganga, since Soren has no unnatural odor. He smells like fresh forest.

"The river is close by," he says. "I noticed it earlier while you were asleep. If we travel in it, they won't be able to track your scent."

While Soren leads me through the forest, I can't remember the last time I held someone's hand like this. If ever. His touch is as cold as snow and his skin feels almost as soft. As long as I don't let go of Soren, I'll be safe.

The darkness is so thick, I might as well be blindfolded. Pine needles grab my hair and poke my face, but I hold on to Soren like he's my lifeline. Because I'm pretty sure that right now, he is.

Soren tugs me to the left. "Careful."

A skeleton nearly bumps into me. *Shit.* The stave conceals sound, sight, smell, but what happens if I touch one? From how careful Soren's movements are, I'm guessing nothing good.

The skeleton is so close, I'm afraid to breathe.

I creep around him slowly, staying as far away as I can without letting go of Soren.

"This way," he says, helping me down an embankment.

My boots squish into soggy mud, surprising me. For some reason, it hasn't frozen like everything else in the forest. It feels almost . . . warm. "Once we find Amma and Skaga, we just need to follow the river to get back to Unden?"

Soren tenses. "I have no intention of going back."

His words stop me in my tracks. "What?"

I blink once. Twice. Why did I assume he would return with me and Amma? Of course he won't. He belongs in Tiveden. Which means the sooner I find Amma, the sooner I'll have to say goodbye to Soren. I don't know why it bothers me so much, but it does.

"Right," I say, shaking my head. "Of course."

Soon, I'll be back in Unden with Amma and Dad. I can do my next injection on time. I can return to Stockholm and finish school and apply to universities and hang out with Zuri again. All the things I stopped doing since Amma went missing. I can continue with my normal, regular life. I should be glad, but I'm not.

"So we're getting close?" I ask carefully.

"Trollkyrka is not much farther. That is where Skaga was left as an offering, so it makes sense her path would lead you there."

My hands feel sweaty. "Trollkyrka . . . isn't that the Fell King's throne?"

"Yes," he says gravely.

Mud sucks my boots down with every step. If Soren already realized where we were heading . . . he didn't need me to lead him after all. This whole time, I've probably just been slowing him down—

I stumble over a rock.

Soren catches me in a swift movement. "Are you all right?"

"It's fine, I just can't see where I'm going in the dark."

When I take another step, sharp pain shoots up my leg.

I swear under my breath. "I think I twisted my ankle."

"Then take this," Soren says, placing something in my palm. The lignite. My feet suddenly go out from under me. Before I know what's happening, Soren lifts me in his arms. "I will carry you."

"Why not just leave me?" I whisper.

Even before now, he could have abandoned me anytime to find Skaga sooner. But he chose to stay with me instead.

"I would not do that to you," Soren says, repeating the same words I told him on the lakeshore.

Now, he's carrying me like he once carried Skaga. Leaning against his chest, I think I can hear his heart beating, so faint and slow, I'm not sure whether I'm imagining it.

I look down at the lignite in my palm. "Will the stave still work if I'm holding it?"

"It should since my blood was used to activate it. Just don't accidentally break it."

As I gently touch the engraved symbol, recognition rockets through me. "This is the first stave you taught Skaga, isn't it?"

"It is."

So it *was* Soren who taught them to her.

That's yet another thing Amma's stories got wrong. Maybe that's why Skaga is projecting the past to me—and possibly Amma—in order to set the record straight. She's revealing the truth to us in Tiveden the only way she can.

"Though I wish I never had," Soren adds quietly. "That stave cost us both far too much."

"What do you mean?"

His throat bobs. "Did you not see that in Skaga's dream too?"

I shake my head. "No."

"That stave I taught her was the first of many. She was very skilled with them, but she soon grew careless." His claws dig into me as he carries me. "Her father found a piece of lignite carved with the helm of concealment inside their house. Once he consulted the village witch and realized its power, he decided to follow Skaga to discover why his daughter kept sneaking off into the woods."

I tip my head up, trying to make out his expression. "So Ramunder found you two together?"

"He was furious as soon as he appeared. He tore her from my arms and dragged her back to Unden. I wanted to stop him, but Skaga begged me not to. She promised she would return." Soren looks pained. "But no matter how long I waited in the woods, she never did."

My heart falls. "I'm sorry."

"So am I" is all Soren says.

Bright eyes dot the darkness all around us. As we continue down the river, I lose count of how many we pass. The closer we get to Trollkyrka, the closer the Fell King gets. The only thing anchoring me is Soren's firm grip. As he walks, the movement lulls me to sleep, until my exhaustion starts to pull me under.

We're safe, I try to remind myself.

But only for as long as the lignite lasts.

NINETEEN

"*You will never set foot in that forest again. Do you understand, Skaga?*" *Father pulls me toward our longhouse, leaves crunching with every step. His ruddy face is full of fury, as it has been since he discovered Soren and me together in Tiveden.*

"*You had no problem sending me there to die!*" *I shout, digging my heels into the dirt.*

The words drain all the fury from his face.

"*I had no choice, little one,*" *he says as he lets me go.*

"*Of course you did!*"

"*Between duty and love, there is no choice.*" *His voice breaks.* "*As Unden's leader, I could not place my own feelings above everyone's survival, even if it killed me, Skaga. I pray to the gods you will never have to learn that lesson yourself.*"

"*You are wrong,*" *I say, unable to stop the words pouring out like a river.* "*There is always a choice, Father, and you made it. You chose Unden over your only child.*"

Unlike Soren, *I add silently,* who has always chosen *me.*

"*I did what was required of Unden's leader,*" *Father says, his breath misting in the crisp air.* "*But even then, your mother returned you to me.*"

"*You are mistaken.*" *I am so angry I can barely breathe.* "*It was not my mother who spared me. It was Soren.*"

"*Do not speak that name.*" *Father grabs my wrist and pulls me inside the longhouse.* "*He is a fjándi!*"

Enemy. Devil.

Fiend.

"Not to me," I tell him.

As I summon my memories of Soren, Father's eyes turn completely white. I know my power is working, so I concentrate my thoughts on how Soren carried me down from the mountain, how he helped me gather food and firewood in the forest, how he told me he loved me and he cannot lie, how he shared all his secrets with me. By the time I finish, my heart is overflowing with the love I hold for Soren, so deep that I could drown in it.

"Now you see he is my savior."

As soon as Father's vision returns, he smacks me hard across the face. The sound of his slap rings throughout our longhouse. "You dare use your power on me? Say nothing else before you heap more shame upon Liv and me. You have not only lied to us but deceived all of Unden. If Gorm or anyone else gets wind of this . . . so help me, Skaga. Not even your precious goddess will be able to protect you."

I am too stunned to speak. Slowly, I bring my hand to my stinging cheek. Father has never hit me or Liv before. She would sooner cut off his hand, but I cannot hurt my own father. All I can do is hate him more than I have ever hated anyone.

Tears spill down my cheeks. "I will never forgive you for this."

"Then do not," Father says, his chest rising. "But as long as I live, you will never see that fiend again. You will wed Torsten and become his problem to deal with."

It was not Torsten who saved me, but Soren. If I am to wed anyone, it should be him.

But that is impossible. I know it and always have.

"I despise you!" I shout before fleeing to my bench-bed.

Sobs send tremors through my body like an earthquake. I feel as if I will fracture completely. Lady tries to console me, rubbing against my leg while I choke on my tears. I draw my cat closer, but hugging her makes me cry harder, until I can barely breathe at all.

Her soft fur reminds me of Soren's fur-trimmed cloak.

It reminds me I will never see him again.

ᘓ

"There, Skaga," Liv says, a note of pride in her voice. "Now you are ready to be wed."

She tucks a loose strand of long blond hair behind my ear and surveys her work. The top of my hair is pulled back by twin braids, while the rest falls free around my shoulders. Liv smiles like I imagine my mother would. "You look as beautiful as Freyja. I hope Torsten knows how fortunate he will be to call you his wife."

I shake my head. I do not feel fortunate at all. When I was younger, I thought I liked Torsten, but those were the foolish feelings of a little girl.

Soren is the only one my love belongs to now.

Liv fusses over the wedding gown she made me, its shade the pale blue of fresh frost. She adjusts the belt of braided rope woven through an iron trollkors symbol, pulling until the dress hugs my hips. Blue fabric flows down my legs and pools at my feet. As Liv pulls my belt tighter, I feel as though I am being tied to the stone altar in Trollkyrka all over again.

Finally, she drapes a plush fur shawl around my shoulders and fastens it to my gown with two silver tortoise brooches. The soft fur brushes my throat, and I am reminded of the first time I saw Soren under the moonlight, his fur-trimmed cloak crusted with snow.

"Come," Liv says, holding her arm out to me like an offering.

"Where is Father?" I ask, looking around the longhouse.

"Fetching your bride-gift," she says simply. "He will join us at the feast tonight once you are wed."

My eyes narrow, but Liv offers me nothing else.

I sigh heavily. "Very well."

My mind has been made up since last night.

I must go through with this wedding.

For my future, and Unden's.

Unable to delay any longer, I take Liv's arm and leave home for the last time. Crisp air greets us as we step outside. The sky is the same pale blue as my gown. Without thinking, I glance toward Tiveden. Many of its trees are as bare as my heart.

As Liv leads me down the dirt path running through Unden, villagers shower us with sunflower petals. Fitting, since flowers are said to blossom wherever Freyja sheds her tears. As I crush the petals underneath my fur-lined shoes, I imagine my tears have turned to flowers.

Torsten waits for me before the lake.

He is dressed finely, unlike the usual tunic and baggy pants I'm accustomed to seeing him in. Torsten looks more handsome than he ever has, but I still do not want him. He shifts nervously from foot to foot, as though he cannot wait to make me his wife. My stomach churns with guilt. Even after I wed him, it will not stop my longing for Soren just as the Bright Lady longs for her lost love.

"Skaga." Torsten takes my hand in his, but I loathe its warmth.

I struggle not to rip my hand away. "Torsten."

The entire village gathers nearby to watch us wed.

Gorm joins us, his long robe trailing behind him. For once, the priest smiles warmly when he sees me, almost as if he can sense my misery. I force myself to return his smile. I must play the part of the joyous bride, no matter how much it sickens me.

"We gather here today for the union of Skaga Ramundersdóttir and Torsten Björnson."

It seems unfair that even on my wedding day, I am subjected to Gorm's words.

I do not wish to be standing here, listening to his hateful voice, anymore.

Last night, I thought of running away.

While Father and Liv slept, I stood over their bed with a piece of polished bone in my hand, marked with a stave. The sleep thorn. Father destroyed all my staves save for this one. Soren gave it to me in case of emergency, and ever since, I've kept it tucked in the pocket of my apron dress at all times. I have never needed it—until now. Even though Liv and Father did not stir, I knew if I tried to leave, they'd hear the hinges and come running. A sheen of sweat covered Father's face, his brow furrowed. Even in sleep, he seemed troubled.

I had never used the sleep thorn before. When Soren first told me of this stave, he said to place it under the pillow of my enemy—or atop their snoring chest, he added with a rare laugh—and the sleep thorn would put them into an extended slumber. One they would not wake from until the stave was removed.

Soren did not say what would happen afterward. Father and Liv were still human. They needed to eat and drink. What if no one removed the stave in time and they starved in their sleep? What if I inadvertently killed my own parents?

I gripped the sleep thorn tighter.

Liv rolled over. I froze, heart pressed against my ribs. Staring into her face, I couldn't breathe while I waited for her eyes to open. How would I explain this? Everything would be ruined. Everything. The sleep thorn still required my blood to cast its spell.

Liv murmured my name. She smiled, reaching out for me. And in that moment, I knew I could not run away. Tucking the sleep thorn into my pocket, I crawled into bed beside Liv. She wrapped her arms around me while I wept, hugging me close to her like I was a little girl again—

"I name you man and wife," Gorm finishes.

Liv stands beside the priest now, carrying a bowl of blood.

I cannot choose myself. Not when Father built our home with his bare hands so we could be a family again: me, him, Liv. While standing on Birka's shores, waiting for his longship to appear on the horizon, I dreamed that Liv and I could sail with him so we would always be together. In Unden, we finally are. Father founded this settlement so I would always have a home, even after he and Liv are gone.

As furious as I am with my father, there is nothing I would not do for either of them.

Tears cloud my vision as Torsten wets the golden ring with blood and slips it on my finger. I catch a glimpse of our reflections in the lake and I cannot help but see an impossible future reflected there, one where Soren stands beside me instead of Torsten.

But that future can never be.

So I take the other ring from Gorm's palm, and I dip it in the bowl of blood Liv holds.

I give my ring to Torsten.

"May the gods bless your union," Gorm says, glancing between us with his kohl-lined eyes. "And may Freyja make your marriage fecund, so you will soon birth a son to carry the weight of your future."

"Or daughter," I add defiantly.

Torsten nods. "I will be overjoyed with any child you give me."

My lips stretch painfully as I smile back at him. "As will I."

All of Unden applauds us in an overwhelming burst of noise. As I look out at the gathering, I realize that not only is my father absent, but so are three of his fighters. I lean closer to Torsten.

Instead of kissing him, I whisper in his ear. "Where is my father?"

He frowns, shifting uncomfortably. "He went into Tiveden, but I'm sure he will be back soon. Worry not, he won't miss our wedding feast."

Liv clutches the bowl of blood in her hands. She told me Father went to get me a bride-gift. But what could he possibly get from Tiveden—

Soren.

Father means to kill Soren or die trying.

Gorm claps our shoulders and cries out, "Come, it's time for the bridal race!"

I grab the long skirts of my wedding dress and break into a run. Houses streak past me, but I do not stop when I reach Torsten's home. My feet cannot fly fast enough as I race toward Tiveden. Others chase me, but I do not look back. All I can think of is Soren.

I reach the forest at last.

Father stands there, axe clutched in his large fist, surrounded by bodies. All his fighters lie facedown on the forest floor. There are also a few trolls, small enough to still be children, their dark blood seeping over the dirt.

Bile burns my throat, painful as poison.

I am too late.

Soren hangs his head, bowing before the deceased trolls. "How dare you," he says, slowly looking up at my father, his voice turning lethal. "You trespass on our home and kill children while they play?"

"Those are no children." Father grips his axe. "They are monsters."

Soren mutters a galdr and throws his hand out.

Father soars as if he weighs nothing, slamming into a tree with a loud crash.

Liv rushes to Father's side.

She must have chased me as I fled Unden.

Soren snarls, baring his sharp fangs. He will kill them both.

"No!" I scream.

Soren looks at me as if he is only now realizing I stand here. "Skaga?" His gaze sweeps over my dress, devastation on his face. "What is the meaning of this?"

"It is as I told you, fiend." Father climbs to his feet. "My daughter never loved you. She seduced you so she could learn your secrets and save our settlement."

"That is not true," I say, my voice rising. "I can explain."

Soren gestures toward the troll corpses. "See what your father has done with the knowledge you've given him."

I shake my head. "I did no such thing!"

But as soon as the words escape, I question their truth. Have I never accidentally shared something Soren told me? I pause. After Father forbid me from seeing Soren, I used my powers of projection to show him the truth. How Soren saved me and has helped me ever since.

By doing so, I must've revealed too much.

"How else would we have learned that our steel can harm your kind?" Father grips his axe so tightly, his knuckles turn bone white. "Or that I must behead you to kill you?"

I have been as careless with Soren's secrets as I was with the staves.

"My daughter will have your head as her bride-gift," Father says, unleashing a furious attack on Soren.

I watch, helpless. I cannot allow either one to hurt the other.

"Stop!" I scream.

Soren obeys as if I used a binding galdr on him.

Father does not. He buries his axe into Soren's chest with a sickening sound.

Soren looks at me, stricken, as though I drove the axe into his chest myself. "Did you truly never love me, Skaga?"

"I did love you," I say, choking on my tears. "I still do."

He is quiet for a long moment. "How can I believe that, when you can lie and I cannot?"

Soren reaches up and rips the axe from his chest, black blood pouring down his leather armor. He looks as if he's ripping his heart out. His expression darkens, and I fear he will cut my father down. But then Soren sends the weapon flying with such force that it lodges into a nearby tree. "I will only believe your actions. If you truly love me, then marry me, Skaga."

"It is too late." I twist the golden ring on my finger like guilt twists my insides. "I am already wed to another."

Father struggles to pry his axe from the tree, but it will not give.

Soren steps closer. "Is it true, then? Did you really ask for my head as your bride-gift?"

Before I can answer him, Liv jumps between us, her sword raised. "Any closer and I will behead you myself."

"Liv, stop." I grab hold of her arm. "Please."

"He and his kind should not exist," Liv says, pulling free of my grip, and the momentum knocks me against a tree.

My back slams against the bark, and I let out a sharp cry.

Soren rushes toward me—

Liv stops him with her sword.

Soren dodges the cold steel of her blade, strike after strike, side to side.

Liv does not relent. She is a shield maiden.

She's never backed down from a fight in her life.

She swings for Soren's neck. He disarms her in a fluid motion. As he does, Liv slips a dagger from her belt. She tries to stab him at the same instant Soren brings his elbow up, redirecting her blow.

It happens so fast, I cannot make sense of what I am seeing.

The dagger finds Liv instead.

A thin line of crimson spreads across her throat.

"Skaga," she chokes out. "Remember who your family is."

Blood streams down her neck, her chest.

She collapses, knees crashing into the dirt.

"Liv!" Father howls like a wild animal.

"No." My arms shake as I pull her against me, her blood soaking the wedding dress she made me. My hands are slippery as I hug her. "Mother."

It feels right to finally call her that, but Liv cannot hear me. I should have told her sooner. The thought is like ripping my ribs apart and exposing my beating heart. I would tear it right out of my chest if I could. Because of this foolish heart of mine, I have lost the only mother I have ever known.

"You see now what he truly is," Father says, taking Liv from me, lifting her limp body in his arms. He looks at Soren with a dreadful expression. "I swear before all the gods, I will make you pay for this, fiend."

"And what of these children you slaughtered?" Soren shouts, motioning toward the dead trolls. "Do their lives not matter? They were part of a family too, no different from your own. If I must pay, then so should you."

As Soren speaks, his fangs appear deadly to me now.

He stares at Liv's blood, looking every bit the monster Father warned me he was.

"Do not speak of my mother as if she is one of your creatures," *I say through stinging tears.* "My father was right. You and your kind are enemies to all living things." *My voice trembles with rage as I rise to my feet.* "I did not want your head before, but I do now."

Soren looks at me with the same shocked disbelief Father wore while watching Liv die. "You cannot mean that."

"I do."

Something fractures between us, shattering like ice.

Soren closes his eyes, as though he can no longer bear the sight of me. Dark blood stains his armor, but I know my words have cut him far worse than my father's axe.

A long moment passes.

Air hisses between his teeth, the only sound he makes. He remains rigid. Darkness passes across his face, like storm clouds gathering, and my breath catches. When Soren finally speaks, his voice is deathly quiet.

"Then I will have your hatred as well as your home," *he says slowly, each word full of pain and fury.* "Know that it was only because of my love for you that I ever tolerated your kind. You humans—you are all the same. Small-minded. Self-serving. Vile and hateful."

I have to bite back my shock.

"*Leave,*" Soren commands. "*Return to your home for however long it remains. But this will not be the last you see of me, Skaga. You have made me your enemy.*"

Standing there in his bloodstained armor, he is nothing like the Soren I know. This is not the Soren who held me in his arms in Tiveden. This is not the Soren who fed me countless berries and kissed me even more. This Soren is all sharp, lethal edges.

The realization sends my stomach plummeting.

Perhaps I never knew Soren at all.

TWENTY

The first hint of dawn paints the horizon gold. Soren must have walked all through the night, carrying me in his strong arms, trudging through the dregs of the river without stopping. My head rests against Soren's chest, not far from where Ramunder once buried his axe. I rub my eyes, trying to clear the sleep from them, only to realize I'm crying.

I can still feel Skaga's agony. Her love for Soren as well as her heartbreak and her hatred. Their impossible love ignited the war between Tiveden and Unden. It was what set the blood oath, and later Skaga's betrayal, into motion. They both wanted to protect their homes. And now I've not only woken Soren, but I'm leading him straight to Skaga.

Who knows what will happen at their reunion?

Tears burn my eyes, but I can't tell if it's from relief or pain or both.

Blinking a few times, I check the stave still clutched in my hand. The lignite is crumbled. Soon it will be dust. "The stave has almost run out."

"We're nearly there," Soren says. "See that mountain ahead? That is Trollkyrka."

I blow out a long breath, looking at the massive mountain.

Trollkyrka is where Skaga was brought to die—and where she first encountered Soren. But it is also the mountain throne of the Fell King. Somehow, it feels inevitable. Like I've been heading here all my life.

"*He'll* be there, won't he?" I ask.

Soren nods stiffly. "Yes."

The Fell King has always terrified me, and soon I'll have to face him to find Amma. As the muddy river squelches under Soren's boots, I'm afraid each step he takes will be the one that alerts the Fell King—

A draugr blocks our path. He crouches, the ridges of his spine protruding from his back as he fills a drinking horn in the river. A bone horn, like Amma always said the Fell King carries.

"Is that him?"

Soren chuckles. "I think not."

"Well, can we get by?" I whisper. Even with the stave protecting us, I can't bring myself to raise my voice when the draugr is less than a meter away.

"We should be able to slip past him."

I don't dare take my eyes off the draugr. His body is so emaciated that I can clearly see his bones, from his long clavicles to each rung of his rib cage. Soren said those skeletons earlier used to be draugar. Do they just slowly waste away?

As Soren goes to step around him, the draugr lifts the horn, nearly knocking into us. *Shit.* My skin prickles with awareness as the draugr drinks deeply, his throat bobbing. Wait. There's only one thing that draugar thirst for, though—

The muddy water is red.

My arms tighten around Soren as I recall the lake turning red in my dream. "Is this *blood?*"

"Hlaut."

Sacrificial blood.

"Like animal sacrifices?" I ask carefully.

He shakes his head. "Human."

Revulsion courses through me as I glance down at the thick, sticky river. We've been walking through human blood for hours.

I still don't want to believe it. "How?"

"The hlaut sustains Tiveden now," Soren says gravely. "Once the gods accept the sacrifice, the blood flows into the heart of the forest. It waxes and wanes according to the strength of the oath's magic."

That must be why the river hasn't frozen.

I try to envision what it must have looked like in the past. A bright red river, flowing through Tiveden like the blood pulsing through my veins. The distance ahead of us suddenly seems so far.

Soren continues through the river. The blood, I remind myself as I stare down at it. Human sacrifices might have been part of our ancient past, but no one does that anymore. Unden is old-fashioned, not *barbaric.*

"The river is nearly dry," I point out.

I must be right. Human sacrifices aren't performed anymore. And from the looks of this river, there hasn't been one in a long, long time. This must be another thing that changed while Soren was asleep.

"Nearly," Soren says meaningfully.

My throat closes up. "How many would have to die to fill this river?"

"Only one," Soren says. "The gods turn the blood into enough to sustain us for nine years."

I think of Amma. How suddenly she went missing. How they barely searched for her. How quickly she was declared dead. I thought maybe her disappearance was being mishandled, but what if it's something more sinister?

"Where are you going?" a deep voice asks behind us.

Soren stills.

My heart pounds wildly as I check the lignite.

It's crumbled to dust.

I look up at Soren and our gazes lock. Even though the lignite's run out, he's still holding on to me. I don't want him to let go. His grip tightens almost imperceptibly, like he doesn't want to either.

We turn slowly.

Another draugr stands in the river, clad in dark leather armor. His beard is silver, like his long hair, and a crown of twisted roots sits upon his head. Skulls rest on each shoulder and leather straps cross his broad, powerful chest. A great bone horn hangs from his hip.

Recognition rockets through me.

The Fell King.

TWENTY-ONE

The monstrous Fell King stands before me.

My breathing turns ragged. The Fell King who haunted my childhood is right in front of me, no longer concealed in the shadows. But his face—his face is familiar. I've seen it too many times before in my memories. And the way he's looking at me—it's like he recognizes me, too. Or he thinks he does.

"Skaga," he breathes. "My daughter."

That voice.

Soren sets me down into the river. "Ramunder."

That name. The Fell King is Skaga's father. Unden's original founder.

"So you have finally returned," Ramunder says.

How is this possible?

I shake my head, recalling all the times I've seen Ramunder in Skaga's memories. However imperfect, he loved his daughter and tried his best to give her a good life . . . not so different from my dad. As I search his face, it feels like Dad is standing before me.

"You are still as young as the day I died," Ramunder continues. "Time has passed differently here. For me, it has been an eternity. Come, Skaga, I have been waiting for you."

"She is not Skaga." Soren moves between us, shielding me with his body. "You will not harm her." His voice is so fierce, so protective, it makes my cheeks burn.

"I recognize my own daughter." Ramunder tips his head to the side. "I will not allow you to corrupt her once more. No one answers to you any longer."

Soren's voice turns lethal. "You will regret this, Ramunder."

I still remember Ramunder's hatred as he held his wife's dead body and swore to make Soren pay. Now that he's a draugr, it seems his hatred of Soren has grown. And if he is the Fell King, he must be even more powerful than Soren.

"Tiveden has changed since you slept." Ramunder holds his arms out. "It is *better* now than ever before. We feast. We kill your precious Folk as we please. The only law is that there are no laws. For now I am the Fell King."

I back away slowly.

"Just because you wear a crown does not make you king," Soren says fiercely.

The Fell King steps closer, exposing his sharp fangs. Slowly, he unstraps the bone horn from his belt and brings it to his mouth. The sound it makes is as loud and deep as thunder. It reverberates through my bones, forcing me to throw my hands over my ears with a scream.

The rocks move, jarring me forward. An earthquake? No—

A skeletal hand shoots from the riverbed less than a meter away, sending a spray of blood and rocks toward me.

I stare in disbelief as a skeleton claws its way to the surface, wriggling like a worm. More emerge all around us. Too many. The closer the skeletons get, the more I can see, and as horrified as I am, I can't look away. Strips of flesh sag around the bones, and the overpowering smell of rot stings my nose.

"Capture Skaga," the Fell King orders. "I will deal with Soren myself."

Skeletal heads snap in my direction, and the deep black holes of their eye sockets stare at me. Their teeth are chattering like they're trying to talk.

Soren lunges for the Fell King. "Astrid, run!"

My pulse pounds in my ears as I turn and flee, splashing through the river. My ankle screams, but I don't dare slow. Before I get far, bony fingers, cold as icicles, grab hold of my leg.

I fall. Hard.

Rolling over, I free my dagger from my coat pocket as the rest of the skeleton emerges from the riverbed. I stab at it, but the blade glances off bone. *Damn it.*

The skeleton rips my dagger away from me, flinging it aside. Bony hands grab at my face, feeling for my eyes. Oh God, *my eyes.* Ramunder said to capture me, not *kill* me. But I guess to a skeleton, eyes aren't necessary.

I twist away, straining for a rock nearby in the riverbed. My fingers finally close around it, hand shaking as the skeleton is about to bite me. Baring my teeth, I smash the rock into its skull with an awful *crunch.*

Kicking it off me, I rise to my feet. I did it—

A bony finger twitches. Another.

The skeleton drags itself through the river, clawing its way closer.

"How the hell am I supposed to kill it?" I shout.

"Dismantle it," Soren calls, wrestling with Ramunder. "Or crush it."

Swearing, I stomp the bones with my boot. The creature shrieks as my foot shatters its wrist. Still, it doesn't stop writhing.

More splash through the river, racing toward me, and I can't even kill *one.*

Gasping for breath, I look up.

The huldra stands there with a swarm of skeletons. Stunned, I stare in disbelief. She must want to finish me off herself. But then vines shoot from her fingers, wrapping around the skeletons instead. They struggle against her, their teeth clacking. The vines crush them until their bones snap like branches.

With the skeletons bound, the huldra turns to me, her eyes two dark pools.

I back away slowly. My dagger. I need my dagger.

But she doesn't come any closer.

"Help," she says in that scraping voice of hers.

She gestures toward . . . my dagger. It lies amid the mud and pebbles.

Another skeleton rushes toward her while she has her back turned.

"Watch out!" I cry, running to retrieve my dagger.

Her back unfolds and roots shoot out, stopping the attack. Unlike her vines, these roots are thick. Powerful. The skeleton starts clawing desperately at the riverbed, trying to escape, realizing its mistake too late. The huldra's roots drag it over the rocks and into her gaping back. Bones crunch, cracking as she devours it.

My whole body trembles. I do *not* want to be killed by a huldra after all. Raw terror seizes me as she approaches. I can't move. Can't think. More skeletons have crawled from the earth, replacing the first wave.

The huldra rips another skeletal arm off with her roots. I dodge darting hands and answer with a rock, smashing through bone. There's no time for precise strikes, not when my life is at stake. I hit whatever I can until finally reaching my dagger. I scoop it up quickly from the river's bloody dregs.

There's a sharp pull at the nape of my neck. I fly back with a scream, losing my footing. What the hell? My scalp burns—shit, my braid. A skeleton yanks my hair like a rope, dragging me through the river with one arm.

Right toward the Fell King.

Soren punches Ramunder in the face, snapping his head back, sending saliva flying. Ramunder staggers back, wiping his jaw, and lunges at Soren. Neither will stop until one of them is dead, for good this time.

Soren blocks another blow. "Astrid!"

I buck against the skeleton, but two more bony hands wrap around my ankles. They haul me in opposite directions until my body is tight as a bowstring, ready to snap.

Suddenly, I thump onto the rocks.

Piles of bones surround me. I gulp mouthfuls of air, blinking through the tears until my vision clears. The huldra stands there, roots spread from her back as she fends off more skeletons.

"Get out of here!" Soren shouts.

I scramble to my feet, pulling free of the bones. Adrenaline propels me as I race down the riverbed, my braid beating against my back.

An awful *crack* echoes.

Soren growls, a low rumble traveling over the rocks.

The sound stops me in my tracks. He's injured. Badly. Somehow, that scares me more than anything else. I look back as Soren collapses, knees crashing onto the river. He tries to rise but cannot. He still hasn't fully regained his strength after the sleep thorn.

The Fell King stands over him.

The Shore is right ahead of me. I'm so close. All I have to do is follow this river until I reach Amma. That's what Soren would want me to do. If I go back and try to help him, I might never make it out of here.

But if Soren is hurt, it's because he saved me.

More than once.

The Fell King leans over him, gripping Soren ruthlessly by his throat. I can't help but recall Torsten's headless corpse. Soren could end up like him unless I do something. Fast.

I have to help him.

While the Fell King is focused on Soren, I creep up behind them. I don't want to harm Skaga's father, not when she loved him so much. But I have no choice. I can't let him kill Soren. Sweat soaks my palms as I grip the dagger. If I'm wrong and this doesn't work, the Fell King will kill both of us. But unless I do *something*, Soren will be gone forever.

And I can't let that happen.

My heart pounds as I lift the dagger over my head with both hands.

Before I can strike, the Fell King knocks me aside.

"Father, stop!" I scream, the sound ripping out of my throat. Only it doesn't sound like me at all.

Ramunder doesn't listen.

The Fell King plunges his claws through Soren.

Black blood sprays over him. Soren's blood.

"Let us return to Trollkyrka," the Fell King says, dropping Soren into the river. "Come, Skaga."

Soren doesn't rise. I stand there, stunned.

"If you will not come willingly," Ramunder adds, breathing heavily, "then that huldra will make you." He clutches his side. So Soren hurt him, too. *Good.*

Maybe, just maybe, I can finish what Soren started.

I have to try. Even if it could be two against one now.

I walk toward the Fell King, dagger hidden behind my back.

The huldra watches me go. For a second, I don't know if she will help or hinder me, but that question is answered when roots shoot out of her back, reaching for the Fell King.

Ramunder gives a surprised shout.

"I told you to get Skaga, not *me.*" He catches one of her roots, using it like a rope to pull the huldra toward him. More roots wrap around him, binding his arms to his sides.

"Stop at once," he commands.

The huldra breaks the roots off her back as if she has no choice but to obey him.

But Ramunder is still bound. I'm already bringing the dagger down toward the Fell King with all my strength, muscles burning. The blade lodges into his neck, cold blood spraying me like ice water. *I did it.* Panting, I pull back—

The Fell King unleashes a furious roar as he struggles to free himself. "Stop Skaga!"

The huldra's dark eyes flit between us, but she doesn't move.

"How can you disobey me?" Ramunder bellows.

I bet I know why. Because I'm not Skaga.

"Run!" I shout at her before the Fell King can figure that out.

The huldra turns and sprints away, her tail swishing behind her.

She helped me. But why? I shake my head. At least I don't have to fight *her.*

The Fell King is still fighting to break free of her roots, but he can't.

Black blood gushes from Ramunder's neck, spilling over the stream like slick oil. My arms tremble as I stab him over and over and over, thinking of all the sleepless nights he terrorized me. Soon the Fell King lies there, motionless, but I don't stop. I keep stabbing him. He was already dead. How the hell do I know if I actually killed him?

Arms shaking, I raise my weapon again—

Blood everywhere. Wounds all over the body. The sight before me isn't so different from Torsten's decapitated body. My muscles lock up at the realization. Maybe it wasn't a monster that did that at all.

Maybe it was a human.

I drop the dagger, and it clatters onto the rocks.

Soren groans, blood spilling from him in a steady stream.

"Soren!" I scramble over to him. "Hey, hey, are you okay?"

"Fine," Soren grits out. "Draugr are not so easily killed. I just . . . need a moment. I still haven't recovered my full strength since . . ."

His eyes start to close. My heart misses a beat. Soren is hurt this badly because of my family. Because of the sleep thorn. Because of *me*.

Wait.

I glance back to the Fell King lying in the mud not far from us. Suddenly, I'm not so sure Ramunder is actually dead. Skaga watched as Ramunder buried an axe into Soren's chest and he still survived. Beheading is the only way to actually *kill* them with steel. But as I recall Torsten, I start to retch. I can't bring myself to do that, not even to the Fell King.

Ramunder remains still. For now.

"Come on," I urge Soren. "We have to go."

Soren doesn't stir, as if he can no longer hear me.

TWENTY-TWO

Even if I knew a healing stave, it's not like I could use it.

I just have to stop the bleeding. Somehow.

A sharp breeze whistles around us, cold air stinging my skin, but I ignore it. I have to find the wound, but his entire tunic is stained black. How the hell am I supposed to stop the bleeding if I can't even tell where it's coming from? I grab my dagger and slice his tunic in half so I can actually *see*. I peel the soaked fabric back, exposing the powerful muscles of his chest, covered in blood.

There. A deep hole in his abdomen.

The Fell King must have punched right through Soren like a massive bullet. A wound like this . . . it would be enough to kill a human. Soren groans, the sound slicing through my thoughts. I have to stop the bleeding. Now.

Maybe I'm imagining it, but the Fell King coughs, wet and thick with blood.

Time is running out.

If I can't get Soren back on his feet and fast, the Fell King *will* kill us.

Setting my jaw, I press against the wound in desperation, applying as much pressure as I can. Within moments, black soaks my hands. *Damn it.* Soren grunts, but his eyes remain shut.

Okay. Okay, this is definitely not working.

I don't know how long until Soren passes out . . . assuming draugr even can.

"Soren. Listen to me. Do you think you can stand?"

Another grunt.

I take that as a yes, so I prop him up as best I can. He wraps an arm around my shoulders, and I grit my teeth. It's like dragging a dead-weight, but we make it one step, then another, before Soren stumbles and his weight topples us over. We crash into the river, tangled together. His arm drapes across my chest, pinning me against the bloody riverbed. I should care, but all I can focus on right now is Soren.

He doesn't move. I can't even tell if he's conscious. "Soren?"

Not so much as a groan.

Oh hell. My stomach lurches. What should I do? We have to get out of here, but he's too heavy for me to carry. I struggle to free myself from him. Once I do, I glance at the trail of dark blood along the riverbed. We've barely made it a few meters.

We're never going to get out of here at this rate.

The Fell King starts to rouse.

Shit. I scrub my hands over my face. I can't abandon Soren. I won't. I pull away, staring down at my shaking hands. Black blood covers my skin, revealing the cracks in my palms.

That's it. My blood.

When we first encountered Torsten and he ran his tongue along my cheek, my blood healed him. So I unwind the bandage slowly before squeezing my fingertip. The stinging soreness is enough to make me wince, but fresh blood wells. I hold my finger above Soren's mouth and a bead of red splatters onto his lips, followed by another and another.

He groans.

Gritting my teeth, I squeeze tighter, encouraging more to spill, but it doesn't seem like enough. His brow furrows a bit, but his eyes won't open. Of course not. He's lost a whole lot more blood than a few drops.

I can't believe I'm about to do this.

Unzipping my coat and tugging the collar of my sweater down, I lean over him, exposing my throat in front of his mouth. "Drink, Soren." My voice wobbles around the words.

I hover there awkwardly, holding my breath. How bad will this hurt?

Soren said he can't get me sick, but I could still get an infection. He could rip out my throat. Drain me. I can't leave him, though. He needs to see Skaga again. Almost as badly as I need to see Amma.

The bite never comes.

"Soren?"

If this doesn't work, I don't know how we'll get out of this.

I lower my neck until his cold lips brush my skin, sending a shiver tracing down my spine, but he still doesn't stir. I can't feel his breath against my neck. I can't feel anything other than panic rising inside me like a wave.

"Come on, Soren," I say, practically begging.

Something sinks into the base of my throat—

His teeth. There's a sudden, sharp ache, chased by pleasure. I flush, my skin hot beneath his cool lips. Soren wraps his arms around me, drawing me closer to his bare chest as a low groan escapes him.

God.

My whole body is tingling, and I have to close my eyes. This feels more intimate than our kiss, than either time he's tasted my blood before. His fingers wind through my braid as he cups the back of my head with his claws. My pulse beats wildly against his lips.

What if he can't stop?

Breathing harshly, I pull away, to see if *I* can stop.

He allows me to move away, but not without gasping. *"Astrid."*

My blood drips from his lips, his two sharp teeth still exposed. I reach for my throat with shaking hands. At least he's conscious. Relief wells, even as warm blood trickles from where he bit me.

"Wait." He pulls me back toward him and licks the blood off me slowly, taking his time as his tongue trails up the column of my throat. "Thank you," he whispers against the sensitive skin there.

Oh God. Goose bumps rise along my arms. When he withdraws, the cold wind nips my skin again. I don't want him to stop. I can still feel his breath on my neck, his arms wrapped tightly around me, holding me against him. Part of me craves his touch. I want him to keep going.

I want *more*.

His wound knits back together slowly, the flesh sealing itself until all that remains of the once gruesome injury is another scar. The injury must've been too bad to fully heal—or maybe he needs more blood.

But I can't give him more. Not when I'm already lightheaded. I'm used to getting a lot of blood drawn, but I need to be able to walk. This will have to be good enough. Plus, he has other scars that stretch across his throat and his palm, so I have to believe he'll be able to live with another.

Some wounds never completely heal.

I wipe away the black blood covering his abdomen, only to reveal a large stave tattooed on his chest. It's elaborate, spanning across his pectorals and down to his abs. I run my fingers gently over it, realizing this must be the stave he was talking about. The one that turned him into a draugr.

The ground starts to tremble under us.

Soren and I look at each other. All those undead we passed last night must have heard the Fell King's horn.

It won't be long until they reach us.

"We need to go," Soren says, breathing heavily. "The Shore of Sacrifices should be ahead."

"Can you stand?" I ask.

He licks his lips and struggles to sit up. "I can manage."

"It's not much farther," I say, hoping I'm right. I hold out an arm, helping him to his feet. The bleeding has stopped, at least. "Just . . . don't collapse again. I can't carry you. You're heavier than you look."

He gives a small bark of laughter and my heart flips.

Soren sags against me, but I don't push him away.

We move as quickly as we can. I don't know how many steps we take—I'm focused on ensuring that Soren doesn't slip. The hard planes of his body press against me while we walk. He's so close, I inhale his scent of fresh mint and wood moss.

I glance back over my shoulder, but the Fell King hasn't moved. Yet.

The forest parts ahead, revealing a wide-open space.

It's no lake. A massive muddy mess stretches in front of us and disappears into the fog. Remnants of a large Viking longship sit wedged in the mud. It reminds me of the grand burials Amma used to tell me of, when they burned the longships along with the deceased, just as the gods did for their dead.

This ship isn't scorched, but rotten. Something covers its sides like snake scales. No, not scales. Those are human *nails*. Fingernails. Toenails. I shudder as I take in the revolting detail. The dragon head carved into the prow stretches toward the sky, snarling to be freed to sail again. But there is no use for it here, not any longer.

This must be the Shore of Sacrifices.

Or what's left of it, anyway.

TWENTY-THREE

The Shore of Sacrifices is nothing like what I expected.

Instead of waves lapping against the shore, an all-but-dried-up bog covers an open stretch of land. Fog blankets the entire landscape, making it hard to see far. Mist dampens my skin like tears as I look around the wasteland. I don't see anyone or anything. Only the abandoned longship rotting before us and the hazy shadow of Trollkyrka looming in the distance. Will Skaga even be here anymore?

Will *Amma*?

Tears burn, but I blink them back quickly.

"The tide must be low because the blood oath hasn't been renewed yet," Soren says, leaning against me. "We should be able to cross easily."

At least I don't have to climb aboard *that* ship. Still, I hesitate as I look out over the Shore. It's not mud at all, but congealed blood that we'll have to walk through.

How far are you willing to go? Soren asked me before I entered Tiveden.

Even now, standing before the Shore of Sacrifices, my answer hasn't changed.

I'll go as far as I have to.

"All right."

Mud sucks at my feet as I step into the bloody dregs of the shore. Despite the chilling cold, the muck feels warm through my boots. Swallowing my revulsion, I keep going, taking one wet, squelching step and then another.

"It's her," someone whispers behind me.

I twist my head but can't see anything.

"She's here," another voice says in a low whisper.

When I look, no one is there.

"Did you hear that?" I ask Soren.

"Hear what?" he asks.

"She's returned," whispers a cacophony of voices.

Suddenly, the fog around us lifts.

Sunlight illuminates the shore, and I can finally see it clearly. Scraggly plants protrude from the muck, and a filthy layer of detritus blankets what little blood remains. Ahead, a longhouse sits less than a kilometer away.

"Look," I say, blowing out a breath. "That must be it."

Amma—and Skaga—wait for us there.

I can *feel* it in my bones.

We slog ahead until we reach a longhouse surrounded by níðstǫng poles. The animal skulls stare at me as I take in the ancient house, derelict and windowless. Sod blankets the roof and tree trunks lean against its sides, propping up the warped, rotting wood.

"Are you ready?"

"Are you?" Soren asks.

I remember climbing the steps to Amma's house back in Unden only to find it empty. The crushing disappointment I felt at her absence. I don't know which to hope for: that Amma will be here, or that she won't.

As much as I want to see her again, I'm not sure I want to find her here. Not at the Shore of Sacrifices. Because if I do, it means Soren might be right about Unden. They could have sacrificed Amma just like the town once tried to do to Skaga, along with Unden's other ill and old people.

But if she isn't here, it means I might *never* find her. It means Dad might be right about her, and the letter she left me could have just been the ramblings of a woman whose mind was no longer all there. I could have been chasing a delusion this entire time.

I force myself to nod. "Yeah."

Together, we approach the rotting longhouse.

Soren reaches for the door handle.

What will Amma say when she sees him? What will Skaga do?

"Wait," I say, grabbing his arm. "If my family is really inside, they may not be ready to see you yet. Let me go in first and explain everything."

Soren considers, looking at me and then the longhouse.

He steps back. "Very well."

We share one last look before I reach for the door.

As I grip the rusted handle, a deer skull watches me from the gable of the roof, the bleached bone chalk white.

"Be careful," Soren says from behind me.

I have nothing to be afraid of. No matter what, they're still my family. Taking a breath, I push on the door. It gives easily, hinges creaking as it slowly swings open.

My skin tingles as I step inside.

The longhouse is dark, but the walls glow with an eerie green biolu-minescence. I reach out, swiping a finger over the wall—the wood feels almost papery, crumbling with decay, but the light comes from within. In some sections, there are growths of fungus covering the wood. They shine the brightest, like neon-green lamps.

Their light bathes the longhouse, painting the place with an unsettling, sickly green tinge, making it feel like a waking dream. There's a sense of wrongness as I walk through the house, like I'm intruding someplace I don't belong.

Despite how small the longhouse appeared outside, the inside seems to stretch forever. Benches run along its sides, draped with furs. I keep walking along the beaten earth floor but seem no closer to reaching the other end. I stumble into a long, narrow fire pit in the middle of the house, my boots stirring up heaps of ash.

This place reminds me faintly of the inside of Skaga's home I've seen through my dreams. As I look around, the whole house seems abandoned, like the longship outside. Skaga isn't here.

Neither is Amma.

Relief and disappointment war within me.

"Soren—" I start to call out, but movement catches my eye.

Someone *is* here.

My heart climbs my throat as I move slowly. A woman stands in one of the shadowed corners of the longhouse. Her back is turned to me, her attention focused on a standing loom, a tapestry of threads, carefully braiding them together with slender, wrinkled fingers and long nails. Despite the darkness, she works assuredly.

The motion is familiar. I already know who it is, even before spotting the white braid running down her back, glowing in the luminescent green light. My mouth goes dry.

I take a tentative step closer. "Amma?"

She turns, revealing her familiar face. A face I haven't seen in nine years. She looks older than I remember. Amma gives a small smile, seeming unsurprised to see me standing before her. I stare at her green-tinged, wrinkled skin, unable to trust my own eyes. It could be another huldra. Or worse.

But then she speaks. "Astrid, you made it."

I would know that voice anywhere.

It's really Amma. And she's been expecting me.

PART THREE

Stave to raise the dead
Stafr til at vekja upp draug

TWENTY-FOUR

Amma is so overjoyed, her blue eyes glow from within.

I step closer, only to falter.

Her lips spread into a smile, revealing sharp, pointed teeth. Ice pushes through my veins as I study her more closely. Her eyes—her eyes were always brown, not blue. And her skin. It's no longer warm and freckled, but pale as a corpse, drained of all color.

All *life*.

Amma wraps me in a hug, her embrace frigid. It feels like being caught in a blizzard, cold burrowing into my bones. I drag in a long breath, but her comforting scent of sweet pine is replaced by the stink of rotting flesh. Claws dig into my back as she holds me.

This—this is all wrong. She isn't like the Amma the huldra showed me, the Amma I remember, warm and smiling and safe. This isn't the person who embraced me when I scraped my knees playing outside. This isn't the person who carefully braided my hair each morning.

This can't be Amma. Because if it is, then that would mean Amma is . . . I can't even think it.

"I knew you would find me," she says, her voice rasping in my ear.

I pull away from her, fighting the urge to retch. This *is* Amma. And that realization is more terrifying than anything I've encountered in Tiveden so far.

"Tell me, what is the date?" Amma asks.

I gape at her, at a loss for words. "Um . . . I'm not sure," I manage after a long pause. I pull my cell phone out of my pocket, but it won't turn on. It must have been destroyed when I fell into the lake. Counting in my head, we arrived in Unden on the thirteenth, I spent the first night at Amma's house, and the past five or so days in Tiveden, so that would make it . . .

"The eighteenth, I think."

But then I realize Amma went missing more than a month ago, so I quickly add, "December eighteenth."

"Your birthday is tomorrow, then," she says. "We can celebrate it together. I'd hoped you'd reach here sooner, but we still have time until the twenty-first."

Midwinter.

I stare at Amma, trying to make sense of what I'm seeing, but it's like I'm looking into a stranger's face. A monster wearing a cheap mask of her, as twisted as Tiveden. "What—what happened to you?" I have to force the question out. *How did you become . . . this?*

Amma grips my shoulders, her claws digging in as she smiles. "You found me in time, Asta. I knew you would."

"Why did you—" I start to ask when the door slams open, startling us both.

Amma's eyes widen. "*You.* How are you here?"

I turn to see Soren standing in the doorway, looking lost.

"What is going on here?" he asks. "Where is Skaga?"

"Amma," I say slowly, but the word sounds hollow now.

Amma scrutinizes me, looking as horrified as I feel. Her eyes are intense. Furious. A look I usually only see on Dad's face.

"What have you done, child?" Her voice is low. Gravelly.

She stares at Soren as she adds, "That is the Fell King."

My heart stops. "No, you're wrong." Ramunder is the Fell King, not Soren.

But Amma is a draugr now—she can't lie any more than he can.

Amma frowns. "I fear *you* are the one who is mistaken."

I turn to him. "Tell her, Soren."

He looks at me with a pained expression. I wait expectantly for him to deny it. But he doesn't. He can't say anything.

Because Amma is telling the truth.

The world tilts violently under me.

Suddenly, it makes sense. Why Skaga would have imprisoned him in the first place. Why Ramunder only claimed he was the Fell King *now*.

"Why didn't you tell me?"

Soren looks stricken. "Because I didn't want you to look at me like you are right now. I did not want you to fear me, as you used to in your childhood."

I gape at him. "That was *you*?"

"He cannot be trusted," Amma hisses before Soren can respond. "You do not matter to him, Asta. He was only using you in order to get Skaga."

Amma is wrong. It may have started that way, but we've become more than that. Soren saved me. And I saved him, too. That must mean something—

Soren storms across the house and grabs hold of Amma. "Where is she? Where is Skaga?"

I almost don't recognize this Soren, even though the way he moves is similar to the first night I found him, when he confronted me. Somewhere along our journey, something changed between us. Now that he's once again focused on finding Skaga, he's forgotten all about me, like I'm no longer even standing here.

The realization stings. Maybe Amma is right.

Maybe I *was* mistaken.

Amma gives a smug smile. "You will not find Skaga here."

"Where, then?" Soren growls.

"You misunderstand." Amma crouches down beside the cold fire pit. "Skaga has never been in Tiveden." She grabs a fistful of ashes and crushes them, letting them slip like sand through her fingers. "She burned her body long ago, just as Freyja once did."

The charred coal scent fills the longhouse, stinging my nose.

Panic spreads over Soren's face. "Impossible."

Amma brushes off her hands, her lips curling. "I applaud her for out-smarting you one last time."

Soren punches the wall, and the entire house trembles from the force, dust raining from the raised roof. "It's not possible," he says, choking on the words. He leans against the wall, his hand splayed. "She swore to me. She cannot . . ."

My chest aches. Even knowing who he is now, the same Fell King whose shadowy presence once terrified me, I start to reach for his shoulder, wanting to comfort him. I know how desperate he was to see Skaga again. I was just as desperate to find Amma. How would I feel if our roles were reversed? If Skaga stood here instead of Amma?

"Stay away from him," Amma demands. "Do not make the same mistake Skaga did. He is our family's sworn enemy. You never should have awoken him."

"I—I didn't know."

"Of course not, Asta." Amma offers a reassuring smile, but her sharp canines make me wince. "There's much you don't yet understand, and I will make that right. I will teach you."

Still, I hesitate.

"Everything I told you is true," Soren says, desperate. "Your family imprisoned my kind. They imprisoned *me*. They are the ones who did this to Tiveden."

"To protect our home," Amma says.

"Tell her how," Soren growls. "Tell her about the sacrifices. You must still do them or the blood oath would not be fulfilled."

Soren can't lie. But I can't make sense of what he's saying. I thought *Amma* was the sacrifice. She died somehow, but as I look her over, there's no sign of an injury that could've killed her. Not like the scar across Soren's throat.

So why is he talking as though Amma is the one who *did* the sacrificing? Swallowing, I suddenly remember what Old Ulf said at her vigil. *We will never forget all the sacrifices she has made on our behalf. . . .* I thought he was speaking metaphorically. Not *literally*.

Amma is the closest thing I have to a mother. She raised me for nine years while Dad was checked out. But if she's at the Shore of Sacrifices . . . Maybe that doesn't mean what I'd assumed. Maybe I don't know her like I thought I did. My memories of her are a child's memories. I was just a little girl.

How well do I really know Amma?

"The blood river has run dry," I say, trying to convince myself, too.

"Not completely," Soren says. "There was still blood. You saw for yourself."

He . . . he's right. And Amma isn't denying it either. She's suspiciously silent now. Something inside me threatens to break. I glance between them, at a loss for words. Suddenly, I don't know who either of them is.

I turn to Amma. "Did you really . . . ?"

My mind revolts against the thought. Amma wouldn't. *Couldn't.* I don't want to consider it, but the truth is right in front of me. It always has been.

The blood oath must not be broken.

"How many?" is all I can get out.

"You should be asking how many I've *saved*," Amma replies.

My chest cracks like a frozen lake.

All my life, I've loved a murderer.

Even worse? I still do.

I don't want to. I would rather rip my heart out—my heart that is capable of loving her despite knowing what she is, what she's done. My heart is already trying to find a way to forgive her, trying to understand her side. I've loved her every moment of my life. I can't just erase that. No matter how much I wish I could.

Soren steps closer to me. "You said you were different from your family," he says, his voice pleading. "Help me break the blood oath, Astrid. If Skaga is gone, then you are the only one who can. You need not become like her."

Amma stiffens. "A blood oath made before the gods cannot be broken. If it is, ruin will come to our family."

I stagger back. "What?"

Soren never mentioned *that*.

"I've had a very long time to consider this," Soren says. "There might be a way around that, a way you can survive."

Amma scoffs. "Performing the sacrifice is the *only* way."

Neither can lie, but I can only believe one. It was always going to come to this—and I'm the only one who didn't know it. Soren wants to break the blood oath to free himself and his kind, even if it means ruining my family. Amma wants to uphold the oath to protect our family and our home, even if it means murdering people.

I have to make a choice. Just like when Skaga had to choose between her family and her home or her love for Soren. Who do I believe? Who do I trust?

Neither.

Both have deceived me. Betrayed me.

"Please, Astrid," Soren says quietly. "I cannot lose you, too."

My chest aches at the desperation in his voice.

I don't want to lose him, either.

"How could you even consider helping him?" Amma asks, her voice haughty.

She expects me to betray Soren just as Skaga did. She doesn't care whether I want to.

"He saved me," I tell her. "I never would've made it here without him."

"We saved each other."

"So long as you walked the path, Freyja would have protected you," Amma says. "As she has protected me, my mother, and all those before us. He must have led you astray."

"We got lost because of *me*, not him. And I care about him—"

"Who do you think he cares for?" Amma asks slowly. "You or Skaga?"

It's as though she still knows my every insecurity. The doubt I've held the entire time Soren and I grew closer. Amma knows me better than anyone, even now. She knows just what she needs to say.

"I . . . don't know," I admit quietly.

I glance at Soren, but he looks uncertain. The memory of his lips closing over mine flashes through my mind. I bite down, making the cut on my lip ache. The moment he saw me, he believed I was her. Then, *You are not Skaga*, he said, alarmed after tasting my blood.

"I care for you both," he says tightly.

Part of me wishes I *could* be Skaga. She will always come first to Soren. I saw it for myself when he barged into the longhouse looking for her. To him, I'm second best. I always will be.

Seeming to sense the shift of my thoughts, Amma adds, "I love *you*, Astrid. Our family needs you. *Unden* needs you. You are our future."

All this time, I've been desperate to be reunited with Amma. Not just because I miss her or because I never got the chance to say goodbye. It's because I'm afraid no one will ever truly love me other than her.

Dad resents me for Mom's death. He can barely bring himself to love me.

Amma is the one who helped me see that.

And she's right about Soren, too. He will never love me like he loves Skaga.

She's always right.

And now, she and I can finally be together again, somewhere even Dad can't keep us apart. Even if she's not who I remember, her blood still flows through my veins. It's like Amma always used to say: *We are nothing without family*.

I am nothing without her.

I need answers, and Amma is the only one who can give them to me. She'll help me make sense of everything like she always does. Soren may not have lied to me, but he never told me he was the Fell King.

I can't trust Soren.

Maybe I never should have.

Wordlessly, I take my place beside Amma—and whatever was forming between me and Soren shatters like frost. Family will always come first. I have to believe that, because if I don't, I will be left with nothing.

Soren stares at me like I just stabbed him.

The same way he looked at Skaga when she chose Unden. After

experiencing her dream, I couldn't understand the choice she made. Not until I had to make it too.

"Do not do this." Even his voice is pained. "*Please*, Astrid."

Words rush out of me before I can stop them. "You only want *me* because you can't have Skaga!"

"That is not true." He speaks slowly, deliberately. "I cared about you because I believed you were *different* from Skaga."

His words settle like sediment at the bottom of my stomach. *Cared.*

"And I was right," he continues. "You *are* different from Skaga. You are *worse*. You saw for yourself what your family has done to this forest—and to me. Yet you still choose them."

He called Amma a murderer—and he cannot lie. But if Soren is the Fell King, how many has *he* killed? He cost Skaga her mother, even if it was an accident. I won't lose Amma because of him.

"She's my family," I offer weakly.

Maybe he's right. Maybe I don't actually know Amma.

But I want to.

Amma reaches for my shoulder and guides me away. "Leave him, Asta."

"You would turn your back on me?" Soren says, his voice turning desperate. "Do not make me your enemy, Astrid. I beg of you. I have had a long time to reflect on the past and my mistakes. I do not want to repeat them."

Amma gives a solemn shake of her head.

I look between them. "I'm sorry, Soren."

"You will address me by my title," he says. His tone turns cold. Cruel.

It feels like a hand is closing around my throat and squeezing.

"You will address me as the Fell King."

I have to bite back my shock. Standing there, bathed in shadow, he looks unrecognizable.

Like the Fell King who haunted my nights.

Soren stalks through the house. "I will be your enemy, if that is what you desire."

He slams the door behind him, so hard the whole house rattles. I stare at the closed door, shaken to my core.

By choosing Amma, I also made another choice.

I've chosen to make Soren my enemy, too.

TWENTY-FIVE

"Let him go," Amma says, resting a cold hand on my shoulder.

Her touch doesn't offer me any comfort. It stings like frostbite as I stare at the door, unable to speak. I ball my hands into fists. Hands that held on to Soren not long ago. But he felt so different. His touch was the kind of cold that invigorates, not destroys.

"You are better off without him, child."

Am I, though?

The longhouse feels emptier without Soren. I can't make sense of him being the Fell King. That he is the one who always terrified me when I was a child. I was traveling through Tiveden with him this whole time and I had no idea. Worse, I'd started falling for him. My cheeks turn hot with humiliation. I feel like such a fool.

But Amma is standing beside me. After all these years, we're finally reunited. I search her face, looking for something familiar, something right, but all I can see are her eyes glowing in the dim light. Seeing her like this is its own kind of nightmare, one I can't wake from.

"What about Johan, hmm?" Amma asks knowingly. "You and he always shared a special bond."

She smiles at me, exposing her sharp teeth.

"We did. Once." I can't help but remember how uncomfortable it was to see him again and realize how much has changed between us. That things will never go back to how they used to be. "But we haven't talked in years."

"Neither had you and I," Amma points out. "Did you know he would visit me often? He always asked about you. He never forgot. Relationships may ebb and flow, but the feelings remain. They can always be found again."

"I suppose," I say, shivering at the sight of her.

Amma's smile vanishes. "You poor thing, you must be freezing."

We both know that isn't why I shivered. She scoops one of the furs off the bench, and I accept it from her anyway, playing along. As I wrap the fur around my shoulders, I recall pulling Soren's cloak around me and wince.

"Oh, Asta," she says. "Are you hurt? What happened?"

I shake my head. "What happened to *you*, Amma? How did you . . . ?"

Die, I can't bring myself to finish. When I tried explaining to Johan why I needed to find Amma, I said it would feel as if she were alive and dead at once until I knew what had happened to her. When I told him that, I never imagined she could actually be both.

Amma sits down on the bench, the wood creaking under her weight. "I will explain everything," she says, patting the furs beside her. "I could not bring myself to tell you so in a letter, but I was already dying long before I set foot in Tiveden."

I hesitate a moment. As if I'm afraid of *Amma*.

Ridiculous. Shaking the thought away, I lower myself beside her. I have so many questions, questions only she can answer. "You were sick?"

"Cancer," Amma says simply.

Guilt stabs me, surprisingly sharp. So Officer Lind *was* right. Until we arrived in Unden, it had never even occurred to me she could be sick. It had felt like we would always have each other. Once I was old enough, I was going to move back to Unden to do all the things we'd missed out on in the past nine years.

"Did Dad know?"

"Even if he did, would it have made any difference? He wouldn't have visited. In fact, I doubt he would have even told you I was sick."

My stomach sinks. She's right about that.

"Which is why I had no choice but to go into Tiveden," Amma continues. "I knew if I did, you would follow me."

She knew what her disappearance would do to me.

She knew I would be so desperate to find her that I would even go into Tiveden—

"You *died*."

Amma pauses for a long moment. "It was a sacrifice I had to make."

My eyes burn. "But why?"

"So you can become the next Seer. I'm sorry I could not help you more, but each Seer must make the journey here herself. It is a rite of passage, not unlike a pilgrimage, so we can see for ourselves why the blood oath must never be broken."

She isn't making any sense. "Seer?"

"Unden's high priestess. Skaga was the first." She turns my hand over slowly, tracing the scar along my palm with a long claw. "All scars tell a story. When Skaga made the blood oath with the Fell King, she sliced open her palm, and now every descendant of Skaga bears that very mark. We are bound by the oath she made that day."

I stare at my hand, at the scar I've had my whole life but didn't know how I'd gotten. Amma holds out her left palm, and an identical scar traces across it. How have I never noticed until now? And Soren—he had the same scar on his palm. I still remember when he offered me his hand and I took it. Our scars lined up, a perfect fit for each other.

But he never explained how I had it too.

"It is time for you to become our Seer," Amma finishes.

"Why me?" I ask, voice rising. "What about Dad?"

"He may bear the scar, but your father cannot become Seer."

Dad has this scar too?

Then again, it wouldn't exactly stand out. He's an auto mechanic. He has a whole collection of scars on his hands and arms. Even if I had noticed, I would've just assumed it was work-related, not because of some ancient blood oath our ancestor swore. "Why not?"

"Only a woman can," Amma says. "As her last such living descendant, you must take Skaga's place as Seer. All of Unden's past foremothers have served in this role as well."

A nervous laugh escapes me. I'd always wanted to become Unden's foremother, just like Amma. But this is different. "You expect me to kill someone?"

Like you have? I don't say.

The unspoken words hang heavy between us.

Amma doesn't smile. Her eyes are hard and cold. "I did what was necessary to save countless more lives. And I expect you to do the same."

She's serious.

I yank my hand back, but her claw scratches my palm as swift and sharp as a razor blade. As sudden as her unexpected demands. I wince as blood wells.

Her hungry gaze is locked on my palm.

On the bright red blood pooling there.

I quickly wipe my hand off on my coat. "How did you become . . . like this?"

"A consequence of the blood oath," Amma says. "The Fell King desired an eternity with Skaga, and now all Seers must become draugar."

Soren is the reason Amma became a draugr?

And not just her. If I become the Seer like she wants, I will too. I thought that anything was better than being dead. But after seeing what Amma has become, I'm no longer so sure.

I shake my head. "He wouldn't—"

But then I remember how certain Soren was Skaga would be in Tiveden and the rest of my words die on my lips.

Soren didn't seem surprised when he saw that Amma was a draugr. He was only surprised that Skaga *wasn't*. It must be why he wasn't more upset when I revealed she was dead. He already knew she would be a draugr.

"He would," Amma says. "He craved her above all else."

Soren said Skaga was willing to do anything to hold on to the blood oath. What was he willing to do to hold on to her? He would have spent eternity with her if he could have.

If she hadn't outsmarted him, that is.

"The Fell King loved Skaga, but that love soured when she chose Unden instead of him," Amma continues. "And so he declared war. He would have destroyed our village, too, had Skaga not tricked him into making the blood oath."

I'm not so sure it's that simple. At first, I thought he wanted revenge for Skaga's betrayal. But I was wrong. Soren loved Skaga while also loving Tiveden. He wanted to protect his home, just like she wanted to protect Unden.

"Is that why Skaga betrayed him?" I ask.

"He is the one who betrayed *her*," she says sternly. "After making the blood oath, the Fell King realized that Skaga no longer needed him. He sought to break the blood oath so he could destroy her home and take all she loved. Skaga used the sleep thorn on him in order to save us all."

Amma says it so adamantly . . . as if she's reciting scripture, a story told and retold through generations. To her, it *is* true, I guess. But she wasn't actually there like Soren was.

Soren never told me who he really was, though. Who knows what else he omitted?

It's difficult for me to reconcile the Fell King with Soren. Soren seemed so different. He can be cold and cruel, but he doesn't seem capable of everything Amma is accusing him of. Then again, I had no clue he was the Fell King.

Maybe I have no idea what he is truly capable of.

"Soren taught her the staves, didn't he?" Not only that, but he found her, alone in the woods, and carried her back to Unden. I saw that much for myself. "Soren—the Fell King, I mean—spared her life too."

"What?" Amma says, her voice harsh. "Where did you get this idea?"

"I . . . saw it."

She leans closer. "I'm afraid I don't know what you mean."

"Didn't you see it too?" I ask slowly.

Amma frowns. "See what?"

"Skaga's life." Amma seems confused, so I add, "I keep dreaming of her. She has the power of projection, right? Well, she . . ."

My voice trails off. If Skaga burned, then she *couldn't* have been projecting onto me like Soren claimed. But why have I been having these dreams? Even if it wasn't Skaga, there has to be some kind of explanation.

"You told me to walk her path, right?" I ask, trying to make sense of things. "The runes. Spiritual connection. When I touched the first one, I felt her. It was as if—as if my own hand carved it. It felt so real. And then—"

"Impossible," Amma says.

She used to say the same thing when I'd try to tell her about the Fell King visiting me, or when I started getting sick. Suddenly, I feel small. As she looks at me now, the disbelief is plain on her face. There's something condescending about her dismissal, the same thing doctors did before I got my diagnosis.

"Unless . . ." Amma shakes her head slowly. "No, surely not. Whatever you think you've seen, it must have been the forest's influence. Or perhaps even the Fell King's." She frowns. "He is our enemy, child. He always has been."

It sure didn't seem that way. I remember how he kissed Skaga while holding her in his arms, looking at her like she was the only thing he could see. How he told her he would do anything for her, and he couldn't lie. . . .

Although because of the ógipta, I can't really trust anything I've seen, can I? But I'm not sure I can trust *Amma*, either.

Uncomfortable, I change the subject. "I thought Ramunder was the Fell King."

"Oh, child," Amma says, patting my leg. "He has only been acting as Fell King. When he died in the war, Skaga brought him back as a draugr. Later, she made him Fell King in Soren's absence, giving him the crown of roots and horn of bone that once belonged to Soren so that Ramunder could protect all of her line who would inhabit Tiveden after her."

"Why would Skaga burn herself, then?" I ask.

Even if she wanted to punish Soren, it still seems extreme.

"Just as Freyja was burned, Skaga burned her own body so she would be reborn. This way, the Fell King could never have her, and Unden would always be protected."

"Why didn't you do the same?"

Amma gives me a small, sad smile. "Because," she says, reaching a clawed hand toward my face. She carefully tucks a loose strand of hair behind my ear. "I knew you still needed me. It's my duty to prepare you as our next Seer. Besides, I love you too much to ever leave you."

"I thought you had," I whisper.

"Oh, Asta." Amma wraps her arms around me, drawing me into her winter-cold embrace. "I've never left you. I never will. You are like a daughter to me, the daughter I never got to have. What did I always tell you? We need no goodbyes."

A tear slips down my cheek. "I didn't want to leave you, either."

"Shhhh," Amma says softly, rubbing slow circles over my back. "I know it was your father who stole you from me. But we are together now, somewhere he cannot separate us. That's all that matters, my brave little Asta. No one will ever take you from me again."

All of a sudden, the past week catches up with me, worse than any fatigue I've ever felt. Everything I went through to find her—awakening Soren, trekking through Tiveden, being attacked by Torsten, being nearly devoured by a huldra, being chased by a nykur, being hunted by the kattakyn, and being confronted by Ramunder . . .

"I'm so tired," I admit, sighing.

"Oh, I'm certain you are," Amma says, guiding me through the longhouse. "It seems you have had a long and difficult journey, I'm sure in no small part because of who accompanied you."

Soren, she means.

But I don't think I would have survived without him. We saved each other countless times.

In the end, it didn't matter.

"Come with me." She pushes aside strings of bones that dangle in a doorway at the rear of the longhouse and leads me into a separate room. A large bed takes up much of the space, heaps of furs piled on it. Amma passes by an ancient-looking chest and pats the bed. "You can rest now, Asta."

My body aches as I climb in.

Amma sits on the edge beside me, pulling the furs up over me gently. "You're all right," she coos. "You're safe now."

She tucks me in as if I'm a little girl again. And for an instant, I glimpse the Amma of my memories: her sun-kissed skin, her sparkling brown eyes, her patient, knowing smile. My eyelids grow heavy, drifting shut.

She's still Amma, somewhere in there.

She has to be.

TWENTY-SIX

"What happened, Skaga?" Torsten rushes over to me.

"It is not my blood," I say numbly, but Torsten looks me over, ensuring I am unharmed.

"Did you change your mind about marriage?" Gorm asks with a wolf-like grin. "The bride is only supposed to run as far as her husband's house, not beyond it."

Everyone in Unden is still gathered, eager for the wedding celebration to continue.

"There will be no celebration tonight," I tell them all.

They glance at each other, exchanging uncertain looks.

"There will be battle," Father says, finishing my thought for me.

He follows me, Liv's body dangling in his arms. Whispers rise around us at the sight of her.

"We fight the Folk tonight!" Father shouts.

Now even Gorm looks alarmed. "What happened?"

"The Hidden Folk have declared war upon Unden." Father is silent for a long moment. "They killed my wife, along with three others. Their bodies are still in Tiveden on the path to Trollkyrka. Go fetch them, so we can bury them before the battle begins."

Father walks down the dirt road, still carrying Liv.

Gorm chases after him. "Where are you going?"

"I will lay my wife to rest in our bed until I bury her," Father says simply.

Gorm stills briefly. Then, sighing, he turns to his followers. "Retrieve the bodies from the forest, but be cautious."

"I will go as well," Torsten says.

"No," I say. "It is too dangerous, Torsten."

I have already lost Liv. I will not lose anyone else.

Torsten turns to me, gripping my shoulder. "Go home, Skaga, and do not worry. I will handle this, so you and your father can grieve."

I glance between him and my father. "Very well."

I follow Father through the streets and into our longhouse. He continues wordlessly until he reaches their bedroom and lays Liv down. Liv lies on the bed like she did last night, when I stood over her holding the sleep thorn. But I cannot convince myself she is asleep, not when she is bathed in blood.

"I must sharpen my axe" is all Father says, but the words are rough.

He disappears into the main room, leaving me alone with Liv.

Tears burn hot trails down my cheeks, and I understand why Father is focusing on his fury instead. If he allows himself to feel this sorrow, it will bring him to his knees. He cannot afford to grieve when we must fight tonight. And it is all because of me.

Because I am a foolish girl who fell in love with a monster.

Soon, the sound of steel grinding against the whetstone fills the house. My teeth grind together in response as I stare at Liv. If I had used the sleep thorn on her last night, would she be alive still? The stave I was terrified could kill her might have spared her instead. If I had used it and ran away instead of marrying Torsten, Father would not have gone to behead Soren and Liv would not have followed me into the forest when I went to stop him. . . .

I cannot allow myself to think it. Such thoughts will drive me mad.

But there is still one stave I can use to help Liv.

The only stave Soren refused to teach me. A forbidden one capable of raising the dead, like his parents once used on him. He said it must never be used again, but right now, I am desperate. He may not have taught me it, but I have traced it on his bare chest more times than I can count. I know that stave as well as I know my own heart.

I cannot lose my mother.

I will not.

My finger trembles as I draw the stave upon her, using the last of her life's *blood. As I finish, I beg Freyja for her help. She always has helped me in my times of need, and I need her more than ever now. I will do whatever she asks of me if she only gives me this. Holding my breath, I wait—*

Liv gives a great gasp like a fish.

Blue eyes open.

Her clawed hands fly to her throat. Where it was sliced open, there is only a scar now. "Skaga? What happened?"

A disbelieving laugh bursts from me. "I could not let you go to the gods, not when I still need you, Mother."

"Oh, Skaga." Liv embraces me, her body cold as ice. "My daughter."

I hug her tightly.

After using this forbidden magic, I know there is nothing I cannot do now. The sound of the whetstone has stopped.

Father appears in the doorway. "Come help with—"

His axe falls to the floor as he looks between us. "Liv? Is that really you?"

She nods. "Your—our daughter brought me back, Ramunder."

Father hurries across the room, and I brace myself for his fury. I have used another stave, even though he forbade it, and turned Liv into a draugr—

He throws his arms around us both, pulling us against him. "My loves. I swear so long as I still breathe, no harm will befall either of you again."

We cry together like we did the night I returned from Tiveden alive.

⁓

"Are you ready?" Father asks us.

Liv reaches for her prized shield, the circular one I carved the stave Ógishjálmr into. The eight arms of the stave extend from the dome in the middle of the shield. Whenever an enemy beholds the helm of awe, they will be gripped by terror and unable to attack. But as Liv touches the wooden bar across the back of the shield, she recoils.

"The wood," she says, looking pained. The handle must be made of ash wood, which means she can no longer use it now that she's a draugr. "Take it instead, Skaga."

Father tosses her shield to me. "Be safe, both of you."

Nodding, I catch it. "You too."

Her shield is far heavier than I expect, as if it is meant to be a weapon as well. I look it over with renewed respect. Hopefully, the metal dome is also cold steel that can harm the Folk.

Hefting the shield up, I follow Liv and Father outside.

The sun has already disappeared from the sky, and darkness will come soon, bringing battle with it. Men and women gather in the streets, their spears and axes and swords ready. They look to Father, waiting for his command.

Gorm stills when he notices Liv beside us. "How? She was as dead as the others. We all saw it for ourselves."

"I used my mother's magic," I say simply.

"You go against nature, girl," Gorm spits at me. "You provoke the gods by raising the dead. They will turn our weapons against us."

"Enough." Father holds up a hand, silencing Gorm. "We cannot afford to fight among ourselves. Our true enemy will be upon us soon—"

A horn bellows in the distance, as loud and deep as thunder.

The Hidden Folk are declaring war.

"Ready your weapons," Father cries out, raising his sword to the sky. "We fight for Unden!"

Torsten is there too, lifting his spear with a shout.

Others join in the battle cry, their weapons held high.

Just because I am no fighter does not mean I cannot make a difference. I set my mother's shield down and slowly make my way to the wooden fence that surrounds Unden. Like this, it will not protect us very well. So I free my dagger and carve the firestarter stave into it. Then I slice my finger, filling the grooves with my blood.

A small flame rises, shooting sparks of gold.

It slithers along the fence like a snake, but it does not devour the wood. The golden flames climb higher, spreading quickly, until the entire fence is aflame with it. It is like no fire I have ever seen before. I reach my hand into the flickering flames, but it does not harm me. It feels like warm sunlight upon my skin.

"This is my mother's sacred fire," I proclaim. "Freyja herself will aid us, as she helped me on Trollkyrka. We will not lose this battle when we have the goddess on our side."

Gorm glares at me but reaches for his axes. Even he can tell this is no longer the time for words.

The time has come for battle.

As I face the wall of fire, heat warms my skin, but I cannot see past the bright flames.

"They are coming," Liv calls, loud enough for us all to hear. Now that she is turned, her hearing is better than any human's.

"Prepare yourself," Father says beside me.

Clouds cover the moon, leaving us in sudden darkness. The fire seems even brighter, bright enough to sear my eyes. An unnatural breeze blasts the forest, pulling through the trees, rattling branches like bones.

Wind slams into us, snuffing out my fire. Choking on smoke, I cannot see anything. But I hear them. Hundreds of Hidden Folk punching through the soil. Snarls and screeches fill my ears, making me shudder as they pour out of the forest and swarm into Unden.

I instantly find Soren at the forefront.

"Do not harm her," he calls, pointing a long finger at me. "Skaga is mine."

It feels as if I have been submerged in ice-cold water as I notice the crown of twisted roots resting upon his silver hair. A large bone horn hangs from his hip, the only weapon that he carries. Realization chills me as I recall the story he once told me.

"You are the Fell King?"

Soren inclines his head. "Not the first, but yes. The Hidden Folk chose me as their protector until the Allfather returns."

I thought he had shared all his secrets with me, but I was mistaken. Now Soren stands before me, his army at his back. That I fell in love with the Fell King only makes my heart all the more traitorous.

"Destroying Unden will not make me love you."

Soren reaches up, and at first, I think he's going to wrap his hands around my waist—but he unlatches the horn from his belt instead. "You are mistaken, Skaga." He lowers his voice, turning lethal. "I must do this in order to protect Tiveden. I never should have allowed Unden to exist, but my love for you made me a fool. Until your father reminded me that humans will always kill senselessly. To you, it matters not who you hurt. So I will abide by your rules."

Soren lifts the horn in his strong hands.

The polished bone glints under the moon, revealing intricate knots carved through it.

"Soren, don't!" I reach out, trying to snatch it away.

He brings the horn to his lips—the same lips that once kissed mine.

Now he uses them to destroy us all.

I glance to my right, where Father stands, clutching his axe. Torsten stands beside him, spear ready. To my left, Liv bares her teeth and claws. I lift her wooden shield to my chest. I am grateful to have both my parents beside me when the battle begins, no matter what will happen afterward.

We are all that stand between Unden and annihilation.

The Folk rush forward like a river, moving so fast their bodies streak through the darkness. My heart lodges in my throat as I wait for impact. They are so close now, I can see their glowing eyes like fixed points. Seconds separate us. I brace myself, gripping my shield, as they burst through the fence, sending wood chips spraying across my face.

With a scream, we race to meet them in battle.

We crash against each other like two mighty waves.

TWENTY-SEVEN

Glowing blue eyes stare into mine.

Sweat beads on my forehead as I shoot up straight. I can still see Soren and his army about to strike Unden. But it's not the Fell King who stares at me. Just Amma. She sits on the edge of the bed, in the same spot she was before I dozed off. As if she's been there this entire time, watching me as I slept.

"How long have I been sleeping?"

"Oh, I don't know," she says. "A while."

It sure *feels* like I slept for a long time. My stomach rumbles.

"You must be starving." Amma hands me a bag of pretzels from my backpack. "This should hold you over for now. I have something special planned for your birthday tonight."

So I lost an entire day. I stuff some stale pretzels into my mouth.

"I guess we'll have to wait until tomorrow," I say once I finish eating.

Amma tips her head to the left. "For what?"

"To go home."

"Oh, Asta." Amma gives a sad smile. "This is my home now. I can only return to Unden on Midwinter."

I blink. "What? But I thought—you said we would be together."

"And we are, aren't we?" Amma says.

"But I need to go home," I say slowly. My next injection is soon. Not to mention I need an actual meal, a bathroom, a warm change of clothes. Most of all, I need to let Dad and Johan and Zuri know I'm alive.

"And you will. On Midwinter."

Conversation over, she might as well be stating.

Dad does the exact same thing. I guess I never realized where he got it from.

"Now come," she says, peeling the warm fur blankets away. "There is much to do before Midwinter. First, we must get you ready to meet the others."

Goose bumps pebble across my skin. "Others?"

I climb out of bed, but my limbs are heavy with exhaustion.

Hopefully not from a flare-up.

"Our family, of course." Amma smiles. "We must present you to them for their approval before you can become the next Seer. They are all eager to meet you."

I rub my hands up and down the sleeves of my coat, desperate for warmth. My undead family, she means. Seeing Amma like this is one thing—I *know* her. But how am I supposed to react to meeting a bunch of dead ancestors? That isn't exactly normal.

Nothing about this is.

"What if they don't?" I ask, shifting uncomfortably. "Approve of me, I mean."

"Don't fret," Amma says, leading me outside the back of the long-house. "I'm certain they will love you as I do. The selection ceremony is mostly tradition now, anyway. It was only necessary back when there were multiple candidates."

The crash of pounding water fills my ears as soon as I step out into the night.

A half-moon hangs overhead, turning the forest a forbidding blue.

"Still, we must make a good impression," Amma continues. "You are not the only one they will be judging. As the most recent Seer, it was—and still is—my duty to prepare you."

I look around, but no one else is here.

Trollkyrka looms in the distance, making the longhouse seem to shrink in comparison. Mist dampens my skin as a powerful waterfall pours down from the jagged cliffs, forming a pool at our feet. The water is surrounded by fragrant flowers, with veins running through the petals and darkening in the center like bloodstains.

"Henbane," I say, smiling to myself. "Like we planted together."

Amma nods, returning my smile. Unlike when we grew them, these flowers have grown wild in Tiveden. Their leafy stems rise up well past my shoulders, impossibly tall. Each blossom is as large as my head. For a brief moment, they look less like flowers and more like bloody faces.

But then I blink, and they're flowers again.

"Go on and bathe." Amma waves a wrinkled hand toward the water. "They should be here soon. I'll gather you some fresh clothes to change into."

It's been days since I showered. I'm covered in blood and mud, soaked with sweat, my hair matted and filthy. Amma heads back to the long house and I shuck off my coat, my dagger still in its pocket, before peeling off my sweater, jeans, and underwear, until I stand there, naked.

Only my trollkors necklace remains, resting heavily on my collarbone. I reach up for it, trapping the twisted steel shape with my palm. Even if the necklace is only useful for its iron, it's supposed to ward off the Hidden Folk. Now Amma is one, and so is the rest of my family here. If I meet them wearing this, what kind of message will that send?

You're safe now, Amma told me.

I slip the necklace over my head and leave it resting atop my clothes.

Dipping a toe into the water, I recoil at once. It's *freezing.*

But I need to get clean, so I force myself to wade into the pool. I'll acclimate to it, just like I will get used to Amma. *I hope.* The cold numbs me to my core, my limbs growing heavy as I swim deeper.

Even the roaring waterfall isn't enough to drown out the thoughts in my head. I was wrong. Unden didn't sacrifice Amma; instead, she chose to sacrifice herself. She became a draugr. *For me.* So we could be together again. Submerged in the cold water, my skin stinging and raw, it's as if I can feel her love all around me, overwhelming me.

And it *hurts*.

Holding my breath, I plunge under the waterfall.

It beats against my head, my shoulders, powerful and without mercy. Amma's words return with the crashing fury of the waterfall. *You are our future.* In the pounding water, I feel the weight of that expectation. How much really rests on me. Soren must have realized too. That's why he wanted me to break the blood oath after finding out Skaga was gone.

But I can't.

I have to become the Seer. That choice was made for me from the moment I was born. Now I can be part of something larger than myself. Something that will continue on long after me, like a river of blood, running through generations, through time itself. The ancient waterfall pours over me, washing away any doubt, any fear, and I stand powerless beneath it.

Our family needs you. Unden *needs you.*

I emerge from the waterfall invigorated.

Awakened.

Amma waits for me on the shore, a long tunic bundled in her arms. She smiles when she sees me. I climb out of the water, cold stinging my skin, but my body is so numb, I barely feel it. My limbs move on their own toward her. My clothes—and my trollkors necklace—have disappeared.

I shiver, standing naked before her.

Amma pulls the coarse linen tunic down over my head, but its long sleeves and warmth are welcome after the chilling swim. Once that's on, she slips a green apron dress over it and fastens the shoulder straps with a pair of intricate gold tortoise brooches. A string of glass beads hangs between them with a small amulet of Freyja dangling in its middle.

"Are you ready to meet your family?" she asks, securing a leather belt around my waist. She pulls the belt so tight it makes me wince.

I don't know if I am ready, but I force myself to nod.

She smiles. "Excellent. They should be arriving soon."

∞

A long line of women stands before me, stretching back into the dark forest. They look like ghosts gathered there, thin moonlight bathing their pale skin, casting their white dresses in an eerie, otherworldly glow. My heart pounds so hard, I can feel the weight of the tortoise brooches pressing against my chest. There must be at least thirty women, if not more. I twist my barely dried braid between my fingers, a nervous habit I've had since I was little.

Amma stands beside me. "Don't worry, I will introduce you to everyone. Remember their names along with their gifts."

"Gifts?" I whisper.

"Ever since Freyja gave birth to Skaga, the goddess's magic has flowed through our bloodline. We all share her seiðr magic, but her power manifests differently based on our individual personalities." Her eyes shine as she asks, "Any idea what your gift is yet?"

For some reason, I'm reluctant to mention my magic-breaking ability.

Amma studies me, her gaze shrewd. She's always been able to tell when I lie, so I shake my head slowly.

Her smile turns tight-lipped. "In some, it can take longer to manifest than others. Some know from early on, but others are not so fortunate. Once you become Seer, you should be aware of your gift. We will not have to wait much longer."

Amma takes my hand in her wrinkled one, like she used to when I was little and we would walk together while she pointed things out and told me stories. Only now, I know her stories are all *real*.

I hold her hand, trying to ignore its chilling cold.

Amma brings me to the first woman waiting. "This is my mother, Gudrun. Freyja has given her the gift of foresight."

My great-grandmother.

Gudrun's eyes glow dimmer, their color more of a milky blue, but her expression is sharp and shrewd as she assesses me. I can't help but wonder what she sees when she looks at me. Can she see my future? The choices I have yet to make? I swallow hard. Whatever she sees, she looks disappointed by it. By *me*.

Amma doesn't seem to notice, though.

"Mother, this is Astrid," she says, an unmistakable note of pride in her voice.

Gudrun gives me a sharp nod. "Great-granddaughter."

There's no warmth to her voice. None at all.

"I'm surprised you have the courage to stand before us," Gudrun continues, "since you were the one who woke the Fell King."

"Mom, don't be like that." A teenage girl stands beside her. "Hi, Astrid. I'm Hilda."

"My twin," Amma says, but her voice is unusually bitter. "We even share the same gift."

My eyes go wide. "You have a sister? You never—"

"I died when we were nineteen," Hilda says. My great-aunt is practically the same age I am now. I look between her and Amma. Twins. One in her sixties, the other never turned twenty. Seeing them side by side makes me uneasy. I can't imagine what it must have been like for Amma to lose her twin.

Then again, Amma has had a lifetime to grieve her sister. Or perhaps she coped with loss like Dad did. Never wanting to talk about it, preferring to act like it never happened. Maybe grief was something Gudrun didn't allow.

Hilda smiles warmly at me. I study her, devouring every detail: loose waves of silver hair; smooth porcelain skin; the sparkle in her blue eyes. Amma must have looked like this when she was my age. But Hilda appears freshly dead, unlike Amma and Gudrun, with their sagging, rotting skin. She's barely decayed even though she died long before either of them.

"Nice to meet you," Hilda says, holding out a hand.

As I shake her hand, I notice a long scar trailing down her forearm.

Gudrun grips her shoulder. "Hilda was originally chosen to become Seer."

Amma winces like it's still a sore spot.

She mentioned that this used to be a Seer selection ceremony. I never imagined she meant for *her*. She must have gone through all this with her twin, but Hilda was chosen instead. No wonder Amma wants so badly to make a good impression now.

"She barely lasted a year," Amma says, her voice turning brittle. "I served as Seer for *decades*, far longer than most, and yet you still bring that up every chance you get, Mother." Sighing, Amma steers me away from them. "Come, there's more welcoming family for you to meet."

Amma leads me down the long line, hand in hand.

She introduces me to *her* grandmother, as well as my great-great aunts and great-great-great cousins. There is generation after generation, more family than I ever imagined I could have. Some smile at me, flashing sharp teeth. Some are old, some are young, all with varying heights and builds and demeanors.

They may be draugar, but they are family.

Growing up without Mom, this is what I longed for. As I greet my ancestors, I search for some sliver of myself in them: pert nose, high cheekbones, rounded forehead, full lips. But I find only uncanny faces, devoid of life, like wax figures staring at me with dead eyes.

"This is Sigrid." Amma stops before a middle-aged woman with long silver hair. "She must be your . . . well, very, very distant aunt, shall we say? Freyja has granted her the power of compulsion."

Sigrid nods. "Hello, girl."

As we continue down the line, their faces, names, and powers start to blur. One has a deep gash across her face, flesh split from a sword or ax. The death blow didn't stop her, though. She holds out a stiff hand to me. Another has bloated skin, as if she drowned. When she opens her mouth to speak, water gushes from her blue lips.

The more ancestors I meet, the more I start to recognize that the older the Seers were when they died, the more monstrous they look now. Some stink of decay. Their flesh sags like rancid fruit; I bet if I reached out and touched them, the skin would slide right off their bones.

Half of one's face has fallen off, exposing some of her skull. At first I assumed that the longer they'd been dead, the more the draugr decayed.

But that isn't the case with Hilda and the Seers who died young.

It must be something else.

But what? All of them made the same choice. They all chose to become the Seer in order to protect our family. Our home. Cold spreads through me along with an awful realization.

The longer they lived, the more people they sacrificed.

That's why the older Seers look so different.

When we reach the end of the line, a woman older than any other I've seen stands there. Skin waxy and wrinkled. Unblinking eyes. Glistening fangs protruding from peeling lips.

"And I am Dagny," the old woman says. "I must say, you bear a striking resemblance to my mother." Dagny steps forward, taking my hands in her rotten ones.

As soon as she touches me, a vision flashes—*I'm screaming as if going into battle, skin soaked with sweat as Torsten grips my hand, and then I'm holding a crying baby girl, covered in blood—*

"It *is* her." Dagny releases me suddenly. "Skaga has come back to us."

Not again. I shake my head, my braid swaying. "I'm not—"

"You've finally returned." Dagny's eyes shine with emotion as she searches my face. "How I have longed to see you once more, Mother."

I swallow hard. Dagny looks even older than Amma, so having her call me mother is . . . unsettling, to say the least. When she looks at me, she sees Skaga, just like Ramunder, Torsten, and even Soren once did. I know what it's like to be so desperate to see your mother, even for a moment. "I'm sorry, but—"

"My mother has been reborn," Dagny proclaims for all to hear, "just as she said she would be."

"Just as the goddess was," Amma says, sounding almost reverent.

"What?" I blink once. Twice. "What are you talking about?"

The Seers whisper among themselves.

Gudrun scoffs. "She is but a child."

"So was my mother once," Dagny says.

"*That* must be why it took another generation to finally birth a girl,"

Amma says at the same time, her excitement growing with each word. "You are Skaga reincarnated."

They're mistaken. They must be.

I shake my head. "That's impossible."

"Not impossible. Improbable, perhaps." Amma swells with pride. "But I always knew you were special, my little Asta."

My chest aches. Of course I've always wanted to hear those words—who wouldn't?—but not for this. What Skaga did doesn't deserve praise, but disgust. She's killed countless people, and so have all the Seers. I wouldn't do that. I couldn't. I won't.

"I'm *me*," I say, unable to keep the betrayal out of my voice. "You of all people know that, Amma."

"We are not individual," Amma says. "People are made up of many parts: our physical form, our mind, our life force, our fate."

"Not necessarily fate," Dagny corrects. "It is more like fortune or luck, and can be reincarnated into one's descendants. Freyja has granted me the ability to see people as they truly are, so I can read these parts separate from the whole. And you not only share her appearance, but your fate belongs to my mother as well."

Her fate. My arms shake as I back away from Dagny. Was I fated to find Soren?

Am I fated to betray him, just as Skaga did?

"You *are* her," Dagny finishes.

I don't believe it. I don't *want* to believe it.

"I'm not."

As soon as the words escape, I question their truth. As much as I hate the idea, it would explain why Skaga and I look identical. Why everyone keeps mistaking me for her. Except, if what Dagny says is true, then it wasn't a mistake. They were right.

"She is hardly the same as Skaga," Gudrun says with a scowl. "The girl may share some similarities with Skaga as you claim, but she does not possess her mind."

I latch on to her words, desperate. "That's right, I—"

"What about those flashes you've glimpsed, hmm?" Amma prompts.

"Those—those are just dreams," I say, trying to convince us both.

"Not dreams," Dagny says with a knowing smile. "Memories."

The ringing in my ears grows louder, until I can no longer hear them. Just like when I first got my diagnosis, I can't make sense of their words. I'm suddenly lightheaded. If what they're saying is true, then does my body even belong to me?

Does *anything*?

Gudrun glares as some of the other Seers gather around me.

"Skaga," they murmur, reaching out for me as if they can touch her.

As if they all want to take a piece of me for themselves. It feels like I'm being ripped apart, torn limb from limb. Not physically, but my entire sense of self. My identity.

My free will.

As their cold hands touch me, each hand bearing the same mark as mine, I realize that *this* is my inheritance. An inheritance of scars. Skaga left her mark on every one of us, on our entire lineage, shaping us in ways seen and unseen. Of all of us, she left the greatest mark on me. I always thought I'd inherited my illness from Mom, but maybe it was actually from Skaga.

Without Skaga, I would not exist.

None of us would.

Family is forever, Amma always used to say. Generations and lifetimes stretch before me. Seeing it for myself . . . awe and terror battle inside my chest. All this time, Soren was so desperate to find Skaga. But she was always inside me, someplace that can never be lost or stolen. Her heart beats behind my rib cage, her blood flows through my veins, her memories linger inside my skull. She is every part of me, ever-present, everywhere I go.

Even if I wanted to, I cannot escape her.

TWENTY-EIGHT

"It is time for you to become the next Seer," Amma says, turning toward me as my ancestors line back up. I can feel the weight of her words, of her expectations, like the waterfall pounding on my shoulders. I don't even know who I am anymore, and already Amma wants me to become something else.

I don't want to be Skaga *or* the Seer. I never asked for any of this.

"Now?" I stare down at my hands, but they no longer feel like my own. The scar across my palm looks suddenly repulsive. It hurts as much as a fresh cut.

Amma nods. "You will perform a blót."

My mind is reeling. It takes a moment to register the word: *blood sacrifice.* The river of blood running through Tiveden. The Shore of Sacrifices. The duty of a Seer. I fear this more than any monster. And *I'm* the one who is responsible for it all.

As Skaga, I've done terrible things—and I can't even remember all of them.

Now Amma is asking me to do more.

"What sacrifice?" I ask, the words falling from my lips.

She studies me. "You must sacrifice a boar, Freyja's sacred animal. By sacrificing it to the goddess, you accept the blood oath as your duty, and officially become the next Seer."

I stare at her in horror. "You want me to *kill* an animal?"

I guess I should be relieved she's not asking me to kill a person.

Yet.

An animal is still a living thing. It doesn't deserve to die. I would never want to *harm* an animal, never mind kill one. If I take a life, *any* life, it will bring me closer to the person I was in my past life. A person I'm not sure I want to become again. Amma isn't just asking me to sacrifice an animal. She's asking me to sacrifice who I am.

I back away from her. "I can't."

The Seers nearby whisper to each other, their agitation growing.

"See?" Gudrun sneers.

"It is no different from butchering an animal for its meat," Amma says more firmly. "No part will go to waste. We offer its life to the goddess, consecrate ourselves in its blood, and then you will feast on its flesh."

I swallow hard. It's not like I haven't eaten meat before, but buying meat isn't the same as butchering it yourself. I would be taking an animal's life with my own hands.

"I . . . I don't know."

"You *must*," Amma tells me, grabbing my arm. Her claws dig into my skin. "If the blood oath is not fulfilled, all of us standing before you will cease to exist. Every Seer will be completely erased, as if we never lived at all, and no one will even so much as remember us."

Her words suck the air out of my lungs. "You mean I'd forget you?"

Amma nods gravely.

So I would not only lose Amma, but all memory of her too? I stagger back. Those memories are more precious to me than anything. I've held on to them so tightly for so long, made them such a part of me, that I don't know who I would be without them.

Without *her*.

"It is what the goddess demands," Gudrun says.

Dagny adds, "We have all made this same sacrifice. Now, so must you."

I catch my lip between my teeth. If I become the Seer, I will share their fate too. Unless the blood oath is fulfilled, I will die along with Amma and the rest of the Seers.

Their gazes are all fixed on me, cold and empty. If I do this, I won't just become the Seer. I will become *Skaga*. More than that, I'll be embracing everything she was: her duties, her desires, as well as her destiny. The thought makes me sick to my stomach.

I look down the line of my ancestors, leading back to the longhouse. If I don't do this, every one of them will cease to exist, including Amma. I fought so hard to find her—I won't lose her again. No matter what choice I make, I'll lose something essential.

"Okay," I say slowly.

As soon as I do, it feels like a mistake, even though it can't be.

Amma gives an encouraging smile. "It will be over before you know it."

My unease grows as our ancestors pass a torch down the long line, until Amma accepts it. She doesn't recoil from the flames or keep a distance like Soren did from the campfire. Amma seems unafraid, almost as if she's forgotten she is no longer human.

"Careful, Amma."

"Fire is nothing to fear," Amma says. *Maybe for a goddess,* I almost point out. *Not for a draugr.* But before I can, she continues, "Freyja herself was burned thrice and thrice she was reborn."

Amma hands the torch to me. "And now we know, so was Skaga."

The flame snaps and crackles, but not even its heat can help with this bone-chilling dread. I was Skaga in my past life, but I don't *feel* like her in this one. This is brand-new to me. Without all her memories, what if I make the same choices as her?

What if I make the same mistakes?

The Seers head into the woods in a slow procession. As they pass us, torchlight carves out their faces, the harsh shadows making them resemble skulls. Even though I'm surrounded by family, Tiveden feels *less* safe now.

Shaking off any misgiving, I follow Amma. "Where are we going?"

Shadows move through the trees as I walk past, making it look as though the pines are moving around me, even though their branches bend with snow. It's unsettling, almost as if Tiveden itself is bowing before Skaga.

Amma is quiet for a long moment, the rustling pines the only sound. "Trollkyrka."

Troll's Church.

The place Skaga was left as an offering.

And the Fell King's throne.

I bite the inside of my cheek until the sharp tang of blood floods my mouth. How am I supposed to face Soren? *I've* been the one he was searching for this whole time. Not only that, but I'm the one who betrayed him. Imprisoned him. Even if I no longer remember doing it, it doesn't change the fact that I did. Or that I could still betray him again.

"Can't we do it somewhere else?" I ask.

"The mountaintop is an ancient altar," Amma says. "It's tradition for the Seer to make her first sacrifice where Skaga was left to die."

"But the Fell King will be there." I shudder. "Is that really safe?"

"I want to see for myself who sits upon his throne now."

The last time Soren and Ramunder faced each other, Soren had been badly injured. If they fought again . . . Soren might already be dead. I don't want that to happen, even though maybe I should. Soren is the Fell King. So why does the thought of him being hurt still make my chest ache?

And this ache—I can't tell who it belongs to anymore. After everything she did to Soren, why does it feel like Skaga doesn't want him harmed either? Maybe she is the reason I've felt so drawn to him. Not because of Tiveden, or Skaga's power, but because I *am* her. My heart knew him even when I didn't.

My fingers tighten around my torch. "If it's Soren, won't he try to stop—"

"We'll perform the ritual under the guise of an offering at Trollkyrka. Regardless of who sits upon the throne, the Fell King cannot refuse an offering. A stipulation Skaga added to ensure that the blood oath can always be fulfilled. So you will do the sacrifice, offering it to the Fell King while ensuring that you become the Seer at the same time. This is the only way we can be certain he won't interfere."

So not only will I have to sacrifice an animal, but I'll also have to do it in front of Soren. *You are not Skaga,* he once told me. I wanted to believe him. But now he will see me the same as he saw her: clutching a dagger, covered in sacrificial blood.

And I'll truly be no different from Skaga.

‡

A towering mountain looms over us like a great god, cloaked by damp fog. Its long shadow stretches over us, bathing me in darkness. As I stand before the mountain, a sense of déjà vu slams into me. *This* is Trollkyrka.

"Come," Amma says.

The terrain grows more treacherous as we make our way up the mountainside. My torch blazes, the hot fire illuminating the lichen-covered boulders. The backs of my legs pull as I climb Trollkyrka just as Skaga once did. Unlike then, rope doesn't rub my wrists raw, and no one leads me to the altar like an animal. This time, I will not be the sacrifice.

Even if I'll no longer be the same afterward, at least I'll return from Trollkyrka.

Hopefully.

"What will we do if Ramunder sits on the throne?" I ask, breathing hard.

"We should hope he does," Amma says. "His goals align with our own: to protect Unden. He may call himself Fell King, but he serves at Skaga's behest, just as we do."

I'm not sure I want to face Ramunder—not after what I did to him. It's almost like I did that to my own father. I've said plenty of awful things to Dad out of anger, but I can't imagine hurting him.

Then again, I might have stabbed Ramunder viciously, but I hurt Soren far worse. The sight of him is still imprinted on my mind, the way he looked at me the last time I saw him, his expression betraying his devastation. The same way he once looked at Skaga. I haven't forgotten the hate-filled promise he made to her—to *me*.

I don't know what either of them will do.

Some rocks seem to move underfoot. No, not rocks, but ancient creatures curled in slumber. Amma steps over one, ignoring it. If she can see it at all. I force myself to continue, hurrying after her. The higher we climb, the more glowing golden eyes seem to watch us from the shadowy crevices.

"Do you see them, too?" I ask, gripping my torch tighter.

"Trolls," she says simply. "They hide in caverns and crevices but have their own kingdom inside the mountain. Trollkyrka itself was once a primordial giant, turned to stone by Freyja's light."

When we reach the top, my breath hitches at the view of the moonlit forest. Tiveden stretches before me, an endless sea of trees. The Shore of Sacrifices is the only interruption, barren and broken. Up this high, it feels as though I could reach out and the moon would rest in the palm of my hand. As though I could become a god just as mighty as Freyja herself.

In the distance, I think I can see Unden and I realize just how far away Johan and Dad are from here. How impossibly farther Stockholm and Zuri are, as if the years I spent there took place in another world.

Suddenly, I've never felt so alone. Almost as alone as Skaga felt while she waited to die, abandoned by everyone she cared about. Unlike then, this is my own choice. It's the only way to protect the people I love, so why do I feel so lonely?

"Allow me to do the talking," Amma says.

I turn my attention toward Trollkyrka. My torch illuminates the jagged cliffside, sending shadows stretching over the rocks like thin, bony fingers. Somehow, this place looks even more terrifying in the flickering firelight. Heat warps my vision as I look around, recognizing the smooth and flat slab of stone before us.

An ancient altar.

The realization sends a quake of fear through me.

As I rub my arms, I can *feel* coarse ropes wrapping around me along with sheer terror. The cold chill of the stone altar as I lie there, powerless. People like Skaga, like me, were the ones that others were willing to sacrifice, as if we are nothing but burdens.

Until Skaga ensured that would never happen again. In a brutal world like that, power is the only way to protect yourself and those you love. So she took power however she could get it. Now I will be the one performing the sacrifice instead of being its victim.

So why do I still feel so weighed down by guilt?

Hidden Folk emerge from the shadows all around us.

Trolls appear first. Some have severe, stony faces to blend in with the mountainside. Others appear almost human, except for their supernatural beauty—and their antlers. A small old woman hobbles forward, her bent back covered by a cloak of moss. There are numerous huldra, too, but their complexions take on different shades of tree bark, ranging from birch white to rich brown oak, and all wear their mossy hair in varying lengths and styles.

The huldra who helped me isn't among them.

These Hidden Folk appear ancient, more ancient than Soren, as if they have always existed in Tiveden and always will. These must be the original spirits of this forest, created by the Allfather of the gods. It makes me wonder how Soren first came to wear the crown of roots, if these Folk bestowed it upon him or if he took it from them.

Swallowing hard, I glance back at Amma.

She remains perfectly still.

The other Seers step closer, circling around us protectively.

"Seize them." A low voice echoes over the stones.

Soren—or Ramunder? My gaze slowly climbs the skeletal throne. I don't know who I hope to find. Someone sits there, watching from high above where my torchlight can't reach. Moonlight silhouettes the treetops around him, glinting on loose silver hair and long bangs.

Soren.

Seeing him lifts a weight from my chest even when it should send one crashing into it. Slowly, my vision adjusts to the darkness, and my relief recedes like the tide as dread settles over me. The crown of twisted roots now rests upon his head. His features are too harsh. His mouth is too cruel. *This* is who is responsible for unleashing his army upon Unden.

For all my sleepless nights growing up. What I still don't understand is *why*.

Soren grips the sides of his throne tightly, his claws on full display. He sits on a massive creature's skeleton, its open rib cage forming the high backing of his throne. Fear prickles my skin. If Soren is here, then what happened to—

Ramunder. His corpse kneels next to the throne. He's been stripped of his armor vest, exposing a back that's been carved open. It almost looks like a huldra's, but his ribs and lungs are pulled out, spread like a pair of gruesome wings. *A blood eagle.* A ritual execution straight out of the sagas, one reserved for royalty. When Amma described it, I could never quite wrap my head around just how horrific it really was.

Until now.

My chest aches at the sight of him. I can still feel the weight of his large hand patting Skaga's head when he was pleased with her. Hear the fondness in his voice as he called her his little one. For a moment, it's as if I'm seeing *Dad* there.

I blink, and it's Ramunder again.

As I stare, his lungs inflate ever so slightly. A cold fingertip traces down my spine. Maybe I imagined it. Or maybe Ramunder is still alive. Still suffering, living in unimaginable agony. What Soren has done to Ramunder is so much worse than death.

But this isn't Soren anymore.

This is the Fell King.

Hatred for him swells in my heart. Not just Skaga's, but my own. I can't forgive him for this any more than she could. We are enemies. Maybe we always were.

"Grandfather!" Dagny cries out, rushing toward Ramunder.

Before she can reach him, a troll takes her down.

One of his huldra grabs me, her rough hands closing over my shoulders. As I struggle, she sends my knees slamming into stone. My torch falls from my fingers and rolls across the rock. The other Seers are restrained by Soren's court and forced to kneel too. The huldra grabs the back of my head, shoving my face toward the rock until I'm groveling like the rest of the Seers.

Like Ramunder.

"Wait," Amma says quickly, pushing her captor away. "We have come to make an offering to you." She stands and approaches the throne, eyeing the other creatures gathered behind Soren. "Fell King, I fear we have started off on the wrong foot. I spoke rashly to you before, in a way that's unbefitting one of your subjects. Now I wish to make amends."

Soren's mouth twitches with disdain, exposing one of his fangs. Amma kept him imprisoned, along with the rest of the Seers gathered here. He knows it too. Even though nothing she said was technically untrue, her words were carefully selected.

His attention lands on me, and he casts me a look as pointed as my dagger.

"And how will you do that?" Soren asks, but his gaze never leaves mine.

"We would like you to witness our humble offering," Amma says, "and to honor you with the first blood of the sacrifice, in recognition of your long-awaited return."

Soren's expression is hard as stone. "Do as you will," he says, but his voice is tight, clearly seeing through the thin ruse.

With a wave of his hand, the Folk release us.

A heavy weight lifts off my shoulders as I get up and grab my torch, surprised it's still burning. The Seers gather around the altar, white dresses dragging over stone. Amma slides something from a pocket concealed in her dress. The dagger. *My* dagger. She must've taken it while I bathed in the waterfall.

Amma holds my dagger between her extended palms, like the statue of Freyja held it when I first found it in the cellar. As she offers it to me, her eyes are as empty as the statue's.

"Take it."

I can feel Soren watching me, making me realize just how hot the torch is as sweat drips down my back. Reluctantly, I accept the dagger. It's heavy in my hands as Gudrun leads over a boar, coaxing it along by a coarse rope tied to its throat. I didn't notice the animal until now, but Gudrun must have led it up the mountain to be sacrificed. Just as Skaga once was.

Unlike me, the boar seems strangely calm. Probably drugged. Gudrun hands Amma the rope and takes my torch. My eyes water as the torch smoke thickens the air. Now that I'm holding the dagger, I don't know if I can do this.

Amma circles me, pushing through the smoke.

The boar looks up at me, at my dagger, as if it understands. In its dark eyes, there's a spark of fear, there and then gone. I stare back at the animal, my stomach working into knots. Before long, it will be a human face I stare into.

"I can't do this."

"You can." Amma grabs the animal by the nape of its neck, exposing its bristled throat. "You *will*."

I search the expectant faces of my ancestors gathered around me.

All of them depend on this. On *me*.

"You have already done this," Amma whispers harshly. "Do not show weakness in front of our family. Especially not before the Fell King."

Soren watches in silent judgment, utterly aloof, as if I'm a complete stranger to him. Right now, he feels like one to me. I've already made my choice. I chose my family, just like I did in the past. Now I have to live with that.

Still, I hesitate.

"I told you," Gudrun says. "She is not ready."

"She is." Amma grabs my wrist, her cold grip shockingly strong. Her claws dig into my skin as I struggle to pull free. She steers my hand closer to the animal's throat and it squeals, writhing in her grip.

"Go on," Amma urges, her voice hoarse. "Please, Astrid."

Gudrun sneers. "You have no one to blame but yourself, Ingrid. You failed to prepare her properly. *This* is why Hilda was chosen instead of you. You humiliate our family in front of the Fell King."

You are not the only one they will be judging, Amma told me. I'd never imagined her own mother would be her harshest critic. But Amma believes in me still. I can't disappoint her.

Swallowing my revulsion, I drag the blade across the animal's throat in a swift, sure stroke. Hot blood pours over my hands, thick and wet. All I can do is watch in horror as life leaves the boar's dark eyes, until only the wavering flames reflect back in them.

Oh God. *What have I done?* The dagger slips from my fingers and clatters against the stone, loud as thunder. I stare down at my trembling palms, slick with red. I killed an innocent animal.

And the next time I hold that dagger, I'll be expected to kill a human.

Amma pats my shoulder. "It's over with."

Is it, though? I feel queasy.

This is only the beginning.

My ancestors cry out, their applause echoing off the rocks and jolting me back to the present. Amma dips her fingers into the animal's fresh blood and drags it down my cheeks. The blood steams on my skin; Amma's fingers are bone-chilling. As she paints my face, all I can see is the animal lying there with unseeing eyes.

This is all *wrong. Wrong, wrong, wrong.*

When she finally finishes, I force myself to look at Soren, afraid of what I'll see. Anger. Disappointment. But it's none of those things. Instead, his eyes swim with sadness. As soon as he notices my attention, any sympathy is wiped from his face. He leans back on his throne, looking bored.

I told you, I can practically hear him say.

I never understood why it was called *performing* a sacrifice. Until now. I'm the star of this sick show. Standing before Soren, feeling more like Skaga than ever, it seems we're both stuck playing parts we don't want. Like we have been for centuries and always will be.

An endless cycle.

Amma removes a curved horn from the belt at her hip. I don't let myself look down at the boar while she catches its blood. It's bad enough that it's drying on my skin, making my face feel tight.

She hands the drinking horn to me. "Offer the first blood to him."

I take it from her and glance down at the thick blood filling the horn. In the dark liquid, my reflection stares back, but I don't recognize myself anymore. Rather, it's Skaga gazing back at me. Ripples distort our reflection as I walk toward the Fell King's throne.

"Go on," Amma urges.

I approach Soren, clasping the drinking horn tightly. "Fell King, I offer you the first blood of the sacrifice."

Soren watches me with a dark expression. When I stop, he holds out a hand and motions me closer with a condescending gesture. As if I am his to command. I suppose once I die, I will be. Gritting my teeth, I stop before his throne, the horn trembling in my hands. Not from fear, but fury.

"Then I will accept your offering," Soren says begrudgingly. "But know that I'm aware of what you have done here. So I will drink the sacrificial blood from your own hands."

The Seers gasp behind me.

I give a questioning glance over my shoulder, but Amma nods stiffly. Of course Soren can demand whatever he desires.

He is the Fell King.

It gives me a strange sense of relief as Soren takes the horn from me. Judging by the Seers' reaction, he never made this demand of Skaga. I hold my cupped palms before him in supplication. He tips the drinking horn forward, letting the blood pour from it. It travels slowly, viscous and thick like honey, a dark stream spilling into my waiting palms. There's something almost . . . sensual about it.

He tosses aside the drinking horn, sending it clattering onto the rocks. I'm focused on Soren. I can't look away.

I lift my hands toward his mouth, and he leans forward in his throne to accept my offering. As soon as his cold lips meet my skin, I gasp. The contact sends a thrill shooting through me, even though it *shouldn't*. Not now that I know who—and what—he really is. Who *I* am. He drinks long and slow, leisurely, his eyes never leaving mine.

While he drinks, I fight back thoughts of the last time I offered Soren blood—my own blood. His lips pressing against my pulse. His teeth softly sinking into my neck. Him tasting me with an insatiable hunger, barely able to pull himself away. I run my tongue slowly along my bottom lip, biting it as I watch his throat move while he drinks.

Soren grasps my hands, tipping them back so he can drink every last drop.

When he releases me, I stagger backward.

Almost mindlessly, my sticky fingers brush over the bruise on my neck. It aches still. From him. *For* him. And I know he's thinking of it too, because he lowers his gaze to my fingertips on my throat. Maybe it's just the shadows playing over his face, but his eyes seem to flicker with desire.

Hot liquid pools inside me in response. Suddenly, this dress feels too tight. Too difficult to breathe in. If I offered him my neck, I know he wouldn't refuse. I could climb onto his lap, and he would drink from me seated on his throne while all his subjects watch—

I retreat to Amma's side.

She clutches the dagger in her hand, blood dripping down the sharply angled blade. This is what I chose, even if I didn't fully understand it at the time. When I crossed the Shore of Sacrifices, I never would've imagined *I* would be performing one.

What have I become?

Or maybe this is who I've always been.

Amma lays her hand on me, heavier than it has any right to be. It weighs down my shoulders along with the legacy Skaga has left me. One I'm no longer sure I can carry. I try to pull away, but Amma tightens her hold.

"You are our Seer again at last."

⟫⟫—TWENTY-NINE—⟪⟪

*"Tonight, we feast in honor of Skaga." The pride in Amma's voice is unmis-*takable. "We celebrate her return eighteen years ago, as well as her rebirth as Seer tonight."

I barely remember the trip back to the longhouse. Since sacrificing the boar, all I've done is relive the moment. The quick slice across its throat. Hot blood pumping over me. Its legs buckling under its own weight as it collapsed. Everything about it felt so . . . familiar. I took a life, but it didn't feel like my first time, and that terrifies me.

Amma hands me a drinking horn. It's so cold in my grip it feels like holding an icicle, but flames are reflected in its polished surface. The wild boar I killed—*sacrificed*—hangs suspended over a blazing fire in the central pit.

Gripping the horn tightly, I sniff the dark liquid contents.

Amma offers a wry smile. "Yours is only mead, don't worry."

All I can see is the boar's blood. I can still feel Soren's intense blue eyes on mine as he drank from my hands. He is the only one who still seems to see *me*, not just Skaga reincarnated. Even if he hates the sight of me.

Laughter drifts through the longhouse.

This is a celebration of death. What once seemed so spacious is suffocating with all the Seers gathered here. As their undead faces glow in the orange firelight, my throat squeezes. The reason my family is celebrating is because I did something terrible.

Soon I will have to do worse.

I take a swig of mead. I don't drink much alcohol, since it can trigger my Crohn's symptoms, but I don't really have a choice right now.

This celebration is for me, after all.

Sort of.

I can't remember the last party I've been to. In Stockholm, it was hard to keep friends. They didn't understand why I kept canceling plans all the time, or refused to attend too-crowded parties, but I didn't want to tell them about my illness. Soon, they stopped inviting me.

I've certainly never been to a party like *this*. My undead ancestors gather around me like I belong here, chattering before the blazing fire about Skaga's long-awaited return.

"What I don't understand is why *now?*" one Seer asks.

"I'm sure my mother has her reasons," Dagny replies.

I don't know any more than they do. Their voices, the haunting music, and the thick trails of smoke—everything moves fast and slow at once. This feels more dream than reality. For a second, Soren stands among the crowd, but he vanishes as soon as I blink.

Instead, Gudrun approaches us, her white dress dragging over the packed dirt floor. She wears death like a fine robe. Regal, but terrifying. Her face is hard, her expression distant, like she's forgotten what it is to be alive. Or maybe it's because of her foresight. She assesses me with her milky blue pupils, clouded by cataracts.

"Seer," Gudrun says, nodding in my direction.

"Hi, great-grandmother," I offer weakly.

Amma barely smiles. "Hello, Mother."

Seeing them next to each other is unsettling. It looks like they could be sisters, not mother and daughter. Gudrun must've died around the same age as Amma, maybe a little younger, and has looked like this ever since. I can't help but wonder what their reunion was like. If Gudrun was happy to see her daughter again or was just as disappointed with her as she's acted since I met her.

Gudrun peers down her nose at me. "At Trollkyrka, I said what was necessary to goad you on. I will not apologize for it to either one of you."

You humiliate our family in front of the Fell King. No matter why she said it, Gudrun can't *lie.* She still believes everything she said about Amma being a failure. They might look similar now, but Amma is nothing like her mother.

"She is our Seer now." Amma pats my shoulder. "That is all that matters, Mother."

Amma is far more forgiving than I would be.

"Even so," Gudrun says, "her hesitation did not escape my notice. Nor did it escape the Fell King's."

Amma loops her arm through Gudrun's and leads her toward the long bench spanning the wall. "When you look forward, what do you see, Mother?" Her voice rises. "What are the Folk doing?"

Gudrun lowers herself onto the fur-draped bench. "I will look."

Sweat beads down my back, and my coarse tunic sticks to my skin. "What—"

Amma holds a finger to her lip. "Shhh."

The Seers crowd around as Gudrun inhales the smoke in the air. Her mouth drops open. She starts convulsing. With each jerking movement, she sucks in a harsh, gasping breath, in time with the beating drum.

"Creatures throughout Tiveden are drawn toward the boundary," Gudrun says in a growling, guttural voice that doesn't belong to her. "The blood oath's protection weakens, and the forest floods forth, waiting with hopes that the oath will at last be broken."

"No," I say, the word escaping before I can stop it.

Gudrun turns to me suddenly. *"You."* Her empty eyes settle on me as though she can see right through me. "You shall be the end of the Fell King."

Her words crawl over my skin, making me shudder. I don't want to hurt Soren. But then I recall how his expression darkened when I chose Amma over him. How he looked at me as though I'd driven my dagger into his chest. I already *have* hurt him. And not for the first time, either.

Maybe she is right. Maybe I will do worse still.

Gudrun exhales an impossibly long breath, smoke pouring from her mouth like fog. She blinks a few times and then sags against the wall, deflated and weak.

Amma looks overjoyed. A smile stretches across her lips and exposes her long, wet fangs.

"To Astrid," she says, raising her drinking horn.

Everyone around us lifts their own cups high. "To Skaga."

I'm still reeling. Would I really kill Soren? Am I capable of that? Their cheers are deafening, reverberating through me. Then again, before entering Tiveden, I never would've believed I was capable of killing anything. Now my dress is filthy with dried blood. Almost as filthy as I feel.

"Can she really see the future?" I ask Amma over the roaring celebration.

"She can." Amma bumps her horn against mine. The sound it makes is as hollow as my chest feels. "Her ability is similar to our sight. The further she looks, the more clouded the details. But she can see the general shape the future will take. There are limits, of course. Like our vision, she can only see so far. But she has never been mistaken. She saw your return to Unden and that we would be reunited."

Some part of me still hopes she's wrong.

Soren deceived me. He threatened me. Maybe I should want him dead. But when I first saw him sitting on his throne, all I felt was relief he was still alive. When he drank the sacrificial blood from my cupped hands, my chest was tight with breathless anticipation. I wanted him. I still do, even though I shouldn't. By caring about him, I am betraying Amma. Skaga. My family. *Everything.*

Soren is the last thing I want to think about right now.

I bring the polished bone to my lips and throw back my drink, trying to drown Gudrun's words. Mead spreads over my tongue, but I don't taste any spices or honey. I can't taste *anything*. How much longer until Tiveden takes my other senses too? The longer I remain here, the less human I become.

"I'm so proud of you, Asta. We all are."

Her words fill me with warmth despite what I did. All I've ever wanted was to make Amma proud. I gulp another mouthful of mead. Maybe it's the alcohol, but I feel strangely pleasant. A little dazed. Is this how the boar felt before it was slaughtered?

"Even Great-Grandma?" I ask.

Amma smiles, her mouth stained red. "Oh, of course she is. Pay her no mind. That's how my mother is." A long pause. "You become accustomed to it."

Maybe I can get used to Amma this way too.

But wait. That's not mead staining her mouth, is it?

Blood. That's definitely blood.

I recoil. I guess she did only specify that *mine* is mead.

"Right," I manage to get out. "Thank you."

Through the crowd, I glimpse Soren standing in one of the shadowed corners of the room. But no one else seems to notice the Fell King's presence. Only I do. Is he actually here, or is this another Tiveden hallucination?

I rise to my feet. "Be right back, Amma."

The Seers writhe and dance before the fire. It doesn't take long until I'm swallowed up by the mass of bodies. Soren stands straight ahead, staring at me as I move through the Seers toward him, bumping into cold backs and dodging sharp claws until I finally reach him.

"Soren?" I whisper.

The celebration around us is so raucous, no one is paying attention to me. His jaw tightens as we look at each other, his attention lingering on my clothes. Dressed like this and bathed in blood, I must look more like Skaga than ever.

"Astrid," he says, but his voice sounds far away.

Hearing my name on his lips sends a jolt through me. No one

responds to his voice—other than me. More than most of the Seers, Soren has all the reason in the world to see Skaga instead. But he still sees *me*.

"What are you doing here?" I ask quietly.

"I saw how you hesitated." His voice is as low as a whisper. "It is not too late to change your mind. You can still do the right thing."

"I meant *how* are you here."

"The blood oath," Soren says. "We are bound by it. We always have been. Because of that bond, I am able to reach out to you, no matter the distance. Regardless of where I physically am, I can appear before you." He hesitates. "As I visited you while I slept in your cellar."

But as I look around us, no one else has noticed him. He must be mistaken. If I'm the only one who can see him, it isn't just the blood oath that connects us.

Soren is bound to Skaga's soul—*my* soul.

"I don't want to see you," I say, trying to convince us both. "Not now, and certainly not then."

Soren takes a slow step toward me. "Do you not? You seemed relieved when you last saw me." He leans in closer, and a chill traces down my neck as he whispers, "I only want to talk, Astrid."

Soren is so close now that I'm suddenly aware of how thin this dress is, aware of every goose bump rising along my body. I'm not so sure that *talking* is all either one of us wants. Last time we were this close, he sipped the sacrificial blood from my cupped palms, his lips cold against my skin as he drank—

"You can still do what is right," Soren says, reaching for me.

My eyes widen when his fingers brush over my braid. The sensation is barely there, like a half-forgotten memory, but I'm surprised I can feel his touch through our bond at all. He trails his hand down my hair slowly, sensually, while he speaks. "I cannot stay for long. Come to me when you're ready to listen, Astrid—"

"Astrid?" Amma calls behind me at the same time.

Soren vanishes.

Whatever bond was connecting us has been severed.

I turn slowly to see Amma standing there, alongside another Seer who carries a platter with the roasted boar.

"Is everything all right?" she asks, her brow wrinkled.

Nothing feels right, but I don't know how to tell her that.

I hold up my horn instead. "Just had a little too much to drink."

"Here, eat this. It will help." Amma slices off a piece of meat with her claws and holds it out to me. "As our new Seer, you must consume the sacrificial boar."

I sit on the bench and take a bite. No salty, rich flavor. It tastes as though it's completely rotten. Even though I'm starving, I have to force myself to swallow one bite after another. The more I eat, the worse I feel.

Amma lowers herself beside me. "Feel any hint of your power, hmm?"

"What do you mean?" I ask once I finish chewing.

"The boar is sacred," Amma says, watching me eat. "Typically, if a Seer has not awakened to her gift already, she will once she enters into the blood oath."

The food lumps in my throat, nearly making me choke.

"What about you?" I ask, changing the subject. "You never told me what your gift is."

"Freyja bestowed on me her ability to take the form of a falcon."

I blink a few times. I'm either drunk or Amma just admitted she can turn into a falcon. Or maybe both. "I'm sorry, *a falcon?*"

"Only for brief periods." Amma laughs. "How else do you think I disappeared without a trace? How I made it so deep into Tiveden? I'm not as young as I once was."

I frown, staring at the dirt floor.

"Fret not," Amma says, patting my leg. "Surely you will share Skaga's power of projection."

Guilt chews at my insides. I know I should tell Amma about my magic-breaking ability, but something has been giving me pause. Now, telling her I don't have the same gift as Skaga will only disappoint her.

"Right," I lie instead. "Of course."

"I'm certain you'll receive it before Midwinter."

Midwinter is in two days. Then she expects me to *murder* someone.

We sit in uncomfortable silence.

"Is there really no other way?" I ask quietly.

At first, I think Amma didn't hear me, but then she says, "No."

"Can't we fight back?"

"We tried once," Amma says gravely. "Making the blood oath was the only way to save Unden. And that was long ago—our enemies have grown stronger while we grow weaker. We are no longer the warriors we once were."

My head feels faint, the house becoming all low sound and flickering light. As I look around, the heat of the fire distorts my family gathered on the other side of the house, their faces going out of focus.

"Who am I supposed to . . . ?"

I can't even bring myself to say the rest out loud.

Amma studies the cup clutched in her wrinkled hands. "Someone from Unden."

My breath won't come. So it will be someone I know at least in passing. Will it be Ebba, my neighbor? Old Ulf, one of our elders? Or maybe Officer Lind? Or, or—

"It will be quick and clean." She clears her raspy throat. "Painless compared to the alternative, trust me. One life will save hundreds."

Revulsion spreads through me like a slow, painful poison.

Amma murdered people with the same wrinkled hands she once used to hold mine. The hands she once painted with. But I can't even summon those memories of her anymore. Now when I think of her, her paintbrush is replaced with a dagger dragging across a throat. Instead of paint, there is only spilled blood.

I was so happy, so relieved to see her again, that I told myself it didn't matter what she'd done. But the more time I spend with her, the harder it gets to convince myself of that. Now that we're together again, I don't know if she'll ever let me leave.

Maybe I made the wrong choice after all.

Suddenly, the door to the longhouse is thrown open, slamming against the wall like a sledgehammer. Moonlight floods in around a dark silhouette in the doorway. Amma goes still as a statue.

All the Seers stop.

Everything stops.

THIRTY

A burly man stumbles into the longhouse clutching an axe. The firelight illuminates filthy brown hair matted over his face, his skin covered in scrapes and cuts. For a moment, I think Ramunder stepped out of one of Skaga's memories. Until the man looks up and his brown eyes meet mine.

My drinking horn slips from my hand. *"Dad?"*

Drenched in black blood and gore, he's almost unrecognizable. He looks like some fierce warrior lord. Nothing like my father. I shake my head. No way. Dad is back in Unden. He refused to go into Tiveden, not even to find his own mother. This must be another hallucination.

"Astrid," he says, breathing heavily.

Amma takes a slow step toward him. "Erik, my son."

This is real.

A sob escapes me. All those times I sensed someone following us, it wasn't just the forest messing with me. It was actually *him*. Dad followed me through Tiveden, despite all its dangers. He went against his beliefs and risked his own life in order to find me.

Wincing, Dad clutches his side with one hand. He's hurt. Because of me. This is all my fault. He'd better be okay. Dad is too strong, too sturdy, too stubborn for anything to ever happen to him. But then I recall what happened to Ramunder.

"Dad. *Dad.*"

He struggles to remain standing. "Come here, Astrid. Right now."

"Are you okay?" I ask, rising off the bench.

I'm about to rush over when Amma steps between us. But she isn't looking at me. She's focused on Dad. "Look at you, my son. Please, let us clean you up."

The draugar close around him, looking more menacing than helpful.

Dad swings his axe with a snarl.

"It's not safe for you here, Astrid," he says, ignoring Amma's pleas. "We have to go. Now."

Amma's expression remains placid, but her body stiffens. Tension pulls taut between them, and I'm caught in the middle of it. I don't know what to do. Again.

"Erik, please." Amma holds up her clawed hands. "Be reasonable. Let us help you."

She's right.

He won't make it far. He looks like he barely made it here.

He needs help.

"Dad, you're hurt," I start, only to stop.

He's bleeding. A lot. And this longhouse is teeming with draugar. All the song and chatter from the party earlier has completely died. Every unnatural blue eye in this place is fixed on him, unblinking.

"Amma will help you." I look over at her questioningly. "Won't you?"

"Of course," Amma says. "None of us will harm him. You have my word."

I rush over to Dad and prop him up with my shoulder. "What happened?"

He sags against me. "I found that note she left in your room, telling you to follow her. I thought it would be safe for you once she died. But as soon as I saw it, I knew where you went. I know you. And I had to find you, Astrid. I followed you through Tiveden. The fires. The markings on the trees."

My throat closes up. Whenever I heard branches snapping or sensed someone nearby, and that time I heard someone calling out to me, it was *Dad*. He's been right behind me the whole way. So close, but still out of reach. "How did you—"

"I've always been strong, stronger than most."

Surviving Tiveden by himself would require *supernatural* strength. But Skaga's blood flows through his veins, just like mine. He must be blessed by Freyja too. I glance at the dark blood covering him and his axe. Torsten's decapitated body flashes in my mind.

Was that Dad too?

"And I had help," he adds, breathing hard. "A huldra."

Like the huldra who helped me? Could it be the same—

Dad coughs, and blood splatters onto the floor.

Panic grips me. *"Dad."*

"Damn draugr got me before I beheaded him," he says through gritted teeth.

I swear under my breath. Definitely not the time or place to admit that in a longhouse full of draugar. Some of the Seers snarl, but others are still too distracted by his fresh blood on the floor. Before things can escalate, I slip his axe from his grip.

"Allow me to help," Amma says, taking his other arm.

The draugar reluctantly clear a path for us as Amma helps me guide him to one of the fur-draped benches. Dad drops with a heavy thud and slumps against the wall.

"Fetch me a cloth quickly," Amma calls out.

Gudrun already has a cloth draped over a wooden bowl.

Amma wipes Dad's face carefully. "Let's get you cleaned up, son."

Dad flinches but says nothing. That's how I know he's barely holding on. He isn't resisting Amma at all anymore. I worry my lip between my teeth. This is all because of me. Dad might be dying because he followed me.

Amma sets the cloth aside, but her eyes linger on the damp blood covering it. She clenches her jaw, then returns her focus to Dad. With one of her claws, she starts tracing a bloody stave over his injury—

Dad snaps awake, latching onto her arm.

"No." He winces. "Don't you dare."

It feels like a punch to the stomach. "Dad, please. Let her—"

"Erik, you must recover your strength," Amma says, pleading. "This is the only way."

"*No.* I want no part of your magic, not after everything it's cost this family."

Gudrun watches, a look of stern judgment on her face.

Amma presses her lips together. "If you insist on being stubborn, at least rest in the bedroom."

Dad tries to stand, but collapses.

Before he can hit the dirt floor, Amma catches him in a swift movement.

"Dad!" I cry out, a moment too late.

Amma hands him off to Gudrun. "Take him to the bedroom, Mother. He needs to recover his strength. Can I trust you to tend to him?"

"You already know I will," Gudrun snaps. "I always clean up your messes, don't I?"

Propping him up, Gudrun helps Dad through the longhouse. By the time they reach the bedroom, his feet are dragging over the dirt floor. A draugr is the one who did this to him in the first place. Can one really be trusted to take care of him? But she's his grandma. *Family.*

As soon as Gudrun disappears with Dad, the celebration resumes.

Amma turns to me. "The Fell King must be responsible."

"What do you mean?"

"It would not surprise me if this was an act of retaliation."

I stare at the bloodstained furs where my dad was moments ago. Soren wouldn't do that to me. Would he? I opened up to him about my dad and our complicated, messy relationship. How sometimes I hate Dad, but I always love him.

Then I remember what he did to Skaga's father. The grisly blood eagle. I saw what Soren looked like, seated high on his throne. The dark root crown atop his silver hair. The cold, distant look in his gaze. The indifference. The cruelty.

I keep trying to separate Soren from the Fell King, but I can't.

They are one and the same.

Just like Skaga and me.

I lean against one of the wooden posts to support myself. "I don't know. . . ."

"Who else would it be?" Amma asks, her tone impatient. "He is the Fell King. You saw him on his throne for yourself. Nothing happens in this forest without his knowing. Have you not listened to me at *all*?"

Her tone takes me aback.

I can't remember the last time Amma talked to me like that. If she ever has.

"I apologize," she says quickly. "It wasn't my intention to be short with you, Asta. I'm worried about your father, that's all."

I nod. "I am too."

If Amma is right—if Soren is responsible for this—then my great-grandmother's prophecy makes more sense. *You shall be the end of the Fell King,* she told me. I didn't believe her then, but if anything happens to Dad . . . I will make sure her prophecy comes true.

Around us, the Seers scream and dance, making my head throb.

Their celebration grows more raucous the longer it goes on.

"I think I need some air," I say, rubbing my temples. "The mead is making me a little lightheaded."

Amma offers me some furs from a bench. "Take these so you don't get a chill."

As I take the furs, all I can see is a dead animal, and I flinch. "Thanks."

"Don't stray too far," Amma adds.

"I won't."

Wrapping the fur around my shoulders, I slip through the still-partying Seers and head for the door of the longhouse Dad walked through not long ago. Outside, the cold air is sobering. There's no bench, so I sit and lean against the rotting side of the house instead. Vibrations travel through me from the noisy celebration inside, but out here, I can finally *breathe*.

Dad found me.

As I look out at the Shore of Sacrifices, I realize some quiet part of me wondered if he would be relieved I was gone. He wouldn't be reminded Mom died every time he looked at me. He wouldn't have to deal with my attitude anymore or raise his voice at me. He wouldn't have to keep making so many sacrifices for me.

Without me, I thought maybe he could be happy.

When I was little, I didn't understand why Dad was never around. I kept asking Amma why, why, *why,* until one day she lost her patience. Even though I couldn't have been much older than five or six, I'll never forget what she said. *Because he resents you for surviving when your mother didn't.*

It was one answer I'd rather not know.

Blowing out a long breath, I lower myself to the cold ground. When I left, Dad followed me into Tiveden, risking his life, risking *everything,* to find me. Exactly like I did for Amma. It's suddenly hard for me to swallow. Dad does love me after all.

Hugging my arms, I look up at the night sky.

He'd better be okay.

As my adrenaline drains away, exhaustion takes its place. I don't think I've ever felt so tired. Not just physically, but emotionally. My entire body aches like the awful, bone-deep fatigue I get during flare-ups. Sometimes it's so bad, I sleep whole days away.

Right now, I feel like I could sleep for *weeks.*

The celebration inside feels far, far away as my eyes drift shut.

Unden runs red with blood.

A giant boulder hurtles over our heads before crushing some of our warriors with a sickening crunch. Trolls that tower over even the tallest among us hold uprooted trees like spears, swinging them through the front lines. More boulders rain from the forest, decimating our forces.

All except for Father.

He sends his axe flying with enough force to behead multiple monsters. Then he grabs the first weapon he finds and runs the spear through a huldra. Moss pours from her mouth like blood. But Father does not stop. He is out for vengeance. He takes a sword next and cuts a path through the Hidden Folk.

As I watch Father fight, I understand why he is feared by so many.

He is unstoppable in his fury.

"Fiend!" Father calls.

He cuts down a troll, but Soren is the one he hunts for.

A draugr charges me.

I duck behind my shield and watch as the monster's feet still before me, stopped by the helm of awe. Then Torsten is there, beheading the draugr in a quick slice. He remains at my side, faithfully protecting me, as we follow in the wake of Father's bloodshed, killing any he missed.

I spot Soren ahead of us, and so must Father. He beheads a draugr standing between them and tosses its head at Soren's feet. Father points his sword straight at him. "I will have your head next."

Soren holds his arms out, welcoming him. "Try and take it."

Father slices his sword in an arc.

Soren feints to the left, dodging easily, and disarms him.

But Father is not finished.

Hatred has driven him wild. He tackles Soren.

My heart stops beating as I watch them struggling against each other.

Before I can stop him, Torsten thrusts his spear at Soren.

Soren grabs hold of the spear with a snarl. The handle must be made of ash wood, but he does not let go. The spear splinters and snaps in two. Soren knocks Torsten aside.

Father grabs the broken spear and drives its pointed tip into Soren's chest like a stake.

A scream climbs my throat.

But Father must have missed his heart.

Soren rises and grabs him by his throat.

"No!" I shout.

My shield drops to the ground, and I fall to my knees alongside it. Bloodshed and screams surround me. I can no longer look. So I clasp my hands together and pray to Freyja. If you can hear me, Mother, I beseech you. Help me as you always have. End this battle now, as you once ended the war between gods—

I do not know how many times I repeat the words.

I keep saying them until I can feel my mother's warmth, however faint.

Dawn breaks over the horizon, bathing the sky in gold.

It is a far cry from daylight, but it's enough to turn a troll to solid stone.

Hearing its shriek, other trolls turn and flee for the forest.

"Fall back!" Soren drops Father and tears the stake from his chest, flinging it aside as blood streams down his armor. "Retreat to Tiveden!"

Torsten grabs the stained stake, ready to defend me to the death.

Soren turns away, his cloak billowing. "This will not be the last you see of me, Skaga."

I rush over to where Father fell. He lies there, unmoving.

"Father," I cry out, shaking his shoulders.

His chest does not rise. My breathing turns frantic. I cannot lose him. I cannot.

So I grab my dagger and cut open his leather armor. I have to fight against the leather as it creases against my blade. Gritting my teeth, I manage to slice down the length of his armor and peel it back, exposing his chest. I cut him, deep enough to draw fresh blood. Onto his unmoving chest, I paint the forbidden stave that returned Liv to me—

Bright blue eyes open.

Father gasps. "What have you done, Skaga?"

"What had to be done," I tell him, tears burning. "Unden needs you. I need you."

When I look up, Soren is already gone, along with most of the Folk. Only a few are still fleeing. A draugr hurries by us, but Torsten stabs the stake through her heart before she can make it far.

I look for the horizon. The sky has turned red-gold, as if the Bright Lady is smiling upon us. Father winces. Not from injury. From the daylight. I brought him back to life, but not without a new weakness.

"They will return tonight," Liv says, shielding her eyes. "Rather than divide their forces and give us the advantage, they retreat for the time being."

"So should you," I tell her. "Return home with Father."

Liv helps him onto his feet.

Squinting, Father looks around us. "Unden needs a leader, now more than ever."

"Then I will lead them," I say, clasping his cold shoulder.

Father nods solemnly.

As he and Liv leave, I face those of us who remain. Men and women stand before me, bloody and exhausted, but they cling to their weapons. There are fewer than I hoped, but at least some survived. I may not be a warrior like them, but Gorm has taught me that even words can be wielded as weapons. I select mine carefully.

"We have made it through the first night." When I speak, my voice is as clear and loud as my purpose. "The Bright Lady has driven our enemies back, but they will return. Until then, Freyja has given us a chance to prepare ourselves for the next attack."

For the first time, I force myself to look at the battlefield Unden has become. Bodies everywhere. So much blood spilled. We have already lost far too many, and this is only the beginning. But there is no turning back. Some Hidden Folk lie among the dead as well.

Tonight has not been without its victories too, then.

"Gather our dead and injured," I say. "Bring them to my home, and I will heal as many as I can with the staves Freyja has given me. Collect their weapons as well. We need all the cold steel we can find." I throw my arm out in command, as I have seen Father do many times. "Now go! We must make the most of the Bright Lady's light while we have it."

To my surprise, they listen as if Father himself commanded them.

We all get to work searching the battlefield.

Torsten follows beside me. "Your father would be proud."

"I still feel as though I have failed him." My stomach sinks as I survey all the dead. "And everyone else here."

"If we win this war, it will be because of you and your staves, Skaga."

My throat constricts. It is because of me that we must fight at all, but I cannot bring myself to tell Torsten that. If I had not spent so much time with Soren, if Father had not discovered us so close, if I had not shared Soren's secrets . . . but I did.

Lifting my apron skirt around my ankles, I crouch down beside a shield maiden. Blood rivers down her throat, reminding me of Liv when she first died. But she has not been drained. Some I cannot bring back, but I can save her still.

So I set to work on the forbidden stave.

When I wake, I'm greeted by the northern lights. I lean against the longhouse, taking in the mesmerizing sight. Streaks of green paint the night sky, swirling and luminous like one of Amma's watercolors. It's . . . beautiful. Even more breathtaking than I remember. Since moving to Stockholm, I rarely get to see them, and never *this* bright.

Even traveling in Tiveden, I never saw them. The northern lights aren't that common here either, and normally I would've been fast asleep by now. Maybe Soren watched them while I slept. The furs Amma gave me brush my neck as I look up at the sky, and I let myself pretend that it's the soft fur collar of Soren's cloak wrapped around me instead.

Soren.

The thought of him is like a swift punch to the stomach.

He made an appearance at the party too. Unlike Dad, Soren wasn't actually *there*. It seemed like he needed to talk to me, but Amma interrupted, severing our connection before he could. Then Dad showed up. What did Soren want to tell me?

Would he really have hurt my dad?

I blow out an unsteady breath. Then again, I saw for myself what Soren did to Unden. As I lean back against the rotting longhouse, the party continues inside, but all I can hear is the screams from the attack ringing in my ears. Looking out at the Shore of Sacrifices, I can still see all the bodies littering Unden. What I saw is worse than any nightmare. It's *real*.

Ramunder, Liv, and everyone else . . . they were warriors and stood no chance.

What hope would we have now?

Everyone in Unden would die. I saw the devastation the Hidden

Folk caused. If it happens again, it will be because of me. The knowledge settles inside me like a leaden weight. If anything happens—to Johan, to Dad, to *anyone*—it will be my fault.

As the lights waver in the sky, so does my resolve. When we first arrived, Soren said there might be another way. A way no one had to die. Whether it's one person or all of Unden, I don't want to sacrifice *anyone*. Before I take a human life and do something irreversible, shouldn't I hear Soren out at least? I'm desperate for an alternative. Any alternative.

If only I could hear what he has to say . . .

When I tip my head back, the northern lights are directly above me, stretching into the sky. It looks like a portal to another dimension. Now I understand why Amma called these lights Bifröst, the bridge connecting our world to the realm of the gods.

Wait. Our connection.

If Soren can appear to me, why can't I do the same thing? I don't know how, but he said the blood oath connected us. Rubbing my thumb over the scar on my palm, I close my eyes and concentrate on Soren, on his soft silver hair and ice-chip eyes. How much I long to see him again, to get answers to all these unasked questions—

My eyes open, but I'm no longer sitting outside the longhouse.

I'm standing before Soren's throne at Trollkyrka.

The edges of my vision blur and waver like the northern lights above us. Soren reclines on his throne, looking as unhappy as he did when Amma and the Seers brought me there to become one of them.

"Soren," I say, his name sounding breathy.

He goes suddenly still, swallowing so hard his throat moves.

Soren has never felt further away from me as his eyes lift to meet mine. "Astrid."

Even his voice sounds cold and unfamiliar.

Hatred seizes me. "I will never forgive you if you hurt my dad."

"I did no such thing."

His confusion catches me off guard, and I falter. The statement is simply worded, so unlike the way Amma speaks. But he still might be leaving out some important detail, like she does. "Did you order him harmed?"

"I did not." His denial is plain. Direct. *Honest.*

"Did you even *know* he was hurt?"

Soren shakes his head.

Was that just another of her manipulations, then?

Now that I think of it, when Amma made the accusation, she phrased it in a way that only made it seem like it *could* be true. There's no way she could have known definitively. She only said it wouldn't have surprised her. And she hates the Fell King.

I approach Soren slowly.

I have to be sure.

"I saw what you did to Ramunder."

"That was the Hidden Folk, not me," Soren says. "Ramunder may have called himself Fell King, but Skaga stole my crown."

"It wasn't your crown though," I point out, recalling the story he once told Skaga while feeding her berries in Tiveden. "It belongs to the Allfather."

"Originally, yes." His mouth twists with displeasure. "But the ancient Folk *gave* me his crown and horn. After I fled to Tiveden, they recognized my power, and believed the Allfather had returned."

"Why would they want to kill Ramunder, though?" I ask.

"A stolen crown does not make a king," Soren says gravely. "The ancient Folk would not obey him. But as long as he held my bone horn, Ramunder could still command the dead, so he ordered them to hunt the Folk. The entire time I slept, Ramunder and his undead army have been terrorizing Tiveden."

"That still doesn't explain why *now*."

"When I finally returned, the ancient Folk pledged me their support. With their help, I was able to regain control from Ramunder. But the Folk are unforgiving, and their memories are long. Since he called himself Fell King for centuries, they gave him an execution reserved for royalty."

"Oh," I say, at a loss for words.

Amma never mentioned *any* of that. But she only arrived in Tiveden recently, and Ramunder has been acting as Fell King the entire time Soren was sleeping in our cellar. Maybe Amma isn't aware of what Ramunder's rule was like.

Soren grips the sides of his throne tightly. "Is that why you have come? To lay more false accusations at my feet?"

I shake my head. "You said there might be another way."

"I told you to find me when you're ready to listen. Are you?"

"I am."

He considers for a long moment. "You have already asked me three questions. I will allow you to ask three more."

There are so many questions I want to ask.

If I only get three, I'll have to choose carefully.

"Besides the blood oath, what other choice do I have?" I ask first.

I step forward, feeling his familiar pull. Maybe it's the bond between us, like an invisible string pulling me toward him. Or maybe I'm scared and desperate for any comfort I can find. Last time I stood here, making the offering to him, I was ashamed of how much I wanted him.

Now I'm ashamed of how much I still do.

"Come closer," he says as if he can read my thoughts. "And I will give you your answer."

Before I realize what I'm doing, I'm climbing the steps toward his throne. I'm not sure if this is really happening or if it's just my imagination. I stop before him, a cold thrill tracing down my spine.

"Closer," he commands.

The throne is big enough for only one person. I don't know if he thinks I won't do it, or that I will. I don't know which he is hoping for. Before I can think better of it, I lower myself onto his lap. He stiffens as if he's nervous. My own heart pounds too loud in my ears.

"Tell me," I say unsteadily.

"You could have been my queen," he says, tempting me. "Ruled Tiveden alongside me."

As I search his face, there's a hunger there. A *need*.

And it's one I share. Did he make Skaga feel this way too?

Our faces are close, barely a breath between us.

As if we both want to see who will give in.

"Perhaps you still could be," Soren continues. "If we break the blood oath together, there might be a way for you to survive." He brushes a cold hand over my cheek, and I can feel the slightest whisper of his skin against mine. The ghost of a touch. "Help me, Astrid. It is not too late yet. We can end Skaga's mistake."

My mistake.

Words catch in my throat, but I can't help myself.

I lean in to his touch.

I want to say yes. Anything to avoid becoming that version of myself. To avoid repeating all my past mistakes. I want to be different, but it might already be too late. I've done awful things in my past, and now my present as well. I will have to do worse still.

I ask my next question carefully. "What would happen to Unden if it's broken?"

"The Folk only want their forest back, free of its poison. That's all they have ever wanted."

"Stop the monsters heading toward Unden, then."

He shakes his head. "That is not my doing. As the boundary grows weaker, Tiveden tries to expel them because of the blood oath's poisoning."

"You're the Fell King," I say, bitter. "You can command them."

"My power is weakest at Midwinter."

Growing up, I always heard he was strongest then. For all I know, he could be misleading me or concealing something vital. Again. I can't trust him. Skaga never should have either.

So why does it feel like my heart is begging me to?

When I shift in his lap, Soren lets out a low noise. "Without the oath, my magic will no longer wax or wane along with it. I will be able to command the Folk again whenever and however I wish. So long as the blood oath is ended by Midwinter, I can protect Unden."

Just because he can doesn't mean he will.

"Will you?" I ask. "I saw for myself what you did in the past. *You* wanted to destroy Unden."

He still does, if Amma can be believed.

"I did, once," Soren says. "But after Skaga used the sleep thorn on me, I realized I had become no different from the humans I hated so much. I wanted to kill their kind so we could live, but so did they. As draugar, our emotions become heightened. If we aren't careful, they can become twisted. My desire to protect Tiveden turned into something destructive."

Like the Seers. I can't help but think of Amma, and how different she is now that she's a draugr. How possessive and controlling she's become. How Gudrun's judgment of Amma seems to have only grown harsher and more hateful. Or how Dagny's love for her mother is more like blind worship.

"But I have changed," Soren continues. "After my time under the sleep thorn's spell, I swore not to take another life. Which is why I wanted to avoid any encounters in Tiveden—otherwise I would be tempted to kill any who tried to harm you. It took all my restraint not to kill that huldra after she attacked you. It's also why I allowed Ramunder to leave our battle alive."

He didn't kill Torsten—or Ramunder, for that matter. Since we've been together, he hasn't killed anyone. Not even Amma or the Seers who kept him imprisoned. But even if Soren won't kill anyone, it doesn't mean the Hidden Folk won't.

I run my tongue along my lips. "I don't know how I can trust you when you never told me you were the Fell King."

"I couldn't bring myself to." He hesitates before adding, "Once you mentioned seeing me in your room, I realized it was you I saw while I slept. It was never my intention to frighten you. I was merely trying to reach Skaga. Instead, I found you."

It makes sense, knowing what I know now.

"Still, why didn't you *tell* me?" I ask, unable to hide the hurt in my voice.

"Because I didn't want you to fear me again."

I shake my head slowly. "You still should have told me."

"I know."

Like I should tell him the truth now.

I know how desperately he wanted to find Skaga. I have to tell him.

The moment stretches out—

Biting down on my lip, I trace the scar across my palm. If I acknowledge our past, we will have no future. Part of me knows these wounds have to be left alone to heal, but another part of me is afraid to let them close up. Even if I told him, what would it change?

I've already made my choice, just as Skaga did.

She and I really are the same after all.

"I can't," I tell him, shaking my head. "Not if it means destroying my family."

As much as I might want to, it's too risky to trust him. Even if he did protect Unden, I don't know whether the other Seers would survive the breaking of the blood oath. Or if I would. Amma seemed certain of the consequences, and she can't lie any more than Soren can. So why does it feel just as risky to trust my family?

Soren's gaze pierces me.

I have to close my eyes against his familiar pull. Some part of me wants to choose his side even now.

"The blood oath is the only way," I say, reciting Amma's words.

But they sound hollow, even to me.

When I open my eyes, I'm back outside the longhouse. The northern lights have disappeared, leaving the sky empty. Almost as empty as I feel. Even the temperature has changed, the air suddenly seeming colder than before. I should be relieved to be back, but I'm not.

The door creaks open and Amma joins me.

"The party is over." She looks out at the horizon, at the first hint of dawn. "Everyone will be going to sleep before the sun rises."

"I'll be right in," I tell her.

She offers a small smile. "Hurry inside before you catch a cold, Asta."

Amma retreats inside as the first sliver of sun appears.

I linger outside a little longer, not wanting to go back in yet, and watch as dawn blooms across the sky like a bruise. Tracing my scar, I can't help but feel like I've made another mistake. A deep part of my soul hurts at the thought. My nails dig into my palms as I rise. *You are different from Skaga*, Soren told me. *You are* worse.

I'm beginning to think he might be right.

THIRTY-ONE

"You've done well, Skaga," Father says, grabbing my shoulder with his clawed hand. "But you must stay here tonight. Leave the battle to us."

I look around at all the undead warriors I've raised, not just Liv and Father. I brought back as many as I could and used my blood to heal our injured. Each of my fingertips has been sliced open today. We have nearly the same number as last night.

"What do you mean?"

"We will ensure that the settlement survives," Father says, "but you must be there to lead Unden afterward. Some of us must live if Unden is to have any future."

"You must survive," Liv says. "As you have survived so much else. Promise me."

"But Mother—"

"You must be protected at all costs," Torsten says, taking their side. "You are the only one who knows the staves."

Liv and Father nod their agreement.

"Very well," I say, sighing.

They turn to leave, but I grab Torsten by his arm. "Wait, Torsten. Let me protect you."

His eyes soften. "You must protect yourself."

"Take this." I hand him my mother's shield, the one carved with the helm of awe. "This stave will make any who face you in battle freeze in terror. But you must cut them down quickly."

Torsten stares at me intently as he accepts the shield. "Of course, Skaga."

He says my name with tenderness, nothing like when Soren spoke to me last. I return his affectionate gaze. After all the cold blue eyes I have seen open today, his warm brown ones are comforting.

"Return to me alive, Torsten."

He grins. "You already know I will."

Soren's horn bellows, so loud even our longhouse trembles.

Torsten takes Father's axe and heads outside with my family.

Bloodcurdling screams reach my ears. The battle has already begun. I long to know what is happening, but my parents and Torsten are right. If we are to stand any chance at all, we will need my staves to raise our dead and replenish our numbers.

Even so, I cannot bring myself to cower here. I pace up and down the longhouse. There must be something I can do. If I must remain here all night, helpless, I will drive myself mad before dawn. I have to see what is happening. I need to know.

I nearly stumble over the fire pit.

Lignite.

I grab a large piece and set to work on carving a helm of concealment into its surface using the small tool I clean my nails with. Perhaps there is something I can do after all. With this, I can resurrect our fallen forces without endangering myself. Already, my head feels light from using so much of my blood today.

As I work, claws scratch over the roof of our longhouse. More screams pierce the air. I force myself to ignore the terrible sounds and focus on my task. My hands shake, but I keep them steady until the stave is finished.

Clutching it tightly, I race through the longhouse.

Blood seeps in under the door, turning the bottoms of my boots sticky.

Far worse awaits me outside.

Corpses everywhere. Blood runs through Unden like a river. Longhouses that took months to build have been destroyed in moments. I look around in despair, no longer knowing where to begin. Or if I can make any difference at all. I spot Gunhild, one of our strongest shield maidens. A draugr strikes her with such force, her shield shatters. Claws quickly slash open her throat.

So many are dead.

Too many. I do not know how I can bring them all back.

As I look at the chaos around me, it's hard to distinguish between our undead and the Fell King's forces. I kneel beside Gunhild, careful not to let go of the helm of concealment.

"It's okay," I tell her. "I'm here now."

But she cannot hear me. She is already dead.

Soren's horn blasts again, but it sounds distant. With my free hand, I start to draw the forbidden stave with her life's blood. Another bellow of the horn adds to my urgency. I do not know what three blasts will do.

Before I can finish, the horn resounds for a third time.

Gunhild rises back to her feet.

She looks my way as though she can see me.

My breath won't come. Has the lignite crumbled already?

She does not move, and neither do I.

Slowly, I look down to the lignite in my shaking palm.

It remains intact. I am still invisible . . . but I do not know how long the lignite will last.

All around me, more of our dead rise to their feet, their movements rigid and unnatural. Torsten and the living warriors glance around, trying to make sense of what is happening. Soren has used his horn to raise our dead himself so that I cannot bring them back to fight for Unden.

"The Fell King has claimed them!" I shout.

But Torsten cannot hear my warning.

No one can as long as I hold the helm of concealment.

Chaos erupts as our own dead attack us. Gunhild charges for Torsten, but he blocks her blow and cuts her down with a swift stroke of his axe. Now the Fell King is making us kill each other. I can barely bring myself to breathe. I'm tempted to toss aside this lignite and jump into the fight myself, but I am no warrior. If I cannot be strong, then I must be clever.

There is only one way I can end this now.

I must find Soren.

I run down the blood-soaked street, searching for Soren, but I cannot find *him in the thick of battle. If he is not here, then there is only one place he will be.*

I take off toward Tiveden.

Liv is ahead, locked in battle with a wicked huldra. She strikes with her claws, but the huldra dodges to the left as her back splits open like waiting jaws.

"Mother!" I scream.

I watch in horror as roots wrap around Liv. There's an awful snapping sound as her bones break like thin branches. Running toward her, I scream and scream until my throat is raw.

The huldra devours her until there is nothing left.

Even I cannot bring Liv back now.

Grief takes root inside of me, grabbing hold of my heart, wrapping around my lungs until I can barely breathe. I will never see Liv again. Never feel her strong arms around me, never hear her loud laughter, never tell her how much I love her again.

Suddenly frantic, I look around from one huldra to another. Soren must have sent more to kill the draugar I have created. Like Liv. Like Father. Panic grips me. I scan the battle, desperate to find Father, but everywhere I look, our warriors are cut down like trees.

By dawn, there will be no one left.

We never stood a chance.

Leaving behind the bloodshed, I race toward Tiveden. As I enter the forest, I glimpse Freyja walking ahead of me. Her hair flows like golden sunlight, dragging over the dirt. She is here to guide me. I follow her path, marking the trees as I go. Something eases inside my chest, lightening my steps. I'm not doing this alone. I never have been.

I don't slow until reaching Trollkyrka.

Freyja vanishes, but I am not afraid as I stand before the towering mountain. My ripped dress glows with bright moonlight. Slowly, I crush the rest of the lignite in my palm and offer it to the wind like ashes.

"Fell King." My throat aches, but I try again. "Soren!"

"Skaga," he says behind me.

As I turn to face him, his lips lift into a cruel grin. "You came."

I hate how much I've longed to see him again. Tears burn as I take in the sight of him, standing there in his leather armor. Disgust and desire wage war inside me. But I have come here with one singular purpose.

I must do whatever it takes to save Unden from certain destruction.

"I've come to make you an offering." I try to calm my racing heart. "I will give you what you desire above all else."

Soren strides closer, his cloak billowing behind him.

"What I desire is Unden's destruction," he says, as if he is trying to convince both of us.

His words are carefully chosen so he can still speak them without lying.

I close the space between us, bringing my face toward his until only a breath separates us.

"Is that really what you desire most?" I ask softly.

Soren brings his lips to my ear and whispers, "You do not have the slightest clue what I want."

A feeling spreads through me, as dangerous and heady as being drunk on mead. I tilt my head to the side, exposing my throat to him. "You want me."

"You repulse me," Soren says, but his eyes darken with desire. He wants me and hates me at once, just as I do him. He leans in closer, breathing in my scent like he's unable to resist.

I hate that I want him despite everything he has done.

"I offer myself to you," I say, reaching into the folds of my dress and freeing my dagger, "just as I once did that fateful day in the woods."

Soren studies the dagger in my hands. Its sharp blade glints in the moonlight.

"What do you mean?" he asks, the words barely a whisper.

Tension binds us as we stand there, facing each other in silence. As I grip the dagger, for the briefest of moments I imagine burying it into him. But I cannot bring myself to kill Soren any more than he can kill me. My love for him is lodged inside my chest.

"One day, we can be together," I say, the words carefully considered. "But first, give me this life. Give me my father's dream of Unden. Give me these two simple things, Soren, and I will give you my love. Forever."

Soren's eyes gleam. "You will become my queen?"

"I must rebuild Unden first." I grip the dagger handle. "You will not meddle with our settlement again. And we will not intrude further on your forest so long as your kind remains hidden here."

His face draws tight. "Unden deserves to be destroyed. They will not stop killing senselessly. You of all people should know that, since they were willing to let you die."

I hold my dagger to my throat. "I'll gladly give my life for them."

He reaches for me.

I back away from him. "Destroy Unden, and I will kill myself right now. Bring me back if you want, but I swear you will have only my hatred forever. I would sooner burn myself than be with you."

"Skaga." My name is a desperate plea on his lips. "Do not do this."

The dagger tip remains at my throat. "Swearing an oath is the only way we can both get what we want."

"And I am supposed to trust your word?" Soren asks.

As I swallow hard, the dagger presses into my throat.

Blood trickles down my neck.

My blood.

Removing the blade, I shake my head slowly. "I do not expect you to. I will make a blood oath so you know I do not speak falsely. If I break my word, then Freyja will strike me dead, and you will get what you want."

"I do not want your death," Soren says, his voice pained. "I never have. I have only ever wanted you, Skaga."

Soren closes the distance between us. He licks the blood off my neck, taking his time as his tongue trails up the column of my throat. A shiver of pleasure spreads through me.

It shames me how much I long to feel his teeth once more.

"Very well," Soren says, his breath cool on my skin. "But I require a sacrifice from Unden now and every nine years hereafter, so they—and you—do not forget who it is that allows them to live."

"Who will choose the sacrifice?" I ask.

"You may, so long as you bring their bodies into Tiveden. They will be *given to the forest as repayment for all the Folk your kind has killed."*

My breathing is unsteady, but I cannot refuse him.

Better one life of my choosing every nine years than for us all to be massacred tonight.

I force myself to nod. "Fine, I agree to your terms."

"Then let us make this blood oath of yours," Soren says—

Hands grab my shoulders, ripping me back to the present. I'm in the longhouse, still sitting on the hard bench I fell asleep on. Dad is kneeling in front of me.

"Astrid," he breathes.

"What's going on?" I ask, disoriented from my dream.

Bright daylight pierces through the holes in the ceiling as I look around. We're surrounded by corpses.

Draugar sleep all over the longhouse, stretched out on the benches and leaning against the rotten walls. In the light of day, there is no mistaking the fact that the Seers are dead. They are completely still, like pale mannequins painstakingly posed around the longhouse. Their chests don't rise or fall. There are no soft snores, no mumbling in their sleep, nothing.

Just complete and utter silence.

"It's going to be okay." Dad's hands are warm and steadying on my shoulders. "I'm going to get you out of here. We're going home."

Home. For the first time, I think of Stockholm instead of Unden when I hear that word. If the sun is already up, that means Midwinter is *tomorrow.* If I want to go home, this is my last chance to escape. But I'm too afraid to move with draugar sleeping on either side of me.

Who knows what will happen if I wake them?

I don't dare find out.

"I can't," I whisper.

"I know you love her, but she doesn't have your best interests at heart. She never has. You need your medicine, Astrid. I can tell you're not well just by looking at you. I'm sure your grandmother can tell too, but she won't let you leave, will she?"

His tone is surprisingly soft. Gentle. It's foreign to me. I haven't heard it since I was a little girl. Amma sleeps on the opposite bench. Unlike her, Dad recognizes me, even if I no longer can recognize myself. He still sees me as a child he can save.

"It's too late." Tears gather in my eyes. "I'm already the Seer. Unless I perform the sacrifice, I will die." I struggle to get the words out. I will have to kill someone every nine years, over and over and over again, until the day I die. Death is the only way this ends.

"I'm sorry," I add weakly. "I should've listened to you."

Dad looks devastated.

But then he shakes his head. "Don't apologize. We'll figure something out. There has to be another way."

Amma's sister found one. I can't help but recall the scar that traced down Hilda's forearm. She must have felt as trapped as I do now. She went through with the ritual, yes, but unlike Amma and so many other Seers, it seems Hilda couldn't live with what she had done. Yet even though she died, she never *escaped*.

I shake my head.

"How can we leave?" I ask, looking around us hopelessly. We're surrounded. Cold crawls through me—it's like a minefield of bodies. If we wake one of the sleeping draugar, who knows what will happen to us? "It's too dangerous."

Dad's jaw clenches. "Trust me. It's more dangerous if we stay."

"What about Unden?"

"They're complicit in this too. Let them deal with its consequences."

Something in me protests against his words. I can't tell if it's Skaga or me.

I chew my lip. "I don't know. . . ."

"You haven't even graduated high school yet," Dad says. "They aren't your responsibility. You're still just a child."

He's right. I never asked for this. I don't want to be Skaga's reincarnation, or to have to bear the responsibility for so many lives. I should be back in Stockholm, worrying about my grades and my health, not blood oaths and human sacrifices. Even a boring life seems so much better than *this*.

"The blood oath has already cost our family enough," Dad says insistently. "I'm not leaving here without you."

It's already too late for me. But if I'm going to die either way . . . this could be my only chance to die as Astrid rather than Skaga. Not like I can tell Dad that, though. But I can go along with him, even as something in me struggles with the thought.

I nod. "Okay."

"Do you know what happened to my axe?" he asks, glancing over his shoulder.

I shake my head. I remember taking it from him, but I can't recall what happened after that.

"It's fine. We'll deal with it. Right now, we need to go."

I rise slowly, but the bench creaks like a gunshot in the silence. I stare down at the draugr closest to me on the bench, expecting to see piercing blue eyes gazing at me.

The draugr doesn't stir.

We move quietly through the longhouse, dodging draugar sprawled on the dirt floor. My heart pounds so loud, I'm afraid it will wake them. We're almost to the door, when—

"Where do you think you're going?"

Amma. I go stone-still.

No one will ever take you from me again, she said. Amma already blames Dad for taking me away once. I don't know what she'll do if she realizes he was about to do it again. Or that this time, I *want* to leave her.

My mouth opens, but no words will come.

"I'm taking my daughter home," Dad says.

"Oh, Erik," Amma says. "You are in no condition to go anywhere. You must rest, my son." Each word is chosen carefully. She sounds exactly the same as she did when she stood before Soren and twisted her intentions into truthful words.

Dad's body goes rigid with tension. "Astrid, go. *Run.*"

But I can't.

All the draugar in the longhouse are wide awake now. The nape of my neck prickles as I look around at their bright eyes. They're all watching me. Waiting for me to make a move.

"If you leave now," Amma says, "you know what will happen."

Her voice is as sharp as her fangs.

My feet remain rooted as the Seers surround us.

I slowly turn to face Amma. "Is that a threat?"

"It's a warning." She looks at me as if I'd struck her. "You cannot escape this, *Seer*. If you do not fulfill the blood oath tomorrow night, it will not matter where you run. Stockholm will not be far enough."

I search her face. "Better to die before I become like *you*."

"Make no mistake," Amma says. "The casualties of your cowardice will be far greater than our lives. Once freed, the Hidden Folk will not stop with Unden, either. Stockholm will not be safe. *Nowhere* in this world will be."

Her words suck the air out of the longhouse.

Zuri and her family. They were always so kind and welcoming to me. They had nothing to do with Unden or its history; they shouldn't have to suffer the consequences. Breaking the blood oath could result in so many more dying than I even realized.

We never should've left Stockholm. I can see what my future there is supposed to be: riding my moped through the streets, decorating my dorm room at university, going out to parties with Zuri and maybe even meeting some new friends, graduating with a journalism degree and an armful of flowers from the proudest dad in the world.

Happy—I could actually be *happy* if I let myself be.

But that future feels impossibly out of reach now.

Maybe it always was. I look over to Dad as two draugar take him by the arms. He struggles against them, but it's no use. He can't break their hold any more than I can break Skaga's. Ever since we left, I've felt pulled back to Unden. Now I understand why. Skaga and I not only share a soul—we share the same fate, just as Dagny said.

I was always going to end up here.

The draugar are too strong for Dad. Without his axe, he doesn't stand a chance.

Neither of us do.

"Oh, Astrid." Amma looks down, studying her claws. "The blood oath must not be broken. You *know* this. Do you really want to unleash the Fell King and his monsters upon us? What about Erik? You saw what one draugr did to your father. Imagine what many could do." She pauses, letting her words sink in. "Or I suppose you don't need to imagine, do you?"

Because I already *have* seen it. Boulders whistling through the air, houses splintering apart, streets running red with blood. I glance over at Dad, bloody, barely holding on, caught between creatures that could rip him apart in seconds—

No. Amma might be talking about Soren, about his army of the undead, but all I can imagine is what *she* is capable of. What the Seers will do to Dad if I try to leave. It's a threat disguised as concern.

"Don't trust a word that comes out of her mouth," Dad says desperately. "She warns of terrible consequences, but she can't tell belief apart from fact anymore. Time distorts things. And so does she."

Dad is right. Of course he's right.

Amma may not be able to lie anymore, but she can still deceive. She withholds information. She manipulates words. She twists meanings. And she always has. Dad knows his mother better than I ever did. I just realized it too late. Can I really trust anything she says?

No one will ever take you from me again. Amma meant that.

All I know is I can't let anything happen to Dad.

"Okay." My limbs are heavy, hard to lift, as I rub a shaking hand over my mouth, unable to believe what I'm about to say. "Okay, let's say I was willing to do it." My throat closes up, but I force myself to continue. "Can Dad and I return home afterward? If Stockholm is too far, we can stay in Unden."

"Of course you can," Amma says with a smile.

I don't have a choice, do I?

Maybe I never did. Or maybe I already gave it up.

"Then I'll do it," I say, even though the words make me sick.

"No." Dad looks panicked. "Don't do this."

"I can't just let everyone die!"

I can't let *him* die. Doesn't he understand that? After all our fights, after all the awful things I've said to him, he still went into Tiveden to save me. Now I have to do this to save him.

Dad shakes his head. "You don't want to become anything like her, Astrid. Believe me."

I look at Amma and the rest of the Seers surrounding us.

He's right. I don't want to become like them.

But I already am. They are like this because of *me*.

"Erik, I'm afraid you're exhausted," Amma says before he can add anything else. She motions to the two draugar holding him. "Take him to get some rest." She turns to me. "You too, Astrid. Tomorrow is an important day for us all."

My stomach sinks as I watch them drag Dad into the back of the longhouse. He'll be safe as long as I remain with Amma. As long as I obey her. I force myself to swallow. Even if she wants me to kill someone tomorrow night. Skaga only made the blood oath because she was desperate to save her home and her family.

If it meant protecting Dad, would I be capable of killing?

Maybe. Admitting it scares me more than anything else. Because of the unspoken truth hiding behind it. The answer I already know, the one buried deep down inside me: *yes.*

I would do terrible things to protect those I love.

I'm not so different from Skaga after all.

THIRTY-TWO

"Who do you choose, Skaga?" Torsten asks slowly.

I search the faces of those who survived the attack on Unden. Torsten, my father, and a handful of his men and women are still standing, along with Gorm and few of his followers. I curl my hand into a fist, blood dripping from the fresh cut across my palm for the blood oath. Now, like one of the Valkyries, it is I who chooses the slain.

"The time has come for you to go to the gods, Gorm."

When he hears his own words repeated back to him, he gives a nervous laugh. "You have not lost your sense of humor, I see."

I offer him a gracious smile. "You do Unden a great favor. We will all be in your debt." I cannot help my satisfaction as I add, "Will you go willingly, or must I force you?"

Gorm looks around, his gaze flicking from face to face. "She should be the sacrifice!"

No one offers him help now.

"Do not forget, I am the keeper of the blood oath. Only I can perform the sacrifices now. The goddess herself spared me. Do you dare go against the gods?"

"You lie," Gorm spits.

Torsten lifts his axe, ready to defend me, but I raise my hand.

"I stand before you, still breathing, do I not?" I ask Gorm. "You experienced yourself the power my mother gave me. You even saw me start her divine fire. What further proof do you require from the gods?"

Gorm licks his lips like he does whenever he struggles to find words.

He knows this is an argument he cannot win. He has no proof of my lies, while my life is all I need to prove my claim.

"So I ask again," I say, my smile spreading. "Will you go willingly, or must I force you?"

Gorm grinds his teeth together. "I will go."

His leather armor is bloody from battle and twin axes hang on his back. No doubt he intends to kill me first. He can try.

"Torsten, strip him of his weapons."

Gorm grimaces but hands his axes over to Torsten. "How will I protect myself?"

"You will be safe so long as you walk with me," I tell him, trusting that Soren cannot break his oath any more than I can mine. "The Bright Lady protects us now."

Each survivor takes a torch.

I lead them toward Tiveden, until we reach the forest's edge. Where Soren and I always met in secret. This spot will do. It seems fitting to make my first sacrifice to him here. I will offer him blood where I once gave him my heart.

The survivors gather around.

"Bind his wrists and feet with rope," I say, my voice as unwavering as their torches. "And hang him upside down from that tree."

Torsten obeys at once.

Gorm tries to flee, but he is no match for Torsten.

Before long, he hangs suspended upside down before me. Gorm twists and writhes, struggling to free himself from the ropes, but he cannot. Now he knows a fraction of how I felt, how every one of those he sent to die at Trollkyrka felt. It gladdens me.

Gripping my dagger tightly, I take my time as I approach.

"Why are the most vulnerable always the first to be sacrificed? Shouldn't we have been the ones most protected?" I ask even though he cannot answer.

Even if he could, no answer would satisfy me. Only his death will. Gorm glares at me. He should suffer for as long as I did while waiting to die. He should suffer as he made every one of his own sacrifices suffer.

I lean forward and whisper into his ear. "Farewell, Gorm. I hope you do not suffer too long."

He once said much the same to me before leaving me to die.

But unlike him, I mean my words.

"Til níu ára ok friðar." I say the words to fulfill the blood oath, as I told Soren I would. For nine years and peace.

With a swift movement, I slice Gorm's throat with my dagger.

Blood spills, dripping over his upside-down face. As I watch the life leave his eyes, it feels as if my entire world has turned upside down. Now that I have taken a life, I swear I will kill only those who endanger our settlement, not those who need its help.

I will lead Unden not with terror, but with hope.

"Bring the bowl," I tell Torsten.

He carries the large wooden bowl Liv once held at our wedding and sets it down at my feet. He remains kneeling, looking up at me reverently as Gorm's blood spills steadily into the bowl. None shall ever make the mistake of harming me again. As I wipe my dagger off on my hands and paint my face with his blood, I have never felt so powerful. If I cannot have love in this lifetime, I will accept this in its stead.

Once the bowl is full, I raise it in my arms.

"Freyja, I offer you this hlaut," I say. "With this sacrificial blood, may you protect Unden and all of us. May the forest and the Hidden Folk both be fed by this offering for the next nine years."

I tip the bowl forward, letting the blood spill into the soil.

The blood oath is fulfilled.

But the bowl does not empty, no matter how much I spill. More and more blood pours forth, until it runs like a river into Tiveden. It is impossible and yet I watch as it happens.

"See for yourselves," I say, trembling with awe. "The goddess accepts my offering. Nine years from now, a stave church shall stand here in Freyja's honor, and there I will perform the next sacrifice. So long as I lead you, Unden will be safe."

Torsten and the fighters strong enough to have survived the siege fall to their knees, as if Freyja herself stands before them. "Formaðr," they whisper.

Chieftain. Leader.

Foremother.

When I wake, the longhouse is empty. I don't see Amma anywhere. The last time I did, she told me I needed to rest, and draped a fur over me while I lay on this bench. I sit up slowly, blinking a few times. I don't even remember falling asleep.

But I can still hear the whispers from my dream, however faint. I can still feel the weight of Skaga's dagger as she slit Gorm's throat without remorse. As I stare down at my hands, they are covered with red, exposing the cracks in my palms. I'm already a murderer. As soon as I blink, the blood disappears, but I'm still shaking.

I don't know how Skaga lived with what she'd done.

Or how I'm supposed to.

Gorm's death was the first of many. Wind rakes over the house and whistles between the walls, sounding like the wailing cries of all those Skaga killed. Darkness blankets the smoke-stained house, smothering every corner in shadows, except for the sickly green glow of the fungus on the walls. How many more died because of what she started? After so many centuries, her victims could probably fill this entire longhouse.

After the ritual at Midwinter, I will add yet another.

What time is it? With no windows, it's hard to tell anymore. I peek out from the small sliver of space between the slats—sudden brightness stabs my eyes like knives. Either I haven't slept long, or I lost a whole day.

I yank away, only to bump into something. My heart stops as I turn and come face-to-face with Amma. Her corpse-pale skin stands out in the darkness. Her cold, hungry gaze is fixed on me.

"Where is everyone?" I ask, looking around the seemingly empty house.

Amma stares at me. "They're already at the stave church, preparing for the ritual tonight."

Tonight. Midwinter is already here.

"Won't the boundary stop them?" I ask.

"Freyja grants us passage every Midwinter, so we can assist with the ritual and ensure its success. Since we intend Unden no harm, we are able to pass through while the boundary is at its weakest."

I glance toward the bedroom. "What about Dad?"

"Sleeping," she says.

Good. At least he's safe. "Can I see him before we go?"

Amma shakes her head. "We must get you ready for the ritual."

"Already? I thought I'd have longer to prepare or . . . I don't know. Something."

Bile burns the back of my throat, and I feel ready to throw up. I don't know if there's anything that *can* prepare me. Especially after what I saw in my dream. My memory.

"You were *supposed* to." Amma moves through the house like a ghost, her linen dress bright as bones. "Normally, the Seer is trained for this moment over nine years. But before I could begin your training, Erik stole you. Time is a luxury we no longer have. The sacrifice must be made tonight, and you will wear this to the ritual."

With a clawed hand, she lifts one of the bench seats and removes a fresh dress, identical to those the other Seers wear. "This dress is designed especially for us. It even has a concealed pocket to carry the dagger."

I stare down at the blood-crusted dress I still have on from last night. Amma wouldn't let me change out of it afterward. *The blood of your sacrifice is sacred.* Now I strip quickly, unable to get out of it fast enough, but Amma takes the stained dress from me and carefully folds it before tucking it away like a treasure.

As I'm pulling on the clean dress, my elbow gets stuck. Amma helps me maneuver through it, the coarse linen scratching my face as I struggle. For the briefest moment, I'm a little girl again, stuck in one of my sweaters, and Amma is helping me prepare for school.

Then her cold fingers tug the dress down.

Linen gives way to reveal her monstrous face. Her thick, waxy skin, drained of life. Her unblinking eyes staring at me. Looking at her is like peering into a casket and seeing the cold, stiff body of someone you loved. They look *wrong*. It's them, only it isn't. Something vital is missing.

This is no longer Amma.

I stagger back like I've been punched. I wanted to find her so badly. But this isn't her. No matter what I do, she will never be the same. It's like I'm losing Amma all over again.

She frowns, reaching a clawed hand toward my face.

I can't help but recoil.

Amma grabs hold of my braid. "We need to do something about this," she says, seating herself on the wooden bench.

I kneel on the dirt floor automatically. She undoes my braid like she always used to, but now her fingers are cold as icicles, making me wince as she pulls at my scalp.

"What's the matter, Asta?" Amma asks.

You. But I can't say that.

"I don't know." The closer the ritual draws, the less certain I feel. Hugging my arms, I admit, "I don't know if I can do this."

"Of course you can," Amma says softly. "You have already done this many times."

I think she means to comfort me, but her words make me feel like I'm going to throw up all over the dirt floor. All I can think of is the hot spray of Gorm's blood splattering my face. The light slowly leaving his eyes as he stared into mine. Nothing about it is comforting.

Thankfully, Amma unbraids my hair quickly.

My blond hair spills down my back, unused to freedom. With my hair loose, it softens me somehow, makes my face seem rounder, my features less threatening. I hate it.

Amma takes a bone comb and starts to brush out my hair.

"You should wed soon," she says, combing my strands slowly. "It's your duty now to continue our line and bear a daughter who will become the Seer after you. Perhaps eventually, you will return again, just as Freyja was reborn thrice."

My mouth drops open. *"What?"*

I've never wanted to have children. My doctor started me on birth control as soon as I was fifteen, saying that if I became pregnant, it would be high risk. I'd have to stop my medications. I could die after giving birth, just like Mom did. I wouldn't want to give a child the guilt I've had to carry.

"Who would I even marry?" I ask.

"Why, Johan, of course."

It isn't his face that comes to mind. Soren's does.

Just like the reflection Skaga glimpsed in the lake as she wed Torsten.

"I told you, he's my friend."

"Your Afi was my friend too. Who better to spend the rest of your life with than a best friend?" Amma says with bittersweet longing even though my grandpa died long before I was born. "Once you marry Johan, you will see. You will come to love him as much as I loved your Afi."

Amma already has my future planned for me. She didn't even bother to ask what *I* want. Suddenly, I recall that line from her letter: *For so long, I begged Freyja to give me a daughter.* As soon as I was born, I became the daughter Amma had always hoped for. She must have been ashamed she only had a son. Maybe that's why her own mother is so cold to her.

I don't know what to say, so I say nothing.

"You remind me so much of myself at your age," she continues. "I still remember how nervous I was before my first sacrifice."

The way she talks about it seems almost . . . fond.

But she's wrong. I'm not nervous.

I'm fucking terrified.

The comb pulling through my hair fills the growing silence between us. "This is tradition. It is not easy, but if it was, then it would be no sacrifice. It is a burden we must bear to protect Unden."

Even knowing what she is, part of me wants to believe Amma. This is the only way. She had no choice. She was doing it for the greater good. I try to convince myself of that while she brushes out my hair. Amma didn't choose this. Skaga—no, *I*—did.

The comb catches on some tangled strands, making me wince.

"Stubborn thing," Amma mutters to herself.

I grit my teeth as she tugs harder, pulling at my scalp painfully.

Some of my hair rips out, and I suck in a sharp breath. *"Ow."*

Abruptly, she stops. "Sorry. I forget my own strength sometimes."

Glancing over my shoulder, I notice red blood staining the white comb. *My* blood. Amma stares down at it, as still as a statue. She must not notice I'm looking, because she slowly brings the comb up, her hand shaking like she's trying to stop herself. But she can't. As soon as the comb reaches her lips, Amma starts to lick my blood from the comb's teeth. Her eyes flutter and roll back.

What the fuck. I look away quickly, staring across the longhouse, fighting back tears.

Amma resumes her task without a word. She portions out my hair, gripping the strands tightly, as if she hadn't just licked my blood off the comb.

My lip curls with disgust.

"Do you ever . . . regret it?" I can't help but ask.

"Sometimes, perhaps." Amma clears her throat. "But with one life, you will save hundreds. Regret never lasts long once you leave the church and look out at all the grateful faces of everyone who will survive thanks to you."

She continues to talk, but I don't hear her over my pounding heart.

When I returned, everyone kept staring at me. I assumed it was because I had become an outsider. But what if it wasn't out of judgment, but . . . *hope?* After Amma disappeared, I was the only one who could become the Seer and perform the ritual. Without me, they would all die.

Unden would cease to exist.

That would mean everyone in Unden knows about the sacrifice. Am I the only one who *didn't?* Even thinking about it, my head hurts. I try to focus on Amma's cold fingers in my hair as she braids it carefully.

When she finishes, she drapes fur over my shoulders and turns me around until I'm facing her. Then she piles the braid on top of my head, wrapping it around like a crown. The weight of it feels almost as heavy as her expectations, and everyone else's. She sets something cold and smooth against my forehead.

After freeing some strands to frame my face, she steps back.

"You're ready," she says.

But I'm not. I'm not.

Amma removes the sheathed dagger from her pocket and holds it out to me like an offering.

My arms shake as I accept it. Not wanting to look at the dagger for long, I quickly slip it into my dress pocket, out of sight.

"You were born for this," Amma says, taking my hand in hers. Using her claw, she nicks my skin until blood wells and her eyes darken with hunger. "This is the blood of the first Seer. It flows through your veins the same as mine. But only you carry the miracle of Skaga's soul." Amma dips a fingertip into that blood. Rather than taste it, she drags it down my cheeks and chin. "Freyja will walk with you. The goddess will lend you her strength."

Amma guides me toward a polished metal mirror on the wall. I don't recognize the reflection staring back at me. The thick fur wrapped around my shoulders. The bright red blood marking my cheekbones and chin. The crown of braids piled atop my head, and a small bird skull nestled above my hairline like a jewel. Now Soren and I both wear the dead as symbols of our reigns.

I look fierce. Powerful. Like a vengeful goddess.

Like Freyja herself.

THIRTY-THREE

"Wait." Amma stops me as I leave the longhouse. *"You need this."*

She takes my hand and drops a smooth, polished stone in it. A stave is painted on it with dark blood—eight long arms radiate out from a central point, each one terminating in a different assortment of lines and symbols.

"What is it?" I ask.

"A vegvísir. Once you give this your blood, so long as you carry it, you will never lose your way before reaching your destination." She smiles. "We cannot have you getting lost again."

Wayfinder. I stare down at the cold stone sitting in my palm.

No, not a stone. Polished bone.

"You'd better take it, then." I hold it back out to her, feeling even guiltier. I still haven't told Amma about my power, but as soon as the stave doesn't work when I add my blood, she'll realize it anyway. I force myself to push through my lingering unease. "It won't be of any use for me."

Her brow furrows. "Why wouldn't it?"

"I can break magic," I say. "That's my ability, not projection. Because of that, my blood doesn't work on staves."

Now it's Amma's turn to look shocked. "Are you certain?"

I nod. "I've done it a few times."

"Why would Freyja grant you such a peculiar gift?"

I shake my head. I can't make sense of it either.

Amma quickly recovers. "Perhaps that's how you awakened the Fell King from the sleep thorn's spell."

"I just picked up the stave that was on him."

She taps her chin. "Skaga was one of the most powerful spákona who ever lived. Her skill with staves was unmatched. Even if you removed the sleep thorn, I don't think that would be enough. *You* must have broken her spell."

"Oh."

"It's no matter." Her claws brush my palm as she takes the stave back. "I will show you the path forward as I always have. Trust me."

Trust her? A cacophony of voices whisper from the Shore of Sacrifices.

"The journey back is always shorter," Amma continues as though she can't hear the whispers. "You will see, we'll reach the church before you know it."

I'm not sure I *want* to. The sooner we reach the church, the sooner I become like Amma. The sooner I become another monster once I die. My throat closes up at the thought. Only Skaga has escaped that fate so far. Maybe I can too.

If I can't, I know what awaits me.

We will be together forever, like Amma wants.

As we make our way across the Shore, every muscle in my body screams for me to stop. I have to force one foot in front of the other. With each step, I tell myself this is the only way. I tell myself I don't have a choice. I tell myself this is for the greater good.

Amma offers me her clawed hand.

I hesitate a moment before taking her cold hand in mine.

It shouldn't offer me any comfort, but it does.

‡

Once the sun sinks below the trees, monsters move through the forest all around us. Amma and I aren't the only ones making our way toward Unden. A half moon rises in the dark sky, ringed by murky light, revealing countless creatures heading toward the stave church.

The Hidden Folk are being drawn toward the boundary just like Gudrun saw in her vision. Hopefully it will hold until I can perform the sacrifice. They cannot be allowed to reach Unden. I've already seen what they would do: rush through the streets like a river, slaughtering all they encounter, until the entire village is destroyed.

But these monsters lack the urgency of my memories. They wander in a trancelike state, their movements jerky and unnatural. We walk through the woods almost as if Amma holds a helm of concealment instead of the wayfinder stave.

"Why don't they attack us?" I ask her.

"They cannot harm you," Amma says, the words full of pride. "Becoming the Seer is akin to becoming the queen of Tiveden."

Soren said he wanted to make Skaga his queen. It seems like that was part of the blood oath they swore to each other. I don't know all the specifics of it, not since the memory was interrupted. As we walk through the woods, I rack my brain, trying to recall its terms. The oath feels right there on the tip of my tongue, but I'm unable to articulate it.

Amma stops before a hollow tree. "Through here."

"Are you sure?" I peer inside the doorway-like entrance. This must be another huldra's tree similar to the one Soren and I passed through when the kattakyn chased us.

"The stave led us here." She nods, holding out the vegvísir in her clawed hand. "This tree will take us to the church."

"Okay," I say.

I step into the tree, and Amma joins me a moment later.

When we climb out, I feel suddenly sick.

The stave church looms on the horizon.

Wooden effigies blaze throughout the village. Dark shapes are gathered on the safe side of the church. All of Unden is waiting for us. For Skaga.

For me.

This is actually happening.

I'm going to *kill* someone.

Not in my past life. *Now.*

When Amma sees the crowd gathered outside, she pulls an ancient headdress on, its long strips of fringe covering the top half of her face.

With her unnatural blue eyes concealed, she almost looks human again. Almost.

"You're coming with me, aren't you?" I ask, panic rising.

"Don't worry." Amma gives my hand a gentle squeeze. "I will remain right beside you. And so will the goddess."

My neck aches as I force myself to nod.

Bonfires bathe Unden in a fiery glow, the same ones we saw being built when we first arrived. The villagers all hold torches, illuminating the path to the stave church and sending shadows stretching over the building like thin, bony fingers. All those years I spent wondering about Midwinter's festivities, and now I will finally be part of them. Not just taking part, but *leading*. Of course, it turns out that those festivities aren't as "festive" as I'd once imagined.

As Amma escorts me, I scan the trees, hoping to see Soren before I do something I can never take back.

He isn't here.

My long white dress drags through the snow as I walk toward the stave church. The fur mantle weighs on my shoulders, reminding me of all the lives depending on this. On me.

"They're waiting for you," Amma says.

Everyone from Unden lines the path, faces lit with hot torchlight. They've all traded their regular clothes for matching coarse linen tunics. I barely recognize them. Then again, I no longer recognize myself. Each step I take is an echo of Skaga's.

Something inside me protests, but I'm urged on by the deep, guttural chants filling my ears. As I walk by, everyone stares at me. Flames are reflected in their dark eyes, along with something unfamiliar. *Hope.* They reach out for my arms, grabbing at my scarred hand, desperate to touch me. Their savior. Their Seer.

The vessel for their goddess.

Old Ulf beats a stretched drum in rhythm with my pounding heart like it's loud enough for him to hear. It probably is—it certainly feels ready to burst free of my rib cage. A familiar face stands beside him, clutching a torch. *Johan.* He's a part of this too.

Of course he is. He's spent his whole life in Unden. Linnea is singing alongside her girlfriend, and Nils towers over the crowd. If Dad hadn't taken me away, maybe this would seem normal to me, too. Maybe it would make this easier.

Officer Lind nods to me. "Astrid, I'm glad you came back. You're doing the right thing." Ever since he left that voicemail on our machine saying Amma had disappeared, his voice has been burned into my memory. *This is Officer Lind from Unden. . . .*

Something snaps into place, seeing him standing here. Why Amma was declared dead so fast before her body could be found. Why Officer Lind insisted Dad return to handle the paperwork. It wasn't some cover-up.

It was to get me.

That was why Dad didn't want to come back and put it off for so long. But *I* insisted. He only relented because I said I would never forgive him if he didn't. Bile burns the back of my throat. I have to look away, focusing on the dark church ahead, and the terrible choice waiting for me within those walls: hundreds of lives to spare one—or one life to save hundreds.

The doors part before me with a heavy groan, as if guided open by Freyja's invisible hands, beckoning me inside. Rows of pews disappear into the darkness, the torchlight only reaching so far into the church. I'm sure the other Seers lurk in the shadows, hidden from sight.

As I step inside, the sharp smell of pinewood stings my nose.

The wooden floor creaks underfoot like a gunshot, making me shudder. Amma is right behind me.

The doors start to close after us, pushed by two draugar. The people of Unden remain outside, their hopeful faces disappearing as the doors slam shut with a sense of finality. Gudrun drops a large beam across them, sealing us inside.

No turning back now.

"Is barring the doors really necessary?" I ask. Something about it seems sinister. Desperate, even. No one had to bar Skaga inside for her sacrifices.

Amma inclines her head. "Only we can be present for the ritual, to ensure nothing goes awry. The rest will wait outside until we give word that the blood oath has been fulfilled."

A weighted silence settles inside the church. None of this feels real as I move down the dark rows and approach the altar surrounded by candles. The carved goddess stares down at me. Candlelight flickers around her, sending long shadows moving over the elaborate woodwork.

Swallowing, I look up. My gaze climbs the twisted tendrils snaking up the tall wooden beams. Something hangs above the altar from the highest reaches of the ceiling, where the light doesn't quite reach—

A man.

Strung from the rafters above, upside down like a pig.

Just as Gorm was. I shake with fear. Despite the frigid cold, his shirt has been removed. His hands are tightly bound together, and a sack cloth covers his head. A large wooden bowl wrapped in runes waits on the floor below.

To catch his blood, I realize, sick to my stomach.

No, I already know. It's the same bowl Liv once held at Skaga's wedding—and Torsten placed underneath Skaga's first sacrifice. The bowl from which the river of blood first flowed.

And suddenly, this is very, very real.

"One life to save hundreds," Amma says.

My pulse pounds in my ears. An awful sense of déjà vu seizes me, as though I've stood here many times before. I can still smell the coppery stench of Gorm's blood. Hear his muffled screams. See his split-open flesh.

Go! my every instinct screams. *Get out now.*

But then I think of Dad sleeping back in the longhouse, recovering from his injuries. I think of Johan standing outside, along with everyone else from Unden. I know I cannot let what Skaga witnessed happen to them too.

One life to save hundreds.

With a shaking breath, I reach into my dress pocket and slide the dagger from its sheath. It's surprisingly heavy in my hand. Roots are etched into its handle, scratching my skin. Outside the church, the village's voices rise like a flock of birds taking flight.

Amma grips my shoulder. "Are you ready, Seer?"

No! I'm not, I'm not, I'm—

"Yes." I have to force the word out.

Amma nods and approaches the man hanging upside down before us. She grabs a fistful of the cloth sack and rips it off, revealing the sacrifice's face.

Dad.

⇒—THIRTY-FOUR—⇐

My knees give out, but Amma catches me by the elbow.

I stare at Dad, stunned. Blood has rushed to his face, turning it bright red, while he hangs upside down before me. He's shouting—or trying to. A thick rope gags him, tied so tight it digs into his cheeks.

"How could you, Amma?" My voice shakes like the rest of me.

"This is what Freyja demands," Amma whispers into my ear. "The goddess allowed him to survive Tiveden for this very purpose. She intends for him to be your first sacrifice."

I turn on her. "Are you out of your *mind*?"

She can't seriously think I'm going to kill my dad. Her own *son*.

"If it was easy, it would be no sacrifice." Amma's eyes turn to cold fire. "He dies either way. Sacrifice him and save us all, or refuse and he will die along with everyone in Unden once the blood oath is broken. You must decide whether or not everyone else dies too. Including you and me."

No. No way.

Dad was right all along: Amma *has* lost it. I glance down at my trembling, white-knuckled hand still clutching the dagger. It might as well be a hot coal. I drop the weapon, letting it thud to the floor.

"Remember, Asta," Amma continues. "He was never there when you needed him. I was the one who raised you. And how did he repay me? He *stole* you. Think of the life we could have had." Amma scoops up the dagger and closes my fingers around the handle. "He's always resented you for taking Alicia from him, and he always will. He must wish you were never born."

Her words pierce me as I stare at the sharp, angled blade.

All those times Dad and I fought, and he screamed at me. All those times I cried myself to sleep in Stockholm because he had taken me away from my life, from *Amma*. All those times I begged him to tell me about Mom and he refused. All those times I needed him and he wasn't there.

My grip on the dagger tightens.

But as I look up at Dad, I remember everything else. He tucked me into bed each night in Stockholm, placing Björn in my arms with a kiss on my forehead. He drove me to every doctor's appointment and made sure I got the best care possible. He sat by my bedside and held my hand when I was hospitalized. He took care of me—however imperfect, he tried his hardest. I know he did.

There are two choices, two paths, laid out before me. Just as there were for Skaga so long ago. In this moment, it feels like I'm staring down at my future as well as her past.

Panic fills Dad's eyes as I approach.

"Speak the words," Amma says. "Til níu ára ok friðar."

For nine years and peace.

The same words Skaga spoke before she slit Gorm's throat.

We are one and the same. Skaga's blood flows through my veins, her heart pumps inside my chest. She walks with me now. I take a step closer, the dagger still clutched in my trembling hand. But as I do, I can feel Skaga protest. I know what choice she would want me to make, and it's not *this*. Everything Skaga did, she did for her family.

I move the edge of the blade closer to his throat. If he's going to die either way, maybe this death is kinder. Swifter. Better a quick slice than being ripped limb from limb by a draugr. I've seen for myself what the Hidden Folk are capable of. I saw what happened to both of Skaga's parents. And Torsten—Dad did that to him.

Wouldn't Skaga want me to avenge her husband?

Chanting builds outside, urging me on. The pounding drums. Rattling bones. Haunting voices. My heart hammers in my ears until it feels like they're about to burst. All our lives depend on this—on me.

"Til níu ára . . ." I struggle to shape my mouth around the words.

"Ok friðar," Amma encourages me.

My tongue feels as rough as sandpaper, but I force myself to try again. "Til níu ára . . . ok friðar," I finish, feeling the words' ancient power.

Hot tears drip down my cheeks as I press the knife tip into Dad's throat, his pulse beating wildly beneath my blade. Blood wells. A bead of red trickles down his face before splattering into the wooden bowl. I hate him. I love him. *He dies either way.*

I lash the knife out—

And slice the gag.

Dad gasps for air, barely able to focus on me. He looks ready to pass out.

Amma's claws dig into my shoulder. "What are you doing?"

Dad glares at us. "Astrid, don't—"

He pulls at the ropes binding his wrists, swaying where he hangs. "Don't listen to her. She's manipulating you. She wants to get rid of me so that I can never take you from her again."

"Freyja herself has chosen him," Amma spits.

Swallowing hard, I force myself to speak. "I—I can't—"

Her voice grows frantic. "*Kill him*, Seer!"

My fingers squeeze the damp knife handle.

"Don't do this, Astrid," Dad says desperately. "What do you think happened to your mother?"

Time stops. *Everything* stops.

Mom? My chest tenses until I can't breathe. Mom died on Midwinter after I was born. Eighteen years ago. It's why Dad never let me attend the celebrations. It felt too much like celebrating her loss.

"What?" I ask, but the word is thin enough to break.

Nobody says anything. Not Dad, not Amma.

"What are you talking about?" I ask again, but Dad's face is beet red. He's been upside down too long.

I grab the rope and start sawing it with my dagger, but it's too damn thick. Amma screams while I work, but I barely hear her over my ragged breathing. She shakes my shoulders, her claws sinking into me. But I know she won't hurt me. None of them will. They need me. I grit my teeth against the sharp pain but keep going.

The last thread frays.

Snaps.

Dad thumps to the floor with a loud grunt, his back slamming against the edge of the altar.

"No!" Amma shrieks, so loud it's head-splitting.

But my relief—Skaga's relief—drowns out her screams.

Glancing over my shoulder, I scramble over to Dad. Amma's face is wild, her hair fraying. The Seers close in. Their shadows shroud the altar and cover me and Dad in darkness. They circle around us like a noose, leaving no escape.

"Dad?" I focus on him. Whatever is about to happen, I need to know the truth. "What did you mean? You said Mom . . . ?"

As color slowly returns to his face, he gives a harsh gasp. "Your grandmother killed Alicia." His breathing is labored. "In a ritual. Like this."

My whole body is trembling. *No.*

He's wrong. *Wrong.* He has to be wrong.

"She didn't," I say, shaking my head. "She died after giving birth to me. Complications from Crohn's. *That* is what you told me, Dad. Both of you did."

"That isn't what killed her." Dad turns to Amma angrily. "*She* did."

"Alicia understood that the blood oath must not be broken." Amma's wrinkled face is harsh in the candlelight. "She volunteered, knowing she would soon die anyway. By sacrificing her, I gave her death meaning. I ended her suffering."

"So you claim," Dad says, barely restraining his rage.

I look between them, suddenly feeling sick.

Smoke from all the candles streaks my vision until their faces stretch and pull, until both Amma and Dad become unrecognizable. The taste of gritty ash fills my mouth, and my heart rate ratchets higher. I spin around, ready to run, but the distorted faces of the Seers hover around the hot flames.

Amma was the closest thing I knew to a mother. Am I supposed to believe she's the reason I grew up without one? That the wrinkled hands I held are the same hands that stole my mother's life?

As I look at Amma now, I know it's true.

All those Midwinters sitting in a dark house with Dad while the rest of the town was noisy with celebration. All those birthdays blowing out candles and wishing I had a mom like Johan did. All those nights talking to the only photo I ever found of her before hiding it beneath my pillow like a secret.

I look up at Amma, pleading. "How could you?"

She didn't just take Mom. She stole the childhood I could have had. The family we could have been. Me, Mom, Dad.

"I did what I had to," Amma says. "Now so must you."

Til níu ára ok friðar.

For nine years and peace.

Peace? I suck in a steadying breath, and underneath the stinging smoke, the smell of pine needles is there, faint as a memory. But it doesn't offer any comfort. Instead, it makes me nauseous. Just how many lives has Amma destroyed?

Wait. Nine years. Mom died eighteen years ago.

Then who . . . It hits me all at once. *Johan.* He lost his mother shortly after we moved nine years ago. Over a week ago, I stood right beside her grave. And now I stand here, in the same spot she was sacrificed.

The same spot Mom was sacrificed.

By Amma.

Something in my chest hardens, like the pent-up tension in a lake as it freezes, sending cracks spreading through the ice. Cracks run through everything I thought I knew.

All at once, my world shatters, plunging me beneath the ice. This whole time, Dad was trying to protect *me* from *Amma.* From this terrible truth. From my legacy.

From who I've now become.

Who I've always been.

"That's why we left in such a hurry," I breathe.

I've never seen Dad look so terrified. His brown eyes are wide. Desperate. "If we stayed, she was going to teach you everything. No child should have to hear or see those things. I couldn't—I couldn't lose you to her too."

His words hit me like a kick to the stomach. *Knowledge always comes with a cost*, Soren told me. He was right. Now that I finally know, I'm no longer sure I want to.

"He stole you!" Amma shrieks. "He knew I was about to begin training you, and he was jealous."

"You mean you were going to *indoctrinate* her."

Amma points at Dad. "She belonged to me, and you took her. You knew how important she was to Unden's future. Without her—"

"It's nothing you and this place don't deserve," Dad says.

He's right. And so was Soren.

If I break the blood oath, I can take her and all the Seers with me. I would rather die than become Amma's possession. It's too late for me, for Unden, but Dad doesn't have to die with us. He can still live.

I lash out, slicing the ropes that bind his legs.

"Run," I scream. "Now!"

"Not without you," he says, grabbing hold of my hand.

However long I have left, I want to spend it with him. I want to have the conversations we never had, so at least when I die, we can be on good terms. And once Amma and I are erased, he can start over. He can live the life he never got a chance to because of Amma.

But we have to get out of here first.

Dad bulldozes through the circle of stunned draugar. He lifts the beam blocking the doors and throws them open with a loud smack. Cold wind sweeps into the church, all the candles guttering out instantly. Choking on smoke, I can't see a thing as he pulls me through the doorway.

We burst outside.

The villagers stand there, waiting for the ritual to be completed. Waiting for me to carry out the bowl of my father's sacrificial blood. No one expected him to be standing beside me, still breathing. They stare at us, stunned.

As we run down the steps, everyone crowds around the entrance, forming a wall with their bodies. Cutting off our only chance of escape. Their sheer number makes them impossible to get through.

Dad and I stop, breathing heavily.

I look over my shoulder and see Amma standing in the doorway, her fringed headdress hastily pulled up again, obscuring her face with strips of cloth. Beneath it, there's a flash of burning eyes. The other Seers fan around her.

We have to *go*. "Dad!"

Scanning the sea of firelit faces, I spot a familiar one among the crowd. *Johan.*

I bolt toward him. "Let us through. Please, Janne."

Dad is right behind me.

"What?" Johan looks between us. "But Astrid, your dad—if he's here, it's because he's been chosen to join Freyja. There's no greater honor."

His words sting like a slap to the face. "You too?"

I swallow hard and shake my head. Of course he knows. He has lived in Unden his whole life. For the first time, I'm grateful I *haven't*. I glance around for an escape route, desperate. Nowhere is safe for Dad, though—not Tiveden. Not Unden.

"Get out of the way," Dad says, sounding as desperate as I feel.

A screech rises from the church, piercing the night. *"Stop them!"*

My blood runs cold. The villagers close around us, tightening like a noose. Dad still struggles, trying to shoulder his way through, when Officer Lind draws his gun.

And points it directly at Dad. *Shit.*

"Can't let you do that," Officer Lind says through gritted teeth. "Come on, Rick. This is what you wanted. You can see Alicia again."

We back away slowly, but there's nowhere to go.

The Seers and Unden have us trapped.

Blazing effigies illuminate Amma's wild face as she nears. "She is not yours to take, Erik. She is Skaga, and she belongs to Unden. This is her *duty*."

"I refuse to believe that," Dad says resolutely. "Astrid will always be my daughter."

Amma grabs Dad by the throat. "You will not steal her from me again!"

A shout bursts from me. "No!"

Amma's face is fully exposed, and she looks crazed. Terrifying. Dad grips her arms, struggling to free himself from her hold.

Even with his strength, he's only human.

She no longer is.

"Amma!" I yell, dagger clutched in my hand. "Amma, stop!"

Her inhuman gaze flicks to me. "The blood oath must not be broken."

I feel as powerless as Skaga did while watching her father suffocate.

Amma squeezes his throat tighter. He makes a choked gasp—

She drives her other clawed hand forward.

Right through his chest.

I *scream*. I can feel it inside me, reverberating through my rib cage. The sound is primal, ripping out of me, my body unable to hold it any longer. My face feels too tight as I scream and scream, wild with grief. Until this moment, I didn't know I was capable of making a sound like that. That anyone was.

Amma pulls her hand free with an awful, sickening squelch.

Blood splatters across the snow.

Dad crumples.

"Oh my God." I crash to my knees beside him, grabbing him with shaking hands. "Dad, no!"

"Don't mourn me. I don't deserve it." He reaches up for my wet face, brushing a tear away with his thumb. "I'm sorry I couldn't save you, Astrid. Just like I couldn't save your mother." He chokes, blood bubbling from his lips. "You have to *live*. Promise me you will. . . ."

His eyes close before I can even respond.

He sags against me, too heavy for me to hold anymore.

No. *No.*

A hoarse sound escapes me. *"Dad!"*

My throat is shredded from screaming. This can't be happening. He can't leave me. I won't allow him to die. Hot tears drip down my cheeks as I shake Dad by his shoulders, desperate. But no matter how much I shake him, he won't move.

Dad can't be dead. He can't.

My chest feels ready to rip apart. His loss feels like a reopened wound, the pain fresh but somehow familiar. As if both Skaga and I are losing our fathers together.

Amma kneels beside us, resting her blood-soaked hand on my shoulder.

It burns me down to my bones.

I pull away from her with a snarl, baring my teeth. "Don't you dare fucking touch me!" I scream. "Don't ever touch me again!"

"You're in shock, Seer." Amma withdraws her hand, looking equally stunned. "With time, you will come to understand my actions. He left me no choice."

"He is your son," I say, unable to hide my disgust any longer.

"He *was*. I labored for hours to birth him, pain like you cannot even fathom, Astrid. But I needed a daughter, not a son." She glances at Dad, her expression turning bitter. "Still, I tried my best to love him in spite of that. And how did he repay my love? By denying me. By denying our *family*. But the one thing I cannot forgive is him stealing you." Her lip curls. "I gave him life; it is mine to take."

As I stare up at Amma, hatred consumes me like kindling. "This was no sacrifice. This was *murder*."

"The girl is right." Gudrun carries the wooden bowl over as the other Seers join us. "Only the living Seer is able to perform the sacrifice. You know better, Ingrid."

Amma rips the bowl from her mother. "That is for Freyja to decide," she says, sounding frantic as she struggles to capture Dad's blood with it. "I have given my only son's life. Surely that must count for something."

Amma desperately scoops up her son's blood with her clawed hands as if that blood is more precious than him. I have never hated anyone as much as I hate her right now.

Amma is a monster.

She always was.

The only difference is, now I can see her for what she is.

"Get away from him!" I cling to Dad, unwilling to let go of him.

Now everyone can see the true Amma as she clutches the bowl of blood tightly to her chest. "This must work. It has to. The blood oath cannot be broken."

Gudrun sneers. "As always, you do nothing right, Ingrid."

"We will select another sacrifice, then." Amma hastily pulls her hood up over her face, but she exposes her clawed hand, still soaked with my dad's blood. "Who of you wants to join Freyja?"

"I . . . don't understand," Johan says, staring down at Dad. He looks shaken to his core, as if he sees his mother lying in my arms instead. "You promised they felt no pain."

Amma presses her lips together.

It takes her a beat to recover. "They do not suffer long, so that Unden can survive. The blood oath must not be broken. You know this."

The villagers exchange quick glances.

Some even nod, trying to reconcile this with their beliefs.

"Now, who will volunteer?" Amma tries again. "If I must choose one of you, I will."

She glances around desperately.

People no longer look so sure. They no longer know what to believe.

"How dare you look at me like that!" Amma snarls at the gathering, her long teeth flashing. She sounds unhinged. "I am your foremother. Your *Seer*. My entire life, I have protected you. Your families. Your homes. *Unden* would no longer exist if not for me."

Ebba Karlsson stares at my father's corpse. "We didn't realize it happened like *this*."

Seeing the brutality must be different. That's why the ritual takes place behind closed doors, with only the other Seers—the other *murderers*—to witness what actually happens. They must know that no one could stomach it, not without questioning what the Seers have told them.

Amma points her bloody, clawed hand around the group. "Do not lie to yourselves now. You all knew what we did. You not only knew, but you also participated. You celebrated each sacrifice. If you believe me guilty, then so are you. All of you."

Firelight reflects in Johan's glasses. "You promised us that Freyja took them in her arms and carried them home." He holds the flame toward Amma, illuminating her monstrous face. "You *lied* to us."

Amma backs away. "You all averted your eyes from the truth."

Unden is slipping out of her control, and she knows it. Using his torch, Johan drives Amma back toward Tiveden. The other villagers follow his lead, wielding their torches like weapons against my family.

"Look what you've done now, Ingrid." Gudrun rubs the deep creases in her forehead. "This is unprecedented. We are without a sacrifice *and* a willing Seer. We must prepare for the worst."

"The blood oath will *not* be broken," Amma says, her blue eyes burning fiercely with her fervor. "My sacrifice will be enough. It has to be."

Amma retreats into Tiveden, still carrying her precious bowl of blood.

Everyone in Unden uses their torches to drive Gudrun and the rest of the Seers back.

"Condemn us," Gudrun says, her voice turning vicious, "and you condemn yourselves. The blood oath that has protected Unden for centuries will be broken at first light tomorrow. See for yourselves the necessity of what we did. By the time you realize your mistake, it will be too late to beg us to come back. We will no longer be there to save you."

The Seers run into the woods until darkness swallows them.

By dawn, they will all burn alive.

And so will I.

I may not be dead yet, but as I hold Dad's body in my arms, I wish dawn was already here.

The villagers linger. They exchange bewildered looks, shake their heads, cry out, comfort each other.

"Everyone, go home," Officer Lind calls out. "Secure your homes and get ready to shelter in place. Find any ancestral weapons you have and prepare to use them. We'll need whatever weapons we can find tomorrow."

Everyone leaves, trickling back into Unden.

Except me.

For the first time in my life, I am completely and utterly alone.

═➤─THIRTY-FIVE─◄═

Dad almost looks like he could be asleep.

Like when I first found Soren. I wish this were because of a sleep thorn, and that if I broke the spell, he would wake up. No matter how long I stare at Dad, his eyelids remain shut. He doesn't move. And his chest holds irrefutable proof of why: the bloom of blood across his abdomen.

Now I understand why Skaga used the forbidden stave on her parents. Maybe . . . maybe I can still save Dad.

Draugar aren't inherently evil—Soren isn't. He was right about the blood oath and everything else. And if it meant I could see Dad again, even as a draugr, wouldn't it be worth it? My throat closes up, trapping all the words I never got a chance to say to him. All the words I might still be able to say if I used the forbidden stave.

I could bring him back. Maybe with Dad's blood, the stave might work. My tears make it hard to see. Skaga hasn't shared her skill with the staves. I never had the chance to memorize the forbidden one that marks Soren's chest.

Dagny was right. Skaga and I share the same fate after all.

We both lost our fathers.

And we will both burn.

But unlike her, I can't bring Dad back.

I hug him tighter, rocking his body back and forth. Dad, who went into Tiveden, knowing its dangers, to find me and bring me home. Dad, who wouldn't have been anywhere near Amma and used as a sacrifice if it weren't for me. Dad, who sacrificed everything in his life so I could live mine.

My entire life, he has been my one constant. In Unden. In Stockholm. It was always him, trying his hardest to take care of me, even though I never made it easy for him. But I could never see that. Why couldn't I just *see* it?

Because of Amma.

I was obsessed with her, even before she went missing. Even before Dad took me away. It was always Amma. Amma who paid me the most attention. Amma who read to me before bed each night. Amma who held my hand and guided me everywhere, pointing everything out to me and teaching me how to make sense of the world.

No, not teaching. *Telling.*

Amma was always telling me what to believe. What to do. Who to be.

That's how I ended up here, isn't it?

Swallowing hard, I study Dad's face carefully, trying to memorize everything about him. His roughly shaved beard. His closed eyes. Skin soaked with sweat. I brush his damp hair off his face. Then I stroke his cheek, stubble scratching at my skin like sandpaper—

His body is already growing cold.

Tears build behind my eyes. Something presses against my skull, a constant, mounting pressure. I want to claw at my chest to get rid of this grief. I can't live with this ache. I can't live without *him*.

"I'm sorry I never listened." My voice breaks. "But I still need you. *Please.* I love you, Dad."

I press my forehead to his. Sobs rack me, climbing into the night sky. As I hold Dad in my arms, I never want to let go. I can't even remember the last time I hugged him. Now I'll never be able to again. This entire time, I couldn't see what was right in front of me.

It was always Dad.

Dad was the one who loved me the most. It wasn't a simple, straightforward love like mine for Amma. It was a painful kind, one that hurt to hold on to as much as a prickling bush. All those times we fought about

Mom and Amma and everything else. All those times we ate frozen din-
ners in uncomfortable silence. All those times he couldn't bring himself
to look at me, so he sat in front of the television instead.

I must have reminded him of Mom. How she had her throat slit by
his own mother. How he failed to stop it. I was a reminder of his greatest
guilt. His greatest shame. But he never blamed *me*. Not like Amma
always claimed he did. Now that I think about it, she was the one who'd
planted that idea in my head in the first place, even though *she* had been
the one responsible for Mom dying. She let me blame myself. As much
as it hurts, I rip out that long-held belief by the roots.

Dad loved me more than Amma ever did.

He'd tried to give me a normal life, a life he never had growing up in
Unden. A life of riding the metro wherever I wanted, attending school,
and making friends, visiting the doctor or hospital whenever I needed.
He sacrificed so much to give me that—

And I threw it back in his face. I didn't understand the gift he had
given me: a new beginning. What I wouldn't give for one right now. One
where I didn't have to go on in a world without my father.

I would go back, back, back.

I would try harder to understand him.

I would spend more time with him instead of Amma.

"A-Astrid?" A soft voice behind me.

Johan stands there, his torch burning low. He's one of the last people
I want to see right now. Johan didn't help me when he could have. Even
if I didn't deserve his help, Dad did.

Tears burn paths down my cheeks. "What do you want?"

I know Johan is hurting too. But as I stare down at Dad's stiff face, I
can't help but hate Johan. I hate *Unden*. Dad was right about this damn
place, just like he was right about Amma. We never really had a chance
of escaping Unden—or *this*—because of who I am.

Johan crouches down in front of me. "To be here for you. Like I
should have been at the vigil. Only I couldn't be because I was so upset.
You hurt me when you pushed me away after you moved, but I know you

need a friend right now. Just like I did when I lost my mother." He offers me his hand. "I'm sorry, Astrid."

I am too. But it doesn't do any good.

It won't bring my dad back.

"Get the fuck away from me," I say, lashing out at him. Even though the person I hate most right now is myself.

Johan shakes his head. "I won't let you push me away again."

"You were *part* of this."

"Only because I didn't know the truth," Johan says, choking on the words. When I finally bring myself to look at him, tears trail down his cheeks too, glowing in the torchlight. "She told me my mother was chosen by Freyja. That it was quick. Painless. And then Freyja would hold her in a field that goes on forever—"

"Well, she fucking lied."

"I know that now." Johan drops his hand. "I was wrong—all of us were wrong. We never should've listened to your grandmother. We never should've let things go so far. But we did because we were terrified of what would happen if we didn't. Every Midwinter, we saw what awaited us otherwise, the monsters gathering near the church."

My chest aches. Amma is the most dangerous monster of all. She has a way of convincing people with her words. But her truth is as twisted as a snake. She manipulates people, using their beliefs, their fears, their *love*, to make them do her bidding.

Even Dad. He remained in Unden for most of his life. He knew about the sacrifices, but he must've believed his mother's lies once too. The sour taste of vomit lingers inside my mouth. He must have woken up only after Amma took his wife from him. After she took my mother from me. Why didn't we leave then?

Can I really blame him? I look at Johan's tearstained face. *Either* of them? Amma had *me* convinced too—I was willing to kill another human being because she told me to. Until she wanted me to murder my own dad. I only realized the truth about her too late.

"You were her victim," I whisper, realizing the truth behind his words.

Warm arms encircle me. My breath hitches as Johan pulls me against him and strokes my head. "So were you," he whispers into my hair. "Let it all out. I'm here for you."

We are all her victims. Dad. Johan. Me. *Unden.*

The realization only makes me cry harder.

My skin is too tight. Too hot. All this time, I wouldn't let anyone close because I was afraid I could get sick. I was so afraid of dying from an infection like Mom that I became afraid of living, too. All because of a *lie.* My chest rises and falls rapidly. It's hard to even breathe.

Johan pulls me against him, hugging me tightly as we cry together. We cry for my dad, for both our mothers, for ourselves, and for each other—two kids caught up in something neither one of us wanted.

My breath comes in quick, short bursts, until it feels like I'm about to rip apart. The only thing holding me together right now is Johan. He rests his chin on top of my head but says nothing. Because there's nothing to say.

Nothing can make either of us feel better.

Dad tried to protect me. He didn't want to hurt me. So he bore his pain, his guilt, in silence, and watched as my mother's murderer took her place in my life. Wasn't that what Amma always wanted? She thought I belonged to her.

Is *that* why she killed my mother?

I know it's why Dad is dead now. Amma wanted me to choose her over him, once and for all, in the most permanent way possible. She wanted me to cut away every piece of myself until all I had left was her.

And that isn't love.

It's control.

From the moment I was born, she wanted to possess me.

I do not belong to her, or anyone else. I belong to myself. Just because the same blood flows through our veins, I do not owe her anything I don't want to give. I do not have to follow in her footsteps, or Skaga's, or anyone else's. I can make my own choices. I may not be able to change the past, but I do still have a say in the future. So I rip the branches from my hair, tear the bird skull off my forehead, and pull my crown of braids free, until my hair is loose and wild.

I can only live *my* life.

No one else's.

THIRTY-SIX

Red blood stains the snow around us. Johan's torch rests nearby, barely burning. Soon its warmth will disappear, unlike my grief. Without my tears, there is only the unbearable reality: I will have to face a world without my dad in it. I'm not sure I'm ready for that yet. So I sit there, staring at the dark forest beyond us. The dying light of Johan's torch flickers over the trees, shadows dancing around us.

Something flashes in the forest—

White dress. Pale skin.

Dread drenches me like a bucket of ice water.

One of the Seers? Or Amma herself?

My hand balls into a fist. I won't let her take Dad from me. Not again.

But it isn't Amma.

The huldra—the one with short hair who attacked me but later helped me and Soren—emerges from the wood. Barefoot, she takes small, cautious steps, silent in the snow. She wears a pained expression as she approaches us. Her tail remains tightly wrapped around her waist like a belt.

What is *she* doing here?

Johan backs away. "Is that—oh gods. That's *definitely* a huldra."

Sweat beads down my forehead as I recall the first time I encountered her. "Yeah. Trust me, I know."

More recently, she assisted me when Soren was fighting Ramunder. Without her help, those skeletons would've killed me. I would be dead—but maybe Dad would still be alive.

Still, I hesitate.

Why would the huldra show up now, here of all places? And how was she able to slip through the barrier?

Johan reaches for his torch, but I hold up a hand.

"Hold on." Amma told me the Seers could only pass through tonight because they intend Unden no harm. If the huldra is here, maybe the same is true for her. "I think she wants to help. As long as she doesn't turn around, we should be safe."

Johan gulps. "I don't know about this. . . ."

"It's okay," I say to both her and Johan.

As the huldra gets closer, I can make out her features more clearly. She isn't disguising herself anymore, as if to show me I can trust her. Moss and lichen spread over her damp skin, her short hair tangled and filthy with twigs and pine needles. She looks wild and feral, one with the woods, but her eyes are black pools of sorrow as she joins us.

I'm no longer afraid of her.

The worst monsters in Tiveden turned out to be my family.

Johan shakes his head. "I don't trust her. If a huldra helps you, it's because she wants something from you."

"I don't know," I say slowly.

The huldra stares at Dad. For some reason, she seems fascinated by him. She crouches over him, studying his features, and traces a long nail down his cheek.

"No!" I shout. "Leave him alone."

The huldra hisses at me, exposing a mouthful of moss. A bug scurries across her peeling bark lips. I hold my dagger out at her, and she retreats a few steps.

But she doesn't flee like she did before.

"See," Johan says. "Told you."

The huldra stands there, waiting for something.

Dad mentioned a huldra helped him through Tiveden, didn't he?

She helped both of us.

I slowly rise to my feet. Even in her natural state, something about the huldra feels familiar. Maybe it's her heart-shaped face, or her pert nose, or the fullness of her lips. I step closer until I can see my own reflection inside her watery black eyes. A tear escapes one, trailing down her mossy cheek.

"Mom?" The word rushes out of me like an exhale.

A small smile curls her lichen-covered lips. She no longer looks so monstrous—she looks like my mom again, wearing her face like a perfect mask. Her freckled cheeks, her large hazel eyes, her short blond hair. Despite the altered surface, her underlying facial features are all the same. Mom smiles, exactly like in the old photographs of her that Dad hid away because they were too painful for him to look at.

I suck in a breath. "Is that really you?"

When she nods, I notice a long, smooth scar around her throat like a necklace.

The mother that Amma took from me. All this time, she's been right here in Tiveden.

A sob escapes me. *"Mom."*

Mom draws me toward her, pulling me into her arms. Her embrace is damp and mossy. But she's warm. So warm. I always wondered what my mother's embrace would feel like.

Now I finally know.

Maybe this is what she wanted all along.

When I first encountered her, I couldn't tell if she was trying to help me or kill me. What if it was just her motherly instinct twisted by her monstrous nature? Maybe Mom just wanted to carry me inside her again like she did eighteen years ago. Maybe she's always been trying to protect me in whatever way she could.

Eventually, I manage to peel away from her.

So it wasn't just Amma and the rest of the Seers who turned into monsters. Do all the sacrifices end up in Tiveden? Do they *all* transform? I know that the Seers become draugar because of what they've done. Both Amma and Soren made that clear.

What if the sacrifices also suffer a similar fate? I look Mom over, like I can find answers in her face. And I do. Unlike the other huldra I saw with Soren, who were naturally beautiful, something about Mom looks . . . wrong. The bark covering her skin is cracked, split open, peeling off. Almost like the diseased trees in Tiveden.

Realization ripples through me.

But that would mean some of the Hidden Folk in the forest . . . are actually people my family has sacrificed. Suddenly, it makes sense why Tiveden is so dangerous. Of course the sacrifices would try to attack me. Not because they're evil, but because of what my *family* has done to them.

I lick my chapped lips. "Are all the sacrifices trapped in Tiveden?"

"Help—" Her voice sounds rough from disuse. "Help us."

"Did they all . . . become like you?"

She nods stiffly.

"*No.*" Johan shakes his head so hard his curls bounce. "Then that would mean my mom . . . she's . . ."

Many of these monsters—they were once *people*. People who lived in Unden. People my family murdered. People Skaga—*I*—murdered. The weight of the realization presses down on me like a fist. There are *so many*. Just how many lives has each Seer taken?

Like what Amma did to my mother. She's been like this for almost eighteen years. My whole life. *That* is why she's barely able to speak anymore or even hold on to her human appearance for long.

Because of *Skaga*.

The oath she made to protect Unden damned the very people she was trying to protect. It's suddenly hard for me to breathe.

No, this is all because of *me*.

How can I possibly atone for this?

I didn't think I could hate Amma any more, but as I see the devastation spread across Johan's face, I do. She not only slit both our mothers' throats, but she turned them into monsters like her.

I rub my eyes roughly. "Dad deserves to be free."

Mom nods.

Once, I thought anything was better than dying.

But now I know there are worse things, after all.

"You all do," I add, choking on a sob as I see what Mom was made into.

She holds her hands out, extending her cracked palms like an offering. "Help," she says, motioning toward Dad.

Mom wants to carry him. My chest aches as I grasp at him, holding him tighter. I don't want to let him go. I can't say goodbye. I can't, but—

I force myself to nod. "Okay."

Mom takes Dad, lifting him up like he weighs nothing. Seeing Dad hang there limply sends a fresh wave of grief over me, so powerful it nearly knocks me to my knees. Is this what Dad felt when he lost her? How did he continue on for so long afterward?

Right. *For me.* He kept living for me.

If I'm able to keep living, who will it be for?

Carrying him carefully, Mom walks barefoot toward Tiveden.

At the edge of the forest, armfuls of branches have been spread across the ground. Mom has clearly been preparing for this. She must have been watching from the woods this whole time, unwilling to reveal herself. Or unable to, if the barrier was still holding her.

She lays my dad down gently on the bed of branches.

A pyre.

My chest pulls painfully, trapping the air in my lungs. She wants to burn his body.

Mom picks up another branch and raises her mossy brows. "Help?"

Unable to summon any words, I nod and gather as many long branches as I can find. Johan helps us too. The branches I choose are sturdy and strong, just like Dad is.

Was.

The branches grow heavy in my aching arms, but I force myself toward the growing pyre. I take my time laying them out, placing each one carefully over his body, a blanket of branches and sticks. Because the sooner I finish, the sooner I'll have to say goodbye.

Mom returns with a handful of pine needles and sprinkles them over Dad. That scent—the one that always comforted me—twists my stomach now. Then Mom turns to me, an expectant expression on her face. She tips her head toward the burning effigy by the church.

Oh. We still need fire.

Then I remember the stave Soren taught me in Tiveden: *firestarter.*

I bend over beside the pyre and start drawing the stave, snow stinging my fingertip. I imagine Soren's hand guiding me. Even the phantom memory of his touch is enough to comfort me. As I work, something awakens inside me, ancient and wild. A rush of heat travels through me, and I can feel it flowing through my veins, pulsing in time with my beating heart.

I slice open another finger and paint the stave with my bright blood. *For Dad.*

But it won't work with just mine.

I glance over at Mom. "It needs your blood too, Mom."

She nods and kneels in the snow beside me. When she cuts her finger with one of her claws, I see she has the same dark blood as Soren. Slowly, carefully, her finger follows the same path as mine.

She stumbles back as a small golden flame spreads over the stave.

The pyre catches. Flames devour the bed of branches, smoke rising around Dad, until the whole pyre is burning a shimmering gold. *Freyja's fire.* It may not burn me, but the fire is hot on my face as tears trail down my cheek like molten rivers. The fire is so warm it feels like I'm the one on the pyre, flames licking over my skin, but its heat doesn't hurt me.

"What is that?" Johan asks, awed.

"Freyja's divine fire."

Dad deserves something special. It's no grand ship burial, but I'm glad I can give him this much, at least. The pyre's light flickers over the forest, painting it in a warm amber glow. Skaga never had the chance to do this for her father.

Mom smiles at me, wearing her human form again. I try to memorize her face. Before I can, she slips her hand from mine. The illusion starts to flicker in and out like the shimmering flames as she walks toward the fire. She's leaving me again.

"No!" I grab her, but my hand comes back empty.

Mom is already climbing into the pyre.

She stretches out beside Dad on the branches as if they were back in their bedroom. Wind rushes over me like a long-held exhale, stoking the growing flames. I glimpse her wrapping her arms around him, holding him in one last embrace, before the bright flames consume them both.

I reach toward the fire, fingertips straining—

It's too late. I have to let them go.

Sometimes letting go is the most difficult thing of all.

I finally release the sob I've been holding, followed by a burning flood of shame. All those awful things I said to Dad over the years—I wish I could take every single one back.

Instead, I would tell him the one thing I should have said all along:

I love you, Dad.

Nothing hurts worse than not being able to say those words to him. I'll never make that mistake again. I can't help but think of Soren. From now on, I'm going to tell the people who matter to me that I love them while I still can. And I'll say it often.

Starting with Johan.

"I'm sorry." I drag my sleeve across my face. "For not being there when I should have been."

After leaving Unden so suddenly, I blamed Dad when I lost all my friends, when really it was *my* fault.

"I should have stayed in touch," I continue. "I was too sick and too busy and all kinds of excuses, but I should have reached out more. You were too important to me not to. Your friendship always meant so much. You were always there for me, and I should have done the same for you, even if it was hard. Even if it hurt."

Johan sniffles, his throat bobbing. "You're here now."

He holds his hand out to me.

This time, I take it. "Always."

I study Johan. My childhood best friend. My new friend.

The fire is reduced to embers before us.

Without the crackling flames, the silence is heavy and absolute. I stare at the smoldering pyre. All that remains of my parents is a heap of ash, steam rising from the melted snow. Smoke pours into the night sky, carrying my parents up with it. Wherever they go next, at least I know they'll go together.

"I can't believe they're really gone."

Johan squeezes my hand. "They will finally be reunited with Freyja."

I want to believe him. I want to believe that this isn't the end for them. I want to believe in something bigger. Just this once. So I close my eyes and do something I told myself I would never do again: I pray.

Freyja, may you welcome my parents home with open arms.

And for the briefest of moments, I can see them, walking through a field together, their hands clasped tightly. Stalks of wheat sway around them in a gentle breeze. Sunlight warms their smiling faces.

Hot tears spill down my cheeks.

Mom and Dad are together again. Something about that feels right. Like a first step toward repairing all the damage Amma and the Seers have done. The heap of ash smolders in front of us. But there's still so much more I have to make right.

I turn toward Johan. "I'm sorry for what we did to you and your family."

He nods wordlessly.

And that's okay. I don't expect forgiveness.

"Your mom deserves to join Freyja too," I tell him.

I think of my mother with her scraping voice as she pleaded, *Help us.* If the blood oath is broken, the dead will only grow more monstrous, not less. The more they kill, the worse they'll become, just like the Seers.

It will never end.

I blow out a long breath. "All the sacrifices do."

"I agree." Johan swallows thickly. "But how?"

"I don't know," I admit. "But Soren might."

He said there could be another way to break the blood oath. One where we both survive. Soren tried desperately to get me to listen. But I wouldn't, not when it came to Amma. Just like I wouldn't listen to Dad.

Well, I'm ready to listen now. I only hope it isn't too late.

Skaga might be part of me, but my choices, my experiences, my *life*—those are all mine. I will do what she never could. Losing her mother was what drove her to make the oath. Losing Dad has made me determined to end it. Even if it costs me my life, I *will*.

Soren was right. The blood oath must be broken.

PART FOUR

Wayfinder
Vegvísir

➤ THIRTY-SEVEN ◄

As Freyja's fire goes cold, I realize Johan and I aren't alone anymore. The funeral pyre was the only thing protecting us. Now it's nothing but ash. The Hidden Folk gather by the forest's edge, waiting for something. Or someone.

I slip my hand from Johan's. He looks ready to protest, but I don't give him the chance. "You need to go home. Now."

"What about you?" he asks nervously.

"I have to find the Fell King."

Johan frowns. "What? No, Astrid. I can't—"

"It's okay." I nudge him. "Please go. I can't lose you, too."

He rakes a hand through his curly black hair. "All right, but be careful."

Johan takes off with a sigh. Once he's out of sight, I turn to face Tiveden. Now I just need to get through to Soren.

As I set foot into the forest, the Hidden Folk are waiting. Huldra, draugar, trolls, nisse, and countless other creatures are gathered, but I don't see Soren among them. Their empty gazes are fixed somewhere beyond me, as if they don't see me at all. They remain motionless, their arms hanging by their sides, standing there like mannequins.

I pass a woman, her once-flowery nightgown stained and shredded. Long hair falls around her face in braids. Recognition rockets through me. Growing up, I saw that face all the time, but now her brown skin has turned ashen and gray. A scar trails across her throat.

I stumble back. "H-Hedda."

Johan's mom doesn't react to my presence, though. If she can hear me at all. She stares through me, her once beautiful brown eyes now turned white as milk. Her lips, smeared with dark fluid like sloppy lipstick, part.

"Varsågod," she says.

The Swedish word has many meanings, depending on context. *You're welcome. Here you go. Please.* I don't know which one she means, but I know it's not her voice. It comes out too high-pitched, almost saccharine, sounding more like a little girl, not a grown woman.

Horror dawns on me. Those milky eyes. The nightgown. The childlike voice. After Hedda was sacrificed, Tiveden turned her into a mara, the giver of nightmares.

And not just her. As I look around, I see that all the Folk standing around me share one thing in common: the gruesome scar across their throats. My skin crawls. These—these are all the people my family has sacrificed. *This is a nightmare. One I can't wake from, because it's real.*

The blood oath has made monsters of us all.

I hurry past them, more desperate than ever to find Soren. The more faces I see, the more I start to recognize, even though it's impossible. They are people I have never seen before, but my mind still supplies their names. *Drífa. Arvid. Frida. Sune. Björn. Thyra.*

Gorm.

I stare into the face of the first person Skaga killed. I can feel the phantom weight of her dagger in my hand, still see his throat slitting open beneath its blade, still smell the coppery odor of his blood as it sprayed my face—

"Why have you come here?" a familiar voice asks.

Soren.

Facing him, I take in his tall black boots, his dark pants and tunic, secured by a thick leather vest. Clad in this black leather armor, Soren looks unfeeling and brutal, prepared for war. His fur cloak billows around him and a polished bone horn hangs from his belt. No weapons.

Not like he needs them.

This is the Fell King.

As I stand before him in my torn dress, he looks me over slowly. I can't help but remember how Soren's cold hand felt in mine, reassuring and strong. My pulse leaps in my throat, but I'm not afraid of him.

Not anymore.

"I know the truth now," I tell him. "All the sacrifices are trapped in Tiveden." Cold air fills my lungs with each painful breath. "And you realized that too."

His face is an unreadable mask.

The Soren I know is in there somewhere. He has to be.

The Fell King lowers his gaze to the blood covering my dress. "It is too late."

In his words, I hear an echo of what I told myself before the ritual. *This is the only way. I have no choice.* It's the same kind of lie I tried to convince myself of to go through with what I thought I had to do. But Soren is a draugr. If he's saying such things, it means he believes it wholeheartedly. But that doesn't mean it's true.

"No, it's not," I say. "I didn't perform the sacrifice."

"That changes nothing." He walks past me, his shoulder barely brushing by mine. "There is nothing I can do now. As I told you, my control is weakest on Midwinter."

"Wait." I grab hold of his cloak. "We can still end the blood oath. Together."

We stand like that for a moment, a meter apart, his cloak held in my hand.

Silence grows like a living thing between us.

"I know better than to trust you again," he says finally.

"I was wrong." I pull him closer and wrap my arms around his chest. My cheek presses into his back, the snow-dusted cloak chilling my skin, but I won't let go. "I was wrong about my family." The words are barely a whisper. "And about you."

Soren stiffens in my arms.

"Astrid," he says in warning.

I don't know what he must be thinking right now. What he must be feeling. I hug him tighter. Soren *saved* me, asking nothing in return. Unlike Amma, who manipulated me, using my love to control me.

"I should have listened to you sooner," I whisper against his back.

His body relaxes, the tension dissipating. My grip loosens, and he turns around, pulling me against him. He slips his arms around me, blanketing me with his cloak. I lean into him.

Soren bows his head, resting his forehead on mine.

"I always should have," I say softly. "Even long ago."

He pulls away, looking at me intently. "What do you mean?"

I study his beautiful face, sharp fangs and all. "Skaga isn't gone," I whisper, taking his clawed hand in mine and guiding it toward my heart. "She's still here, inside me."

We stay like that for a long moment.

Soren's breath hitches. *"Skaga."*

He hesitates like he's struggling to find words.

His eyes are like a frozen lake, tears pooling along his lashes. "I have waited so long for you."

When he finally speaks, his voice is soft. "Even after what you did, I never forgot you. And I know you did not forget me, either. I heard everything you confessed in the cellar, and I forgive you. For you, I would forgive anything."

He traces a finger along my brow, trailing down the line of my jaw and leaving ice in his wake. So many feelings well up inside me, I don't know what to say or how to react.

"All I want is to be forgiven," he says.

His gaze is so intense, as if he can see through to my soul. "Forgive me, Skaga. Please."

I lean into his touch. "She already has."

Somewhere deep inside, I can *feel* how true the words are.

"I loved her so much, but I'm no longer the same person who did. While under the sleep thorn's spell, I had nothing but time to reflect. I changed. And when I met you—I couldn't make sense of what I was beginning to feel for you. It felt like I was betraying her memory by caring for you. Love like that is only supposed to happen once. But now . . ."

"I know. I'm not the same person either." I let the weight of the words sink in. "Skaga may be part of me, but I'm still my own person, separate from her and who she became."

"We are both different," he breathes.

Finally, we're on the same side.

But not for long.

Even if we break the blood oath, I only have until dawn.

"So what now?" I ask him.

"Do you remember when we made the oath?"

I shake my head and he continues, "When Skaga asked me to make the blood oath with her, she came to me in tears, desperate to end the conflict between our kinds and to protect the settlement her father dreamed of having here. I could not refuse her. I never could."

Like I couldn't refuse Amma.

I would've done anything she asked of me.

I almost did.

"So I made the blood oath with her," Soren continues. "Such a thing is a human custom, but Skaga insisted so I would know she wasn't lying. I didn't question it, even though I should have. I only intended for the oath to last as long as her life, not forever. But because it was a blood oath, any who shared her blood could fulfill it."

"Any could?" I ask slowly.

Soren nods.

A choked sound escapes me. So *Dad* could've become the next Seer all along.

All this time, Amma resented her son for *nothing*.

As that dagger was handed down from generation to generation, the truth grew distorted. Freyja replaced Soren in the narrative. The Fell King was reduced to his role as villain. Somewhere along the way, belief overtook truth.

I shake my head slowly. "Did Skaga know what would happen?"

That one choice would ripple through generations? Making the blood oath destroyed so many lives, including those of Dagny—her own daughter—and grandchildren and great-grandchildren, on and on and on, until reaching Amma, Dad, *me*.

"Neither of us did," Soren admits. "The sacrifices were given to the forest. Tiveden itself must have decided to use their bodies to repopulate the Hidden Folk lost to Unden. But the blood oath twisted the sacrifices, so they became something new instead. Something different.

"No longer human, but not Hidden Folk either. Their ógipta was more powerful than anything I had ever seen. Even back then, they were infecting Tiveden like a disease. But because of the oath, they were trapped with the rest of the Folk. Once I realized, I begged Skaga to break the blood oath. That's when she used the sleep thorn on me."

"Because the blood oath must not be broken," I say heavily.

Just like Amma, Skaga would never let anything stand in the way of that. They were both content to mislead everyone in Unden in order to protect their home. The cost of their legacy didn't matter to them. They could never admit they were the ones who were wrong.

But I can.

"The blood oath has cost us enough," I say, looking up at Soren. "I want to end this once and for all. And I know that's what you want too. Whatever you needed Skaga to do, let me do it in her stead. Even if it costs my life."

"There might be another way. I've had centuries to think on this. If we make a new blood oath to each other, you might still survive."

Might.

But it's better than the certainty that I will die at dawn.

"Do you think that will work?" I ask him.

"If we make a new oath to each other, perhaps we can override the original one and return things to how they once were." Soren hesitates, looking me over. "We will have to return to the stave church, however."

He means I'll have to return to the place where Amma murdered Dad. My stomach drops. "Why?"

"The oath must be made before the gods, and the church is ideal, since most of the sacrifices took place there. We know Freyja will bear witness to our oath."

"What will happen to Unden?" I ask quietly.

"The blood oath will not be broken until dawn, so the earliest the attack would happen is tomorrow night. I will do everything in my power to keep the Folk from attacking. But if I fail, you will still have the daytime to get everyone out of Unden."

It's a solid plan. I nod, determined. Together, we will make this right.

The blood oath has destroyed enough lives already.

I won't let it take any more.

THIRTY-EIGHT

Unden is as still as a grave field.

Massive effigies still blaze throughout the village, but the bloodred houses in the distance remain dark. Everyone is sheltering at home, waiting. The blood oath's protection will only weaken more as the night goes on, until these burning effigies will be all that protects us.

The nearby effigy illuminates the path toward the stave church. Its bright flames sear my eyes, making it hard to see anything else as we approach. But we aren't the only ones who have returned here.

Voices drift from ahead.

"If the Seer will not cooperate, we must make her. I will not let my daughter ruin everything we have worked for."

Gudrun. My great-grandma.

"Will it be enough?" another Seer asks.

"We must try," Gudrun responds. "Before it is too late."

Another unfamiliar voice. "Hjördis and Olga, get us another sacrifice, willing or not. Gudrun, retrieve your granddaughter."

"There's no need," Gudrun says, like she knows we're coming.

Like she's already seen our arrival using her gift of foresight.

A small gathering comes into view, surrounded by bodies. Countless corpses lay scattered around the stave church, their faces pressed into the snow. Some draugar must have slipped through the weakening boundary. The Seers probably had to stop them before they reached Unden, but not without casualties. Fewer than ten remain.

"Let me handle them," I mutter to Soren.

This is *my* mess. I should be the one to deal with it.

Soren nods wordlessly as we move closer.

Gudrun stands with her back to us, still as a statue. "So you've finally decided to join us."

From her tone, she's been expecting me. I don't see Amma among the gathered Seers. Their dresses are ripped and soaked with dark blood. Not just their dresses. Their claws, their faces—they're bathed in blood.

My mind finally catches up to what I'm witnessing.

Those bodies at their feet. They are all *Seers*.

"Where's Amma?" I ask. As soon as the words escape, I want to swallow them.

She's still the first thing I think of. It's instinct.

"She failed in her duties." Gudrun faces me. "I made sure she will never disgrace me again."

I feel suddenly sick, realizing the meaning of her words.

Some of the dark blood they wear belongs to Amma.

They killed her.

My chest tightens painfully as I think of Dad. Mom. Johan. Soren. *Me.* Amma has hurt so many people throughout her long life. I hate her. I do. After everything she's done, I should be glad she's dead.

But I'm not.

Angry tears spill down my cheeks as I search for Amma among the fallen Seers. It makes me sick to think I am capable of loving the woman who murdered my parents and countless others. But my love for her is lodged inside my heart like a splinter.

As much as I hate her . . . I love her too.

My face must betray me, because Gudrun says, "You have only yourself to thank, girl. This is all because you were too weak to do what needed to be done. What you did is unforgivable."

"There was some . . . disagreement about what comes next," one of the other Seers adds. "So we settled the dispute among ourselves, even if it meant thinning our ranks."

"The blood oath must not be broken," another Seer says.

Now only Gudrun and those who agree with her remain.

They must have turned against each other when they realized the sacrifice failed. Most of the Seers now lie facedown, their dark blood staining the snow. But how were they killed? Their bodies are still intact, which rules out beheading or burning. Maybe they were stabbed through the heart. Taking in the harrowing scene, I can't shake my misgiving that these fallen Seers could still rise at any moment.

Soren shifts closer to my side.

Gudrun's milky eyes flick from me to Soren. "Perhaps you can still atone, great-granddaughter, so long as you fulfill the prophecy."

Prophecy—she means killing Soren.

"You're the one who needs to atone." My voice trembles with pent-up rage. "You killed your own daughter and all these Seers, for what? Skaga would never want *this*. Everything she did, she did to protect her family."

Gudrun looks me over with a disgusted expression. "You are no Skaga."

"You're right," I say slowly. "I'm different from her. She may have started all this, but I will be the one to end it."

"We will never allow that." Gudrun gives a small, cruel laugh. "I will tell you what is going to happen. You will kill the Fell King, as Skaga should have done long ago," she says with the surety of someone who has seen the future. "Afterward, you will perform the sacrifice, whether you want to or not. The blood oath *will not* be broken."

"Like hell I will," I snarl.

"You will not have a choice." Gudrun waves her claws toward one of the other Seers. "Now, Sigrid."

Gudrun was stalling this whole time, but I realize it too late.

The Seer—Sigrid—is focused on me with unnatural intensity.

Her eyes bore into me as she says, *Kill the Fell King.* But her mouth never moves. Her voice is in my mind. I shake my head back and forth, as if I can get rid of it. *Kill the Fell King,* she continues. *Kill the Fell King.* She chants the words again and again until I cannot tell her chanting from my own thoughts.

My body moves on its own, turning toward Soren, and freeing my dagger from my dress.

"Astrid, what—?"

I drive the blade at him before he can finish.

Soren catches my wrist, stopping my strike from landing. "What are you doing?"

My arm shakes as I struggle to bring the dagger down on Soren.

"It's not me," I say through gritted teeth.

Kill the Fell King, Sigrid continues chanting in my head.

Right. She has the power of compulsion, to control people through their minds. So that's what Gudrun meant. *If the Seer will not cooperate, we must make her.* To them, I've always been a tool to use and nothing else.

But I refuse to be used.

This is just another kind of magic. I can break it.

I search Soren's face, but his eyes swim with sadness. Like when we lay on the frozen lake together, staring up at the cold stars, our hands barely brushing each other against the chill of the ice. Now he holds my wrist in his cold grip as my hand drives the dagger toward his heart. *Kill the Fell King. Kill the Fell King.*

I don't know if Sigrid is just too strong, or I'm too weak.

Tears burn as the dagger tip draws closer to Soren. "I can't stop it."

"I know." Soren is barely resisting me anymore, even though he could easily crush my wrist if he wanted.

"Fight back, damn it," I say.

Soren shakes his head. "I will not harm you."

"But they're using *me* to hurt you." My voice turns pleading. "You have to stop me."

I glimpse my reflection in his wet eyes. With my hair down, I look more like Skaga than myself, and I wonder which of us he's seeing right now. The Seers are trying to make me betray him just like she did. Is this how Skaga felt when she used the sleep thorn on him?

Did he allow her to do that too?

My hand trembles as I try to resist Sigrid. But the dagger finds his chest, its sharp point pressing into his leather vest. "Please, Soren."

Soren grimaces as the blade breaks skin. "I would sooner let you kill me than hurt you."

Something inside of me cracks like ice.

I won't do that to him, not again.

Never again, I hear Skaga saying.

In his eyes, I see her. I see both of us, our reflections layered on top of each other.

Skaga is with me. I hear her voice in my head. A lifetime of things said and unsaid floods into me like a burst damn, until her voice drowns out Sigrid's incessant chanting. Skaga's memories are like a river rushing over me, her love like the waterfall pounding upon my shoulders—

I yank the dagger away before it can go deeper.

"I won't hurt you again," I say, but my voice isn't just mine. Skaga speaks through me now.

"She broke it." Sigrid stumbles back. "I don't know how—"

"Guess I forgot to mention I can break magic." I face the Seers, my dagger held toward them. "Just like I'm going to break the blood oath. Now get out of my way."

"Never," Gudrun says, her voice trembling with rage.

The nine other Seers flock behind her, standing between us and the stave church.

I brace myself as their claws extend like knives.

Soren positions himself in front of me protectively, but there are too many of them.

They attack. Soren is there to stop them. One struggles against his hold, but Soren grips her with bone-crushing force, sending the others flying back with a galdr.

I race forward—

Gudrun blocks my path. As if she knew exactly what I would do before I did it. Amma said her foresight works like our vision. She can see the immediate future more easily.

Shit. "Are you—"

"That's right." Gudrun's eyes turn white as milk. "Glimpsing a few seconds into the future is no trouble."

I shudder. No wonder she survived the schism between the Seers. If she can see everything her opponent will do before they act, that makes her unstoppable. All the other Seers bear gruesome wounds, but not Gudrun. This power is why she and her faction of Seers came out on top.

Behind us, Soren holds the other Seers in a binding galdr. But there are too many. Some are almost as ancient as he is. He won't be able to hold all eight of them for long.

I have to do *something*. Fast.

Gudrun's lips quirk. "Do you truly think you can defeat me, you petulant little girl?"

I slash out at her face. "I can try."

She blocks the blow effortlessly, as if she saw my attack coming.

I try again and again. How am I supposed to land a blow like this? As soon as I decide to strike, she sees what I'll do.

This time, Gudrun comes at me.

I barely dodge in time.

She missed me. She must not be able to attack while looking into the future. That's why she couldn't predict my exact movement. I can dodge her, at least.

Gudrun strikes again—

A falcon shoots down from the sky and sinks its talons into her hand with an earsplitting screech. Gudrun howls in pain. Clearly, she didn't see that coming. She must only be able to see one person's choices at a time.

"How *dare* you, daughter!" Gudrun yells.

My breath catches. "Amma?"

But no. Gudrun killed Amma. This must be Hilda, who Amma said shared her gift.

With a screech, Hilda claws her face, tearing flesh. Gudrun throws her arm up, shielding her eyes. Hilda shreds her arm down to the bone. Gudrun screams but doesn't lower her arm.

Her eyes.

Without them, she won't be able to see the future, or anything else.

Another Seer knocks Hilda down, taking Gudrun with her, and they crash to the snow in a tangle of fangs and claws.

This is my chance.

Gudrun is wide open. Gripping the dagger, I plunge it into her eye with a scream. I feel almost unhinged as I drive it deeper. She howls as I rip the dagger out, black blood spraying over me, and stab her other eye. Blood gushes from her eye sockets, streaming down her white face like oily tears.

I raise the dagger high with both hands, over my head—

And hesitate.

This is Amma's mother sprawled before me. Suffering. Screaming.

She twists her head toward the other Seers. "The blood oath must not be broken. Destroy the Fell King at all costs."

She's still a hateful monster.

As long as she survives, she will never let go of the past.

I won't let her take the future from us.

So I bring my dagger down, driving it into her heart. There's an awful, wet sound as it sinks into her flesh, reminding me of the squelching sound as Amma plunged her hand through Dad's chest. But I have to do this.

For Amma. Gudrun mistreated her, and that cruelty shaped how Amma treated Dad. A vicious cycle—one Dad could've easily continued but broke instead. He loved me without expecting anything in return. Gritting my teeth, I drive the dagger deeper, fueled by rage.

"I curse you." Gudrun coughs, wet and thick. Black blood spews from her mouth and streams down her chin, pouring over her stained dress like a waterfall. "I curse you, wretched girl."

"You already have," I say, shaking.

What has the blood oath been if not a curse?

A curse she and every Seer chose to continue.

Until me.

"I shall see you soon in Sessrúmnir," Gudrun says viciously. "You will not live past dawn."

Gudrun goes stiff. Unmoving. The gaping holes of her eyes stare at me like two dark pits. Her chest is ripped apart, the flesh torn open where I stabbed her heart. *I* did that. I start to retch.

Soren growls behind me.

The Seers have him surrounded, and Hilda is nowhere in sight. Soren fends them off, his eyes turning onyx and his claws lengthening. For a moment, I can't even recognize him. Behind him, the effigy burns, warm light wavering in the darkness. And I recall Gudrun's hateful words: *Destroy the Fell King at all costs.*

The Seers are certainly trying to.

Soren clearly doesn't want to kill them. I have to help somehow, but there are too many for me to fight. Hilda's help is the only way I was able to kill Gudrun. I'll never be able to defeat them all. Especially by myself.

As Soren struggles to drive them away, I look around, desperate.

Only then do I realize that the fallen Seers around me are actually *moving*. They drag themselves over the snow, smearing blood in their wake. They don't seem interested in me, though. They're pulling themselves toward the surviving Seers.

And Soren.

The others haven't noticed the fallen Seers approaching.

A loud *crack* fills the air.

The burning effigy behind them blazes in the darkness. Through the scorching heat, the base of the massive structure starts to buckle. The whole thing seems ready to topple over at any moment. If I could just get it to fall in this direction, it would crush the Seers and burn them all.

Fire-resistant ropes are all that keep the massive effigy standing.

The ropes. That's it.

I run toward the effigy and saw one of the ropes with my dagger. But the damn rope is thicker and stronger than normal, meant to withstand the blaze as long as possible. The fire singes my skin as I struggle against it. Finally, the rope breaks.

One more.

Soren can barely hold off the Seers, and the fallen ones have nearly reached them.

I have to hurry.

Sweat rolls down my back as I race to grab the rope on the other side. Gritting my teeth, I start cutting it as quickly as I can. I not only have to cut through, but use the rope to try to steer the effigy toward the Seers. This is my only chance to catch them off guard.

I give a quick glance over my shoulder. The fallen Seers are closing in.

My blade grows more frantic, until—

The rope snaps.

Before the wind can take it, I grab hold and wrap it around my hand. The wood groans louder, cracking and snapping from the heat. But it hasn't fallen. Yet. Pulling the rope, I run toward them, trying to bring the burning effigy down with me.

"Soren!" I shout.

Everything happens at once. Soren is beside me in an instant, just as the massive wooden structure starts collapsing. I release the rope, and Soren hooks his arm around my waist, carrying me to safety as it falls.

At the same time, the Seers all look up as the effigy topples toward them. They try to run, but the fallen Seers finally reach them, closing their hands like shackles around the ankles of the other Seers before they can flee. They were never going after Soren, but *each other*.

In a sudden burst of heat, the effigy crashes down.

The Seers shriek as it crushes them all.

Their blood turns the fire bright gold as they're consumed like kindling. Smoke rises in great white clouds toward the dark sky along with their screams. As I watch, I can't help but feel Freyja's hand in this. Those effigies were erected to protect Unden in her stead. Now they finally have, from the true threat.

Even before the dawn, Freyja burned them.

Firelight paints the stave church a bright orange as Soren and I walk toward it. With each step, my guilt only grows. But how many lives have those Seers taken? Maybe this is what they deserved: to die outside the very place they claimed so many lives in. Sick satisfaction fills me. It feels like a small justice. So I will take it.

Now I might be the only Seer left.

And it's time to make sure I'm the last.

THIRTY-NINE

"Are you ready?" Soren asks, his long cloak pooling around him.

"I am."

I take another slow step toward the altar, the wooden floor creaking underfoot. The journey to this moment has spanned centuries. The candles burn low, and the only sound is their soft crackling. The church remains empty, bathed in the warm glow, the doors barred shut. No one is gathered here for this. Only us. And somehow, that feels right. Inevitable.

Because it's always been us.

The Fell King and the Seer.

Soren watches my every movement as I approach, until I'm standing across from him in front of the altar. He studies me wordlessly. All at once, I'm aware of how close his face is to mine. Barely a breath separates us. The little hairs on my arms rise as a tingle travels over my skin.

"It's just you and me now," Soren says, trailing a cold knuckle down my cheek. "As it should be. As it was at the beginning and will be at the end."

We stare at each other, each really *seeing* the other.

"It's been a long journey," he adds softly.

"So it has." I remember when I first woke Soren in Amma's basement, unaware how much my life was about to change forever when I found him. Never in my wildest dreams would I have imagined standing here across from him now, the Seer to his Fell King. Equals.

I slip my dagger from my dress. I know better than anyone the ripple effect even one life can cause, like a stone dropped into a lake. My entire existence has been shaped by the choices of others: Skaga and every Seer after her, but especially Amma. I stare at my reflection in the dagger's blade.

Skaga was the first Seer, but I will be the last.

This is my legacy. The legacy I choose.

Soren inclines his head and lifts his fingers to rest against my jaw. "Hold out your left hand."

I do.

Soren holds out his other hand, the scar there a mirror image to my own.

"I, Soren, make this oath to you: I shall no longer require sacrifices to serve my throne, just as the Hidden Folk shall no longer be bound to Tiveden, so that balance will be restored once more." His eyes don't leave mine as he brings his claw to his palm and drags it slowly across his scar. "I swear this oath on my blood, the most powerful of oaths. So help me Freyja and Freyr and the Almighty Vanir."

Dark blood beads on his pale skin like onyx jewels.

His next words are so quiet I almost don't hear them. "Now you must make your oath."

I pause, unsure at first what to say. When I really listen, it's as if I can hear the oath Skaga made to Soren long ago, a faint whisper in the back of my mind. The words are there, waiting for me to hear them, to accept them—to undo them, this time.

I nod. "I, Skaga, make this oath to you: I shall no longer serve as Seer. I disavow my duty of offering sacrifices, and the protection it has granted Unden, so that balance will be restored once more."

My hand trembles as I bring the blade to my open palm. Its sharp tip kisses my scar. I'm not just doing this for Unden, but for Dad. Johan. Soren. *Myself.* I cannot change what I have done, but I can choose differently now. I press the dagger in and reopen the old wound. Hot blood wells in my palm, but the pain is dull in comparison to all that I'm feeling.

"I swear this oath on my blood," I say, breathless. "The most powerful of oaths. So help me Freyja and Freyr and the Almighty Vanir."

Soren gently takes my hand in his, his palm comforting like an early winter's night. He weaves his fingers through mine until our hands are locked. Everything else falls away, and suddenly it's just me and him. Our blood flows, mingling together. Bright red and deep black. Both an end and a beginning.

"Your blood now flows through my veins," Soren says, the timbre of his voice low and rich.

Something spreads through me as our gazes meet.

I inhale sharply. "As your blood flows through mine."

My head feels light, but Soren grips my hand, tethering me to reality. My whole body tingles at his touch. His certainty. His strength.

The very air around us changes.

The church comes alive with ancient magic, as if the gods themselves are here to witness our oath. When I look up at the wooden statue of Freyja, her empty eyes watch me. Blood drips down her carved cheeks like tears.

One trail is bright red, the other midnight black.

I suck in an unsteady breath. I can still smell the church's sharp scent of cedar, but now another scent fills the space: the earthy smell of damp soil, like the roots twisting through Tiveden. Something else shimmers in the air. The cloying scent of fragrant flowers as they bloom and slowly shrivel.

Soren brushes loose strands of hair from my face, tenderly tucking them behind the curve of my ear. "Do you feel that?"

The way he's looking at me makes me think he's not just talking about the ancient magic. He's talking about us. About whatever is growing between us, fragile as fresh ice. About what we might become if we survive this night.

And with sudden clarity, I realize *I love him.*

I love Soren.

I love him more than I can bear to put into words. I loved him in my last life. I love him in this life, and will love him in any other. My heart beats for his, and his heart beats for mine. They always have. They always will.

"I do," I whisper.

But terror follows in its wake.

Everyone I've ever loved, I've lost. And I don't want to lose him, too.

I pull away from him. With my other hand, I apply pressure to my palm, more than I probably need to stanch the bleeding. My pulse pounds wildly against the pad of my thumb. I swallow past the lump in my throat, trying to fight these feelings.

"How will we know if it worked?" I ask, but my voice comes out too breathy.

The question hangs in the silence of the church.

"We won't until the morning," Soren says.

If unmaking the oath didn't work, I will die at dawn.

I swallow hard. "Then this might be our last night."

"Are you all right?" he murmurs.

Blinking, I realize he misunderstood. He's standing close by; his eyes don't leave the blood dripping down my wrist. But this doesn't hurt. Not like the thought of dying now that we've finally found each other.

I hold my palm out to him.

An offering.

Soren releases an unsteady breath. He looks at me with reverence, the same way churchgoers worship. He captures my wrist and brings my hand to his mouth. Gently, he presses his lips to my palm.

All I feel is contrasts: his cool lips on my skin and the radiant heat of the candles surrounding us; tears dripping down my cheeks and goose bumps rising along my arms; my belly turning liquid hot as his cold fingers caress my skin.

I have to close my eyes against his touch.

"*Soren,*" I breathe.

Over my hand, he looks up at me, his pupils blown wide. My stomach lurches uncertainly. I don't know what he will do next. What I *want* him to do.

His tongue flicks over the sensitive skin of my palm. His fangs flash, but he's being careful not to harm me. He's restraining himself, even though the scent of my blood must be driving him mad. He pulls away like he's barely able to.

"Don't leave me," I say, my voice thick.

I don't want to be without him. No, it's more than that. I *want* him. Want to feel his hands on my hips, his lips closing over mine, his skin against my skin. Heat pools inside me, like the slow drip of the melting candles around us.

Soren reaches for my face. "I won't."

The pad of his finger feels rough against my chapped lips, but his touch is featherlight, barely there. As if he's afraid of hurting me.

I'm not afraid of that anymore.

I gaze back at him. Soren leans closer, his fingers lingering on my skin. I can't help but remember when he drew me against him and bit my neck. My blood still stains the corner of his mouth.

I push up on my toes, trying to reach him, to close that distance between us. Soren lifts me by my hips, seating me on the altar before him like I'm something to worship.

If this could be our last night, I'm not going to waste it.

Mere centimeters separate us, but somehow, it's *still* too far. I want him closer, close enough that we become one, close enough that the same heart beats inside us. I want him, more than I have ever wanted anything before, more than life itself.

Before I know what I'm doing, I wrap my arms around him, pull him against me, and finally, *finally* press my mouth against his.

A rush of exhilaration courses through me the moment our lips meet.

Soren gasps in surprise, but then within seconds, he's kissing me back with just as much force, crushing his body against mine, the altar digging into my legs. But I don't care, not when my hands are on his shoulders, sliding down his clothes; not when he's grabbing a fistful of my hair.

The kiss tastes like blood, and the way Soren's tongue swipes over mine feels like he's trying to break through all the flesh and bones separating us until there's nothing left but our beating hearts and our souls crying out to be together.

My lips are already swollen and sore from kissing him, and I still want more. Soren's eyes are piercing as he stares at me. His hand cups my cheek, cold and comforting.

I reach for the pin that fastens his cloak and slowly undo it. His cloak falls to the floor, a spill of fur at our feet. Wordlessly, I begin unlacing his leather armor, starting at his neck and carefully working my way down his chest.

Before I pull the final lace free, he grabs my hand in his.

"Astrid," he says, his voice rough. "Are you certain?"

I nod, shucking off his armor vest and pulling off his tunic until the bare skin of his broad chest is exposed. I trace a finger over the stave marking him, and he sucks in a sharp breath. His eyes flutter closed, as if the sensation of my touch is too much for him to bear.

This is the stave that made him what he is. A draugr. I take in its entirety: a rectangle spans across his chest, with a series of lines and circles reaching down from his pectorals to his abs.

The symbol is strange and beautiful.

Just like Soren.

I slide the fur mantle from my shoulders and let it fall to the floor with his cloak. He watches my every movement, a hunger in his eyes. Then I capture his mouth with mine, my hands wandering over his bare skin. The feel of his corded muscle beneath my fingertips is overwhelming. I kiss him harder, desperate, and he returns the kiss with equal intensity. He pauses only to pull my dress up over my head and discard it on the floor.

Then he's kissing me again and I'm kissing him.

He picks me up, and I wrap my legs around his waist, needing to be closer to him. A low groan escapes him, and his lips cover mine. I run my tongue along one of his fangs, and he growls, laying me back against the furs spread over the floor like a soft bed. The fur brushes my back, light as a feather, as the hard planes of his chest press against my body.

Now that I've finally kissed him, I can't stop, like I'm under a stave's spell. But then his hands grip my waist and I feel his body crushed against mine, fitting me like he was made for me, and I realize I'm wrong.

This feeling is more powerful than any stave could ever be.

⇒⟶FORTY⟵⇐

"Skaga, this cannot continue," Soren says. "We must break the blood oath."

"I didn't know," I say weakly, as if that is any excuse. "I have only done as we decided."

I thought I understood Freyja's will, but maybe I was mistaken.

"Are you certain something is wrong with the sacrifices?" I add.

Soren nods gravely. "They are unlike any of our kind. Nothing about them is natural. They have more ógipta than I have ever seen before. It is so great, I did not know anything could possess so much maliciousness. Their ógipta already infects the forest, twisting Tiveden itself."

Even in Unden, I have noticed more going amiss. Birds dropping out of the sky like stones. Cattle collapsing, bones snapped like branches. Berries rotting more quickly, fish spoiling no matter how much we salt them.

I shake my head. "But there have only been two."

The knowledge that soon it will be time for me to make another hangs heavy between us.

"Tiveden cannot handle more," Soren says.

I bite my lip as I consider his words. "Could it be because the sacrifices were not willing? Perhaps if they die cursing their misfortune, that is why their ógipta is so great."

Maybe that is where I went wrong. The sacrifices I chose served as a means to dispose of any who threatened Unden. After I killed Gorm, his spákona wife began to cause a commotion. Thyra was even more meddlesome than her husband. She tried to poison me countless times and nearly cost my daughter her life when she was still inside my womb. Thyra taught me how dangerous blood feuds can be, and how quickly those feuds amass casualties.

Thyra was my next sacrifice.

Of course she and Gorm would continue to trouble Unden even after their deaths.

"I will use a willing sacrifice this time," I say.

"Skaga, you are not hearing me." Soren raises his voice. "The blood oath cannot continue. There must not be another sacrifice."

Does he understand what he's asking of me? I search his face. It's unsettling, seeing him like this. I have aged, but he still looks the same as when I first saw him, even though his years far surpass my own.

"There must be," I say. "You swore to me Unden would thrive, and it has. It has grown even beyond my father's wildest dreams. I will not forsake my home, not even for your forest."

Not even for you, I almost say.

"You do not mean that," Soren says furiously.

I stare at him. Soren has been quicker to anger since the oath, more volatile than ever before. Is the ógipta affecting him as well as Tiveden? I cannot explain the changes in him otherwise. He has been growing more temperamental and impatient after our oath, not less.

"Lower your voice," I scold. "We cannot be overheard, especially not here. No one in Unden can know we sometimes see each other still. If we must argue, we will do so in the cellar where none can hear us."

I lift the cellar door and look at Soren expectantly.

"Fine." He walks swiftly down until he disappears into the darkness.

Grabbing a torch, I follow him down the creaking steps. This cellar has always felt like the inside of a burial mound, but I cannot risk Torsten or my daughter discovering us together.

Firelight moves over the packed dirt walls as I face Soren. "You promised me I could live out my life in Unden."

"And you have," he says slowly, "for nearly eighteen additional years. Is that not enough?"

"It is not."

Torsten has given me a daughter, but I have never told Soren that. He would not understand that she is part of Unden's future. I birthed Dagny to entrust this settlement to her one day as my father entrusted it to me. But she is still too young. She needs her mother, as I need my daughter.

"If I die, what will become of Unden?" I ask him. "As soon as the blood oath no longer binds them, Gorm and Thyra will destroy my home with their ill will."

Soren paces the packed dirt floor. "So you would forsake me instead?"

"I would not." I capture his forearm with my free hand, stopping him. "You know I love you still. We will be together one day, but not yet." I slip my hand into his, where it still fits perfectly. "I need more time, Soren. I want to live. Isn't that what first made you love me?"

Soren grips my hand. "How much longer will you make me wait?"

I caress his cold skin with my thumb. "I don't know," I admit. "My death has already been decided by the gods, but I will not know until I reach it. One lifetime, that is all I have ever asked."

"I do not have long," Soren says, his voice pained. "I swore to protect Tiveden. When I had nowhere else to go, the Hidden Folk welcomed me into their forest, accepting me for what I had become. Not merely accepting. They revered me, as if I was the Allfather himself. And how have I thanked them? Because of the oath I swore to you, they are all trapped, and Tiveden is dying."

"I am sorry, Soren," I say, aching for him. "But the blood oath cannot be broken."

"Even if I will be executed for it?"

I gasp. "You are their king."

"They made me Fell King to protect them. I have failed in that duty. Now I must face the consequences: ritual execution. Unless I can free them, they will sacrifice me to the Allfather as soon as I return."

I gasp. "But that would mean . . ."

He nods gravely. "The blood eagle will be carved into my back."

The most brutal execution there is. So brutal, few can stomach performing it.

"No, Soren." I stumble toward him. "I cannot lose you."

Soren steps back, firelight casting shadows across his face. "Now you know how I felt when you first forced me to make this oath."

"It was wrong of me," I say. "I should not have threatened my own life, but I was desperate, Soren. I do not want to lose you or Unden." I step closer. "Can I not have both?"

Soren shakes his head. "You must choose."

Once, my father said he hoped I never understood the choice he had to make when he let Gorm sacrifice me in order to save Unden. But as I stand here before Soren, I'm beginning to. I know what I must do to protect Unden, but it is not what my heart wants.

"Then I choose you," I tell him slowly.

Soren smiles then—actually smiles, full and brilliant. My breath hitches. For once, his happiness is unguarded. He trusts me, I realize, wholly and without question. It only makes what I must do so much harder.

Soren opens his arms to me.

I run to him, but not before slipping my hand into my pouch of staves.

There is only one I have never used before.

Until now.

Soren pulls me against him tightly, pressing his cold lips to my hair. "I love you, Skaga."

"As I love you." I reach for his chest, placing my hand—and the sleep thorn—over his heart. "Never forget that, Soren."

His eyes widen as he realizes my betrayal.

Soren goes slack in my arms. I ease him to the dirt floor as best I can.

"What have you done?" he manages to get out, struggling to stay conscious.

"What I had to do," I say through tears.

As I hold him in my arms, the look of devastation on his face breaks something inside me.

My tears splatter his cheeks until I can no longer tell if they are his or mine.

A sob racks my body. "I cannot allow you to destroy Unden—or yourself."

"Skaga" is all he can say.

But it is enough. In that single word, I hear his every emotion: rage, agony, devastation, but above all else, love. A love that would outlast even the gods if

I let it. But I cannot. Not when I finally understand the words my father once said to me: Between duty and love, there is no choice.

"The blood oath must not be broken," I whisper to him.

As his eyes close, I kiss Soren for the last time.

FORTY-ONE

I wake in Soren's arms.

His embrace is cold and comforting and familiar, as if I have been held in his arms hundreds of times before. As I drape my arm across him, needing to be closer, his skin reminds me of when Skaga held Soren for the last time. She loved Soren, even as she betrayed him.

She never stopped.

I can feel her love for him even now. As I lay stretched out beside him on the church floor, now I know it isn't just her love, but my own as well. *This* is where I belong.

I belong with Soren.

Pulling his fur cloak around me, I sit up slowly. His eyelids flutter slightly as I stir, but he doesn't wake. I linger on his face, his harsh features softened by sleep. Long lashes graze his cheeks, his silver hair spilling around his face, his bangs skimming the bridge of his nose.

This is the first time I've seen Soren sleep.

Well, the second time.

When I first discovered him sleeping in the cellar, it had been centuries since Skaga laid him to rest. It seems right, somehow, that I was the one who woke him. As if Freyja herself foretold it. Now he looks different from when I first found him. He looks happy.

A smile spreads across my lips as I gently brush his bangs aside.

Our clothes lie strewn over the altar, and the candles surrounding us burn low, their warmth wavering like the flames. After last night, part of me never wants to leave this sanctuary. Or Soren. Even now, I find myself resisting the idea of getting up to get dressed, despite the chill in the air.

As I look around, the church is still. Quiet. *Peaceful.* There are no distant screams. No sounds of destruction raging outside. A sliver of weak light shines in through the gap between the doors.

Dawn.

Drawing in a long breath, I look down at my trembling hands. The cut running across my left palm, bright red and tender to the touch. Alive—I'm alive. A small laugh escapes me.

I grab Soren's shoulder, shaking him awake. "It worked."

Soren's eyes open, his gaze softening when he sees me. My heart skips a beat. Heat pools inside me as I remember our last night. No, not our last. Our first of many together—I hope.

"It's finally over," I say, pressing my forehead against his, my nose bumping his. The words don't feel quite enough. "We ended it."

Some of the tension slips out of him as he touches my cheek gently, his cold fingers trailing across my skin. "We did."

I want to press my lips to his again and draw him against me. Feel his muscles beneath my fingertips, his body moving over mine. But we have to save Unden first. So I peel myself away from Soren and pull my clothes back on while he gets dressed.

The crack of light between the doors disappears.

A faint scratching sound. So quiet, I can barely hear it.

"What is that?" I ask, the floor creaking as I walk toward the doors.

Claws. Claws drag over the wood.

I shake my head. No, I must be mistaken.

The beam blocking the doors cracks down the middle. It splinters. Snaps.

The doors burst open.

I stumble backward, but Soren is there to catch me. Early morning light spills in around the silhouette from the doorway. It takes a moment for my vision to adjust—

A draugr.

The silent church fills with an awful clicking as her head swivels until she's staring straight at us. I take in her twisted neck and corpse-like skin. The ropes of long silver hair.

Dagny.

I stare in stunned silence. This isn't possible. The last of the Seers died.

But she is Skaga's daughter. She is the oldest of them all. The most ancient—and also the most powerful. If anyone had survived the infighting, she would.

"What have you done?" Dagny asks.

I take Soren's hand in mine, threading my fingers through his. "We unmade the blood oath. Together."

"No, no, *no*. This cannot be." Dagny looks stricken. "How could you? If the blood oath is broken, then you have killed us all."

"We have a plan," I say, shaking my head. "Soren is going to negotiate with the Hidden Folk. If that fails, we still have all day to evacuate Unden until we can figure something out."

Dagny's eyebrows raise. "All day?"

I nod. "There's still plenty of time. The sun hasn't even risen yet."

"The sun is not rising," Dagny says slowly. "It is *setting*."

"What?" I ask, staring at the red sky behind her. If it isn't sunrise but sunset, then that would mean . . .

"We slept through the entire day," Soren says.

Dagny frowns. "You meddled with powerful, ancient magic. Did you think it would cost you nothing?"

Now that the doors have been thrown open, screams and shouts echo through the church.

Behind Dagny, Unden is under attack.

"Soren, do something," I say, turning toward him. "Stop them."

He nods, reaching for the horn he uses to command them. "Cover your ears."

I clamp my hands over my ears as he brings it to his lips. A loud blast echoes around us. The piercing sound rumbles through me. The church shakes violently, jarring me like an earthquake.

The carnage continues.

I look at Soren. "Why isn't it working? Why aren't they stopping?"

Soren drags in a long breath and tries again. The sound is like a powerful blast of thunder. It keeps going and going, traveling through the church and toward Unden until the horn's bellow cuts off abruptly.

"I don't know," Soren says.

"We have to stop this," I say, panic rising.

We run for the doors—

Dagny blocks our path. "You are not going anywhere."

"We have to help Unden," I tell her. "Move out of the way."

"Before you left, you instructed me clearly." She steps toward us like a predator closing in on her prey. "The blood oath must never be broken. I devoted my life, my entire *existence*, to upholding it."

Now that it's undone, there's nothing to stop her from killing me.

I destroyed her legacy.

My dagger is still lying beside the altar. Soren positions himself in front of me, but I reach for his shoulder and shake my head. Right now, Dagny needs her mother more than anything else. "Go help Unden. I'll take care of this."

Soren runs outside, leaving us alone in the stave church.

I turn to Dagny and say the words Skaga should have said. "And I was wrong."

She gives a disbelieving laugh. "Wrong? *Wrong?*"

Before I can even react, she lashes out.

I duck behind a pillar, and wood explodes where I was.

Wood chips spray across my face.

"I performed the sacrifices as you taught me." Dagny swings at me desperately, driving me toward the back of the church. Away from my dagger. "I said the words just as you told me to. I did what was necessary to ensure the oath was never broken just as you did."

I can't get a word in, not when I'm focused on avoiding her attacks.

I grab a tall candlestick beside me and stab it like a spear, keeping her from getting too close.

She snarls. "Unlike you, I did not abandon my daughter to figure things out on her own."

I thrust the candle again, but the flame sputters out.

Her claws flash, dicing the candle. "I did not burn myself but went into Tiveden as you instructed."

I swing the candlestick toward her like a baseball bat, but she dodges the blow easily.

"No, I *helped* my daughter." Dagny rips the candlestick from my hand and throws it across the church. "And her daughter, and every Seer after."

I need my dagger—

No time. She attacks again.

I roll out of the way with seconds to spare, grab hold of a broken chunk of wood on the floor, and split off a sharp, pointed end. I climb onto my feet, holding the scrap of wood between us like a sword. "Everything I did, I did for Unden. You must hear their screams. They need us now."

Dagny suddenly stops, her hands dropping to her sides. "Tell me, where did I go wrong, Mother? Did I not do exactly as you wanted? If I did not, then what have I given my entire existence for?"

She doesn't actually want to hurt me, not really. *She* was the one who has been hurt.

The scrap of wood falls to the floor as I embrace Dagny.

"I'm sorry," I say, hugging her against me tightly. "I was the one who was wrong, not you. It was my mistake, and I never should have asked you to continue it for so long."

Dagny shakes with sobs but says nothing.

After a long moment, her cold arms encircle me. "What could I have possibly done differently? I sacrificed so much. You have no idea how much. It was so difficult, Mother, waiting for you all this time, hoping you would be pleased with me."

Skaga might not understand, but *I* do.

I cradle the back of her head. "No one should have asked that of you."

"But you did," Dagny says through her tears.

"I'm sorry." I pull back slowly, wiping her tears away with my thumbs.

"I know you did what I asked, but times have changed. We must change with them."

The screams are growing louder outside.

"You did all this to protect Unden, right?" I ask Dagny. "So help me protect it. We both want the same thing."

Dagny searches my face. Nods.

Together, we leave the church. The sun has dipped below the horizon, leaving the sky a bloody red. It looks like the midnight sun, only more sinister.

"Something is wrong," I say. "Very, very wrong."

When I didn't die at dawn, I thought we'd succeeded in unmaking the blood oath. And we did. But its damage still remains, like all the damage my family has—

"The sacrifices," Dagny and I say at the same time.

"The blood oath was what bound the sacrifices to the Fell King, right?" I ask. "We thought that without the oath, they would become regular Hidden Folk, not the twisted, poisoned versions. We thought Soren would be able to command them."

Dagny shakes her head. "That would not work. They never actually *became* Hidden Folk. They are something hitherto unseen. Unnatural abominations created by the blood oath and ógipta."

Besides Skaga, she is probably the person who understands the blood oath best.

Soren wouldn't have realized that—not when he was asleep all this time.

I blow out a long breath. "We have to stop them."

FORTY-TWO

The deeper we go into Unden, the louder the screams grow.

I look around as the town is torn apart by the sacrifices. People are being dragged from their homes by fistfuls of hair, thrashing and screaming. Blood runs through the village, streaking the streets, staining the snow red. Whole houses have been ripped apart, neighborhoods decimated.

As I look around, I can still remember the village coming alive with celebration every Midsummer. Instead of flowers and laughter, now there are only screams and slaughter. This is what Amma and all the other Seers wanted to prevent. What they sacrificed so many to stop.

Now those sacrifices are destroying Unden.

I spot Soren among them. Black blood sprays him, reminding me that he's fighting his own kind to protect Unden. How must he feel? He glances at me, his face streaked. There's no ounce of regret, only razor-sharp focus. My breath catches. Somehow, he still looks beautiful, even in battle.

Dagny barrels into the fight, her long silver braids flying behind her.

I bolt toward Soren—

A massive, horrifyingly familiar creature cuts me off. Flayed flesh. Powerful, predatory muscles. A shriek rips from the kattakyn, sending ropes of saliva flying from its maw. I duck beside one of the houses, flattening myself against the siding.

I don't dare move a muscle. I can hear the kattakyn's heavy footfalls punching through the snow, until it stops abruptly. My breath comes hard and fast. If the kattakyn hears me . . . I clap my hand over my mouth, but I can't quiet my pounding pulse.

Another moment passes.

The kattakyn appears, staring at me with its large, glowing eyes. Trembling, I press my hand harder against my mouth to keep from screaming. A menacing rumbling noise rises from the kattakyn. *Run!*

The kattakyn winces as two bright headlights shine toward us.

A plow slams into the creature, sending it flying.

Ebba rocks forward in her seat from the impact. Instead of snow, blood sprays over the truck and splatters the windshield. The wipers squeak on, smearing dark fluid back and forth. I've never been so glad to see my nosy neighbor.

With a growl, the kattakyn swings a massive paw.

Soren grabs me, pulling me away as the snow plow veers toward the spot I was in moments ago. Metal crunches under the weight of the kattakyn as it climbs over the hood of the truck. The windshield shatters, pieces flying like hailstones. Ebba screams and screams. Soren tries to pull me away, but I can't stop staring at the awful sight as Ebba is shredded to death.

Once the kattakyn finishes, its glowing eyes land on me.

The creature springs forward.

"Astrid!" Soren screams.

"Soren—"

All of a sudden, he's there.

Soren traps its jaws with his bare hands.

The kattakyn struggles against his hold.

"We have to stop it," I say, staring at the crumpled truck.

"I will not kill it," Soren says through gritted teeth. "But perhaps I can still command it."

"It's worth a try, right?"

He nods as he pushes the kattakyn's jaws open wider.

"Return to Tiveden." His tone turns commanding and powerful.

The kattakyn starts closing its jaws.

"It won't work," Soren says, struggling against the kattakyn. "It's been infected by ógipta."

That must be why it looks so hideous, its flesh flayed, raw muscles and sinew exposed. But ógipta is another kind of magic, isn't it? Misfortune magic. If that's why it won't obey Soren, then maybe I can break it. Its teeth keep getting closer and closer to Soren.

I have to *try*.

Swallowing my revulsion, I bring my palm to the kattakyn's neck. The creature's muscles are wet and slimy as it strains to close its jaws on Soren. I squeeze my eyes shut, focusing on the feel of its neck muscles bunching and pulling under my palm, on the low rumbles of rage in its throat, on the steady drip of saliva from its glistening teeth.

Beneath it all, something else pulses. The ógipta. It isn't cold like Soren's galdr or burning hot like Skaga's stave. It's something . . . *wrong*. The hairs on my neck stand on end. It feels like the infected trees in Tiveden, how they break like bones and run with blood.

What is the opposite of misfortune?

I think of Skaga lying atop Trollkyrka, warm sun bathing her skin as she realized the truth of who she was. Her mother's tears showering her as the goddess told her to survive. Sunlight is bright behind my eyelids, its warm glow as comforting as it was when I walked the safe, sunlit part of the woods with Amma, my small hand clutched in her warm, wrinkled one. The sense of wonder and possibility I felt back then.

The joy my heart held—

Joy. That's it.

All at once, the tension is released from the creature's muscles.

The kattakyn withdraws as if only now realizing it was fighting the Fell King.

I pull my hand back slowly. "Try now."

"Return to Tiveden," Soren says with all the confidence of a king.

The kattakyn lopes toward Tiveden, dodging one of the burning effigies with feline grace before disappearing into the forest.

"It worked," I say breathlessly. "I broke the ógipta."

As we return to the main street, I look around us. "Maybe I can heal all the sacrifices."

Soren's expression turns grim. "Careful, Astrid. All magic has its limits. That kattakyn must have been infected recently, unlike most of the sacrifices, who have been poisoned by the blood oath for centuries."

I can't help but feel disappointed. "We unmade the oath, but not its consequences."

In Tiveden, I saw how many sacrifices there were as they stood there in a trancelike state. Breaking *all* their magic would be impossible. I was barely able to break Sigrid's spell. On my own, I couldn't have. Her compulsion magic would have made me kill Soren. But Skaga helped me stop her.

"Even with your ability, you're still one person," Soren adds. "No individual can save everyone."

He's right. I know he is.

Even with the blood oath unmade, undoing all its damage is impossible.

No matter how much I wish it was.

"Can you call the ancient Folk to battle?" I ask, suddenly desperate.

"I will not ask the original Folk to pay any more for my mistakes." Soren shakes his head. "Many have already died, hunted by Ramunder and the sacrifices that were under his command. Because of the blood oath, the sacrifices would have had no choice but to obey him, even if the pre-existing Folk refused to acknowledge him as Fell King."

Now it's the opposite for Soren.

Without the blood oath, he can no longer command the sacrifices.

A draugr appears in front of us.

He wears a wolfish grin as he carries Old Ulf's body down the street. Gorm.

Skaga's first sacrifice.

He's no longer in a trance like the last time I saw him. Gorm drops the body with a heavy thud. Old Ulf sprawls facedown, his back shredded, his blood pouring over the snow. Gorm kicks him over and skewers him with a shrill, gleeful laugh.

My legs shake and give out under me, sending me crashing to the snow. I thought I hated Ulf, that I hated them all, but there's no satisfaction in seeing this. Only a sickening, sinking feeling. Unden is being destroyed by the people my family have killed. People *I* killed.

Gorm smirks, red blood staining his mouth and chin. "*There* you are, Skaga."

I scramble onto my feet.

"I hoped I would see you again," he says, amused. "So I could do this."

With a bloodcurdling scream, Gorm expands all at once.

He swells to the size of an ox.

Bigger.

He grows rapidly, bursting through his leather armor, until he towers over us.

"Can draugar even *do* that?" I gasp.

"In a blood-frenzy," Soren says. "Blood strengthens us, but consuming too much drives draugar mad with its power."

I stare at him, trying to wrap my head around his words, but I can't. If these sacrifices destroy Unden, they will become even more powerful. More lethal. By the time they reach Stockholm, or Gothenburg, or anywhere else—they'll have fed on so much blood, nothing will be able to stop them. *That's* what Amma meant.

The world won't stand a chance.

Gorm lashes out, but Soren holds up a hand, muttering under his breath. Gorm stops moving, his motion cut off mid-swing. He stands there, still as stone. Galdrar can stop him.

Behind Gorm, something else moves.

"Now!" Officer Lind shouts, unloading his gun into Gorm.

The bullets must be steel, but it's not enough.

Another sacrifice slams into Soren, and the galdr stops. With a scream, Gorm brings his fist down. The ground shatters where I stood seconds ago. I barely managed to roll out of the way in time. Gorm is about to strike again while I'm still sprawled out—

Someone bolts in front of me.

Gorm freezes mid-strike.

Johan stands before me, holding his coat open like some kind of superhero, a sword held in one hand.

Then Nils is there, burying a large battle-axe into Gorm's ankle like a tree trunk.

Gorm remains motionless.

He can't even scream as Nils hacks his other ankle open.

Gorm collapses as Johan turns to me.

"You're welcome," he says, helping me onto my feet with his free hand. When I let go, I realize his fingers are bloody. Not only that, but a bright red stave is painted on his T-shirt.

Ǿgishjálmr. The helm of awe.

The same stave Skaga once carved into Liv's shield.

A draugr runs toward us, but as soon as Johan faces them, they stop.

Not breaking eye contact, Johan stabs his sword through it.

I stare at him, stunned. "Since when can you use staves?"

"Your grandmother taught me them," he says, offering me an exhilarated smile. "After you moved, I used to visit her and ask her how you were doing."

Gorm howls, struggling to rise to his feet.

"Like I tried to tell you," Johan adds, "a lot changed since you left. With your grandmother getting older and no new Seer in training, Lind had us all preparing in case something like this happened."

I was wrong. Some of us are still warriors after all.

My breathing turns harsh and ragged as I look around. Linnea chants nearby, and the short staff she's holding extends, lengthening itself. She twirls the full staff in her hands before knocking some of the sacrifices away. Nils fights back-to-back with Officer Lind. Johan runs over to join them, stopping any enemy he sees.

More sacrifices swarm into Unden, and Gorm rises to his feet.

"There are too many," I say through gritted teeth.

Nils brings his axe down, dark blood spraying over him. "We have to break through."

Linnea is breathless. "How are we supposed to do that?"

A cold hand grabs me—Soren.

"Astrid, you have to go," he says, drawing me away from the others. "I can't protect you and fight at the same time."

"I can't." My whole body trembles with adrenaline. "I can't leave you *or* Unden."

Soren twists a draugr's neck with a sudden movement. "You must."

The draugr collapses to the ground, unmoving.

"I cannot kill them," Soren says, "but I will hold them off until we can figure out what to do."

With every sacrifice they bring down, more seem to take their place.

I wondered how many my family has killed. As I look around Unden, despair takes hold of me as I see the answer for myself. So many. Far too many. My breath won't come. They all used to be human, like Mom. Now they're fighting their families, their descendants, their neighbors, their friends. We're killing each other. Unden was once their home too, and now they're destroying it. I can't stop shaking. No. *No.* Unmaking the blood oath was supposed to solve everything, but the sacrifices aren't free.

Soren grips my shoulders. "Astrid."

His cold, steady touch brings me back to myself.

Smoke from the effigies pours into the night sky—

Fire. *Freyja's* fire.

Mom climbed onto the pyre to burn alongside Dad so she could be freed of what the forest had turned her into. So she could finally be reunited with Dad, and they could go to join Freyja together. The goddess's divine fire cleansed her of the ógipta poisoning her.

"Tiveden needs to be saved," I tell him. "The sacrifices won't be able to move on until the ógipta is destroyed." I can feel the truth of the words as soon as I say them. "But it means we'll have to burn the forest."

Soren frowns. "Tiveden is the only home I've known. I am sworn to protect it."

I know how hard it can be to give up a home. I was never able to let go of Unden, even after living in Stockholm for nine years. Can I really expect him to sacrifice the forest he's called home for so much longer?

"But it's the only way to save it," I add. "Freyja's fire should only burn the parts of the forest infected by the ógipta."

Soren searches my face slowly. "Very well. I will go with you."

"You can't," I say quickly. Freyja's fire could kill him, too. I can't lose him.

"You need my blood for the stave," Soren says.

My blood won't work by itself. Even if it could, his is more powerful than mine.

And to purify the ógipta, this stave needs all the power we can give it.

Realization dawns on me. "I already have it. Your blood flows through my veins now," I say, repeating the words we spoke when making the blood oath.

"At least let me help you get there." Soren grabs me in his arms, sweeping my feet out from under me and drawing me against his chest. "I need to make sure you reach Tiveden."

I look over Soren's shoulder, watching his back while he runs.

Gorm chases us in giant strides.

My breathing is hard and quick. "Gorm is coming."

"Hold on," Soren says.

He pushes off, sending us flying forward. Momentum drives me into his chest, and I instinctively wrap my arms around his neck, holding tight. His speed—he's so fast. Soren races ahead, his footfalls heavy.

Gorm pounds after us, the ground shaking underneath him. More sacrifices follow, racing over the rooftops. Trying to cut us off, I realize. Panic pulses through me. They run fast, faster than I ever could, but not as fast as Soren. I hope.

The stave church gets closer.

Closer.

But Gorm is right behind us.

A falcon soars overhead—*Hilda*.

She swoops down with a cry and gouges out one of Gorm's eyes with her talons.

Gorm gives a sharp howl of pain, momentarily distracted.

Soren sets me down on the ground. "Go. We will make sure Unden still stands when you return."

When I manage to speak, my voice is hoarse. "Be careful."

"You too," he says.

I give Soren a quick kiss before tearing myself away from him.

Tiveden still needs saving, and this one is all up to me.

⟫⟩─FORTY-THREE─⟨⟨⟨

I walk toward Tiveden as Skaga once did long ago.

The fallen effigy still smolders, smoke billowing before me like a curtain. I can smell the sickening scents of charred flesh and burned hair, all that remains of the Seers now. Somewhere among them lies Amma. I push through the heaviness weighing on my heart.

This has to stop. Now.

I navigate Tiveden until finding an infected tree. I bury my dagger into it, dark sap spilling down the tree like blood. Bark peels around the blade as I draw the lines of the stave. Even though he's back in Unden, I can practically feel the weight of Soren's hand on mine, guiding me like he did when he first taught me this stave.

I wait to add our blood to it.

Instead, I start on the next tree, carving the stave as quickly as I can. To give the best chance for the fire to spread, I'll need to—

A branch snaps behind me.

My blade stills. "Soren?"

I look over my shoulder, but it isn't him.

Amma stands there, leaning against one of the trees.

"Astrid," she rasps.

I hate that the first thing I feel is relief.

But then I notice how she clutches her side, barely able to remain standing. Her dress is soaked through with so much blood that the white linen is almost black. She pushes off from the tree and approaches me slowly, one of her legs dragging through the snow.

"You survived," she says, her breathing labored. "þǫkk sé Freyju."

Praise be to Freyja.

"Amma," I say, finally managing to get the word out.

She's not dead—not completely. Not yet.

But she's definitely dying.

"What happened?" My voice betrays my concern, which only makes me angrier.

"I failed in my duties." She coughs, wet and thick. "Some of the Seers turned against me. But in the chaos, I was able to flee."

Amma frowns as she looks me over. Her gaze goes to the dagger clutched in my hand and then rises to the tree behind me—at the stave carved there. "What are you doing?"

"Saving Tiveden."

"You wouldn't." She limps closer, searching my face. "You would be betraying me. Our family. You have already caused great strife among the Seers."

I grip my dagger tightly. Those deaths aren't on me.

I didn't kill countless people.

Unlike her.

"You betrayed *me*," I say, my whole body trembling with rage. "You took both my parents from me. And for what?"

She howls. "Because the blood oath must not be broken!"

My face burns. She's *still* trying to justify what she's done. After everything she has taken from me, she isn't sorry at all. "The blood oath is no excuse. It was still your choice to make."

Amma could have walked a different path if she'd wanted to, just like Soren did this time.

But she didn't. She chose to become a murderer.

"The blood oath is no more," I say, reminding myself of it too.

"What? No." She shakes her head. "Impossible. You would not be alive if you had broken it."

Wordlessly, I hold up my left palm. The slice running across it, red and angry.

Amma looks stricken.

She checks her own palm, but it's scarless. I can see that from here. Even if I couldn't, her terrified expression tells me everything.

"What have you *done*?"

I press a finger into my injured palm, blood welling when I do. "What someone in our family should have done a long, long time ago."

Amma stumbles toward me.

"My mother would've seen it. She would've stopped you." Amma latches onto my stained dress with shaking hands. "Where is my mother?"

Slowly, I tip my chin in the direction of the stave church. "Dead."

Her claws sink into my skin. "How could you?"

Wincing, I rip free of her. My dress tears as I back away. "How could *you*? How many people *have* you killed?"

"As many as I had to," she says, panting heavily.

I glance down at my bloody palm.

Enough of this. I stab the dagger into the tree with a sense of finality and carve the last line, wood peeling around my blade. Now that the stave is complete, I bring my hand toward it—

"Don't you dare, Astrid." Amma's voice rises with panic. "*Please*, don't do this to me. To us."

For a moment, it isn't the draugr I'm seeing, but my grandmother. As if she stepped out of my memories and stands before me. She looks so vulnerable, small, and frail now. So easily broken. I remember her wrinkled hand brushing over my braid while she smiled at me.

We need no goodbyes, she told me once.

But if I do this, it will be saying goodbye in the most permanent way. Not just to what she's become, but everything she used to be to me. The two are inextricably linked.

"I'm sorry," Amma says, reaching out, her fingers grasping for me. "For everything. All I wanted was for us to be together again, Asta. I love you. I would do anything for you. Please, don't leave me again. I need you now and always."

Everything she's saying—it's what I've wanted for so long too.

I hesitate, sucking in a deep breath. The familiar scent of pine still lingers, however faint. As I stand here, my insides feel as hollow as a huldra. My arm aches as I bring my trembling palm closer to the tree bark.

I can't remain imprisoned by the past any longer.

I press my bloody palm against the stave. "Goodbye, Amma."

Golden flame hisses to life, too bright for the bleak morning. Pine needles smoke and smolder as Freyja's fire snakes across the branches and climbs rapidly up the tree trunk. Soon the whole tree is aflame, curling and black. There's a loud whoosh. Hot flames explode, and I leap back.

Amma shrieks. "No!"

My feet start moving on their own.

I run for the other tree, smearing my blood across the stave there.

The sudden brightness sears my eyes, but I can't look away as divine fire devours the forest. Flames leap from one infected tree to another, quickly spreading. Once it starts, it can't be stopped. That's how change is.

I race out of the forest—

A hand latches onto my ankle before I can get far.

I fall down face-first, crashing onto my hands and knees so hard my teeth clack together. Snow stings my skin as I try to get up, but Amma grips my ankle like a shackle.

I struggle against her hold, kicking at her hand with all the force I can muster. No matter how hard I fight, her claws only sink deeper into my flesh. I bite back a scream.

The fire is so hot now it feels like baking in the sun on a sweltering midsummer day. Thick smoke clogs my lungs, making me choke. Freyja's fire won't kill me, but its smoke might.

"No one can separate us," Amma says frantically. "Not even you."

She isn't going to let me go. Even if it kills me.

With a great groan, a flaming branch plummets down toward us.

I try to shout, but smoke pours in instead. Coughing, I cover my mouth with my elbow, my lungs burning. I have to get out of here.

The branch crashes down—

Crushing Amma.

She howls, her grip loosening enough for me to pull free.

Choking, I struggle onto my feet.

Amma's face cracks and splits from the heat. Tears track down her cheeks like two molten rivers, steam hissing over her face. Her flesh starts to bubble off her bones as she burns, blood boiling like lava inside her. My heart stops as her screams pierce my ears. The acrid stench of charred flesh and hair fills my nostrils, making me so queasy I retreat another step.

For an instant, the Amma from my memories is standing there.

A smile spreads across her sun-kissed, wrinkled skin. "Goodbye, Asta."

And then she disintegrates, becoming ash.

Becoming nothing.

I clamp a hand over my mouth to keep from screaming. Tears slide between the valleys of my fingers, the flames hot on my skin. I'm shaking. I can't stop shaking.

She's gone. Amma is gone.

The heat turns scorching. Flames lick toward me, stinging my skin, but I'm still staring at the spot Amma stood moments ago. Another massive tree is brought to the ground by fire, slamming down so hard the earth shakes under me.

The forest burns, Freyja's fire turning the world into a golden haze. My head spins from lack of oxygen. I can't see more than a meter in front of me as I stumble through the forest, no longer able to tell if I'm heading toward Unden or going deeper into Tiveden.

Before I get far, I crash to my knees, coughs racking my body.

I can't get up. Can't breathe. Can't think.

I collapse to the snow.

My ears are ringing now, drowning out the sounds of trees snapping and popping as they burn and break apart. I struggle to keep my eyes open, staring at the bright flames, until everything goes black.

Darkness swallows me.

‡

"Must you leave me, Mother?" Dagny asks, tears trailing down her cheeks.

I hold her face close to mine.

"Do not weep for me." I wipe a tear away with my thumb, careful not to cut her with my claw. "Soon, I will see my mother again. Freyja will hold me in a field that goes on forever, surrounded by golden wheat swaying in a warm breeze, someplace the sun never sets."

Dagny's lip trembles. "I will miss you too much."

"Shhhh, my sweet." I press my lips gently to her forehead, though I can no longer feel her familiar warmth. "One day, we will see each other again. Until that day comes, you know what you must do."

Dagny nods, gripping the dagger carved with my name against her chest. The dagger my father once gave me now belongs to her. My daughter is a grown woman herself, with two daughters of her own.

"I know, Mother," Dagny says slowly. "The blood oath must not be broken."

Nodding, I hold my daughter's face in my hands one last time. She has Torsten's brown eyes and my flaxen hair. But when she smiles, it is all her own, like sunrise spreading through the sky. That is why I chose the name Dagny for her.

A new day.

I pull her into my arms. "Take care of Unden for me and your father."

"You know I will." Dagny buries her face in my hair as she sobs. "I love you, Mother."

Many years have passed since we lost Torsten. He was all I could hope for in a husband and an even better father to our daughter. After everything he had done for me, I could not bear to burn his body. So I used the forbidden stave one final time to resurrect him, though he could not remain with us. He bid us both farewell and went into Tiveden to join my father, where all the dead must go now.

I stroke the back of her head with my clawed hand. "As I love you, my new day."

With that, I pull away from her. One day, Dagny will see Torsten again in Tiveden. She can finally meet her grandfather, too. But until that day comes, I hope her life is long and full of joy.

Only I will not be there.

All of Unden has gathered before the stave church to watch me depart on my final journey. What they do not know is that I have already died. Sometime last night, sleeping peacefully in my bed of furs, I took my last breath while I dreamed of my first and only love. I woke this morning with eyes as bright blue as his.

The oath we swore to each other will allow me to live forever.

But I do not want to spend eternity without him.

As I draw my final stave onto the ground, I think only of my love. His gleaming silver hair and cold, strong hands. My throat is thick with emotion as I paint the stave with my blood, which is now the same dark color as his. I cannot even think his name anymore, for it fills me with such great shame.

The goddess's fire ignites, burning my eyes with its glittering brightness.

"The time has come for me to join my mother," I call out to the onlookers. "Freyja burned thrice and thrice was reborn. One day, so will I be. I do not know when, but know that I will return to lead Unden once more."

Dagny will be waiting for me. My mother's magic flows through her veins as it does mine, though her power manifests differently than my own. Instead of projection, Freyja has granted her the ability to see a person and all they are made of. Seeing their essence makes her skilled in understanding people. Mine is so familiar to her by now, I know she will not forget it, no matter how long it takes me to find her again.

I look to Dagny. "Until then, I leave Unden in my daughter's care."

She will rule Unden, just as my father rules Tiveden. After wedding Torsten, I learned at long last why Father had been exiled from Birka. He killed the king he'd sworn to serve because he coveted his crown. So I gave him his own, laying the twisted roots upon his head. Father will now serve as the Fell King to protect our new home.

Swallowing hard, I face the fire fully.

I have taken care of everything.

Well, most everything.

There is one person I cannot bid goodbye to.

He still lies asleep in my cellar, where I have visited him over the years. I hated how I grew older, yet he remained unchanged. Even if I had chosen him, as I sometimes wish I had, time was never going to stop for me. To live means to change. We never had a future, merely fleeting moments.

But when I talked, he would always listen. So I told him things I could tell no one else. I told him how each sacrifice grew more difficult for me, how I wished he could have been my daughter's father, how I longed to be the silly girl I once was, who lived for love and not duty.

I do not know if he heard any of it.

Even if he did, I cannot bring myself to face him as I am now. I fear I am no longer the girl he loved, but an old woman who has led a long and difficult life. As I stare at the wavering flames, I tell myself that I regret nothing. That I did what was necessary and I would do it all over again to protect Unden.

Yet as I walk into the flames, I regret everything.

The fire engulfs me. I can feel its heat upon my skin like sunlight, as if Freyja is holding me in her embrace. It does not hurt like I feared. It is nothing compared to the ache in my chest as I think of the life I chose and the one I did not. As I begin to burn, I can see Soren as clearly as that first day in the forest.

And I smile.

Next time, I will do it all differently.

"Astrid," a familiar voice says. "Please, wake up."

Strong arms carry me, cool against the suffocating heat of the flames. When I open my eyes, all I can see is Soren as Tiveden burns around us. He winces but fights his way forward as he carries me out of the forest, like he once carried Skaga when he spared her life centuries ago.

I lean against his chest. "What happened?"

"It worked. Unden is safe." His breathing is harsh. "The sacrifices disintegrated, cleansed by Freyja's fire, along with their ógipta. When you didn't return, I found you unconscious here."

Words won't come. He risked his immortal life to save mine.

Soren tightens his grip on me. "You did it."

"*We* did."

The entire forest is lit up, beautiful as shimmering golden flames reach into the sky like Skaga's funeral pyre. *This* is what Skaga wanted. She died with regret in her heart, hoping one day Freyja would return her so she could walk a different path. The Seers were mistaken about her, like so many other things.

Skaga no longer wanted to continue the cycle. She wanted to break it. She just didn't know how.

As the glittering smoke rises into the sky, so does the sun. Its bright light turns the world a warm gold around us, driving back the darkness. With a powerful blast, the fire explodes in a burst of heat behind us before we can reach the stave church.

Soren lets out a sharp gasp and stumbles forward.

Panic shoots through me. "Soren? What's wrong?"

He sets me down and then collapses, falling onto the snow.

"Soren!"

Freyja's fire climbs his body. Embers have already eaten away his cape and charred his clothes. No. *No.* He's been slowly burning this entire time because he's a draugr. He must have known this would happen, but he went into Tiveden anyway. To save me.

Soren grimaces, barely holding on.

I kneel next to him. My thoughts are racing. All I can see is what happened to Amma, skin melting off her bones. Blood bubbling like lava. Body disintegrating. I've already lost too much—I can't lose him, too.

I *can't.*

The flames are still small but are spreading over his arms and legs. But something seems to be slowing Freyja's fire from claiming him. Reaching through the flames, I stroke a hand over Soren's face. His skin feels hot, but he's not burning the same way Amma did.

Tears blur my vision. I have to help him, but how? Unlike when he was badly injured before, my blood won't work this time. Wait. Just as his blood flows through my veins, allowing me to use the stave, mine also flows through his. With both of our blood, he is neither fully draugr *nor* human. And Freyja's fire won't harm living things.

My blood is the only thing keeping him alive right now.

If I could just turn him fully human—

The stave. That's it.

I broke the sleep thorn. I can break this stave too.

With shaking hands, I unlace his leather armor and rip his shirt open. The stave still stretches across his chest, so I spread my palm over the symbol, trying to ignore how burning hot he is to the touch. Nothing like the calming coldness when he held me last night.

As I look over his pained expression, something stops me.

Soren's parents never gave him a choice.

But I will.

"Soren," I say, voice trembling. "I can break your stave. If I do, it will save your life, but you'll be human."

His blue eyes search mine slowly.

I clench my teeth tightly. But it's his life, his choice to make.

"Do it," he says.

Relieved tears slip down my cheeks.

But I still have to save him.

Concentrating, I reach into that place deep inside me, where something ancient dwells. I focus only on Soren. How he looked when I first found him, lying in the darkness of the cellar, asleep for centuries. How he saved me. I recall the feel of his cold arms encircling me, holding me against him before the shattered lake. The candles burning low inside the church as we worshipped each other's bodies. I think of the future I want to have with him—

Something shifts, moving underneath my palm.

When I lift my hand, his chest is bare. Unmarked. Just like the scar on Amma's palm disappeared once the blood oath was broken, the stave scarring Soren's chest has vanished as if it were never there. Now his skin is as pale as the snow surrounding us.

The fire covering Soren extinguishes itself, but not before it burns away his crown of roots.

But his chest still doesn't rise.

My tears splatter onto his skin. "Soren?"

And finally, his chest rises under my hand.

Relief rushes through me like a burst dam.

His eyes flutter open, but they look different. Still an icy blue, but they no longer glow unnaturally bright. And his skin—it's warm and vibrant, no longer waxy and cold. My heart thuds against my chest.

"Astrid," he says softly.

When he speaks, his fangs are gone.

I spread my palm over his chest, feeling the steady drumbeat of his heart beneath my hand. It no longer sounds distant, barely beating. It's strong and sure. He captures my hands with his, but he no longer has claws, either.

"Have you always been this warm?" he asks.

A small laugh escapes me. "You're alive."

He blinks, glancing down at his large hand covering mine. "I . . . am."

"Are you really okay with this?" I ask. I don't want him to regret his choice. "Being human also means dying."

Soren pulls me against him, drawing me into his lap as he sits up. "One lifetime with you is better than an eternity without you."

He presses his lips to mine.

This time it's different. Softer. Slower. Warmer.

"Who am I to you?" I whisper against his lips.

"Astrid."

I lower my forehead to his. "Say it again."

His voice is tender as he says, "Astrid, I—"

Before he can finish, my lips cover his. I bury my fingers in his soft hair, where his crown of roots once rested, and pull him closer to me. I don't need words to tell him I love him.

I never did.

When I finally manage to pull away, we both look toward Tiveden as it burns. Now that we're a safe distance from the forest, it looks almost beautiful as bright flames stretch toward the golden sky. Through the billowing smoke, the sun starts to rise. A new dawn. Instead of an ending, this is another beginning.

Now that Soren is human, he'll no longer be the Fell King.
Gudrun's prophecy did come true after all.

But she didn't realize I would end the blood oath, too.

"What now?" Soren asks, taking my hands in his.

As I press my palms against his, our skin is no longer scarred, but soft and smooth.

I smile. "That's up to us."

FORTY-FOUR

SIX MONTHS LATER

"Are you ready?" I call out to Soren, adjusting my flower crown in the mirror, when I catch a glimpse of him walking into the living room.

Soren pulls his arm through the sleeve of his navy tunic. "Of course."

When I turn around to face him, he stills.

His gaze sweeps over me. "You look . . ."

His throat bobs as he takes in my long tunic and green apron dress. To celebrate the solstice and honor our past, we all wear traditional garb. Even though he's starting to get used to wearing T-shirts and jeans, I think Soren prefers these old-fashioned clothes. They certainly suit him.

I can't help but smile. "You too."

He strides over to me and pushes a strand of hair from my face. His finger grazes the shell of my ear, sending a thrill through me.

"You forgot something, though," I add.

Soren gives me a questioning look. "Did I?"

I scoop the flower crown off a nearby table and stand on my tiptoes to place it on top of Soren's silver hair. It's one of the only things that never changed when he became human again. I can't say I mind, though. I love it. The green leaves and flowers pop against the silver strands, bringing out the blue in his eyes. "There," I say, grinning. "Perfect."

Soft pink spreads across Soren's cheeks. "I was hoping you forgot."

I love that blush of his too.

"No such luck," I say, giving him a mischievous smile.

He leans down and plants a quick kiss on my lips. "We're going to be late."

"Okay," I say, flipping off the lights. "Let's hurry."

The screen door snaps shut behind us.

As soon as we step outside, the smell of fresh grass fills my nose. Everywhere I look, it's bright, vibrant green. I pause and glance back at the house. *Our* house. It once belonged to Amma, and Skaga long before her. The house meant too much to me to let it rot. So Soren helped me make some much-needed repairs. The roof is fixed, and old wooden chairs sit in front of it, surrounded by Amma's favorite flowers and Skaga's favorite berries.

Now Soren and I live here together.

Though he never goes down into the cellar—and who could blame him?—I still do sometimes. It was where I first found Soren, after all. The whole house is full of memories, new and old. I like to think that Amma would be proud of me for saving this place. Despite everything that happened, some part of me still loves her and always will. And that's okay. Because two things can be true at once.

"Astrid?" Soren asks, taking my hand in his.

His warm touch brings me back to the present. "Yeah. Sorry."

We walk together, hand in hand, passing newly repaired homes.

Unden comes alive every Midsummer. A giant Maypole stands proudly in the middle of the village, festooned with hundreds and hundreds of bright flowers, welcoming us back. Picnic tables are pushed together, forming a long row, long enough for all the survivors in Unden to sit and eat together. Plates of pickled herring, fresh potatoes, and strawberries drenched in cream cover the long table. And of course, plenty of glasses of aquavit.

As I scan the line of familiar faces already gathered at the table, I realize I'm searching for someone who won't be there. *Dad.* Missing him hits me like a punch to the stomach. It's been six months since he died, but I still look for him everywhere. I'm sure I always will. I never stop missing him, but I'm learning to live with the grief somehow.

Days like this are always harder. A little rawer. As I see the kids dancing around the Maypole, holding hands and laughing, I remember what it was like to be one of them. When I could laugh so easily and freely until my cheeks hurt. How when I was dizzy from dancing and my dress was covered in grass stains from falling down, I'd run back to the table, where Dad had saved a spot next to him. He'd hand me the best fresh strawberry he could find, and then let me double-dip it into the sweet cream myself and savor its taste on my tongue.

I don't think anything will ever taste as good again.

I take the seat beside Johan that he'd saved for me, and Soren sits on my other side, holding my hand beneath the table.

Johan smiles when he sees me. "Hey."

"How are you liking Stockholm?" I bump his shoulder with mine. After he moved there a few months ago, we started joking about how we've switched places. But unlike before, we actually stay in touch this time.

"Great." Johan laughs, exchanging a long look with Zuri, who sits on his other side. She helped me with Johan's move, and the two of them hit it off. Zuri smiles brilliantly at us. She wears my apron dress better than I do, the white linen like snow against her dark brown skin.

"But I'm glad to be back here, too," Johan adds. "And that Zuri could come with me."

"Me too," Zuri teases. "Now I *finally* see what all the fuss is about."

She rests her head in her hand, long black braids framing her face as she laughs. "But seriously, I mean it. I already have some new ideas for paintings. You were right, Astrid. There's something special about Unden."

I can't help but smile. "There is."

Unden has always been my home, just as it was Skaga's.

I belong here. That's why I chose to finish my high school classes online instead. Part of the reason, anyway. I also did it so I could stay close to Soren. He may be human now, but there's no record of his birth. This is the only place he can really live without being asked a lot of questions.

Well, that's not quite true.

I still ask him plenty, but he's used to it by now. As part of my college applications to study journalism, I'm writing a piece about Skaga's life. He helps me fill in what the world was like back then, how life used to be, along with everything else. Because I don't want to forget the past. I want to learn from it.

As Linnea passes me a bowl of strawberries, my throat closes up. I try to swallow, suddenly feeling sick, but my mouth is as dry as sandpaper. I smile, accepting the bowl while blinking back tears. I know she doesn't mean anything by it, of course, but the reminder of Dad still hurts.

Soren leans toward me, his voice low. "Are you all right?"

"I'm not hungry yet." I reach for my glass of aquavit. "Can we go for a walk first?"

"Of course." Soren stands up, pushing his chair back.

More than a few people at the table stare at him. Or maybe *glare* is more accurate. Some of the older residents haven't forgotten who Soren is and what he'd once done long ago. It doesn't matter to them that he helped save Unden. Others, especially those who lost someone in the attack on Unden, still haven't forgiven either of us for what we ended, wanting to hold on to the past for as long as they can, because the false safety of the blood oath was all they knew.

But then there are people like Johan, who finally told his dad he wanted to move to Stockholm and apply to medical school. After how close Unden came to being destroyed, he realized life was too short to live for anyone else.

Now, when I have to go back into the city for my infusions, Johan meets me at the hospital, usually with Zuri. After everything that happened, I had another bad flare-up, and my injections couldn't get it under control. Thankfully, the infusions work. Even though I have to go back for them every month, I don't mind. Johan and Zuri will sit beside me, keeping me company for the two-hour visits, and we end up talking the whole time, catching up about their life in Stockholm and mine in Unden.

I slip my arm through Soren's as we walk the woods together, holding my glass of aquavit in my other hand. We reach the stave church before long. It still stands in the same spot Skaga built it, between Unden and Tiveden. Freyja's flames didn't burn it down, as if the goddess herself spared it. We still worship her regularly.

But when we reach the church, we don't stop.

We keep going into Tiveden.

There is only a wide clearing now where the corrupted parts of the forest once stood. But some things haven't changed. The Hidden Folk still remain, but only those ancient enough to predate the blood oath. They are the ones who made Soren their king. They have always lived in Tiveden and always will.

Even though he is no longer Fell King, they still meet with Soren.

Thanks to him, Tiveden and Unden are finally able to coexist peacefully.

We understand the Folk rather than fear them.

I pour out my aquavit, an offering to honor them.

The soil is still blackened in a lot of places, but it turns out the ash is good for growth. It helps revitalize the forest. Johan explained it all to me, but apparently fire can be rejuvenating. It returns nutrients to the soil more quickly than decomposition ever could. And after the fire, the open spaces allow for more sunlight, so Freyja can give new plants a chance to grow.

Among the burned husks of trees and ashen soil, something green has sprouted. I crouch down, unable to contain my excitement. "Look, Soren!" I point at the seedling, glancing up at him to see a smile pulling on his lips.

The new tree is still small, but I know with enough time, it will grow into something beautiful.

ACKNOWLEDGMENTS

As an aspiring author, one of my favorite things was to read the acknowledgments at the back of books and see how many people are part of bringing a story to life. I always dreamed of the day I'd get to write my own—and after pursuing publication for nine years, now I finally get to write mine.

Thank you first and foremost to my incredible editor, Sarah McCabe, for believing in me and this book. Your passion and insight helped me transform this into the story I always dreamed of telling, and I'm so incredibly thrilled with how it came out. I'll be forever grateful to you for helping me share Astrid's (and Skaga's!) story with the world. Thank you to Anum Shafqat for all your help (as well as appreciating how Soren is a total simp haha). The brainstorming sessions with you both were invaluable, and I've been amazed by how perfectly our visions have aligned throughout this process. I'm so fortunate to have found the perfect editor for this story!

And thank you to everyone at McElderry Books/Simon & Schuster for taking such wonderful care of this story, including Justin Chanda, Karen Wojtyla, Anne Zafian, Bridget Madsen, and Elizabeth Blake-Linn. To everyone who helped market this book, you have my sincerest gratitude: Chrissy Noh, Caitlin Sweeny, Lisa Quach, Bezi Yohannes, Perla Gil, Remi Moon, Amelia Johnson, Ashley Mitchell, Emily Ritter, Saleena Nival, Trey Glickman, and Elizabeth Huang, as well as the exceptional publicity team Lisa Moraleda, Nicole Russo, and Anna Elling. Huge thanks also to Christina Pecorale and her sales team, as well as Michelle Leo and her education/library team. And to Valerie Shea for her thorough and insightful copyedits. Thanks also to the immensely talented Marcela Bolívar for the gorgeous artwork on the cover (I may or may not have a poster of it beside my desk) and to Greg Stadnyk, cover designer extraordinaire, for creating the perfect cover. I couldn't have dreamed of a better publishing experience, and I owe it all to everyone on the S&S team. Thank you for everything you do.

A huge thanks to my agent, Quressa Robinson, and everyone at Folio for helping make my dream come true! I also want to give special thanks to Laura Crockett for seeing this book over the finish line with me. I can't wait for what's next!

I never would have made it this far without the help of my incredible mentors. Skyla Arndt, thank you for your endless enthusiasm and support of this story (and me!). Alex Brown, thank you for all of your invaluable insight into plot, not to mention all the great horror recs. And of course, Tashie Bhuiyan, thank you for being the first person to believe in this book and for all your help with this story, especially the romance (as well as introducing me to *The Untamed*.) This story wouldn't be what it is today without your guidance, and I'm forever grateful to each of you. I'm so lucky to call you not only mentors, but friends.

To the Wildcats, who have been there since the beginning, I love you all so much and I'm so incredibly lucky to know all of you. Swati Teerdhala, our fearless leader, your passion and wisdom is always appreciated, even if it means you're stuck flying the plane sometimes, sorry. Chelsea Beam, your enthusiasm and kindness mean so much, and I can't wait to hold your book in my hands one day. Never stop giving me Webtoon recs, please. Rosie Brown, you're one of the most talented and hardworking people I know, and also happen to have the best sense of humor. Blue Lions/Dimitri for life. Tanvi Berwah, your support and friendship is unmatched, and I'm so grateful you're always there for me, and we get to scream about *Game of Thrones* or our latest obsession together. Sansa Stark always.

To Team Trash, the best group of feral raccoons a girl could ask for: Elle Tesch, Shoshana Grauer, Michelle Milton, Jenna Miller, Jenna Voris, Monica Gribouski, Melody Robinette, SJ Whitby, Mallory Jones, and Andy Perez. You're my favorite raccoons and I don't know what I'd do without you all. Special shout out to Elle Tesch for all your level-headed insight, reading my book countless times, and always being there to listen. I hope you like your fox onesie.

To the HexQuills, thank you for adopting me, and always being so supportive and uplifting: Skyla, Rachel, Olivia, Brit, Kara, Kalla, Mackenzie, Shay, Juliet, Kat, Holly, Phoebe, Cassie, Helena, Kahlan, Marina, Darcy, Morgan, Sam, Wajudah, Livy, Maria, Abby, Alex, and Lindsey. You're all the best, and bring so much sunshine and laughter to my day. Shout out to Rachel Moore for understanding my special brand of anxiety and always being so supportive.

I'm so grateful to Alexa Donne for creating Author Mentor Match, which has helped me on my journey not only once, but twice, and led to me meeting so many incredible writers and lifelong friends. Alexa, you continue to be a source of wisdom, and I appreciate you so much.

Thank you also to Allison Saft, for supporting me and this story over the years. Roan, I can't believe we've known each other for so long?! You're not only a talented writer, but a talented artist. Nat, I've learned so much from you and value your friendship. Thanks to Roz Foster for believing in me from the beginning, and to Katelyn Larson, Gita Trelease, Ashley Darling, and Kim Bea for your support early on. More recently, thank you to Alicia Sparrow for seeing the potential in this story.

Pitch Wars also played a huge role in my journey, and I've met so many wonderful people through the program, especially: Kara A. Kennedy, Tauri Cox, Sana Z. Ahmed, Christine L. Arnold, Emily Charlotte, Megan Davidhizar, Clare Osongco, Anna Mercier, and Natalie Sue. You're all incredibly talented writers, and I love talking craft and learning from you all! Shout out to everyone in the last Pitch Wars class—I can't wait to read all your books.

Lena Jeong, thank you for always screaming with me and being so awesome. Thank you also to Pascale Lacelle and Andrea Max for keeping me sane. Rachael A. Edwards, you're the sweetest and I'm so excited for your book. I really hope I haven't forgotten anyone, but I probably have, so I'm sorry in advance. After pursuing publication for so long, so many people have been a part of my journey, and I'm grateful to each and every one of you.

Thank you to Maria Winkworth for always being so enthusiastic about my book. And to my therapist, Kim, thank you for your encouragement and excitement! I also wanted to give a special thanks to my second grade teacher, Mrs. Cashman, for collecting all of my *Sailor Moon* short stories I wrote instead of doing vocab homework, and making me feel like a writer for the first time.

Allyson, I can safely say this book wouldn't exist without all your support. Thank you for brainstorming with me for countless hours, for giving me your opinion on which word or name works better (Saga still says hi), for always talking me down from spirals, and for everything else you do. We may have met outside of the Tragedy and the Tragic course, but our friendship has been anything but. Thanks for all the hours chatting in coffee shops, screaming about video games, crying-laughing at *Riverdale*, and reading every iteration of this book. I'm so fortunate to call you my best friend, and I'm forever grateful for your friendship.

Lastly, and most importantly, thank you to my family. Mom, for being the kindest, most loving person, and always supporting me no matter what. Dad, for not only raising me on stories and encouraging me to write my own, but also for all the sacrifices you've made for us and your steadfast belief in me. I'm so glad this book meant almost as much to you as it means to me. I love you both more than I can put into words. Amber, don't worry, I promise none of these characters are based on you this time (also hi Claire!). And to Duke, the best boy, for always keeping me company while I wrote, whether you were sleeping under my desk or climbing onto my lap or trying to add some words yourself, I'll love you forever and miss you even more.